Child of the Knife

Torenium Chronicles: Book 1

By: T. David Sergent

Child of the Knife
Torenium Chronicles:
Book 1

Print ISBN: 978-1-7345167-3-9
EPUB ISBN: 978-1-7345167-2-2

Dedication

I would like to dedicate this book to my family who have spent countless hours listening to character development, running through ideas, reading revisions, and telling me to put these books out for public consumption. I thank you all and appreciate you more that you can know. Thanks for having faith in me and the whole Torenium Empire!

TABLE OF CONTENTS

Map of The Torenium Empire

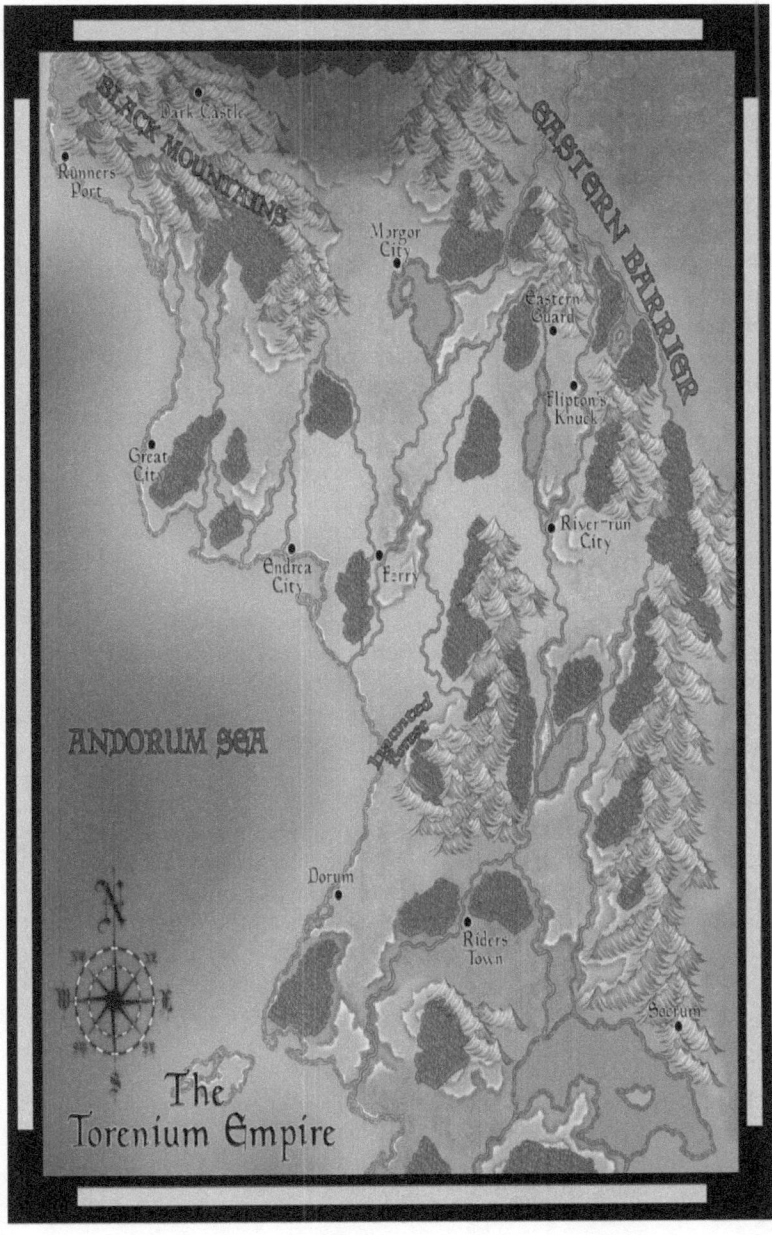

Prologue

"Yes, I very much do believe it has meaning," she said. The tall woman was brushing aside long strands of black hair from her now glaring eyes as she sighed.

"Perhaps it does." The little man replied, plopping heavily into a massive chair by the roaring fire. "But there is a very good chance that it means nothing at all." He scratched at his beard, losing himself to his thoughts as he stared into the fire. "Besides, why would this have anything to do with us? *They* have existed with very little involvement from us for a very long time." He moved to the edge of the chair, stretching his hands toward the fire, feeling the warmth.

There was a sudden rush of air in the room that did not faze either of them. The only acknowledgment the woman gave was straightening her long white gown as it flared from the whirling air. Her elegant dress flowed from high on her throat, to far past her feet, to the floor. She repositioned herself with a tight jawline, knowing what was to come next.

The little man by the fire huffed a deep breath, knowing who was in the room with them now. He knew even the fire wouldn't warm him, as a chill ran up his spine.

"There had better be a good reason for summoning me, yet again, to these pointless meetings!" a deep voice announced as a tall, slender man materialized in the room near the table. He was the exact male replica of the woman in the white gown, but he wore a high-collared black tunic and black riding boots. Both were beautiful creatures and perfect in their own right.

Shama leaned back into the chair, wanting to disappear into the thick cushions. So big was the chair that his lower legs and feet stuck straight out of it toward the fire, as if he were a small child. He really didn't mind, though. He rarely took human form anymore, and he was enjoying the feel of it. Fingers were indeed a beautiful thing, he thought as he raised his hands and wiggled his fingers as he watched them.

"Come now, ole' boy. Couldn't you think up a more appealing flesh bag than that?" the man asked, letting a sarcastic smile spread across his face.

"It appeals to *me*, and that's all I care about," Shama said, looking back into the fire and wishing he were anywhere but here.

The Lady of the Light cleared her throat and stepped graciously between them—a place she occupied most of the time when the three of them were together.

"We have a matter to discuss and I think it is time we get started."

Her voice was smooth and delicate, and Shama enjoyed it almost as much as he detested her twin brother.

"As long as we are not going to talk about that ridiculous prophecy again." The Dark Lord's shoulders slumped slightly, and he gave his sister a sulking look. "The simple ones are always trying to predict the future by writing down their wishful versions of it. Almost always, they are wrong, and only by pure chance do they get one prophecy right in a millennium. Tell me we are not putting any credibility in those insignificant slugs' words?"

"This is different and you know it," the Lady said delicately, though now with a hint of annoyance in her voice.

Shama didn't say a word. Most of their meetings began this way. He knew it was just a matter of time before the black-wearing dandy would turn on him.

"And why must we always have to have *him* here?" the dark lord nodded his head toward Shama.

Here it comes, Shama thought, pressing himself into the cushions of his chair.

"He is insignificant ... when it comes to these matters," the Dark Lord said, giving Shama a sideways glance.

"I thought you said this was just a ridiculous prophecy?" Shama shot back at him, without looking up from the fire.

"Watch your tone, toad, or you will find yourself being one of my pets." The Dark Lord tried to side-step his sister to get to Shama, but she quickly moved in front of her brother, floating like a ghost.

"Why do you protect him?" the Dark Lord complained, his face red with anger. "He is one of hundreds of his kind. Why him?"

His sister just sighed and took a moment to gather her composure.

"Again brother, you know why. He has some role to play that we cannot yet understand. And you know very well that there are not hundreds of his kind left."

"HA!" the Dark Lord shouted into his sister's face. "Why not just bring back the fool who wrote this thing, and then we can ask him what the blazes he meant by it? I'm sure it came from some grand magical place like some tree-loving druid's temple. What a fascinatingly boring little group they were!"

"Because," Shama interrupted, his words dripping with sarcasm. "we don't know who specifically wrote it, My Lord,"

"Okay, let's get started, shall we?" the Lady asked, seeing her brother's face turn a dangerous shade redder at Shama's jibe.

She gracefully pulled a chair from under the large table and sat, smoothing her gown beneath her. Waving one of her small delicate hands at the fire, she caused it to spark up in a shot of light. Shama yelped and pulled his feet away, wincing.

"Like brother, like sister," he muttered under his breath, not meaning for it to be heard.

They did hear it, however, and it brought dark looks from both. Shama could not help thinking how much they looked alike in that angry moment.

Shrugging his broad shoulders innocently, he came to the table as fast as his short legs would take him.

The Lady once again waved a hand, and a large slab of stone appeared on the table in front of them.

"That's it?" the Dark Lord asked, disappointedly.

Neither his sister nor Shama missed the look in his eyes when the slab appeared, however. The Dark Lord assumed a very bored and uninterested look. Still, Shama could see his upper arms moving as he unconsciously rubbed his hands together under the table.

The stone was made of pure marble and was very old. Letters were carved into it, but they blended so well into the rock that Shama could not make them out. He squinted and climbed up closer in his chair to make them out.

The Dark Lord saw Shama struggling, and with a roll of his eyes, he touched one of his long fingers to the cold rock. The ornately cut slits lit up in red flame, as though molten lava flowed through them. There was only one sentence because the stone had been cleanly sheared off by something powerful and sharp. It read: "Watch for the loyal, as he is the one."

"Where's the rest of it?" the Dark Lord asked, not even attempting to mask his excitement now.

The Lady of Light smiled gently at her brother. "I will share it in due time, brother. For now, we must work out each section and its meaning."

"Shama, does this mean anything to you?" she asked, turning her gaze to the little man across from her.

He scratched his beard absently, thinking that his human hands felt exquisite.

"Without seeing the rest of it… It could mean anything," he said.

The Lady sighed and studied the rock, putting her chin on her folded hands.

Her brother waved a hand, and a goblet of wine appeared in front of him. "You waste my time, sister."

He took a loud sip to emphasize his annoyance. "When you are ready to share the whole pebble, do let me know." He took another sip, locking eyes with her and vanished.

With his exit, Shama immediately began to feel better. "He will search the meaning for himself, you know," he said, using the opportunity to gaze into the Lady's perfectly beautiful dark eyes. She returned his gaze, smiling kindly.

"I know my brother, little friend, and I know how to pull his reins in the direction I mean to go." She smiled wider and Shama couldn't help but smile back.

He hadn't the vaguest idea what she was talking about, but he did enjoy looking at her as he rested his own chin on his hands. "Sure-sure, you know what is best," not even caring that he sounded like an idiot even to himself.

Later, and deep in his own thoughts, Shama flew through the clouds with his enormous leather wings stretched out to catch the wind. These were always some of his favorite moments. He knew The Twins still frowned on him for exposing his true self, but it was one of the things he truly lived for.

He let the cold wind take him in any direction it wanted to. He knew that he was high enough that none below would see him. Shama felt more himself being a dragon, and he for sure knew that was the form he had once been born to. But that had been so long ago that he could not even remember, or maybe he just blocked it out.

He rarely liked to think about the past; however, he knew he was from the natural world and always felt better being among all the creatures in it.

The others thought all the wonderful things below him were meant for their amusement and to do their bidding. And it was true that he too was once worshipped, but he had found it too exhausting and heart-wrenching when his people suffered.

Though most of the time they had caused the pain themselves, and the wars, deceit, and murders were what had finally convinced him to just exist in a solitary way.

The air at the height he was flying was more relaxed, but the sun was more potent, and he could feel it on his wings and long, scaled neck. It felt excellent. He suddenly had an urge to quickly swoop down and send a shock of terror through everything below, but he knew that would only lead to a lecture from The Twins. He sighed, which sent a long plume of smoke out of his nostrils and through the air behind him.

The Twins are experiencing some real angst over this prophecy, he thought, as he started turning, rolling, and falling, only to catch the wind again beneath his wings.

He knew they usually had little or no interest in the goings-on of the world-bound. But this... This was getting a lot of attention, and to make things even worse, one of them was sure he was somehow involved.

His keen eyes spotted an eagle riding nearly as high as he was, and he put the suggestion of a chase in its mind. The eagle replied with great enthusiasm, and he tucked his wings and dropped like a stone. When he popped out of the cloud, the eagle shrieked in delight and took off. Shama spread his massive wings ever so lightly to shift himself in that direction.

The words on the stone had been bizarre. What the Lady had chosen to show them had said: "...watch for the loyal as he is the one." Admittedly, it was a strange thing, but then humans had been writing strange things since there were ... well, humans. Why would The Twins, especially the perfect and pretty versions, get so worked up? She does seem to have more of it in her possession, but if she has all the words, why include her brother and me, and why not dissever it herself? This was precisely why he preferred leaving the dealings of Gods with The Twins.

The eagle shrieked again, this time with annoyance, and Shama realized he was near atop the small thing. He swerved off, barrel-rolled, and came out of it, sailing off in another direction, sending a thought of apology to the bird.

The bird responded in the cocky and self-important way of the eagle.

As reparation for his absent-mindedness, Shama took away cataracts that were forming in the old eagle's eyes.

The bird squawked loudly with appreciation and immediately went to find a juicy snack.

By that time, Shama was far too close to the ground, but as he started his ascent, his keen ears picked up the sound of a human baby crying. He had not heard that sound in centuries, and curiosity got the best of him.

The sun was low in the sky, and he was sure he was moving unseen, so he circled the area and watched as two men in hoods rode their horses hard with one of them carrying a small child in his arms. The one holding the child seemed, by the look of the gray hair flapping out of his hood, far too old to be the father. And the other ... the other was different.

Shama concentrated, and the man in the black cloak looked straight up and at him. Shama threw up his wings, stalling himself in midair.

There was no way anyone should have been able to see him this far above the ground. He started to drop so he spread his wings again.

There was something very familiar about the look in that one's eye, he thought. It reminded him of … but it could not be. That one must be long dead!

Shama decided that he'd best leave this place right away when another cry from the child sank deep into his heart. He made a mental imprint of the child's mind. He felt a strange connection with it. It was like two pieces of a puzzle coming together and making a click when pressed into place. It was not, however, an altogether pleasurable feeling, because suddenly Shama felt as if something had begun-something over which he had no control.

He swooped off and let the air beneath his wings lift him higher. He was feeling watched again and searched the ground beneath him, but there was nothing there. He remembered the look that was on the man's face, and it came to him where he'd seen it before. He had seen it many centuries ago on a certain ambitious man who had wanted to be a god. But the Dark Lord himself had destroyed that man. Or had he? What is he up to? Or better yet, what are *they* up to?

Chapter 1 - Sebastion

Sebastion sat by a small bubbling brook, watching the water meander busily through mossy rocks and rotted tree roots. His head was heavy in his hands as he reflected upon his short life. He was short and very thin for a boy of his age. He wore old clothes and battered, worn-out boots. Scars from a life already filled with violence covered his arms and legs. He traced the scars with his finger trying to remember where, specifically, they had come from. He remembered the day his keeper had told him he was big enough and nearly adequate in training to kill a man. The fierceness of training had become more severe from that day on, but to Sebastion, it also meant that he was no longer a helpless boy. It was an indication that he was growing and one day possibly leaving these forests. The trees and hills were all he knew. As early as he could remember, he had wanted to run away and no longer be with the cruel man who had never bothered to give himself a name.

The only pleasure the merciless and bent old man had provided the boy was the books he kept in his trunk. Reading had come easily to Sebastion, and he read those old books with a voracious appetite. It was his only way of escaping his sad reality, and he read as often as he could.

Even though he did not understand most of the things that happened in the strange tales, he did enjoy the pleasures they provided. He had no understanding of things outside the world he lived in.

Still, there were times his imagination would allow him glimpses of another life. The words in the books let him think there could be more to life than violence and the harsh ridicule of the man he called Keeper ... because that was all the man was to him.

It was quickly getting late in the morning, and although Keeper usually slept late, he would be waking soon. Years of constant mistreatment had nearly destroyed Keeper's body.

He had been taking small doses of poison, and now his body could ward off nearly any poison that a would-be assassin might concoct. But it had taken its toll.

"When I leave this dark blasted hell for another, it will not be from poison," the frail, bent man liked to say. Then he would drink down many vials, wincing at the taste and following them with a swallow from a significant skin of wine.

Keeper was not the only one to force down the many evil mixtures. Sebastion was instructed to drink down whatever his master would hand him. He was never told what he was drinking, but he suspected it was some of the same poisons that Keeper was drinking.

Whether it was to build immunities or not, all he knew was that he hated the feeling he got after drinking those foul-tasting brews. When he was younger, he had tried to object, but he had soon found that the awful feeling he got was far better than what would happen if he resisted.

The training was constant and brutal. Mercy was not something Keeper acknowledged. If Sebastion put himself in a position that left him open, his master and trainer painfully let him know it.

The nights were the worst. Keeper always said that their trade was best performed in the cover of night and in the shadows. He would go on about how darkness would be Sebastion's closest and most reliable friend. His instructions included Sebastion standing for hours in one place and, allowed to move a single muscle. If a muscle twitched, it would be met with a sharp slap from a stick.

Each time that Keeper demonstrated what he wanted Sebastion to do, it was as if the man could disappear altogether, even in the daylight. He could be right there in front of Sebastion, yet Sebastion would feel an urge to reach out and see if he was still really there. This trick was even more emphasized when the old man was wearing his forest green cloak.

He blended so well that Sebastion could not help but be impressed with his master's talent. Keeper also always stressed the importance of moving slowly without being noticed. He always explained that it was much more important than moving quickly when stalking one's prey.

Pulling a knife from a sleeve or in a hidden pocket was an essential part of 'The Art.' Sebastion would practice all these things and more every day and evening, with Keeper constantly impatiently pushing him on.

The weapons practice was especially challenging. Sebastion's body always felt sick and weary from the poison and the lack of a good night's sleep. His keeper simply explained it would make Sebastion a better fighter and teach him how to refine his thrusts and cuts so as not to expend his energy needlessly.

Keeper was a master at this too. There was no "play" in their weapons play. Keeper was very adamant that each thrust or slash must have a purpose, even if it was not immediately recognizable. Every one of his movements was made with the same care as that of a vulture picking a bone clean of meat. No move was ever wasted and no opening un-exploited.

Sebastion was taught that only a little movement was necessary when fighting with the knife. The knife was the favorite tool of an assassin and one that only the most experienced could master. They would sometimes spend hours circling each other, looking for openings and lurching out when they thought they saw an opportunity.

Sebastion would always be on the defensive, but there were times he was sure he could have scored a slash or a quick thrust. He still had to weigh this against the repercussions of making Keeper angry. Nothing was ever gained by making the man angry.

His master not only taught with weapons, but at times would infuse prolific words of advice to help the one-day assassin,

"When a sword or knife is drawn, there can be only one of two outcomes: your death or your enemy's," or another favorite of his masters, "Most fights are not lost because of an idiot's lack of skill, but because of lack of commitment."

When giving this particular lecture, he would look down at Sebastion with his cold, bloodshot eyes. "If you are too much of a coward to commit to killing, you must not begin the fight. If you draw your sword or knife, be prepared to kill someone. If you are not prepared to kill, there is no shame for someone like us in walking or running away. Remember, you can always kill them later when your target isn't expecting it!"

Keeper always chuckled at that, or at least until one of his coughing fits would overtake him.

"But what if our weapons are drawn for practice? Should I run then?" Sebastion had asked once, trying to be funny. He remembered that he could not stop the words coming from his mouth and even placed a hand across it once the words were out. The sarcasm was always in his head, but that time it had just snuck out.

"Are you testing me, rat?" Keeper had asked. Sebastion lowered his gaze as he always would, hoping the act of submission would be enough. Besides … it kept his Keeper from seeing the hate that burned there for him.

"No." Sebastion replied that day. Keeper must have thought he still heard a trace of rebellion in his voice and had sprung. Sebastion let himself be smacked in the back of the head, as he had many times before. It was better than the sting of a stick or the pains of going hungry, and he was grateful for that, at least.

***

There was no sharing of chores. Sebastion was responsible for all the things that revolved around day-to-day duties. He did the cleaning, cooking, wood chopping, and anything else Keeper instructed him to do. Between that and his training, he had very little time for himself. There were times when he was sent to do the hunting, and he would have had time for personal reflection but for the feeling of guilt he had for killing the animals.

Over the years, he developed a kind of understanding and even fondness for the animals around their small wooden dwelling. The animals also, in time, developed a tolerance, and he was able to observe them. He actually felt more of a connection with them than he had with his cruel master.

One sunny afternoon, Sebastion had come upon a fawn standing by itself in a small clearing of grass. He silently watched from the cover of a tree. Insects danced around the fawn as it ate lazily, picking up its little head from time to time to look around. Sebastion was grateful the birds had not given away his position as they so liked to do. He was getting better every day at moving through the forest undetected.

The day seemed so perfect looking out at the field and watching that he sighed quietly to himself. Two large heads rose from the grass around the fawn. One of them had many rows of sharp-looking antlers. It was a big buck, and it was looking right at him. The buck snorted a challenge and got to its feet slowly where it had been napping. The doe that was with him bounced off with the fawn in toe, disappearing into the trees beyond. The buck stayed behind with his head high, looking at Sebastion angrily.

Sebastion knew this would have been an excellent time to have tried to bring down the buck with an arrow, but the look in the deer's eyes made him think of only retreat. He gently took a step backward, but as he did, the deer took one forward. Sebastion decided then that it was best if he ran and turned and put all his energy into his feet.

He ran for some time before realizing the deer had given up the chase. He leaned against a tree and sucked in air as a particular thought came to him. That big buck had sacrificed his safety by letting the doe and fawn run off as he faced whatever was there. If he were a predator, the doe and fawn would have been safe, but the buck may have been killed. Actually, he was the predator, he thought.

What would make something want to sacrifice its own life for another? He knew enough of the animal world to know about offspring and the ones that bore them. His thoughts came back to himself, as they did very infrequently. He thought about where he had come from and, if he had a father once would he have stood up and protected him from a predator. He decided he wanted to try again to find out.

Sebastion convinced himself to ask Keeper about whether he had a father. No matter the consequences, he needed to know. Keeper would, of course, become very angry, as he always did when Sebastion asked questions that did not pertain to the Art. Still, he felt he could deal with the anger if he could just get an answer. He did ask about it, but all it got him was an empty stomach and a bloody nose.

Throwing a dried leaf into the stream, he lazily watched it float off beyond his sight. He knew he should get back and prepare something for Keeper to eat, but this morning was starting so perfectly ... with the lulling sounds of the stream and the warmth of the sun as it peeked through the trees above.

He rubbed his swollen eyes, not knowing that as a young boy as he should not have red, swollen eyes and aching joints. To him, the feeling was as normal as eating or sleeping.

With a groan, he pushed off from the tree he was leaning against and started heading back. He did not whistle or sing or even hum along softly to the songs of spring. Instead, he went over the numerous stances and intricate maneuvers required for this day's training. He always used these early hours before Keeper awoke to organize his thoughts. If he didn't and was not prepared, Keeper would un-mercifully thrash him. The bent old man was cruel but very effective in making a point. *Be prepared or face the consequences.* That was how he trained.

When he got to the cabin, he noticed with a cold sinking feeling that the front door was open. He was always cautious not to leave it open as he had done it once before and thought he would lose his life. He knew that it could only mean that Keeper was up early and had awoken to find Sebastion missing. No breakfast prepared, Sebastion's heart sunk, *oh, no. Please,* he thought.

"What have you been up to?" Keeper's voice came from nowhere and cut short Sebastion's thoughts.

Sebastion looked around in all directions. "I was out think-" He knew it was a mistake as soon as the words left his mouth.

Sensing movement to his left just beyond his vision, Sebastion turned, but it was too late. Keeper's staff jabbed him hard in the stomach as he turned. Sebastion went down onto his knees, coughing into the hard, dirt-covered ground. As much as he tried, he couldn't get air inside him.

"FOOL! You stood there like a chicken ready to be slaughtered!"

Sebastion knew this had nothing to do with his abilities. This was payback for not having Keeper's food ready when he awoke.

"Y- Yes," he was finally able to get out, between desperate gasps for air.

"Yes, what!" Keeper screamed down at him.

"Yes, I am a fool. I should have listened … and been more prepared." He wheezed out coughing and spat onto the ground. "I'll learn from this … and do better."

"You bet you will," Keeper said, walking back to the cabin. "And get me my food, maggot!" he shouted over his shoulder before slamming the door behind him.

Sebastion struggled to stand up, still bent, and waiting for nausea to pass. When he didn't get sick, he hurried to prepare Keeper's food. *There will come a day when all this will be behind me, and I will never have to think of it again!*

***

It was a foggy, chilly morning in early spring. The forest was becoming more alive as the ground thawed after the long cold winter. It was as if every tree was competing to be the first to bloom. The race would take days, maybe weeks, before the winner stole the light and the loser would wither and die.

A very enthusiastic mother inside a hollow tree was attending to a small litter of squirrels. She cleaned each one carefully and gave the same careful amount of attention to each. The little squirrel mother took much pleasure in her work, ignoring the adolescent boy watching from a hole in the log.

He watched the little creatures helplessly crawl around their mother. He had brought with him some flatbread he had made a few days ago and threw in a small piece. His aim was off, and it accidentally bounced off the little mother squirrel's head, and she barked angrily once at him before gobbling down the bread.

"You are welcome," Sebastion said, smiling.

Keeper had sent Sebastion out to find some meat to replenish their depleted stores from the long winter. Sebastion had been curious how his little friend had fared through the winter and stopped to check. The fact was that he was procrastinating doing what he knew needed to be done. Keeper never cared much about where the meat came from, only that there was plenty of it.

Sebastion took his time with the squirrels before wandering the forest to collect his thoughts. It was a gift to be away from his constant training, though he would have traded training for hunting. The foraging for meat had become more and more difficult as he built his trust further out among the animals.

An understanding between them had evolved that Sebastion would not hunt the animals within a certain range of his living area, and that was being expanded. But Sebastion was practical and knew that he needed to find food. He liked all the animals in the forest, but like them, he needed to eat. He took up his bow and walked on.

Today, he decided to try the area beyond the creek. He had not been there before because Keeper had made it perfectly clear, he was not to 'even look too long in that general direction.'

Sebastion moved silently through the forest, more like a ghost than a malnourished boy. He was extra cautious, as he had never been in this part of the woods before. He was hoping to get lucky and stumble upon a buck just beyond the creek. He couldn't help but notice the forest here was strangely quiet. Even the insects barely made a noise.

As he moved farther from his familiar territory, he saw that the trails seemed to be more used and not just by game. Even with the air being warm, goosebumps started running up and down his body, and Sebastion's hands began to ache from gripping his bow so tightly. He decided that if he didn't find any evidence of a deer in the next few minutes, he would turn back and just face Keeper's wrath.

Just then, he heard a rustling in the brush nearby. He was moving slowly to peer over the small ledge and into the bush. He caught the sound of what must be people running and yelling, coming from only a short distance away.

Without warning, a huge buck burst out of the bushes, nearly landing on top of him. He recognized it to be the same buck he had seen years ago with the fawn and doe. Only this time, it had several arrows poking out from all sides of its body, it stopped and looked at Sebastion, panting.

It appeared to be near madness from pain and exhaustion, and it was about to lung forward to reap revenge on whoever was in its way. The buck lowered its head, its antlers looking as big as spears. It charged forward, its hooves hitting the ground like thunder.

Sebastion reached behind him to grab for an arrow at his back. He knew he was moving too slowly, and any chance was quickly disappearing. Still, he just couldn't move any faster, he was so scared by the look in this huge animal's eyes. Such hate and rage.

Sebastion closed his eyes and held his breath for what was to come next. Something whisked by his ear and then something else. He heard a thud, and he opened his eyes.

The buck lay near his feet with something like arrows, only smaller and barely visible poking from its body. Sebastion could only stare, not believing his luck.

He heard what must have been the people coming toward him, and he started to move. He knew Keeper would be furious when he found out Sebastion had been here and even more furious if he knew other people had seen him.

"HOLD, THERE!" Someone yelled from a short distance away.

Chapter 2 - The Boys

It was near dusk, and a cool breeze was slowly exhaling fog-filled breath into the forest. Birds flew from tree to tree twittering angrily. Sebastion thought the trees seemed bigger and more imposing in this part of the forest. It could be, however, that he had never before had to look up at a tree while he was tied to it. On the other side of his tree, the large buck hung as the young hunters gutted and prepared to skin it. Sebastion was sharing the same rope. Only a few loops around a branch kept him from being lifted into the air by the buck's heavyweight. He felt the rope pull and loosen as the deer was being taken apart.

The blood ran around the tree in small red rivers over the hard dirt and protruding tree roots. Sebastion was tied in a sitting position against the big tree, his hands tied off with a separate rope. The deer's blood made it to his side of the tree and started to soak into his pants and boots, feeling very warm against his skin. He was terrified, and the forest was getting cold. He was shivering so badly that he almost welcomed the warmth the deer's blood provided his skin as it ran in crimson streamlets past him and into the forest beyond.

The boys that made up the hunting party were discussing what to do with him. He could only understand a few words of what they were saying because the boys spoke quickly and with an accent. One suggested they treat him the same way they had the deer and bring back even more meat. Sebastion wished he hadn't understood that part.

The boys laughed and joked, all the while pointing at him and jabbing him with their feet. He had been warned not to come to this side of the forest, and he didn't know which was worse; that Keeper would be very angry or that he did not even know Sebastion was there.

As he hung his head, Sebastion's eyes filled, but he tried not to cry. He thought the boys might beat him, but some seemed frightened of him, saying things like "wild boy" or "forest spirit." The smallest boy, who seemed a couple of years younger than the rest, was looking at Sebastion with such disgust that he thought he would surely kill him.

The tallest one, the apparent leader, leaned against a tree as he watched the others work on the deer. He was big for his age, already as tall as a grown man, and it was plain that he used that to his advantage. His face was covered with acne, and his teeth were broken and prematurely rotting. The clothes he wore were so small for him that he looked like he must have grown many inches just that day and his hair and eyes were presumably as dark as his thoughts. The leader stared at Sebastion with revulsion as Sebastion gave in and wept silently with his head down.

The large boy then snapped his head up. "I got it! I know what we can do with this … weepy girl." The others stopped working and looked up. Their hands were covered with blood, and their faces no cleaner.

"What you want to do?" the littlest boy asked, wiping his hands on his ragged pants.

"We'll test him." The leader smiled and scratched at his swollen pimples as he thought. "We'll see what kind of man he is."

"What you mean by that?" asked another boy.

The leader smiled his most evil grin.

The others exchanged confused looks.

The leader gave them a disgusted look, his annoyance taking over when the others just stared blankly at him.

"You'll see. By the dark, y'all are a bunch of IDIOTS!"

***

Sebastion could not feel the rope moving any longer, and he looked up to find the boys huddled together. They were jabbering and laughing hysterically. Some were even bouncing up and down excitedly. His neck was starting to hurt from peering around the tree to see what the motley bunch of boys were up to. Some of them were now shaking their heads and complaining. Suddenly, the smaller one stepped into the center, and all started hooting, hollering, and slapping him on the back.

The leader walked up to Sebastion, untied him and he started to get excited at the thought that they might just let him go. The tall boy in the small clothes spoke slowly, but Sebastion was too excited at the prospect of being freed to pay attention to what he was saying. The leader stuffed a small stick about the size of his forearm into his hand and pushed him in the direction of the other boys, who were standing there very eager. Sebastion nearly stumbled over a root but regained his balance in time to avoid hitting the ground. He just stared at the stick in his hand, not understanding what was going on.

They surrounded him in a circle, the half–gutted, hanging deer swung side to side slowly, now forgotten. They stared at Sebastion, hollering and making noises like a pig, but stopped suddenly and parted to let in the small boy with hate in his eyes. Sebastion did not understand what he could have done to make that boy hate him so much. He had only been in their path. He did not try to take down the deer they were chasing. He had only attempted to notch an arrow because the colossal beast was going to attack him.

The boy strutted into the circle with his shirt off. He had a stick about twice the size of Sebastion's in his hand. He twirled it around, smiled confidently and Sebastion's hopes of freedom faded.

This boy, the smallest of the group, was a head taller than Sebastion. He had muscles where Sebastion was skin and bones.

One of the boys stepped forward and violently tore off Sebastion's shirt. This sent them into hysterics as they fell about themselves in laughter.

"He looks like a twig!" One cried.

"Yeah! Which one is the stick?" Another jeered.

This set the boys off again as they pointed. The one inside the circle only chuckled and never let his eyes leave Sebastion's. He walked up to Sebastion, still smiling, placed his stick in his left hand, and with his right, he backhanded Sebastion with a loud slap, sending him into a spin.

Sebastion hit the ground with a thud that he heard more than felt. The air left his body, and he felt the world begin to fade. It was almost as if he had left his body. He didn't feel anything; not bad, not good, nothing. He was no stranger to this type of abuse or even to being knocked nearly unconscious. Many times, he had stepped too close to Keeper's staff or said something he didn't like.

Opening his eyes, Sebastion saw a small ant on the ground carrying a dead insect. He wondered how it could just be going about its business when all this was going on. It could have been so easily crushed. Then he was kicked in the ribs, and the world tilted again as what little air that was returning left him again.

The boys were yelling and screaming, and he felt things that could only be stones bouncing off of him. They hurt, but he was still too far away from himself to really feel the biting impact of them. He rolled into a fetal position and waited for another kick.

Keeper's words came to him, in that labored and always on-the-verge-of-rage way he had of speaking.

"It's not the size that wins a fight; it's who wants it bad enough. If you're not committed, then there is no shame in running."

Sebastion shot up quickly with all his speed, looking everywhere for a place to run, but the boys were still surrounding him. They saw him desperately looking for a way out and began to laugh and point again. He knew what he had to do.

He wanted to run, but that option was obviously out. He only had one other choice. He needed to commit himself completely, as Keeper had told him. He had to go into this with everything he had. He had to fight.

The boys watched as their companion ran around the circle with his hand raised above his head. They all cheered him and laughed—and then they stopped.

When the excited boy no longer heard the cheering, he looked to see what was wrong. He realized their eyes were not on him now but on the skinny boy in the center of the circle. Turning, he thought the boy standing with his stick in his hand looked somehow different. It was as if he had grown, but it was the skinny boy's eyes that really seemed to have changed. It was as if all fear had run out of him.

The champion of the circle of boys spat on the ground and moved forward.

"He wants to be tough now. I'll make him cry again!" he said. He ran forward and he couldn't help but think the skinny twig of a boy stood so strangely still. He curled his hand into a fist and sprang, but Sebastion moved fast out of the way. The other hit the ground hard, but the boy was no stranger to fighting, and he curled up standing again in one motion. He had grown up with the orphans, had been the youngest and had to continually prove himself. Fighting was as natural as eating or sleeping. As he found his footing, he found Sebastion just inches from his face.

With a loud crack Sebastion struck the boy in the face with the stick. The boy doubled over and Sebastion kicked him hard in the knee. Sebastion stood over him waiting to see if the boy would make an effort to get up.

After just a few seconds, the boy attempted to stand, but Sebastion shot out like a snake, hitting the boy in the back of the head with his stick again. The boy went down and this time he lay still and did not move.

Sebastion looked up and found all the boys staring at him with shocked expressions. They recovered quickly, however, and their looks of amazement quickly turned to anger.

The leader stepped forward and yelled, but the only word Sebastion understood was "kill." The leader shot forward, grabbing Sebastion by the throat faster than he could react.

He tried every trick Keeper had taught him, but the larger boy just wouldn't loosen his grip. He tried kicking him in his soft parts, but it did nothing. He tried to reach his face to gauge his eyes, but the bigger boy's arms were far too long for Sebastion to reach him. He wasn't getting any air and he was starting to see stars as the world began to tilt again. Sebastion fell to his knees with the boy's hands still around his neck. The leader let go with one hand and pulled a knife from his belt.

Sebastion began to panic and tried to concentrate on not passing out, looking around for anything that could help him. He could just make out a small knife in the boy's boot.

With spots in front of his eyes now, he knew he didn't have long. He let go of the boy's hand that was squeezing the life out of him and grabbed the little knife. The grip on his throat tightened, and he thought he would pass out for sure. With a desperate last effort and economy of movement he has been trained for, he lashed out at the boy's hand that held the knife. Then the pressure stopped.

The knife dropped to the ground beside him as Sebastion rolled to the ground, along with two hefty fingers. Blood began to shoot into the air; the leader of the boys screamed in pain and anger.

One of the boys picked up a bow that was lying nearby and notched an arrow.

Sebastion tried to regain his breath as the air burned his throat.

A knife flew through the air and the boy's arrow fell to the ground as the string of the bow was severed.

"You boys have had your fun," Keeper said, standing there as if he had been there the whole time. "You putrid children will be leaving now, or ... I will cut off more than fingers." He moved forward with his head barely visible within his cloak, advancing more like a ghost than a man.

The boys were so surprised by his mysterious appearance that they didn't move at first. Even the leader was staring at him, forgetting his severed fingers and the blood that was still running down his shirt as he held his hand close to his chest.

Keeper stopped moving, his cloak blending with the forest so that he almost seemed to disappear. He looked hard at the boys before speaking.

"If you remain, I am going to kill you ... all of you. Do you understand?" He watched as they exchanged looks. "IDIOTS! LEAVE! NOW!"

Those words shook them from their stupor, and they started grabbing their gear and running back into the forest. The last one out of the small clearing stopped and looked at the buck hanging from the tree. He looked back at Keeper, who gave him a vicious grin under his hood. The boy quickly jumped into the brush after the others.

Keeper turned to Sebastion, who was slowly getting to his feet now. He thought the troublesome rat of a boy was looking even frailer with his shirt off, as he looked him over with disgust.

Sebastion felt the welts on his face and body, most of them from the rocks the boys had thrown at him. He ran his hand through his hair that was knotted and had sticks and leaves tangled in it from rolling on the ground.

Keeper noticed blood on his pants. "Are you hurt?" he asked, without a hint of concern in his voice.

Sebastion looked down at his pants. "It's not mine."

Keeper smiled, and Sebastion knew he thought it was the blood of one of the boys on his pants. He didn't have the strength to explain, so he left it at that.

Keeper eyed the deer hanging from the tree. "Did you kill that monster?" He asked.

Sebastion looked over at the deer. "No." He replied. "It almost killed me."

Keeper looked over at Sebastion and gave him a hard stare. "You disobeyed me."

At first, Sebastion looked at the ground, but then raised his head to look Keeper in the eye.

"I know."

Keeper's eyebrows lifted nearly to his receding hairline.

"What's this? Are you challenging me, boy?"

Sebastion lowered his gaze once more, too tired now to fight.

"Can we go home?" he mumbled.

"We can after you make a litter to carry this giant creature home with us." Keeper pulled a pipe out from somewhere inside his cloak and started stuffing tobacco into it.

"Let me know when you are ready and I will instruct you on how you will prepare my venison stew." With that, he lit his pipe and walked off into the forest.

***

Things changed for Sebastion that day in the forest. The encounter with the boys had been the only contact with people he had ever had, other than Keeper. Having nothing else to base an opinion on, he decided he hated them all. He thought he must be something different from what Keeper and the vicious boys in the forest were.

He knew nothing of the outside world … only the small parts from reading Keeper's books. But he felt he knew enough that he did not want to be a part of it. From watching the forest animals, he knew that the older and weaker would eventually die. Sebastion knew that one day Keeper would no longer be around and that he must learn to defend himself against the world of people.

He never wanted to feel as weak and helpless as he had in the grip of the large boy strangling the life out of him. He knew that if he was to survive another encounter, he would have to be prepared. Never again would he allow himself to be in that position.

Sebastion threw himself into Keeper's instructions and committed himself to learning whatever he had to teach. Never again would he let them make him feel the way they had that day. He would become like his Keeper and scare them off with just a look and a few choice words. Since the reading and writing came naturally to him, he needed to spend little time on them, and his keeper was more than happy to focus on The Art. In fact, the old man was delighted.

In the following cycles, the forest changed very little. Some trees fell, and some new ones grew to take their place. New animals replaced the old and weak. The summer turned to fall and then to winter again. The changing seasons were like just another breath in the forest's lungs. Birds sang their songs, and plants reached for the sky. Some things died, and others lived. Each passing day life came and went, and the forest breathed its life-giving breath, and another day would come on the heels of the last.

One warm summer night, as the frogs sang their lustful songs, and the insects were busy going about their work, Sebastion lay in a soft patch of dry moss just on top of a hill. The sun had been strong that day, and the green spongy moss still held its warmth deep inside.

His body was sore and lying there always helped his back when it ached. This knoll had always been one of his favorite places, and he came here often to watch the stars move across the sky.

He had grown, and his clothes were now far too small and worn almost to rags. His vest lay open to the sky as the breeze rolled over him. He had grown long and lean and was already the height of a man, though far too thin for his height. His dark hair was wild and unkempt as usual. He stretched and followed a shooting star as it blazed and then was gone.

Today his Keeper had left the forest to get supplies, which meant he would be gone for days. Sebastion used this time to practice the things he found most interesting. He loved practicing with Keeper's sword.

It was old and rusty, but the balance seemed good and he loved the feeling of it in his hands. Keeper told him, "the Art has little use for the sword, but some knowledge might be useful." Sebastion took this as the freedom to practice it as often as he liked.

He enjoyed it very much and would use it against invisible foes that would use a variety of different weapons against him. He imagined many encounters and he tried to incorporate his maneuvers using the old sword.

He had already studied hard to use different knives and staffs, as well as different archery and hand-to-hand techniques. It had not been too hard to translate these into using the sword.

He lay there letting the warmth soak into his back, running drills in his head while staring into the sky. Then he started to entertain his favorite dream of running away and living in the forest far away from here and free. He would roam the woods and just watch the animals as they went about their days. He had always had these dreams, but lately, they were accompanied by an uneasy feeling that something was going to pull him from Keeper and the forest. He knew nothing of the world, other than Keeper and his training, but Keeper himself has been treating him differently of late.

Looking back, Sebastion was sure it had started one particular evening when Keeper was drinking. He always did when he was in a foul mood. Sebastion asked him if he had grown up in the forest. His head had snapped up from his glass, and he had fixed Sebastion with a stare full of menace. Sebastion was familiar with this behavior, but he knew that sometimes in his rage, Keeper would slip and let out some pieces of information. Usually, they just created more questions, but even if he were beaten again, it would be worth the small bits of information about the outside world and where he had come from.

"Another word, worm, and I'll make you wish you were never born," Keeper had snarled.

Sebastion had thought about this for a moment.

"If I was born," he scratched his head, thinking, "then I must have parents. You said I didn't have parents."

Keeper came around the table like the wind, slapped Sebastion across the face, and was back in his seat, smiling a self-satisfied grin, before Sebastion could turn his head back from the blow.

"Do you care to go on, insect?" He had asked.

Sebastion sat there as if nothing had happened, returning his look. The only evidence of the blow was a swelling on his cheek.

"What was my mother like?" he asked as if he had never been struck at all.

Keeper was surprised only for a moment. Then fury took him. His face went pale and his eyes squinted to slashes in his face.

"Your mother?" he asked in a whisper of a voice. "She is an impetuous brainless mongrel like the litter the bitch bore." Keeper sat very still as he searched for a reaction. "Anything else?"

Sebastion had thought on this. He knew that asking anything else would probably take Keeper too far. Looking at Keeper, he said, "Thank you."

Keeper pulled a knife from his sleeve and hurled it at the side of Sebastion's head.

Without thinking, Sebastion grabbed the knife out of the air, instantly realizing this would most likely take his Keeper too far. He knew the knife was not meant to mortally wound him, and he could have just let it hit its mark, an ear perhaps, but instinct had gotten the better of him. He placed the knife on the table and left the cottage. Not only did Keeper not stop him but, from that day forward, Keeper never again laid a hand on him other than in practice.

Sebastion knew that their relationship had changed that day, but he did not know why.

It was getting late, and Sebastion remembered he had chores to finish but then he recalled that Keeper was gone and decided to stay just a little bit longer. He really enjoyed these nights, staring into the sky. They were very few with the non-stop work around the cabin and training.

He could not help thinking of Keeper's comments about his mother, and he often reflected on them. Did Keeper really know her? He said she had a litter. Does that mean he might have sisters and brothers?

What a fantastic thought! Would they be like him or like the boys he had run into in the forest? Why would his mother, if he genuinely had one, give him away to Keeper? Maybe it was because he wasn't like the rest of the "litter" as Keeper had called them. Perhaps the others were all like the boys in the forest, and he was different, and that is why she gave him away.

He was sure that had to be it. He had seen animals of the forest reject the offspring that were different. Usually though, those were deformed in some way. He was not deformed in any way he knew of, but he was sure that had to be it. He thought it would be nice to see what his mother looked like, though.

He played with these thoughts every night. He wanted to risk asking Keeper for more, but he was afraid. Not afraid that Keeper would strike him again, but fearful that Keeper might say he did not have a mother. He had thought about this so often that he did not want Keeper to take her from him.

The mosquitoes were becoming far too aware of his presence. He decided it was time to go. He picked up the rusty sword and headed back toward the cabin.

Two days went by without his Keeper around. There was a time when Sebastion would have felt frightened at the cabin alone. He had wondered if the boys would come looking for him, but as the years passed, his worry had slipped away. He now loved the freedom of being alone and away from the wicked little man.

There had been times when he was gone as long as a month, and sometimes Sebastion would wonder if Keeper would come back at all. But he always came back without any explanation and resumed the training as if he had never left. Most of the time, though, he was only gone for a few days. He would return with some supplies, and that would be that.

After the incident with the boys in the forest, Sebastion had stopped asking to go with him. He never wanted to be around people again. Yet he couldn't help feeling that he was missing something. It was like being very thirsty, but no matter how much water you drank, the thirst never went away. He was feeling more anxious than usual, and his body was going through many different changes. He could never ask Keeper about it, so he just attributed it to one of the many things that must make him so different. He wanted to leave, but he was still afraid of running into people. One day, however, he would be ready and would go and never look back. Every day he asked himself, "Is today that day?"

The next day, early in the afternoon, Sebastion was heading back from gathering wood for his evening fire. He was lost in his thoughts when he heard voices not far off. He froze, listened, and concentrated as hard as he could, but he lost it. He thought perhaps it was just his imagination. However, curiosity got the best of him, and he carefully and without a sound put down the bundle of wood and went to investigate.

He was not sure exactly where the voices had come from, but he moved in what he thought was the right direction. He was trying very hard to move soundlessly through the trees, but his heart was racing from excitement, and with every twig that snapped under his feet, he flinched. Concentrating on using the things Keeper had taught him, he focused on moving without being noticed.

He crested a small hill and spotted two men not far off walking close together, so he moved slowly down the slope using all the natural camouflage he could. When he got near the deer path the two were following, he put himself in position and waited for them to pass.

He watched them approach and recognized Keeper's bent figure under his heavy cloak as leaned close to the other man, speaking softly. The other was taller and seemed to have a long smooth gait. Sebastion thought the thick gray cloak strange attire for such a warm day and it hid most of his body. Only strands of long white hair flowing out of his hood were visible as he walked.

Sebastion could tell by the way Keeper was moving that the man with him had some authority over him. He had never seen Keeper show any sign of submissive behavior and found it strange. He tried to hear what they were saying, all the time trying his best to mimic Keeper's ability to hold so still he disappeared into the background.

"He is very good," the strange old man said in a deep, soft voice.

"Who is?" Keeper asked.

The older man just chuckled and kept walking.

The two men passed, and Sebastion trailed them from a distance. He tried to learn something about the man by watching his every step and concentrating on the inflections in his voice. Keeper was always trying to make eye contact with the man, but the old man's head was down and deep in his hood.

When they approached the cabin, Keeper ran forward and opened the door. The man—without saying a word—strutted into their home.

The man in the gray cloak fascinated Sebastion. He had never met anyone other than Keeper and those boys that had tried to kill him. He wondered why Keeper would bring someone here now, after all these years. He contemplated listening at the window but thought Keeper's keen ears would give him away. He decided instead to go get the firewood and come back to the cabin as if he knew nothing of their arrival. Quickly he retrieved the logs prepared for his act.

Sebastion came to the front of the cabin and he thought his heart would pop straight out of his chest. He juggled the wood he was carrying so he could work the handle to the door. When he walked in, he could smell the odor of some kind of strange tobacco that the old man was smoking by the fire. He came in and tried to seem as if nothing was out of the ordinary. Placing the wood by the fire, he started preparing the evening meal as he always did. Keeper ignored him as usual and continued talking to the man by the fire.

"I don't believe him at all," Keeper said, with a twinge of anger in his voice.

The big man continued to puff out clouds of smoke from the pipe that stuck out of his deep hood.

"There is not the time since I remember that he has spoken the truth," Keeper continued.

The man grunted his agreement.

"If I were ... back, I would have him explain to me where he gets these insane ideas! I would—"

"Enough," the man commanded quietly and without removing the pipe from his lips. He turned his head only slightly in Keeper's direction. "You will continue to do exactly what you are told to do." There was a short pause. "Someday, when you are running things, you can make all the decisions. Until that time, show some respect. He is not one to take to disrespect ... as you will recall."

Keeper reached up and touched an old white scar that ran across his pale-yellow cheek.

Sebastion could tell that Keeper was taken aback by this, but he said nothing. He did wonder why Keeper was so afraid of this man? Who is he and why was he here? And who is this other the big man spoke of? Sebastion's head was buzzing like a beehive with all the questions he had.

The strange old man gently knocked his pipe against the fireplace, and the tobacco that was still there fell onto the floor. There was a small burning ember in the dirt on the floor, and he squashed it under his boot. Sebastion noticed that the man wore what looked to be riding boots. Not the soft type of shoes his keeper would wear to soften noise. These looked to be something a soldier might wear. The old man turned slowly to Sebastion. "Okay. Let's have a look at you, then."

Sebastion was suddenly more nervous than curious and looked over at Keeper, who just ignored him, looking into the fire.

"Don't worry, boy; you won't need your nursemaid for this," the stranger continued.

Sebastion could see Keeper's eyes give away his anger, but he said nothing.

The man looked him up and down. Sebastion could still not make out his face. "You are not feeding him enough." The man grabbed his arm and Sebastion tried to pull away, but the old man tightened his grip like a vice.

Sebastion started to get angry and began to resist more strongly, but the old man leaned in close and whispered, "Do not be afraid. I am here to take you from this place. Soon you will experience things you've only dreamed about. For now, just relax." The old man's words froze him as still as a rock. He could not believe what he had just heard.

When he was able to move again, Sebastion turned to Keeper, who was now giving the two of them a very suspicious look.

The old man loosened his grip slightly and gently pinched the skin on the back of his arm. He leaned close and studied Sebastion's skin.

"You have begun the dosing far too early." The old man scowled and gave Keeper a hard look from within his deep hood.

"It is no wonder the boy cannot put on weight."

"The boy is growing too tall anyway," Keeper said, mumbling almost to himself.

The old man ignored him. "What do you call him?" he asked.

Sebastion decided it was time to speak, "My name is Sebastion."

Keeper flew at him in a rage and backhanded him across the face.

Sebastion quickly shifted his weight so that most of the blow went right by him. Being used to this treatment, Sebastion just looked to the old man for a reaction to his name.

The man just looked at him, smiling a strange knowing grin.

For the first time, Sebastion was able to see his full face within the hood. The man was even older than he had thought. The man's smiling face had so many lines and wrinkles that Sebastion had to smile back at him. Sebastion somehow thought that man even looked familiar in some way. Though he knew that was impossible.

"Your mistreatment of this boy should have turned him into a whipped dog." He turned his gaze to Keeper, and his smile disappeared as quickly as it had come.

"Instead, you have a wolf cub. And I suspect he is not far from returning to his natural ways." He pulled his large hood off his head. "And I wager that will go very badly for you. It is good I came when I did," he said, turning to Keeper to make his point.

Sebastion stared in astonishment at the old man's completely bald head. The long white hair that was coming from the man's hood was sewn in. The hair was still there hanging down his back from the hood he had let lay behind him. Sebastion's thoughts began racing again. Why would somebody do that? This man is so strange. What did he mean when he said he would take him from here?

Keeper saw Sebastion staring at the old man's head and rolled his eyes.

The old man, however, was still smiling.

"So, your name is Sebastion, is it? Where did you get that name?"

Sebastion thought about that, but he could not remember when he had first heard his name. Surely, Keeper had named him. If not him, then who?

Sebastion turned to Keeper for help. "Don't look at me. I've never given you a name nor heard you call yourself one."

The man was looking at him intensely now.

"Names are a sign of individuality, and that is something that can be very dangerous for the likes of us … Sebastion." His gaze hardened. "You will keep that name secret, am I clear?"

"But... " Sebastion started.

The old man straightened, and it seemed to suddenly get cold in the small room. In an instant, the old man became more imposing than Keeper had ever been.

Sebastion just lowered his eyes and stepped back.

"Am I clear?" the man asked again in a voice that was more commanding than Sebastion had ever heard or thought possible.

"Yes," Sebastion quickly answered.

Keeper chuckled to himself by the fire at Sebastion's reaction.

The next four nights, Sebastion had a great time hearing stories of the outside world from the old man. Keeper kept to himself and only came to them when it was time to train. The man would watch closely when Sebastion and Keeper fought and went through their drills. Keeper was trying to push Sebastion to show the stranger what they were capable of.

On the fifth day, the old man began to shake his head angrily as they trained. They were practicing with dull knifes circling each other and making lunges. It was Keeper's turn to be the aggressor, and Sebastion was blocking his thrusts easily. Without thinking about it, he was allowing Keeper to make small hits, as he had for many years now. He knew that blocking all of Keeper's attempts to make contact would enrage him, and that would mean no supper.

After watching Sebastion let Keeper make two small cuts to his arm, the old man stood up, furious, "Enough of this show!"

The satisfactory look on Keeper's face faded into confusion. "What's wrong?" he asked, spreading his arms defensively. "You can't expect the boy to block every blow. I have far more experience and skill than this ... clumsy ape."

The old man rose from the log he had been sitting on and slowly walked to Keeper. "This 'clumsy ape' is playing with you."

Keeper laughed sarcastically. "All due respect to you, but that is ridiculous." He shook his head and gave Sebastion a smug look.

"Really?" The old man's simply replied, one single eyebrow-raising on his wrinkled head. Sebastion thought the expression made him seem more like a predator than a man. As if by magic, a knife was in his outreached hand. "You will take this knife, and you will draw blood from this clumsy ape." With a flick of his hand, the knife was protruding from the ground at Keeper's feet.

The old man locked eyes with Sebastion. "You will defend yourself to the best of your abilities. Your Keeper will be the very least of your problems if I think for a moment you are still puckering holding back."

Sebastion looked deep into those intense light-colored eyes and believed him.

Keeper smiled as he circled Sebastion. He was very confident and moving like a serpent looking for the opportune time to strike.

"Keeper, I don't—"

"Be silent, boy!" Keeper yelled back at him. "I was given an order, and if he wants you to bleed, then by the dark, so you shall bleed."

Sebastion tried to keep a safe distance, but Keeper kept coming closer as he circled.

The old man was thoroughly enjoying watching. He had sat back down on the log with his hands behind his head. He was delighted and wore a broad grin in his white beard and impossibly wrinkled face.

Keeper made a lunge, and Sebastion moved backward, tripping over a root. He went down, and Keeper was there with his knife.

Like a flash, Sebastion grabbed Keeper's wrist inches before the knife plunged into his chest. He lifted his leg hard and flipped Keeper over him and jumped up to face him.

Keeper stood up slowly, holding his arm across his chest. His confident smile had faded and was now replaced with a snarl of rage and hatred.

"I've been here wasting my life on you, worm, living my life taking care of a snot-nosed little ... nothing! And that is what you will always be!"

He came on Sebastion in a fury; however, every slash, kick, or punch was met with a block. Keeper backed off to take a breath.

"You have been holding back on me! I will know why, insect!"

Sebastion did not know what to say; he had always submitted to Keeper. Holding back in practice seemed only natural. He never thought he could beat Keeper, and he had sensed Keeper's need to believe himself to be the superior fighter.

Keeper moved in again, and Sebastion was half-heartedly blocking his blows as he played with the thought of beating Keeper for the first time in his life ... all those years being afraid ... all those beatings and insults. It was Sebastion's turn to get angry now. All those nights going to bed hungry and sick.

This time it was Sebastion's eyes that were beginning to flare in anger. "Do not show me your temper, BOY," Keeper said, between clenched teeth. "I will cut you in two, I WILL!"

Sebastion just stood there staring at him. He felt as if he was seeing him for the first time. His Keeper was prematurely aged and bent. He had many lines on his face from frowning, his eyes cruel and cold. His body was discolored from the poisons and far too thin, and his hair gray and lifeless, as was his heart.

"So many years you have told me I was nothing," Sebastion took a step forward. "Though I admit I don't know much, I do know that no one should beat a small boy when all he asks for is scraps from your plate."

"SHUT UP! You'd better not say another damn word!" Keeper was frothing at the mouth now as anger took him.

The old man sat at the edge of the log like he was watching a show. He had his chin in his hands, and a wide grin still on his wrinkled face.

Keeper charged at Sebastion like a crazed boar.

Sebastion stood there—his eyes starting to well from tears of realization that it was only his own fear that had kept Keeper abusing him. He whipped out his fist, and Keeper ran right into it, snapping his head back. Falling backward, he landed hard on his back. Sebastion heard the sharp wheeze of Keeper's breath shooting out of his lungs when he hit the ground.

No stranger to fighting, Keeper recovered quickly. Not long after he hit the ground, he was rolling on his way back up. This time he had a knife in each hand.

Sebastion couldn't help but wonder where the new knife had come from. Keeper's words came to him then. "Always have a surprise up your sleeve. It may just save your life one day." A cold chill ran down Sebastion's back as he realized that he would be facing Keeper as an enemy now and not as a teacher.

Keeper did not say a word but began to circle Sebastion like a hungry cat.

Sebastion glanced at the old man, who gave him a sign to look at the ground near the tree. Lying there, he saw his training staff. He knew if he was going to live through this fight, he would need to find a weapon to defend himself, other than a small dull knife.

Keeper, however, saw Sebastion glance at the staff, and he moved to the weapon first and put himself squarely in front of it.

Sebastion took a step backward, knowing he did not have a chance if he could not find a better weapon to defend himself. He took another step back, and his foot hit something that caused him to nearly fall. He cautiously looked down and saw Keeper's old, rusted sword. Picking it up, he held it before him nervously.

Keeper laughed, delighted that Sebastion could find only a rusted sword to defend himself. "Ho, there little boy, what do you expect to do with that?" he taunted, but his eyes never left Sebastion's.

Sebastion felt cold anger rising inside him now. Keeper's words came to him then as they had that time in the forest with the boys. He knew what he had to do. He had to commit.

"I think I will repay you for some of those scars you gave me," Sebastion said, clenching his teeth.

Keeper's knives disappeared back into his sleeves, and he picked up his staff. Sebastion put his own knife away and concentrated on his sword, lowering his body and taking a defensive stance.

Keeper rushed forward, and the two of them went into a dance of strikes and blocks. They each fought fiercely, and neither showed any sign of giving in.

"You have been practicing with that butter knife," Keeper said breathlessly. "Another secret you have kept from me, boy," he accused. He charged again, swinging his staff in so many directions that it was a blur.

Sebastion met them all with blocks. The sword in his hands seemed to move by itself, always finding the staff to block it. All the practicing and committing the moves to memory was now paying off better than he could have imagined. Some of the ways it twirled he didn't even remember learning.

The old man, meanwhile, was stuffing tobacco into his pipe quickly, trying not to miss any of the show. He was still smiling and still quite pleased with himself for initiating this fight.

Sebastion's hands were beginning to sting from blocking all of Keeper's blows, and he was not sure how long the old sword would hold out against this type of punishment. He could feel the blade becoming loose within the Pommel. He decided to change his strategy and let Keeper's blows slide off the edge rather than absorbing the entire force of the strikes.

Keeper swung the staff hard at Sebastion's head. Sebastion slightly angled his blade, and the Staff easily slid off. Keeper had to take two steps to regain his balance.

The eyebrows of the old man on the log shot up in surprise, and he clapped his hands with delight, clenching the pipe in his teeth.

Keeper was having problems compensating for Sebastion's new technique, and every time he connected with the staff, he would lose his balance ... and Sebastion was gaining confidence. For the first time, Sebastion started taking the offensive rather than just defending himself.

Keeper was becoming more desperate with his blows and leaving himself open. His confident attacks were being replaced with off-balance sweeps and jabs.

Sebastion tipped his blade in a manner that Keeper thought was too low, and the wicked man tried to drive the staff into Sebastion's face.

He took a step forward and found that Sebastion had feigned the opening and had something else in mind. Keeper had moved quickly, but before he could react, the flat of Sebastion's sword hit him hard on his backside.

The old man watching from the sidelines coughed out a large cloud of smoke. He laughed between fits of coughing and wheezing and was slapped his leg and pounding his feet on the ground.

Keeper backed off, rubbing his wounded backside furiously, and threw the staff to the ground. He watched as the old man laughed, thoroughly enjoying himself. Not at my expense, Keeper thought. Turning to Sebastion, who was watching the old man with a hint of a smile on his own lips, Keeper reached deep into his sleeves.

Sebastion watched as the old man had his fit. He looked so happy that Sebastion could not help but smile back at him. In an instant, however, the old man's face froze, staring in Keeper's direction. Sebastion snapped his head back, and as he turned, he instinctively moved out of his original position. A knife flew by, right where his head had been only a second ago. The second knife was right behind it, and this one embedded itself deep into Sebastion's forearm. He dropped his sword, and Keeper rushed forward, picking up the staff.

Two new knives swished through the air past Sebastion's head. Keeper screamed, not moving. A knife now protruded from each of Keeper's feet, pinning him to the ground. Keeper could not even fall to the ground without the blades cutting his feet more.

Sebastion could only stare at him, his eyes wide.

Keeper dropped the staff and put his hands on his head, not knowing what to do.

Sebastion forgot for the moment that a knife was embedded in his forearm. However, it was not long before the pain overcame his surprise. He was seeing stars and things were going dark.

Suddenly, there at Sebastion's side was the no-longer-smiling old man, saying something slowly. Still, Sebastion could not understand any of it. The old man gently pushed Sebastion to a sitting position, and he went down with a thump. Then, walking to Keeper, he pulled the knives from the former teacher's feet as if he were pulling forks from a roasted pig.

Keeper yelped and collapsed to the ground.

***

"I know it is sometimes easier for us to use names, so I will give you a name to call me, but rest assured it is not my real name. Nor will you ever know my real name. Names can kill, and they have power you cannot understand yet. You must not ever reveal your real name unless you trust the other person completely. Even then, you should be cautious. For now, you may call me... " The strange old man paused for some time thinking. "You may call me Rayor, for now." The old man smiled to himself at that. "Yes, that seems appropriate."

Sebastion watched as some kind of bitter humor washed across the wrinkly old face. He thought he saw a flash of sadness, but it happened so quickly he could not be sure.

Nearly a week had gone by and Keeper had not spoken or even looked in his direction. On the sixth day, Keeper collected as many things as he could carry and limped off toward the trees.

Sebastion went out on the small porch to watch him go. He wanted to say something but nothing came to his lips.

Before disappearing, Keeper turned and the two locked eyes. It was some distance, but Sebastion could see the expression on his face and it disturbed him. It was almost like ... empathy. Sebastion felt confused—he had never seen that expression on Keeper's hard face before. Didn't he hate him?

Keeper looked down and began to turn away. Still, as if forgetting something, he turned back quickly, mouthed two words, and disappeared into the forest.

They were two words Sebastion was familiar with, but he still had no idea what Keeper meant. He pondered them, running the words repeatedly through his mind. What could he have meant by that? And why that look? Going inside, he grabbed the rusted sword Keeper had left behind. He always thought better with the sword in his hand. He twisted it around and around, walking the floor in front of the empty fireplace. Knowing he would probably never see Keeper again somehow made him feel sad. Not that he would particularly miss the cruel man, but it meant that the only person he had really known throughout his childhood was gone. He looked at his bandaged arm. In a way, it meant his youth was gone as well.

"Choose well" were the two words Keeper had said. "Choose well."

Sebastion was still pacing when the old man who now called himself Rayor came lumbering back into the small cabin.

"Where's the sour man?" This is what Rayor had begun to call Keeper after the battle between student and teacher. Rayor looked around and saw some of Keeper's things were missing. "Did he leave?" Rayor asked, surprised.

"Yes, I believe he is gone … for good," Sebastion said, still a little sad.

Rayor looked at him, raising a brow. "Don't tell me you're going to miss him?" he questioned, screwing up his face. "Because if you do, then your brain has already turned to mushrooms before even puckering growing old."

Sebastion smiled and shook his head. No, he would not miss Keeper, nor miss the beatings and hungry nights.

He certainly wouldn't miss the practices where he felt he had to let Keeper cut him once or twice nearly every evening just to avoid an argument …` or worse. "No," he answered the old man simply.

Rayor was angry that Keeper had left. He kept mumbling things like "stupid" and "foolish" and "ignorant" throughout the evening and part of the next day. When the third day came, however, Rayor announced that they would be leaving in one hour. Sebastion was to pack whatever he wanted and could carry "that won't slow you down" and be ready. Rayor went off in the forest and did not come back until almost an hour was up.

When he returned, his face was pale, and he was breathing fast.

"All right, boy. Let's move out."

Sebastion hoisted a blanket full of books and one more pair of pants onto his back and made for the forest in the same direction that Keeper had gone.

"Where are you going?" Rayor asked.

"What?" Sebastion asked, stopping and giving him a confused look.

"What do you have in the bag?"

Sebastion told him, and Rayor rubbed his head within his deep hood.

"And do you expect to eat books and drink pants?"

Sebastion thought on that. He was not stupid and got the point.

Several minutes later, they both started out again. This time Sebastion still had the blanket he'd fashioned into a pack, but now it contained not only the books and pants, but all the dried meat, all the bread, and two throwing knives. Additionally, there was a small bladder of water strapped to his belt, along with Keeper's sword.

Rayor had requested he leave the sword, but Sebastion would not. Apparently, seeing something in Sebastion's eyes that said he would not leave it behind without a hassle, maybe even a fight, Rayor did not insist, believing he would have had more trouble convincing the boy to come with him. After all, they had met only days before, and now he was changing the boy's world completely.

Although the world Sebastion had known before was not great, it was the only one he knew, and he felt relatively safe in it, even with the sour man's temper and poisons. Where he was going now, he would be in far more danger, but he would also be able to live more like a boy than a battered servant and training partner.

Rayor had to slow several times as Sebastion looked back. The sun was high above them and Rayor knew they had a long way to go yet.

"Have you never been away at all?" he asked the skinny boy who had no right to be as tall as he was.

Sebastion just shook his head.

"Not even to go hunting?"

Sebastion thought of the boys in the forest and shook his head in denial more vigorously.

"Well then, it looks like you will be having quite the adventure coming up." Rayor smiled. The wrinkled man's eyes sparkled inside his hood.

Sebastion looked at him and had to smile too.

"I guess," he responded, unsure and a little frightened.

They traveled the rest of the day before coming to a small town. Standing atop a hill, they looked at it from the shelter of the trees. There was a light breeze, and Rayor's hood kept filling up with air and ballooning out. The days were still warm, so neither had any need for a cloak, much less a hood, but Rayor wore his every day that he and Sebastion were together.

The old man told Sebastion that, since they needed supplies, he would be going to the town. He did not ask Sebastion to join him, and that was fine with him because he had no desire to see more people like the boys he had already met years ago.

"I will be back shortly. If someone comes by, just tell them your father is in town getting supplies and is expected back at any moment."

Sebastion shook his head. It would seem strange calling Rayor his father and he was not sure he could say it convincingly. In fact, he was not sure he had ever said that out loud before.

"Okay, but..." He started but didn't finish.

"Oh, for The Lady's sake, just spit it out already!" Rayor said, annoyed.

"It's just that, you know, what if they don't believe me?"

"What?" Rayor asked, confused.

"I mean that you're my ... you know."

"Your father?"

"Yes, my Father."

"They'll believe it. Now just go to the bottom of the hill and stay silent ... the way your Keeper trained you."

Sebastion nodded and headed down the hill before stopping. "Rayor," he called.

"What?"

"Do they have books?"

Rayor shook his head and turned toward the town, thinking that the boy should be a scribe, not an assassin. He's too tall anyway! Though he knew that he was considered by most to be a tall man.

Chapter 3 – Melodia & The Road

When Rayor reached the town, he found it to be nondescript; it had the main road with the usual general store, tavern, and jail. Some small houses were lining the main street, but not many. Most of the people that came here were farmers who had to travel to get to the town. The roads were quiet, as Rayor had suspected they would be.

His gray-hooded form moved quickly down the street to the store. He stood in front of the door for a few seconds, listening and, heard no one inside and no one close by. The only sound he heard was a loose shutter banging on a house further down the street. Somewhere even farther off, a dog was barking half-heartedly. Reaching for the knob, he pushed the door open. The big bronze cowbell made a dull "bong" from the top of the door.

Rayor flinched and grabbed the ball in the middle before closing the door. He made his way to the counter, searching the store for movement. The store itself was dark, and a lot of the goods looked like they'd been there for a long time. He heard a rat skitter under one of the shelves.

Arriving at the counter, he heard the breathing of someone asleep on the other side. He leaned over and saw the shopkeeper sitting in a low chair with his legs crossed in front of him. The black leather smock that he wore was faded in the middle. He had no shirt on underneath, and his hairy rolls folded in crisscrossed patterns under his smock. His chin was resting on his chest so that Rayor could see only the top of his head. The shopkeeper had grown his hair long on one side and flipped it over to cover his baldness. The hair there was so greasy that it looked to be glued in place.

A rush of loathing for the man shot through Rayor, and he had not even spoken to him yet. Almost instinctively, he picked up a trinket from the counter and promptly bounced it off the shopkeeper's head. There was an audible "thwack," and the fat shopkeeper came awake.

Reeling at the assault, the grotesque-looking man nearly fell out of his chair. When he did finally get his legs underneath him, he stood upright, wide eyes full of rage.

"Who ... what the ... " he muttered, rubbing his meaty hand across his greasy head.

Rayor stood there silently, waiting for the man to compose himself. He had tucked his hands into his sleeves and let his hood fall forward to cover his face.

All the shopkeepers could see was a tall, cloaked figure, with strands of gray hair coming out of his hood.

They stood there as if the shopkeeper was trying to ascertain whether this figure was really there or if he was just dreaming. Confirming this, the shopkeeper reached out to touch the old man.

"Touch me and not much of that hand will be returning," Rayor said before the hand could make contact.

The shopkeeper jumped back, startled.

"Forgive me, kind sir," he said in a raspy voice that made the hair on the back of Rayor's neck stand up. "I was not sure if I was still dreaming or not. Something had … awakened me." He cast a suspicious eye at Rayor.

"Can I help, ya?" he finally asked rather bluntly, regaining some of his composure.

"I'm here for supplies," Rayor said flatly.

The shopkeeper suddenly rubbed his hands together, greedy with the prospect of a sale.

Rayor could not help thinking he looked like a fly ready to lunch on a pile of dung.

The shopkeeper leaned forward slightly, looking into Rayor's hood, and a small medallion previously hidden under his smock slipped out by his armpit.

Rayor sighed audibly.

"Somethin' da' matter, my lord?" the greasy man inquired sarcastically.

Pulling the hood from his head, Rayor faced him.

The shopkeeper crossed his arms and looked him over. "Well, now," he mocked. "What kind of man sews hair into his hood?"

"The kind that is not interested in your stupid questions," Rayor retorted sharply. He reached into his cloak and pulled out his own talisman, holding it out for the greasy man to inspect.

The shopkeeper's face took on a new look. No longer was there a sideways smirk in the unwashed rolls of facial skin. Instead, there was obedience and fear … yes, Rayor saw fear there as well.

"It seems we have something in common." Rayor had an overwhelming urge to puke on the shopkeeper's boots, but instead, he just put his talisman back and returned his hood to his head.

"Yes, it seems we do," the shopkeeper replied, bowing slightly.

The two spoke for some time, slowly, and at times there were long pauses.

Their conversation was of nothing important, but inquiries such as "Do you think it will be a moist summer" or "Does the town have a market day?" All the while, however, their hands were moving rapidly, first one man's and then the other's.

The expressions on their faces would, at times, grow grim or elated, seemingly out of step with the conversation, which stayed simple and without real importance. They continued talking with their mouths while communicating with their hands until the door swung open and two dirty boys walked in.

One of the boys was missing some fingers from one hand. He was a large boy, and Rayor thought his hair was light underneath all the dirt and grime that was caked on. He went about stocking the shelves with this and that. The other boy started pushing a filthy mop around the floor. Neither would even attempt to make eye contact with the shopkeeper.

"They're mine if you want to give them a go," the greasy shopkeeper signed to Rayor in the silent language.

"They're your sons?" Rayor asked back, his fingers flittering.

"No, no. They're mine." He said it this time, smiling a smile that made Rayor almost lose his dried meat from this morning. He understood and wished he didn't.

"Where does the woman we spoke of live?" Rayor asked out loud, wanting to drown out the words he had just heard.

"She lives down the road in the red house. You'd best knock, as she has a lot of guests this time of the day. Not that I'm a regular visitor," the shopkeeper said, winking.

Rayor had a sudden urge to put a knife in this man but knew that would be unwise ... primarily since they both served the same master.

Writing down a list of things and handing it to the shopkeeper, Rayor told him to have the supplies ready before he came back at dusk and to leave them outside the shop. He was hoping not to ever look into the disgusting man's face again.

After he left the shop, he must have rubbed his hands up and down his cloak fifty times, but he still felt that they were dirty somehow. I may be an assassin, but that man makes me look like a... Like what? He asked himself. What the Light are you?

Pulling his hood more tightly over his head and feeling particularly ornery, he walked silently down the street.

When he came to the red house, it was tucked away behind a huge weeping willow tree. He stood there, taking it in.

The front porch was hanging onto the house like a drowning man would a floating piece of wood. The beams underneath had long ago buckled and broken. The front walk was utterly overgrown with crabgrass, making it very evident that no one had either entered or left through the front in a very long time.

Hearing someone coming down the side path, Rayor turned to see who it was. A middle-aged woman, pregnant and practically dragging a child by the hand, looked at him and spat on the ground before crossing the dirt road.

He looked back at the house, smiling. Nice to see I still have a way with women, he thought. He knew the woman's reaction was more about what went on in the house in front of him than with him personally, but he still found it funny.

He followed the well-used trail around to the back and found a small door several feet below the surface. It was apparent this was the door that was most used. He heard soft voices speaking, and he concentrated on hearing what was being said. Soon there was a creaking sound and then a rhythmic pounding.

Rayor went off to a nearby line of trees and waited. The pounding became increasingly louder, faster, and more desperate, and then it stopped. He could hear there was softer speaking now.

A few moments later, a black-haired man in expensive clothes came out, looking shameful and a little scared.

If he's married to the woman he just saw on the road, he should be scared, Rayor thought.

The man was still tucking in his shirt when he disappeared into the trees behind the house. He walked quickly by Rayor, not even realizing he was there.

Hearing movement inside, Rayor moved closer to the house and heard someone going up the stairs to the main floor. He went down the stairs to the red door and listened. When he was sure that no one was on the other side, he put his hand on the door handle and gently turned it.

Rayor peered into the room. It, too, was red in color, and incense was burning not far off. Feeling an urge to sneeze, he took a moment to regain control. There were chairs in the room and a small hallway that led to another room. He assumed that was where the bedroom was.

All of the windows had blankets nailed over them. This gave the room an eerie glow from the sun that was trying desperately to get through. On a wall to the left, there was a large tapestry that caught his eye because it moved in uneven patterns.

Closing the door behind him, Rayor moved silently to the tapestry. On it, there was a forest scene with a great huntress on horseback chasing down crazed wolves or wild dogs of some sort. The canine things were frothing at the mouth as if they were rabid. The movements of the tapestry made the huntress almost seem alive. He looked it over for a few more seconds, but he had not come to this spot to examine the art.

Rayor reached around the tapestry and pulled it aside. As he expected, there was a door behind it. He tried the handle, but this door was locked. Reaching into his sleeve, he pulled out a small box. Inside were little pieces of metal that he used to pick locks. He studied them and drew one out and he pushed it into the lock. As he slowly turned the knob, there was a satisfying click and then the sound of someone clearing her throat behind him.

He nearly jumped out of his skin. He whirled around, quickly reaching into his sleeve again, this time for a dagger. But the face that came into focus was familiar.

"YOU?!" he exclaimed in unconcealed shock.

Melodia just smiled, brushing her auburn locks from her face. She was holding her robe closed with one hand and trying to keep her curly hair at bay with the other.

The old man looked her up and down, and Melodia gave him the time to do it in silence.

"You haven't changed a bit," he said with a touch of jealousy.

She smiled again, and this time it reached her deep, dark eyes. She was barefoot and most likely had been in the middle of washing when she detected Rayor's presence.

"It's been a long time, K—."

"Do not use that name," Rayor said quickly. "I am no longer that person and never will be again."

She looked at him sadly and nodded.

He could not take his eyes from her face. She was still as beautiful as he had once known her to be. Perhaps there was just a little more wrinkling around the eyes, but nothing more than that. He had always suspected that Melodia was far older than he, but she never mentioned age ... even during that short time long ago when they had been more than friends.

"What a pleasant surprise, K—" She stopped herself and made a face at him. "What should I call you?" she asked in a playful tone.

He was not in a playful mood, however. "I don't give a damn, priestess." He let go of the tapestry and it fell back to its usual position covering the door. "I was told you ... sometimes saw the man that was with the boy?"

"You mean the cranky old man that always smelled to be rotting?"

Rayor shook his head in acknowledgment.

"Yes, I 'saw' him pretty regularly. What of it?" She shifted her weight from one foot to the other, trying to get comfortable. Her robe was coming undone and Rayor was finding it distracting. She sensed his uneasiness.

"How about we go upstairs and have some tea?" she asked.

"Would you not be more comfortable down here?" His sarcasm was unmistakable.

Melodia bowed her head, and Rayor saw a flash of shame cross her face. He suddenly wished he hadn't said it.

Yup, still got it with the women! IDIOT.

"Yes, let's have some tea," he said cordially, even smiling a little inside his hood.

The upstairs was much different than the rooms below. Here things were neat and well ordered. The furniture was not of high caliber, but everything was in its place and shined with fanatical cleanliness. Even the cloth napkin she offered him at the table did not show the slightest stain. He suspected she kept the upstairs this way to balance the downstairs.

"So, what brought you here?" he asked.

She was bringing the hot glass of tea to her lips and stopped.

"That's a ridiculous question." She took a sip and put the glass down. Then she wiped the table in front of her, in case any liquid from the glass might have spilled.

"I am here for the same reasons you are, whoever you are these days." She gave him another playful look. "Are you ever going to take off that hood? I know that is not your real hair. I think I would know your real hair, Ki—"

"Not my name," he said again, this time with just a touch of humor in his voice. He pulled the hood back from his head and leaned back, crossing his arms for her to see him.

"Why, you have no hair at all!" she exclaimed, her eyes wrinkling at the corners as a smile took over her entire face. "You can't know how nice it is to see a familiar face," she told him, the smile fading slightly.

"Even mine?" he asked seriously.

"Especially yours. You might try to disguise yourself with wrinkles and a bare head, but I will always see you … always."

He let that sink in, and it felt very sad.

"Why this?" he asked, sweeping his hands around.

"I was instructed to come here and watch. I was not told how or why, though I suspect the why." She took a long sip of her tea. "The how was not obvious to me at first. No, that was quite difficult. However, men have always taken a liking to me." She did not say this in a self-important way, but in a way that said that's just the way it was.

And Rayor knew it was true. He knew all too well.

"How else could a woman like me come to a town and be inconspicuous?"

He started to come up with answers in his head, but they all were pushed back down. This did make sense, though it did not mean he had to like it. "It's crap," he said, interrupting his own thoughts.

She looked at him, surprised. "What is?"

"This whole thing! The Lady allowing you to defile yourself to serve her selfish purposes, for one thing."

She looked angry when he said that, but he meant it.

"You're a priestess and a fine person, better than most I've ever met." That was a lie. He knew very well that she was the best person that he had ever met, but there was no need to let her know.

"It makes me want to..." He stopped then, squeezing the air in front of him with his big wrinkled hands. No man in this village would be good enough for her. That included him, and he knew it. The thought of those toothless buffoons doing what they were doing. The hot blood was rushing to his face.

"You still make rash judgments after all these years. Nice to know some things don't change," she said sarcastically. "And who are you to tell me I'm being used selfishly? It seems to me you're being used in that same way. The only difference is I'm being made to feel bad about it." Her face was now turning red as well.

The old man had a flashback to those times when they had spent so much secret time together.

"Same old Melodia," he said, smiling and letting the wrinkles fold up around his face.

A more natural color started returning to her face.

"Same old jackass. You always could play me like a flute." She winked at him, and he couldn't help but blush a little.

Taking a deep breath, he sipped his tea and decided it was time to get into it.

"What did the rotting man tell you, Melodia?" he asked her.

She shrugged her shoulders, sipping her tea.

"Not much. The most I could get out of him was that the boy was alive. Sometimes he would talk about leaving him there and running off with me to someplace or another. It was all bed talk, you know?"

Rayor shook his head, trying desperately not to let his head picture the boy's keeper with her.

I could kill him!

"He never let on much, and I tried not to push him too much. I was never told to get involved, so I didn't. Is the boy all right? Have you seen him?"

"Yes, he's fine." That was the problem with the blasted Lady of Light. She let the world think she loved them all and that love would save them all, but she would never get involved. Oh, no!

She couldn't ever dirty those precious hands! What a different life the boy would have had if The Lady had lent him one of her priestesses or even if he could be in one of the orphanages that The Lady was well known for.

No, that would not do for this poor little bastard. It took his master to intervene against "the rules" ...or some such nonsense. They never knew that the rotting man, as Melodia called him, was one of them. They thought he was just some random fellow that volunteered to be a nursemaid to the child. "It must be by chance. We must let things be as they will be." They would say. Bunch of gibberish. If the Lady even really cared about anything but herself, and he suspected she did not, at least not in a way that people believed. She would be somewhere weeping over dead butterflies while the people in the world fight for their lives. By the stars and everything that's up there, how could *she* have let Melodia do this? Why her. She is the one good thing I've come across, and The Lady uses her like a rag to wipe herself.

"K— Hey, you there?" Melodia brought him back.

"What? Oh, yeah. Sorry."

"I said, 'I wonder what he's like now?'" She asked, looking at him, concerned.

"He's fine." Rayor suddenly felt restless and wanted to leave. "I must be on my way." He got up a little too quickly and spilled a little tea.

Melodia was at his side in an instant, wiping the atrocity away. "Must you go already?" she asked without hiding her loneliness.

He wanted to tell her that she did not have to stay in this town a single second more. That he was taking the kid away from this place because his master was actually doing something, unlike the never-present Lady. He wanted to take Melodia in his arms and kiss those full red lips and say, "you will never have to do that again," but he couldn't. She must not know he was leaving with the boy. Because "It must be by chance; we must let things be as they will be," and all that godly poetic rubbish.

"I'm afraid I must, Melodia. I have a long journey ahead, and I fear soon the wind will begin to bite." He smiled at her and began moving toward the door.

"The boy is significant," she said behind him. "More so than you can imagine."

He turned back to look at her. "I know he has some role to play, but he is still just a boy."

"You like him. I can tell," she said, smiling again.

Rayor thought about that. "Yes, I guess I do. He reminds me of someone I once knew in another life."

She shook her head, knowingly. "Yes, I heard rumors of his lineage. I would expect you to see a familiar face."

Rayor whirled and crossed the space between her and him in a blur. They stood face to face, his eyes red-hot lava in his head. "I do not have a lineage, and neither does that bastard child. Do not mistake fondness for anything more than what it is. I am fonder of my knife than of anyone I have met thus far. I am not like you. We found that out long ago."

Melodia held her ground, looking up at him.

"Are we really all that different?" she asked.

Rayor made a disgusted sound in the back of his throat.

"If your priestesses did not have food brought to them, they would starve to death praying for wine and sweetmeats," he replied, his mouth dripping with sarcasm.

"I do more than pray," she said sadly.

Some of the fire left him, and he grabbed her arms.

"You are the one who should be worshiped. I see more iron in you than a hundred of your priestesses. Where is your Lady? She's as absent as her priestesses are useless!"

Melodia pulled away from him harshly.

"BLASPHEMY!" she yelled. "You will not speak of her in that way in my presence."

He waved a hand dismissively and headed again toward the door, his long strides taking him there quickly.

"Wait," she said in a small voice.

The door was partially opened, and he squeezed the knob hard in his hand. He did not speak but waited for her last barb, for her last word that would score its mark and leave him feeling empty and sad.

Instead, she ran up behind him and hugged his back tightly.

She smelled so good. Like herbs and vanilla. He closed his eyes and tried to burn the memory of her sweet scent into his very being.

Letting go a little, Melodia rose up on her toes. She kissed the back of his head ever so lightly.

"She has never stopped loving you ... and neither have I."

She let go, and the wrinkled old man walked out, making a point that it was through the front door this time.

***

It was getting dark when Sebastion saw the old man coming up the hill toward him. He had begun to wonder if he was coming back at all. By the way he was walking, Sebastion could tell he was upset about something.

When he came to where Sebastian was standing, he just signaled for him to follow, and they were off.

They walked in almost total silence for what Sebastion felt was a very long time. They camped, ate, and slept.

It was not until early afternoon the next day that Rayor finally murmured something more conversational than "watch out" when a branch swung behind him. Now he asked Sebastion if he knew any songs. He said he could use something to keep his old eyes from shutting.

Sebastion doubted that though, and instead thought Rayor was trying to help him pay attention. Never having done this much walking, Sebastion had tripped many times. He could fight for hours, but his body was not used to this kind of exercise, nor was he very good at it yet.

"I don't know any. There were some in Keeper's old books, but I can't remember any of them."

Rayor glanced back, giving him a strange look. "All right, then. I will see if I can remember any. It's been a long time. A very long time."

He said this in such a strange way that Sebastion looked up at him, but he could see only Rayor's back.

A few minutes later, Rayor shot up a finger and announced he had thought of one. He seemed very pleased with himself for being able to dig this out of his memory.

How very strange that I had to think that hard for the memory, but now that I have it, I remember it completely. He shook the thought off. "Okay, I will sing it once, and then we will sing together until you get it ... got it?"

"Uh, huh," Sebastion replied.

"All right; here goes. Pay attention," and Rayor started singing the song in a clear, deep voice.

> *"There once was a man from Tal-stad,*
> *He had an old horse and mean 'ole dog,*
> *A wick-ed wife and a jolly 'ole hog,*
> *This was the man from Tal-stad.*
>
> *Well, one day his horse up and died,*
> *His dog ran away, and that was just fine,*
> *You know his wife, she was no find,*
> *Yelling and shouting and very unkind,*
> *That was the life of the man from Tal-stad*

Well, one non-particular day,
Liking the hok og more than his dog,
Working to d'a bone for his home,
He packed his things and collected his hog,
No dog, no horse, no wife, and no strife,
And so it went with the man from Tal-stad,"

Sebastion had remained quiet for the entire song. At the end, he stopped walking.

Rayor heard him stopping and turned around to see what was wrong.

Sebastion was covering his mouth and bending over.

"Are you all right, boy? Are you sick?" Rayor asked. He walked closer and turned Sebastion around.

The boy was more than all right; he was laughing hysterically. He was trying to muffle the laughter.

"It wasn't that funny," Rayor said, smirking.

With that, Sebastion gave up and started laughing aloud.

"Keep it down. You'll alert every cut-purse and back-stabber from here to the Great City!"

But now Rayor was starting to laugh too.

When he started, Sebastion stopped to watch the ridiculously wrinkled man laugh and then went into another fit.

"Come now; I wasn't that bad. Was I?"

Sebastion just put his hand out, waving for Rayor to stop. Then Sebastion stopped suddenly and ran into the forest.

Rayor could hear him relieving himself a short distance away. He could hear him still laughing as well.

A big, genuine smile crept across Rayor's face. He had smiled before, of course, but it had been a long time since he had felt genuinely … happy. Yes, he felt happy. It had been so long, he had almost forgotten what it felt like. It scared him, but he also didn't want the feeling to go away. Having something he liked meant it was something someone could use against him.

The old man looked at the boy coming back from the forest, still chuckling, with utter amazement. He was enjoying himself. Rayor knew this would end badly for both of them and that he should put a stop to it … but he didn't want to.

They often talked from that point as they journeyed south. Rayor avoided personal questions about his past, like where he had come from and where he had been, especially questions about where they were headed. Still, they talked about other things—mostly about Rayor's adventures and things he had seen.

Sebastion knew that most of the stories were made up, but he did not care; he was having too much fun.

But it could not all be fun.

Rayor decided they would be traveling by night, leaving daytime for training—specific hand-to-hand training.

Sebastion could not believe how strong and quick the old man was. He knew so many tricks and strange movements that it soon became Sebastion's favorite time of the day. He began feeling better each day. He was no longer taking Keeper's foul-tasting brews, and he was regularly eating. He found that at times he was nearly holding his own with the old man ... although he suspected Rayor sometimes let him do better to boost his confidence.

Several days into their journey, under a huge elm tree, the two were huffing and sucking air into their exhausted lungs. They had gone through a particularly grueling exercise of grappling and throwing each other around a small clearing. Both were winded and bent over with their hands on their knees. Smiles were fixed on both their faces.

Rayor looked up and winked. "You're getting better quicker than I'd hoped. I thought I would at least have a few more weeks of being the master."

Sebastion just laughed quickly, and only because that was all his lungs would let him do. He did not want Rayor to know how much this last burst of energy had taken out of him.

Let him believe that I am advancing as fast as he thinks, he thought slyly, not knowing that the next time Rayor would expect the same level of committed effort or more ... most likely more.

When his breath started coming back to him, Sebastion stood up straight, and a thought came to him. Keeper had implied that he had siblings. He had said, Sebastion's "bitch of a mother had a litter," or something like that. Maybe since Keeper was able to tell him that much, then Rayor could elaborate on that. Then a thought broke through his defense like one of Keeper's staffs, would Rayor get upset or even mad at him? He did not know how to approach it; the question was like a fire that was burning in the back of his mind. If he ignored it, it would only get bigger before consuming everything in its way.

Standing up straight, he put his hands on his hips. While he struggled with whether he should proceed with the question, he stood there for some time, thinking over the right words to voice his questions.

"Are you constipated?" Rayor asked, chuckling to himself.

Sebastion did not know what that meant, but he was pretty sure that wasn't his problem.

"No, I don't think so."

Rayor laughed and crossed his arms to mimic Sebastion, facing him.

"I know you have questions," Rayor said in a sensitive tone. "But I cannot answer any at this time. There are ... things that must happen on their own before anyone can give you what you need."

Sebastion thought on that for a while. What were "things," and why would "anyone" care about him? He decided he didn't care and would ask the question that was on his mind anyway.

"Do I have any siblings? Am I part of a *litter*?"

Rayor cocked an eyebrow at him.

"A litter? Where is this coming from?" Rayor asked.

"Once, years ago, Keeper said my 'bitch of a mother had a litter' ... or something like that."

A dark look crossed Rayor's face.

"What else did he say?"

Sebastion thought, but he could not think of anything else Keeper had said that referenced his family ... if he had one at all.

"I think that ... I might be something different," Sebastion said, the words just coming out of his mouth. He wished he hadn't said that. It was as though the words popped out before he had even thought them through.

Might as well not stop now.

"I have met very few ... people. I don't like them. That is, until you. I do not think I am like the others. You know, Keeper and the boys in the forest."

Rayor nodded his head, understanding. "No. I do not imagine you are anything like your Keeper or the boys you met in the forest." Rayor sat down and pulled his pipe from the sack next to the tree.

"There are many things at work around us, boy." He lit his pipe using the small tinderbox he had.

Sebastion started pulling out his own pipe when Rayor grunted and waved it off.

"Too young and too skinny. You should not smoke until you at least have hair on your chin."

Sebastion scowled and put the pipe away. "Not that it matters anyway," he mumbled to himself.

"Oh, it matters, boy. It matters quite a bit."

Sebastion sat down a short distance away. "What matters, Rayor?"

Rayor looked up at the sky for some time before answering.

"The world is a strange and complicated act of balance, with many levels. We are a part of one level, while there are many above and below us.

If I was a farmer and I owned a goat, that goat's existence would be balanced by me. Its destiny would be almost completely ruled by me. If I were hungry for milk, it would be milked and allowed to wander the enclosure of my farm. If I wanted meat, then its destiny would be different. So it goes with the gods. Unfortunately, we are the goats."

Sebastion thought about this. He had no foreknowledge of farms, but he pretty much got the point.

"I don't think I want to be the goat," Sebastion said. His voice cracked, and the last part came out deep and in a commanding tone.

Rayor shot him a look of surprise.

"Sorry," Sebastion said, clearing his throat.

"Don't be. And I have a funny feeling that you don't have a goat's destiny."

Just then, a squirrel jumped into the shelter of the trees and chirped angrily at Rayor.

"Leave us alone," Rayor said, waving his hand at it.

"We could eat it," Sebastion whispered.

The squirrel stopped immediately and looked over at Sebastion as though he understood what he had just said.

"I think he heard me," Sebastion said, a small smile spreading across his face.

Rayor did not smile back.

"No, I try not to eat rats."

The little squirrel turned its head slowly toward Rayor as if it understood the insult. It chirped something that they were sure was an insult in the squirrel language.

Rayor spat at it, and it ducked and hopped slowly away, turning back to give Rayor a dirty look.

Sebastion had never seen a squirrel act like that, and he watched the place it had been long after it was gone. Glancing back at Rayor, Sebastion found him puffing his pipe and also looking at the place the squirrel had been. He had a dark, perplexed look on his face.

"What—" Sebastion started to ask, but Rayor just tossed him a glance that stopped the question from springing from his lips. Then they packed their things quickly and continued on their journey.

Sebastion was bursting with questions that whirled like tornadoes in his head, but all he could do was watch Rayor's back as he followed him.

It was not until morning and after a hot meal of rabbit that Rayor had killed with a sling that things were back to normal.

Sebastion sensed the opening and struck out with his question like a viper strike.

"So, what was it?"

Rayor laughed at his obvious pensiveness.

"Have you been turning that around in your head all this time?" he asked.

Sebastion didn't answer. Instead, he made that tell-tale sound with his tongue on the roof of the mouth that adolescents make when they don't get their way.

"All right, boy. No need to get worked up. What was what?"

Sebastian's eyes nearly popped out of his head. "What do you mean, what was what?" he exclaimed, exasperated. "What was with that squirrel thing, acting like an angry human?"

"Probably just crazed from some illness," Rayor shrugged ... but he knew that was not the truth. He had never seen an animal act like that before. It had definitely been acting like it understood them, and that disturbed him. Although he knew his master may have the power to do that, he felt somehow that it had not been him. It was something else, and that concerned him even more.

"We need to keep going," Rayor said, grabbing his bag and hoisting it onto his back. He kicked dirt into the small fire, putting it out, and they left.

The next few days were uneventful, but Sebastion enjoyed himself all the same. The farther south they journeyed, the stranger the trees, plants, and animals became. The trees here were much taller and less sparse. They were also much older. He could feel their ancient aura and felt very insignificant around them. To these trees, he was little more than a blip in time, a speck of dust. He had an overwhelming feeling that he wanted to climb into them and sleep. He even stopped several times, staring up at them longingly.

Rayor, however, was always there, pulling his tunic and urging him forward.

"Can't we just stop for a few minutes?" he pleaded.

"Keep moving, boy," Rayor growled.

"Please, I am so tired and these trees... " he trailed off, yawning into his fist.

"You will keep walking; MOVE!"

But Sebastion was losing feeling in his feet, and the trees sounded like they were singing to him in some lulling soft voice.

Rayor looked over his shoulder at Sebastion and rolled his eyes. "You must keep moving. I did not want to warn you about the trees because I thought you might be able to ignore their song. They are calling you to their limbs."

Sebastion's eyes began to close, and he turned, taking a step toward one particularly enormous tree. Its branches extended into the sky farther than his half-closed eyes could see.

Rayor walked over to Sebastion angrily, and slapped him hard on the side of his head.

"Ouch!" Sebastion cried out, putting his hands to his head. "What was that for?" he asked defensively, and a little angry.

"Maybe your Keeper was right about you, little boy!" Rayor roared at him. "Maybe you are just a weak little nothing! Is that it? Are you 'a nothing'? ARE YOU?"

Rayor attempted to slap him again, but Sebastion was too quick. He threw a hand up to block ... but the blow never came.

Instead, a smile spread across Rayor's face.

"You awake now?" he asked, amused.

Sebastion's face was red with anger, and he was confused by Rayor's strange reaction, but he still managed a "Yeah."

"Well, good. How about you take a look around now and see why I did what I did." Rayor's voice dripped with sarcasm.

It was strange to Sebastion hearing this tone coming from the old man.

"Look around at what?" Sebastion asked.

"Look around at what? Open your eyes, boy!" Rayor growled.

Sebastion shook his head and looked around. The anger he still had inside of him seemed like it was being sucked away by the tree song, but he held onto it as he gazed around.

"That's it," Rayor said, watching the boy's face.

Sebastion's brow furrowed as he concentrated on keeping himself angry.

The forest in front of him began to change before his eyes. The large, majestic trees suddenly became looming demon-like things with stretched out hands. The limbs were full of rotting mold, and the trunks of the trees were cracked and bleeding out sap-like blood from gaping wounds. Giant black beetles ran up and down the bark, feeding on the sap.

The song was changing, too. It no longer soothed him in gentle tones but now yelled at him ... no, it screamed at him.

For the first time, Sebastion noticed that there were no birds. The rotting trees extended high into the sky, and yet there were no birds. He couldn't even hear any close by.

"The ground," Rayor said in a low, patient voice.

Sebastion looked at the ground and saw the mold growing everywhere. It covered everything as if it were pulling the broken branches and pieces of sticks down into the dirt to die with it.

And there was something else. Between a few of the patches of mold, he could see white sticks jutting up out of the ground.

No, not sticks ... bones!

Sebastion felt the reality of his surroundings coming to him. Then the scene in front of him changed again. His eyes widened in horror, and the tree song now rumbled deep with fury. Turning in a tight circle, he saw the contours of the ground were not mold-covered sticks and branches but animals ... and people.

Close to the trunk of one tree, he could see the partially decayed head of a man, its dried peeling face frozen forever in a scream of terror. One of the man's arms, which he had previously taken to be a branch, was jutting upward and to the right, warding off some unknown horror.

"What... " The words left his lips in a whisper.

"We have to go, boy," Rayor said uneasily. "They wake up at night, and I don't plan to be around for that."

Sebastion couldn't peel his eyes away, though. Not far to the right was what looked to be a dog and to the left a corpse of a small horse. He did not know if the other half was under the mold or just gone.

Glancing at his feet, he saw he was standing on another skeleton's hand. He yelped and jumped off.

When his feet hit the ground again, they slipped apart on the slick mold, and he went down on his belly. On the ground now, he was facing the rotting face of the man in the mold.

Sebastion screamed and jumped up in mad terror.

Rayor grabbed him, but Sebastion pushed him off and ran as fast as he could. He heard the crazed laughter of the trees as he ran towards the light that was breaking between the trees some distance off. He vaguely heard Rayor yelling, but he could not stop running any more than he could stop screaming. He ran with all the strength his legs would give him.

The trees whirled past him. He thought he could feel the tree limbs reaching out and trying to grab him as well as the mold pulling at each foot as it came down. He forced himself to focus only on the small break of light that seemed to be a lifetime away.

His foot either hooked a root or the root caught it, but Sebastion fell. He felt the trees' elation more than heard it. Knowing the anger was still in him somewhere, he reached in and grabbed hold of it like a drowning man clutching a floating piece of wood. He held on to it tightly, threw his hands out, and rolled.

In an instant, he was up, Keeper's old sword slapping him hard against the thigh where it was buckled, and he started running again.

His head was woozy from flipping over so fast, but he pushed on with everything he had. He no longer screamed, but he pressed his teeth together and pulled his lips back like a snarling dog.

He heard Rayor yelling again, this time closer. His head was still spinning, but it was starting to clear.

"They're closing it!" he heard Rayor yell.

His eyes focused, and he saw the opening of light, but it looked like he was somehow farther away. No, the sun wasn't getting through as much... The opening between the branches was closing.

"THEY'RE CLOSING IT, THEY'RE CLOSING IT!" Rayor yelled.

This is madness! Rayor thought. As long as he had been coming here, the trees had never moved in the day. The trees always hunted the same way for as long as he could remember. They would lull their victims to their limbs with their soothing song. Their prey would fall asleep, clutching the branches like to a mother's breast. Then the night would come...

"RUN!" Rayor yelled.

But he could see the opening was closing too fast. He could feel more than hear the other branches moving, closing any other possible escape route they could take.

Through it all, Rayor did have to admit the boy was moving like a gazelle. His long legs were taking him faster to the opening than Rayor had hoped.

He's going to make it. By the Lady, he's going to make it!

The opening was no more than a small gap now. Rayor heard the trees howling triumphantly.

But the boy was not giving up. He ran straight for it. He jumped onto a protruding root and dived for the closing gap the way Rayor had seen men do from cliffs into deep water.

As Sebastion's toes cleared, the gap closed.

Rayor was alone.

The old man stopped running and stared at the place the boy had jumped through. It was now just a jumbled section of twisted branches and slimy mold. The mold was dripping from the limbs like bleeding bodies after some gruesome battle had taken place high in the branches. He looked around and saw that the rest of the tree limbs were still worming about slowly, closing off any escape for him.

Previously, he had felt the trees had no interest in him but had wanted the boy only. He didn't know why, but he knew the song wasn't for him.

Now, however, the boy was gone, had escaped their trap, and the trees were angry. He could feel them watching him, wanting to take their anger out on him.

His head moving slowly from side to side, still hopelessly scanning for an opening, Rayor heard a scream of rage coming from Sebastion on the outside.

He began to move closer to the spot that he had disappeared through when suddenly Keeper's rusted sword pierced through the trees. The blade jutted in like a sliver of lighted hope.

Rayor knew this was impossible. When the trees came alive, their limbs were like steel. He thought about the old proverb of the trees from his childhood. Of course, then he had considered these trees were just legend.

It went, "On through the day, there is a song, but come the night you all will be gone."

The sword disappeared, and the scream came back, back came the sword, but this time slicing away a tree limb.

The trees screamed with pain and rage. The sound was like hot nails in the ears and Rayor covered his ears with his hands. It is not night yet ... it's only the afternoon! They have come alive too puckering soon. He noticed the tree limbs were alive but did not seem to come directly for him.

Rayor ran forward, pulling the short sword from underneath his cloak. The boy's progress making a hole was slow, and yet ... he was making a hole! Rayor joined in the hacking at a feverish level. The tree song was now more like a rabid beast's snarl.

Each time they hacked, a new branch would come to fill the spot. Soon, however, they were coming back tentatively, slower, as if knowing they would be cut to pieces.

Roots began to surface from the ground. Slowly they attempted to wrap around Rayor's feet, but he was too quick for them. Between his hacks at the branches, he would side-step the roots. He knew they meant to pull him into the earth forever.

The hole was getting bigger. Almost big enough for him to dive through as the boy had.

Rayor was tiring, but Sebastion was like a crazed animal. He had a clenched-tooth grin, and his eyes were huge and bright in his head.

There is such anger and raw ferocity in this boy, Rayor couldn't help but think between bone-wrenching blows to the limbs. He thought that perhaps the hole was big enough when two hands reached through the hole and pulled him hard.

Throwing his hands forward, Rayor ducked his head down, and the boy pulled him almost entirely through. Rayor made it the rest of the way by rolling up into a fetal position and pulling on Sebastion's shoulders.

Sebastion, trying to turn to one side as he pulled, lost his balance and fell onto his side, and Rayor landed beside him. They rolled onto their backs, staring straight up into the last of the day's light.

Breathing heavily, they lay there, not saying a word for some time.

Rayor could no longer hear the songs of the trees and was thankful for that. He saw the hole closing back up. The sound of metal made him look up, and he saw his short sword being sucked into the closing hole. He lunged up quickly, pulling it free, and laying back down.

Sebastion, still lying next to him, was panting loudly. Rayor thought he could hear the boy's heart pounding out of his chest.

"You all right?" he asked, trying to catch his own breath.

The boy looked back at him from the grass, smiling from ear to ear.

Rayor raised his head off the ground to look at him.

The boy was looking happy, very happy.

Holy Light, he is actually enjoying this! Rayor rolled his eyes at him and lay back down. "I am getting far too old for this." He said to the blue sky as he lay on his back.

The next several days were without incident. After the trees, Sebastion's questions came faster and became harder to answer for the old man. Sebastion wanted to know about everything.

It was exhausting for Rayor to keep coming up with answers. He found he liked talking, but sometimes the boy's questions were too direct, and he knew the boy suspected he was keeping many things hidden.

They still traveled during parts of the night. The landscape kept changing from forest to dense jungle to long, spread-out plains. It was when they were crossing a large river, however, that Sebastion had to face people again.

They heard and smelled the river before they saw it. Rayor had broken out of the small game trail they were following and found a road that led to the river's edge.

Sebastion walked on the road with growing apprehension. He knew it must have been people who made this road, and he had no intention of meeting any of them.

After walking on the road for some time, he spotted a small house with smoke coming from the chimney. He stopped to observe it.

Rayor stopped a few yards off and looked back questioningly.

"What's wrong?" he asked from within his hood.

"Are we going *there*?" Sebastion asked.

Rayor turned to look the house before looking back.

"Yes," he said simply.

Sebastion shook his head in acknowledgment.

"All right. I'll stay here and wait for you," he said, thinking this would be like the small village Rayor had gone to so many days before.

Rayor just stared at him for a few seconds before speaking as Sebastion headed for the forest on the other side of the road.

"Not this time, boy," Rayor said.

Sebastion stopped and looked back, confused.

"You're coming this time," Rayor said more sternly.

"I'd rather not," Sebastion said, rubbing his hands together and feeling very nervous now.

Pulling his hood off his head, Rayor frowned.

"We need to get across that river," he thrust a thumb over his shoulder, pointing behind him, "and to do that we BOTH need to take the ferry across."

Sebastion felt his fear growing inside him. "Can't we go around?" he asked, his voice sounding childish even to himself.

"No." Rayor shook his head in wonderment.

The boy had done battle with possessed murderous trees, but now he's afraid of a ferry master?

"Swallow your fear, and let's move. We'd best be across that river before nightfall."

"Why?" Sebastion was obviously stalling for time.

"Because there are more things that can hurt you than trees." Rayor said, and Sebastion nodded sadly that he understood.

Rayor walked to him and momentarily rested a hand on Sebastion's shoulder. "You'll be alright. I'm right here with you. Let's just go and get this over with."

Reassured, though only slightly, Sebastion followed Rayor down the road the rest of the way to the Ferry Master's house.

The house was small and made out of wood and what seemed to be river mud. Wafting from the house were odors of something cooking that made Sebastion's mouth water. He still did not want to be here, but he couldn't help imagining how whatever was cooking must taste.

The door opened before they could knock on it.

A short man with huge shoulders and massive arms stood in front of them. He had a long black beard that looked like it had enough meals left in it to last the next month. Crossing his arms, he regarded his guests with a frown.

"You two don't look to be from around here," he said suspiciously. "Though you do look a little familiar," he said to Rayor.

The man's speech was hard to understand because his sentences were punctuated by the sound of saliva being sucked through the empty spot his front teeth used to occupy.

Rayor looked up, revealing a portion of his face.

"Ahh, yes, I do recognize you. Always a tip from you, there was. Come in and share some of the stew … for a price that is."

"Of course." Rayor nodded politely.

Walking into the house, Sebastion was shocked at how much it resembled his own small home with Keeper. He heard a noise and looked behind him to see another man, taller but with the same bulging shoulders and arms, putting down a crossbow from behind the door. His beard was not as long as the first man's, but it was just as dirty.

The younger man went to the stew pot and scooped out two big bowls of meat and potatoes. The bowls were steaming when he handed one to each of them.

Rayor and Sebastion went to a small table and sat down.

The shorter man cleared his throat, and Rayor tossed him a coin.

Sebastion saw a flash of elated surprise pass over the man's eyes.

"I've no change for something like this, I'm afraid."

Rayor waved a hand at him and blew on the stew.

Sebastion saw a quick look exchanged between the two men with the dirty beards.

With one hand, Rayor pulled his cloak up, revealing his short sword, while with the other he scooped up meat and carefully deposited it in his mouth.

Sebastion took little care of the exchange as he was now busying himself with eating. He could not believe the experience his mouth was having with the food. His head swam with it.

The short man smiled at him, seeing his obvious delight.

"It seems your boy likes my son's cooking."

They're related. Of course! Sebastion thought, surprised. They did look it, though the younger one was taller. Sebastion regarded them more closely.

The younger shifted his feet uncomfortably, but the older one returned his look, just as curious.

"You've never seen a man and his son before, boy?" he asked.

"No," Sebastion replied truthfully.

Rayor looked up at him and urged him to pay more attention to the stew.

The two men exchanged another glance between them.

"Let's go get some more wood," the father suggested to his son.

The son nodded and followed the older man out the door.

Rayor looked toward the fireplace and saw two large piles of wood near it. There was plenty for the night and most of the next day.

Leaning in close to Sebastion, he said, "Say nothing more to these men. I may have made a mistake giving them that coin. It's probably more than they make in a year. Damn! I should have been more careful." Rayor cursed himself.

Sebastion swallowed the last of his delicious food and leaned forward as well.

"Shouldn't they just be thankful then?" he asked.

Rayor smiled at that and pulled his hood farther forward on his face.

"If they try anything, stay behind me and out of the way."

Sebastion choked on a last piece of potato and coughed into his hand.

"Take it easy, boy. You had better get used to this sort of thing. I have a feeling your life isn't going to be all soft pillows and butterflies."

The two men came back with a strange look in their eyes as they invited their guests to spend the night explaining that the river was moving too fast right now and would be impossible to cross.

Rayor said nothing as he contemplated his options. He did not like them right now.

If they stayed with the men, it was almost sure that the two would rob them and most likely kill them for good measure. If they slept in the forest, they would still be in danger of being cheated by these two but might have a chance in the darkness. If he killed them both right here, it was likely Sebastion, and he alone, could not pull the ferry across the river. These two ferrymen looked as strong as oxen.

Rayor sighed and nodded, agreeing to something that only he could understand.

"We will stay in the forest outside and go across the river tomorrow. Will the river be all right to cross in the morning?" he asked.

"Oh, sure it will. In the morning, it will be fine."

Rayor could hear the sarcastic amusement in the man's voice. The big man was not even hiding the fact that he had lied about the river in the first place.

The thought of killing them came back into his mind.

Why would they care about robbing an old man and his emaciated grandson ... damn!

"On second thought, I've changed my mind," Rayor said in a low, dangerous tone. Pulling the hood from his head, he stood to his full height. Rayor was a tall man, but he did not get the response he was looking for from the men.

"Oh, you have, have you?" the father asked in an unimpressed tone. He puffed out his chest and stepped forward. The man's muscular chest was the size of a water barrel.

"You know, I've changed my mind too. We'll be taking the rest of the coins you have stuffed away in that pretty gray dress of yours." The man's semi-toothless smile was ominous as a looked up at the old man.

The other one stepped up behind him, doing his best to also look imposing.

As far as Sebastion was concerned, he was doing a good job.

Rayor turned and looked at Sebastion.

"Boy, this is a good lesson for you. These two men outweigh me, and each is quite possibly twice, maybe three times, stronger than I."

"I'd say quite a bit more than that, old man," the father said, the smile now leaving his face.

"You see," Rayor went on, ignoring the menacing man, "He is already underestimating me. This is a sign of someone with more confidence than sense ... untrained, and yet sure that he will be the victor in this fight."

The taller man started laughing, but Sebastion could see that the father was getting angry.

"That's about enough talk, ole' timer. Hand over the coins or we'll thrash you ... and 'dat pretty little girl of yours, too."

Rayor turned back to face him, crossing his arms like an angry parent as he looked down at the man.

"I'm not going to kill you because I need you to pull the boat across the river." Rayor scratched his chin thoughtfully, thinking. "So, what do you think of this: If I beat you both in a fair fight, will you agree to take us across the river tonight?"

The two big men looked at each other, surprised and a little amused.

"If you can take us both at the same time?" the father asked in a shocked voice.

"You two cows up to it?" Rayor challenged as he moved toward the door.

The son made a grab for him, but Rayor just batted it away like he would a fly and walked out the door.

Both burly men looked at Sebastion and he looked back at them, confused.

"Your pappy is about to get a hell of a beating," the father said, walking out the door after Rayor.

"You're next, little *girl*," said the son, following his father and smiling cruelly.

Sebastion got up and moved to the door to watch. He heard the father begin to speak again, and then he heard a loud slap. Quickly jumping to the door, he thrust his head out and looked.

The father was holding his face, looking surprised again, and yet at the same time, furious.

"Watch, boy. These are some of the same things I have been teaching you. Practice is different than application. You have the tools, but how to use them..."

Rayor lunged forward pushing off on one foot faster than Sebastion could believe and slammed a fist into the father's eye.

The man's big head snapped back.

The son yelled and charged. Rayor grabbed his arm and pulled him closer. Only at the last minute he moved out of the way, and pulled him again, flipping him hard onto the ground using his own momentum.

At this point, the father had recovered, saw his son's predicament, and charged Rayor.

Rayor kicked him just above the knee. He knew if he had hit the knee, he would have shattered it, and the big man would have been useless on his ferry. Instead, the father went face-first into the ground as a result of the shift of balance caused by his charge and hit the hard-packed dirt and small rocks in a hard dive.

Sebastion could not believe how easily Rayor seemed to be controlling this fight. For every move one of the men made, he had a countermove that either put his opponent on the ground or made him step back, seeing stars. He even gave them time to recover and come back to him for more.

Moreover, and the strangest thing of all, Rayor had not even broken a sweat, though these men were younger, bigger, and stronger than he was.

Finally, the two men decided to come at him as one.

Rayor grabbed the wrist of one and twisted in a way that flipped him onto his back and, as the other came around, Rayor kicked him hard in the crotch.

Both would-be assailants lay on the ground now, rolling and moaning in pain.

Sebastion watched with enormous fascination, realizing that every move his hooded mentor made was indeed one of the things he had been taught during their journey. He never would have guessed how effective they could be.

Rayor brushed off his cloak and walked to Sebastion. He was only slightly winded and looked well pleased with himself.

"Do you understand now? Training is the key but knowing how to apply what you have been taught is what unlocks the door.

Of course, if I had become injured or significantly weaker, that may have changed the outcome ... but probably not." He said this last part giving the two on the ground a disgusted look.

"All right!" Rayor announced, speaking as the obvious master of the situation now, "We need to get across the river. There has been too much time here at play."

Rayor walked up to the father, who was getting up by this time and whispered something into his ear.

Sebastion saw the light come back into his eyes and a slight smile appear on his bloody lips.

"Collect your things and come to the river's edge," Rayor yelled to Sebastion.

When Sebastion reached the river, he was fascinated by a new sight.

The ferry was big. It was constructed of many trees tied together by rope. Some even still had branches protruding into the water. The wood was slippery under their feet. While Sebastion thought he would slip right into the river even while trying to get on board, the two ferrymen walked on it as if it were dry ground.

There was a rope tied between the two shores of the river. They could see the other side in the dim light, but it was a reasonable distance off. The water was still, unmoving, unlike what the two men had said earlier.

Sebastion quickly sat down on the wet wood and prepared to be pulled across.

As the two men started pulling, Sebastion could feel the big wooden ferry slide forward. This was a new experience, and he dug his finger into the bark of a tree underneath him for support. He was scared but even more excited. He had never seen this much water, and it fascinated him. There was a splash next to him, and he jumped.

Rayor snickered at him, grinning.

"Watch out, the fish here have sharp teeth and might get you," he said teasingly.

Picking up from the tone of Rayor's voice that there was nothing to worry about, Sebastion continued to watch the water less cautiously, and there was a splash on the other side of the ferry. He spun his head, but all that he could see was the rippled water.

"Ain't you ever seen a fish before?" the taller man pulling the boat asked in a disgusted tone.

"Not in this much water," Sebastion replied honestly.

"You need to get around more, girl."

The man's tone, as much as his words, irritated Sebastion. Heat flashed into his face. "My time has been spent learning to kill people," he answered in a low tone.

The tall man looked at him, then looked away and did not speak again.

Rayor put his hands on his bald head and tried to rub the pain that was there away. *Idiot boy.*

On the other side of the river, Rayor tossed the ferryman two coins.

The muscular man caught them both in the air and smiled from ear to ear.

The tall son leaned in to see what they were, but his father quickly stuffed them into a pocket, still smiling.

Sebastion and Rayor began to follow a trail that led away from the river when Rayor stopped, looked around, listened, and headed into the forest.

Not long after, they started a fire and made some hot tea before bed. Rayor smoked on his pipe, and Sebastion flipped through Keeper's dusty books, which he had read over and over ever since he had learned to read.

Keeper was a good reader, and in a rare moment, had shown approval of the quick way Sebastion had picked it up. From time to time, Keeper would come back with books from his trips. Sebastion had looked forward to these books more than he ever let Keeper know.

The books were how Sebastion had learned all he knew of the world. He knew that people fell in love. He knew that people went to war and fought massive battles for honor. The book he was reading now told of a vast sea and places where people discussed ideas and thoughts. He would like to find this place.

He wanted to have adventures of his own. He remembered the haunted trees and goosebumps ran up his spine. There had been fear, but there had also been something else. That feeling in the back of his mind was excitement and wonder.

Sebastion was enjoying his time with Rayor, and he did not want it to end. He knew that they were heading somewhere special, but Rayor would not say what or where it was.

Still, when he thought of it, Sebastion could not help feeling a little frightened. In the beginning, when he had asked Rayor where they were going, the old man would get a strange look in his eye.

He would never answer, and he'd just say, "You'll see when you get there" and not another word. Sebastion had finally learned to leave well enough alone.

"You read a lot, for a boy in your circumstance," Rayor said, still looking up at the stars.

Sebastion smiled and looked over.

"Most boys I've known would rather hunt and chase girls. Though you might be a little young for the girls."

Sebastion thought on this.

Why would they have to chase the girls? Do girls not want to be around boys? If the other boys were anything like the ones he had met, Sebastion could almost understand why some boys would have to chase the girls.

"What do they do when they catch them?" he asked Rayor in a concerned voice.

Rayor looked over at him, confused at first, and then smiled in a way that made his eyes slits in his face. "Oh, you'll find out soon enough." He laughed to himself, taking a deep drag from his pipe.

Sebastion did not want to chase anyone. In fact, he just wanted to be left alone. However, he was having some strange feelings of late. Sometimes he would think about the women in his books, but these thoughts only confused him and made him uncomfortable, and he tried to block them out of his head as much as he could. They were more potent at night and sometimes he found it difficult to sleep.

Maybe I am meant to chase them? Perhaps they would be hard to catch. The thought was giving him a headache, or maybe the problem was from trying to read by firelight. Whichever, he decided to put away the book and his thoughts and go to sleep.

"What is your very oldest memory?" Rayor asked in a strange voice.

Sebastion opened his eyes and thought.

My oldest memory? He closed his eyes and thought some more. "Sometimes I dream of soft, white pillows and of something ... I don't know."

"What? What is it?" Rayor urged him to go on.

"It's more like the smell and ... you know ... like a touch or something. It sounds crazy, I know."

"It does not sound crazy. Try to put yourself there." Rayor sat up, crossed his legs, and faced Sebastion. "You have given yourself a name; where did that name come from? But first, tell of the soft pillows and the other."

Sebastion tried to pull the dream forward in his mind. It was full of bright white cloth and soft pillows that were like clouds.

"I remember a voice too ... singing or something. It's where that smell of ... I can't explain ... like flowers or ... I don't know."

Rayor rubbed his chin thoughtfully. "Does the voice say anything to you?"

Sebastion thought more. "It just sings, but I never could make out the words."

"Can you hum it?" Rayor asked.

"It goes something like this." Sebastion started humming, and Rayor knew the song immediately. It was the same song his mother sang to him. Guilt stabbed his heart like an assassin's knife.

If I have not yet sealed my fate, I surely will when I deliver this poor child. He's just a poor bastard boy adrift in someone else's dark blasted game.

"Okay. That is enough for tonight. Get some rest." Rayor went to his bedroll, taking his dark thoughts with him.

Sebastion, however, could not sleep. He could not get the thoughts of the dream out of his head. The white sheets and the smell that made him light-headed and safe ran through his head. He had never heard a woman's voice, but he suspected the song in his head had been sung by one. He did not know why he would have a woman's voice in his head if he'd never heard one, but it was there. It had always been there. There were some nights that he would go to sleep very sad and alone, and that voice would sing the song to him. He would close his eyes, the white cloth and the sweet smell would surround him, and he would feel a little better.

There were other dreams too, though. He did not like those dreams. They were of dark creatures that were always chasing him. Sometimes the landscape would change, but the creatures were still the same. They wore long cloaks that would flow behind them when they ran. Sometimes they would run on two legs and sometimes on four. The clawed arms that protruded from the cloak sleeves were covered with green scales. The hood would flop up and down when they ran, but Sebastion could never see the faces inside. The creatures would always hiss at him and, at times, tell him that the running would do him no good, but he would not stop.

He remembered many nights waking up with his body covered in sweat and the hiss of the creature's voice still in his ears.

Sebastion sighed deeply, running his hands through his hair. He thought he might tell Rayor about these dreams.

"I sometimes have dark dreams," Sebastion said.

Rayor rolled over and listened to Sebastion's dreams. He realized Sebastion was more or less describing the under-wraiths without ever having seen one. The dreams were most likely his Dark Master's doing. They even haunt him in his sleep, Rayor thought, the guilt returning … not that it was ever very far away.

When Sebastion had finished, Rayor got up and put two more logs on the fire and pulled something from his bag. He came over to Sebastion carrying a small bottle.

"Take a sip of this," Rayor said in a gentle voice.

Sebastion started to move away, thinking of Keeper's brews.

This made Rayor feel even more sad.

"It will not harm you … I promise. It will help you sleep; that is all."

Sebastion moved forward and took the bottle.

"Just a small sip, now," Rayor said.

Sebastion did as he was told and handed the bottle back. He lay down, and in a few minutes, he felt more relaxed than he had in a long time. His eyes stung from being open for too long, so he closed them for just a second, but they did not open again as he expected. He was asleep for the night and snoring lightly.

Rayor stared at his young companion, feeling old and sad. What has become of me? And what will become of this poor child? Too long … too long I have carried this weight. I no longer wish to do this … and be what I have become.

The stars were bright this night and seemed to burn through Rayor's eyelids. He twisted and turned but found it impossible to get comfortable. Resigning himself to going into that half-sleep he needed, he rolled onto his back and took a deep breath. They both would need their rest to be alert when crossing the Death Plains.

He cleared his mind and relaxed his body. Soon he could feel the tension leaving his limbs and his mind becoming calm. Still, the stars were too damn bright!

Grunting, he threw his arm over his eyes. He was taking in a deep breath when Melodia's scent, from their embrace so many days before, hit him like a brick to the head. His calming mind absorbed it and it smelled of herbs and vanilla. He soaked it up like a drunk savoring his first cup of the day.

As if being shot out of a catapult, Rayor was transported to an earlier time in his life. He knew it would be useless to try to shut out these memories … besides, so few memories ever made it to the surface of late … so he not only opened up to them but also embraced them and let them wash over him.

***

"Your choices are your own," Melodia was saying in earnest.

Both of them were on their knees, facing each other and holding hands. Shirtless and covered in sweat, he had been dreaming in their bed.

Rayor was familiar with the dream that had awakened him, but Melodia was looking into his eyes with genuine concern.

"Perhaps if you would tell me about these dreams, I could help, my love?"

He just shook his head.

"I can never remember what they were," he lied.

"They're killing you," she said, her heart breaking in her voice.

He smiled, leaning into her, kissing her deeply and passionately.

She pushed into his embrace, and soon they were back on the bed in a mesh of limbs and touching. From time to time, she would whisper breathlessly in his ear, "I love you."

Rayor would pull her to him, as if trying to embrace her into his very being, hoping in some way her goodness could balance out his wicked deeds.

As ecstasy washed over him, so did his guilt. He began to pull away to drown in his torment, but she wouldn't let him. Her arms were iron as she held him to her.

"I do not deserve this," he said to her in a whisper.

She loosened her grip a little to run a hand across his face to brush back his long brown hair.

"You do, my love … you do."

Even in her loving embrace, the guilt would worm its way back in.

"The Lady would not approve," he said to her in the same sad voice.

She breathed a heavy sigh and touched her forehead to his as they lay on their soft pillows.

"You underestimate the Lady's ability to forgive. She would not forsake me for loving. She is love."

He looked into her eyes and smiled.

"Would she forsake you for whom you love?"

He remembered she was beautiful there, looking into his eyes. Her long auburn hair spilled out on the pillow behind her and swept down her back. Her skin was porcelain with freckles he could trace for a lifetime. But it was her eyes that put life back into his heart, a life that he had no right to have. Every day he felt coldness creeping into him, and every night she would chase it off.

He would not have voluntarily left her any more than a moth would leave the light of a flame, but he knew it was inevitable.

"I cannot stay here, Mel." He was holding her shoulders tightly in his grip.

"You mean you *won't* stay," she said back in an accusing tone.

He let go of her and stepped back, seemingly taking a moment to pull his clothes on, but really to compose himself.

Back under the stars on the hard ground, Rayor shifted his body slightly in his bedroll, wondering if it was wise to continue with this memory. As the details of those days came back to him, so did the old feelings. He did not like feeling this way again, but he knew he'd already come too far to stop the memories.

***

"Is that it, then? Do you no longer have feelings for me?" Melodia said, sniffling. "Because if it is, it's better than knowing that…"

"That what? That I may be a murderer or worse?" he shot back at her.

She was taken aback, but only for a second. "You are none of those things."

"How can you be so sure, Mel? Never have I told you why people are always searching for me. Never have I told you what happens in those dreams that wake me almost every night, sweating and wanting to die!" A tear was welling up in one eye, and he angrily brushed it aside.

"I will never stop feeling the way I do about you, but that is why I must leave."

"That makes no sense," Melodia said, anger now touching her own voice. "Why would you run from this when we could deal with it TOGETHER!?" She yelled.

He sighed deeply and once again put his hands on her shoulders, kissing her forehead. He could feel that her body was still tense with anger. "I could never burden you with my deeds."

Pulling away, her eyes hot with anger, she challenged, "Couldn't or wouldn't!" She put her hands on her hips and faced him, more like a soldier than his lover. "I have given you my heart; at the very least, you can give me the TRUTH!" Her face was nearly as red as her hair now.

Despite it all, Rayor had to be impressed by how intimidating she could be. There were some in the congregation who always gave her distance, and he had never known why. Now he did.

When he was able to compose himself again, he faced her in his faded cloak with a tied blanket containing all his belongings at his feet.

Looking into her eyes, he thought she was ready to slam a fist into his face.

He thought about what he could say to her to calm her, but before he realized what was happening, the truth began spilling from his mouth. He couldn't stop it.

Melodia's angry expression was turning to shock. Still, he could not stop himself.

When he told her, who had taken him in and whom he now served, she covered her mouth and let out a soft cry.

When he finished, he stood there and waited for a reaction, but she just stood there, her beautiful deep blue eyes staring back at him. Her hand still covered her mouth as if she was afraid of what would come out.

"Now, you know. So, what do you think, 'my love?" He said, using sarcasm to hide his pain. "Is that what you wanted to hear?"

When she still did not reply, he brushed another angry hand across his wet eyes. He looked up into her eyes one last time, and he wished from that moment on that he had not. That look would haunt him for the rest of his life. Even to this very day under the stars that had no business being so bright.

Slowly lowering his hands to the bag by his feet, he listened for a response that never came. He stepped back, away from her, waiting for her to stop him.

Her hand twitched, but she pulled it back, quickly covering her throat.

"Goodbye, Mel," he had said, feeling his heart breaking in his chest. "I love you, but I can no longer pretend to not be what I am ... now."

He had turned and walked away. Stopping a short distance away, but without turning, he remembered saying, "You could not have known. You are blameless. It was I who deceived you into believing I was ... worth being saved."

He had flung open the door, stepped through, and then slammed it behind him forever.

***

Rayor did not know what happened to Melodia after that. Through many lifetimes, he had held her in his arms again, but only in his dreams.

He sat up, tired and emotionally drained, rubbing his swollen eyes. Rayor shook his head, disgusted with himself for letting youth's wild passion get the best of an old man trying to get some puckering sleep.

Strange how dreams could take you back to any time and make the coldest heart feel alive again.

A cold breeze blew in and Rayor tightened his cloak. Putting the sleeve across his face, he breathed in and let her wash again into his mind. He leaned back and shut his eyes, this time only letting in the memory of the good times before the door was slammed shut. Soon he was warm and a tight smile spread across his wrinkled face under the night's sky.

Chapter 4 – Faith

Melodia sat at her small table, sipping tea. She was still wearing her muddy boots and cloak. It had been raining for days, and it had taken her nearly a full day to get to the small, dreary hut she had sought. It was not that hard to find, and she was not surprised to find it empty and abandoned. Her head was so full of questions that she could hardly recall the walk back to her home.

Taking another sip of her tea, she tried to let it wash away her anger. Her knee was bouncing uncontrollably, making the tea slop over the side of the glass and spill onto the table. Ordinarily, this would have sent her off looking for a rag to clean it up, but today she did not even notice. She took a deep breath and tried to steady herself, but soon her leg was shaking again and her brow wrinkling.

He knew the boy was gone, and he let me stay here thinking everything was as it should be. Tears came to her eyes, but they were not from sadness. She held onto her teacup, white-knuckled, her knee still bouncing.

When she heard the door downstairs open and close, a cold smile spread across her face. She hoped it was someone in particular. With the boy gone, there was no reason to stay, and that thought excited her.

Without taking off her boots and cloak, she hurried downstairs.

Waiting for her was a short, pudgy man with a receding hairline and pockmarked face. He stood there, impatiently waiting for her.

"Where you been, whore?" he said, spitting on her floor. "Stunts like that will get you kicked out of my house; yea know?"

She knew he was here for his payment. Once a month, he would collect her rent and then his "treat" as he called it. More than once, he had come in a foul mood and left Melodia nursing bruises and cuts. That would not be the case today.

Melodia faced her visitor with a small smile on her lips.

"You happy to see me, bitch?" he asked, unbuttoning his trousers. "Don't think that little smile is going to save you any silver. The rent is what it is, but the treat will be extra special if you know what's good for ya."

He stood in front of her fully exposed from the waist down, his hands on his hips.

"You waiting for an invitation?"

He clapped his hands in front of himself.

"Here bitch, right here," he said, as if calling a dog.

Melodia began to laugh in a low tone that was more a growl.

The man's face flushed even redder. For the first time, he seemed to notice that she was dressed for travel rather than pleasure.

"You going somewhere?" He took a wider stance and put his hands behind his fat, thick head. "Cause we got settling to do before that happens."

"Yes, we do," she replied, the smile disappearing from her face. "Lady, please close your eyes to me now," she whispered as she charged forward.

The fat man suddenly saw the woman in front of him change from the subservient whore he had known to a charging warrior, and his face went from crimson to pale white in the instant it took for her to reach him.

Melodia filled the pack she had brought to the town so many years ago with the only things she had brought with her. She wanted to keep nothing from this place. Her heart felt as black as this night. Stuffing the knives and various other weapons into her clothing helped her feel better, though. She put the pack on her back and tied everything off.

The bruised and bleeding man on the floor started to come to and began to whimper.

Quickly walking over to him, Melodia kicked him in the teeth carelessly with the heel of her boot. More than one bloody, broken tooth slid across the floor. Opening the door, she stepped outside and slammed it shut. She did not look back, but walked steadily up the dirt road.

A woman was walking towards her with two dirty children in tow. The woman spat at her feet as she walked by and this time Melodia smacked the woman's forehead with the palm of a hand.

The woman fell on her rump, dragging the children with her. All three stared after Melodia in shock as she took long strides towards the forest.

She thought of how she had been treated this way for years and had never fought back, not even once.

That felt good.

Melodia decided she had one more stop to make, and then she would be done with this awful town forever. She could see that the light was on in the little store and walked straight toward it. She found the ugly fat man behind the counter, stocking a shelf with what looked to be rotten apples.

He turned in her direction when he heard the cowbell rattle above the door, and then he made a sour face.

"And what brings you here, milady?" His tone of voice conveyed that "milady" was some kind of personal joke, and he snickered to himself.

Melodia did not respond but instead crossed the space between them in three smooth strides and jumped across the counter that separated them. Her knife was in her hand before her feet hit the ground. With one hand, she pushed the greasy, foul-smelling man against the wall, while with the other hand she held the knife to his throat. She winced at the feeling of the hairy shirtless chest touching her palm.

Instinctively, the man raised his hands, but she put more pressure on his throat with her knife. His hands went down, and he smiled submissively.

"Something I can do for you?" he asked very cordially.

"Yes, there is." Her big blue eyes, like possessed sapphires, stared hard into his dull brown orbs. "Tell your master that I'm coming for him."

"And what shall I—" the fat man started.

She pushed him harder against the wall, feeling the urge to vomit from being so close to him. Several brown, soft apples fell to the ground and rolled around her feet.

"Tell him nothing more, and understand you live only to relay that message."

Her hand darted away and sliced once between his legs, and she was over the counter again.

Melodia threw the defiled knife onto the floor and grabbed a cloth from her belt. Having scrubbed her hands with it, she let that fall to the ground as well as she walked. With that, she opened the door and left like the wind.

The grubby shopkeeper put his hands between his legs and screamed. She could hear him all the way down the street, and even when she turned into the trail. She knew very well it was not a very Priestess thing to enjoy the screams of another in pain. However, she also knew she was not perfect, and all had their moments of faults.

She was feeling better than she had in a long time. Her one purpose now was to free the man she loved. She had not expected to find him again after all these years, but even with his ancient looks and the changed name, she would have recognized him anywhere. She had loved him for a very long time, and not one day had passed during which he was far from her thoughts.

The guilt she had carried with her for so long had now turned to desperation. She had let her love for her god lose him once. She would not make that mistake again. If he thought that his allegiance to his master would keep him from her, he was mistaken. She would find this master of his and convince him to release Rayor, or whatever he called himself now. And if he did not free him, she would cut his master's head from his shoulders.

Silently Melodia whispered a prayer to The Lady but stopped mid-sentence. No, The Lady will have no part in this. This is my burden to carry, and I will see it through … to the end this time, if need be. I will not abandon him again, not this time. He did leave her in this town. He did not tell her that the boy was gone, and she would have words with him about this but … there had to be a reason why he was there crossing paths with her again. She was going to free him and then they will discuss his leaving.

Shrugging her pack into a more comfortable position, Melodia resigned herself to her journey. She felt strength and conviction come into her with this single-minded purpose. She would not rest until the next day, traveling through the night. Her boots barely made a noise as they moved across the rock-strewn earth.

She marched on in silence, somehow knowing where she was going. No one had ever told her where she would find this dark master, but something inside her was pulling her North. She had felt similar sensations when in the service of The Lady, but this was different. It was something … dark.

The tall, beautiful, auburn-haired priestess of the Lady of Light did not care, and her long muscular legs carried her quickly through the forest. Any passerby that might have glimpsed her would have been startled. Her hood was down, and her long hair swirled and whipped like flowing flames over the long green cloak flying behind her. She would have seemed more a haunted spirit than a woman on a mission to mend a broken heart, as she silently slipped through the trees of the forest.

Chapter 5 – Roansters

Rayor woke up in a foul mood, and Sebastion noticed it immediately. Skipping their morning exercise, they continued on their way. Rayor decidedly walked in front, rather than walking side-by-side with Sebastion as they had these past days.

The day was gray and dark. For some reason, Rayor was having them travel by day now. Sebastion asked him why, but all he got as an answer was, "you'll see" or "just wait and see." It was not actually raining, but the moisture in the air was making Sebastion's clothes cold and wet. He could almost watch the rust grow on Keeper's old sword as it slapped against his thigh.

Instead of stopping and eating their noontime meal, Rayor only slowed to let Sebastion catch up and handed him a piece of dried meat rolled in a leaf.

Sebastion accepted the meal without a word.

It was not until late afternoon that Rayor started becoming himself again.

"You'll need to start collecting kindling soon to make sure it's dry enough to light a fire by the evening."

Sebastion shot a confused look at his back.

"You'll see," was Rayor's only response again.

Sebastion could sense, more than see, a smile on Rayor's face. He did as he had been told and started gathering sticks under the blanket he was wearing as a cloak to stay dry.

A few hours later, they stopped and Sebastion was grateful for that. His feet were sore from going so far and not resting.

The spot Rayor picked was peculiar. They were on top of a hill with an incline at every angle. There were small pits dug into the ground at three points around them. Rayor busied himself with cleaning out these pits and making sure they were dry. He then gathered Sebastion's dry kindling and made a small fire in each pit without saying a word.

"Umm, sorry … but can't people see the light of these fires on this hill?" Sebastion asked.

Rayor laughed a low, grunting noise.

"If people are close enough to see these fires, they won't be around long enough for us to worry about them." As he continued feeding the flames, he instructed, "You'd best go find as much dry wood as you can. Bring back as much as you can carry, and then go get more," he instructed without looking up.

Sebastion turned to leave.

"Wait. One last thing." This time Rayor turned to meet his eye. "Don't be out after nightfall. Get the wood and come right back. Make the second trip only if you think you will be back before dark. Do you understand?"

Sebastion nodded, a little taken aback by the tone.

"Is that a yes?"

"Yes," Sebastion answered quickly.

"Good. Off you go then."

With so much moisture in the air, he knew it was not easy to find dry wood. He found a spot under a pine tree where some dry tree limbs lay and studied the ground out of old habits. He noticed what looked to be holes in the ground around the tree as if someone was stabbing a large stick into the dirt. He grabbed as many twigs in his arms as he could carry and headed back.

Looking around, Sebastion now saw that those same punctures in the ground were not only under the tree but also everywhere he looked. He was getting very curious and put the sticks down to more closely inspect the strange holes.

Having been raised in the forest, he was familiar with what a hole used by an animal would look like, and these did not have any of those signs. He stuck his hand into one of the holes and found that it did not go very deep and ended in a point. What could be jammed into the ground that ended in a point? A large spear? But why would someone stab the ground so many times with a spear? Moreover, who would have the strength to stick a spear of that size into the land that far?

Sebastion had lost track of time and looked up to find the sun making its descent. He grabbed the armload of sticks and ran back to Rayor, remembering his promise to be back before dark.

Rayor was still feeding the fires with all the sticks he could find close by. He gave Sebastion an angry look when he came back, but Sebastion also thought he saw a quick flash of relief.

Sebastion dropped the pile and started heading out for a second when Rayor stopped him. He gave Sebastion instructions to keep the flames going and walked off himself to get wood. A short time after that, Rayor returned with a load twice the size Sebastion had brought.

"This is what I meant. Not four sticks and a couple of leaves. How could we keep these fires going all night with your load?"

Sebastion wanted to answer, "How should I know you wanted to keep three fires going all at once and all night?" or "If you don't tell me anything, then how should I know?"

Instead, picking up a nervous twinge in Rayor's voice that he did not like, he remained silent. If there was something out there that could put this old man on the edge, then Sebastion wanted no part of it.

That evening was spent sitting in between the three fires. Sebastion felt ridiculous doing so, but Rayor told him not to move under any circumstances. Rayor, meanwhile, was furiously making sure all three fires were going at a healthy rate. When one would flicker, he was there blowing on it and feeding it fuel. He did this throughout the night.

At some point, Sebastion fell asleep and dreamt that a crazed giant was driving a large spear into the ground all over the forest. There were times when he would be awakened by what he swore was the sound of the spear plunging into the ground, but then it would be gone again. Other times, he would be awakened by the smoke of one of the fires, which caused him to cough until the wind took the smoke away.

Just before the sun began to rise, Sebastion awoke again.

Rayor looked the worse for wear. He was sweating and panting from running from place to place, but he also had a satisfied look on his face.

"I think we are in the clear now, but keep the three going," he said, sitting in the center with a huff.

Sebastion could not help but feel a stab of guilt, since he had slept most the night while Rayor fed the fires, for whatever reason.

"Is it really necessary to keep the fires going now?" Sebastion asked carefully.

"Yes, it is!" Rayor answered sharply.

Just half an hour later, Rayor pulled off his hood and stretched. The sleeves of the tunic he wore under his cloak rolled up his arms as he reached toward the sky, groaning and cracking.

Sebastion saw that the old man's arms were tightly wrapped with thick muscle. He did not expect the old man to be in such good shape since his face was covered in wrinkles, and he, at times, walked in a hunched and sickly way.

Rayor saw him looking and smiled.

"Not everything is always what it seems, my boy."

He winked and pulled his cloak over himself, once again becoming the frail old man.

Sebastion shook his head, considering this to be just another strange thing about his new traveling companion. He shook his head, a smile coming to his face.

"So, will we wait until the sun comes out to travel?" Sebastion asked, wondering about whatever was out there that had caused Rayor to spend so much effort in keeping a fire going ... three, in fact.

"To travel, yes, but I want to be sure you see something, and you're most likely going to see it in the first breaks of light," Rayor said, still being painfully vague.

"Okay, then." Sebastion leaned down to pick up his belongings.

"That won't be necessary right now," Rayor said, waving him impatiently.

Sebastion stopped what he was doing, but he still tucked Keeper's old sword into his belt.

Rayor rolled his eyes and waved at him again. "I don't think that rusty twig is going to help us much where we're going but come on; let's go."

Sebastion followed him into the darkness although some small amount of light was coming from the sky, but not much yet.

Rayor walked slowly and very cautiously. Several times he stopped and stood very still, listening and holding a hand out, signaling for Sebastion to do the same. When Rayor was satisfied, he would move forward, always letting his feet touch the ground quietly as he went.

Sebastion followed nearly as quietly; however, his heart was beating so fast he was sure if anyone would be out there they would hear it.

Rayor stopped again, suddenly, and Sebastion nearly ran into his outstretched hand. He stopped short, and a twig snapped under his foot.

Rayor physically winced at this, as if it was one of his bones that had snapped in the silence. He didn't move but held very still and listened.

After some time, they started forward again, and Rayor looked back, shaking his head.

Sebastion felt a rush of embarrassment flow through him, and then it turned to anger. Why were they sneaking through the forest like mice? What could be out here that Rayor could not handle? Having seen what he could do with the ferryman and his son, Sebastion wondered, Why all the stopping and listening?

He was about to say something when Rayor stood and started jogging up a hill, following a small trail. There was a rock ledge to the left of him and nothing but brush to the right of him.

Sebastion, startled by the quick movement, forgot about what he was just going to say and concentrated on following Rayor up the hill.

The top of the hill had one large tree that Rayor kneeled next to as he peered off into the darkness.

Sebastion came up next to him and also kneeled.

Rayor leaned in close and whispered into his ear, "There are two limbs in the tree above us. They are side by side. We will climb the tree and lay flat against the limbs looking that way." He pointed off into the darkness.

Sebastion nodded his reply, just seeing which way Rayor was pointing, all thoughts of complaining now replaced by excitement at finding out what was out in the darkness.

Rayor signaled, and Sebastion climbed the tree quickly and took his position on one of the parallel limbs. When he looked down at Rayor, he found he was no longer there.

Looking hurriedly all around the tree, Sebastion found Rayor on the other limb next to him. Sebastion stared at him, astonished by his quickness and agility.

Rayor just rolled his eyes and pointed out in the darkness as if to say, "Look there, idiot."

It was not long before the first light of morning started to peek into the sky. Sebastion was beginning to make out what lay before him. There was a large natural field with very tall green and brown grass. Huge trees at the edge of the forest surrounded it.

In the dawn light, he wasn't sure whether he could see dark shapes moving in the grass or whether his eyes were playing tricks on him. Soon, however, the light came up a bit more, and he was sure that the field was alive with large animals moving about.

He had never seen animals like this before. They looked like the deer he'd seen in the forest, only much more substantial and with thick horns growing out of their heads that looked more like weapons than the slender antlers of the deer.

Disappointed, Sebastion thought, surely this cannot be what Rayor was so afraid of. If these animals were something to be afraid of then the old man has obviously gone mad! The excitement and stress in his muscles started to dissipate. He suddenly felt tired and a little foolish sitting in a tree hiding from oversized deer. He looked over at Rayor, who was looking even more intensely down the hill at the same dumb, lumbering creatures.

Sebastion started to sit up a little when Rayor's hand shot out and pushed him back down. He did not even look at Sebastion; he only stared out into the field.

"There," Rayor whispered so low that Sebastion barely heard it. "In the trees." He pointed.

Sebastion concentrated on the thick trees but saw nothing. Just as he was going to ask, the trees seemed to move out of alignment and back again. He concentrated hard on the part that had moved and thought he could see a shape there blending into the trees like a chameleon. Whatever it was it was, it was big ... about the size of a horse and wagon. Maybe even bigger, he thought.

The deer sensed nothing and were grazing right toward it. One lifted its head and seemed to be looking directly at it.

Sebastion was sure it must have seen whatever was making that shape in the trees, but instead, the deer-like thing shook its burly head and walked right next to it and started grazing again.

Sebastion looked at Rayor.

"Keep your eyes on that one," he said in a whisper, pointing slowly toward the animal. "They are called Crangos. They are like deer only much meaner!" Rayor whispered with a smile but not taking his eyes off the creature.

It lifted its head again, but this time its white tail went up, and it sniffed the air cautiously. It turned as if to flee when a large piece of the forest seemed to break off and shoot toward the animal.

It was huge ... even bigger than Sebastion had first thought. As it charged forward and no longer had the trees behind it, Sebastion was able to see it clearly now.

Its body was like a colossal ant, only it had a large shell on its back. It ran on four legs that punched into the ground.

He realized then that these creatures were making the holes he had been so curious about.

Two more legs waved in front of its head as it ran but these legs looked more like long blades than something to run on.

"Roanstors," he heard Rayor whisper beside him.

The monster insect was moving so fast that it was nearly on top of the doomed deer. The Roanstors front legs slashed up and down, and the animal split into three parts, falling to the ground, the pieces still moving as if it could again run. The Roanstor stood over its prey, its sword-like legs continuing to unmercifully slash. The grass was too high to see the animal it had killed, but pieces of flesh, fur, and gore rose and fell as the Roanstor continued to slash the way Sebastion would while dicing an onion for stew. Blood splashed the giant insect and the surrounding grass.

It was horrific, but Sebastion could not look away. Rayor touched his shoulder, and he nearly fell out of the tree. Steadying himself, he looked in the direction Rayor was now pointing. Two more Roanstors were running down the poor Crangos.

These two Roanstors were the dull brown color of the grass but otherwise the same as the first.

The giant insects must have been standing in the grass the whole time!

They were running full-on across the field now, their long deadly legs slashing. The Crangos screamed as they ran, but the Roanstors were too quick. The ground shook as their heavy legs hit it.

It was not long before one caught up with their prey and was slashing it into pieces like the first one. Sebastion watch the last one of them jump forward and slash, sending one of the Crangos' decapitated head spinning into the air. Then the slicing just like the others; it used its sharp legs in downward chopping motions, spraying blood as it pounded the creature into the dirt.

All three were now standing over their prey, their front legs busy. The grass was covered in blood, and the Roanstors were either wholly covered or changing color to match their surroundings. An eerie, low, buzzing sound came from the Roanstors as they worked. Sebastion and Rayor could feel it vibrating through the tree.

Suddenly, Sebastion wanted to be anywhere else but there in that tree, feeling the vibrations from the Roanstors echoing through his body. He had an overpowering urge to run as far and long as he could. He looked over again at Rayor to tell him so, but the old man was gone.

Sebastion looked around frantically, but his companion was nowhere around the tree. Panic started to grip his heart when he saw Rayor's gray cloak a distance away on the hill, as he was slowly moving toward the Roanstors. He had his hood up, and he looked more like a rock than a person. The grass was high, but he still had to bend to avoid being seen.

From Sebastion's vantage point in the tree, he could make out what he thought Rayor was heading for. A large portion of meat had flown far from the Roanstors and was lying in the tall grass. It seemed Rayor meant to grab that piece for them.

It was insane, and Sebastion shook his head, sure that Rayor was indeed as mad as he had previously thought.

Why would he risk being seen by those things for that? It's insane!

Rayor moved as quietly as he could. The sun was almost in the sky now, and he knew he would have only a few moments to complete this and get back before the giants headed back to wherever they had come from. He knew the creatures' journey homeward might take them right over the spot which he was now moving to. He had burned the image of the meat and where exactly it was into his mind and headed straight for it. He was sure the Roanstors had forgotten about it.

This is madness, he thought to himself, but he couldn't keep the smile from spreading across his face. It had been a long time since he had felt the blood run so freely through his veins. He had thought these feelings were lost forever, and yet here they were. He was doing something foolish and very irresponsible … and he loved it.

It's the boy. Something about him makes me feel like ... like the person I used to be. He stopped and listened and then moved slowly on to the spot that held their next very special meal.

From the tree, Sebastion watched Rayor slow and start over and over again. His neck was hurting from looking back and forth between Rayor and the giant insect things that Rayor called Roanstors. Why would any god create such an awful creature?

The Roanstors were now using their sharp front legs to alternate between shoving Crango into their salivating mandibles and stuffing pieces under their shells, first on one side and then the other. Green ooze leaked down the Roanstors' backs every time they would press the pieces of meat under their shells. All three were now the color of the grass.

If Sebastion had not been witness to the massacre, he would have been hard-pressed to see them now, even in the daylight. If it weren't for the movement and the light-colored liquid running down their backs, they would be invisible.

The other Crangos were on the other side of the field, huddled together and looking suspiciously at the Roanstors. Sebastion could not believe they had not run back into the forest to hide. Instead, most were already eating again, only slightly agitated by just having a part of their herd ripped to pieces in front of their eyes.

Sebastion's pity for the creatures was turning to disgust. If they're just going to accept it, then they deserve it. He felt a pang of guilt but swallowed it and turned to trace Rayor's progress again. He was slowly making a line through the grass.

Sebastion settled into a more comfortable position when he saw another trail being made in the grass away from the Roanstors. It was heading toward the same area as Rayor. He concentrated on the line in the grass, and when he thought it was no longer moving, the grass again started parting and moving in Rayor's direction. He could not see what it was, but it was moving faster and then stopped again.

Sebastion held his breath and watched. It was still some distance away, but it was definitely moving toward the same thing Rayor was. Squinting his eyes, Sebastion tried to get a glimpse of what it was.

Slowly, a sizeable canine head lifted out of the grass and peered, not in the direction of the piece of deer meat, but directly at where Rayor had stopped to also listen. Sebastion saw the long-pointed ears stretch, and the black nose aimed to the sky, and then it was gone beneath the grass again.

Soon the grass was bending again, and the canine was moving, but this time it was not heading for the deer meat. It was now headed straight for Rayor, and Sebastion knew Rayor had no idea.

Almost to the spot he remembered the meat to be, Rayor realized that this was a lot closer to the Roanstors than it had looked from the tree. Every nerve was alive as he moved forward at a crawl. He was even now on his hands and knees, trying to stay as low as possible. Several times he looked back at the tree, but he could not see Sebastion through the high grass. He started to get an uneasy feeling that something was wrong, but he just chalked it up to nerves. He was crawling towards giant predatory insects, after all.

At one point, he had decided to keep a knife in one hand, but crawling had made it too difficult, so he tucked it back into his sleeve again. He could hear the chomping of the Roanstors, and the sickening squishing of the meat being pushed under the shells. Wiping the sweat from his brow beneath his hood, he kept moving.

Sebastion was down from the tree and moving through the grass. He kept low and as silent as he could, but he felt he might as well have been jumping up and down, yelling, "Come eat me." He had the rusted sword in his hand, and he was nearly running full-out, even bent over as he was. He didn't dare risk a look to see if the two paths moving through the grass had crossed yet, but he suspected he would hear it if it happened before he got there. He hoped he would be the first to get to Rayor, and he hoped the rest of the body that belonged to the canine head that had peered over the grass was not as big as the head indicated. He quickly changed hands with the sword, wiping his right sweaty palm on his trousers and switching back.

Rayor heard something coming quickly behind him and pulled two knives from his sleeves. He hoped it wasn't what he thought it was. Crouching down, he waited to see what would burst through the thick grass.

He wondered if Sebastion could see what was charging toward him and risked a glance up at the tree, but he saw that he was gone. He knew whatever it was, it was nearly there, and Rayor braced.

Sebastion exploded out of the tall grass and ran past an open-mouthed, confused Rayor. He skidded to a halt and jabbed his sword forward, just as a large wild dog charged them.

The dog leaped at his throat.

Sebastion rolled backward, jabbing the sword upward and piercing the dog's belly.

The dog yelped and landed, mortally wounded, at Rayor's knees, while the old man crouched there, surprise turning to bewilderment.

Rayor looked up at Sebastion in awe to find him looking in a similar fashion behind him. Rayor quickly turned to see one of the Roanstors rearing into the air on its hind legs and staring down at them with its huge black eyes.

It let out a loud chirping sound and crashed back to the ground with a thud that made the ground shake.

Rayor did not hesitate. He got to his feet, still bending, and started running. He grabbed Sebastion, and they ran in that fashion as fast as their legs would take them.

The ground rumbled from the sound of the Roanstors' legs as it moved towards them.

They heard a yelp from the dog and knew one Roanstor had ended its life. Another, however, was still moving and was close behind. Rayor zigzagged through the grass, hoping to lose it with Sebastion still close behind. The Roanstor, however, would just raise up and see them, chirping angrily.

Rayor and Sebastion gave up running bent over. They stood and poured everything they had into their feet. Unfortunately, however, they were far into the field, and the forest was just too far away. Their only hope was to out-run the monsters.

Rayor led the way, his older legs carrying him faster than Sebastion would have believed. The tall grass was whipping past him and both prayed that there would not be a hole that would trip them up.

Sebastion risked a look back and saw two Roanstors coming quickly … too quickly. He realized there was no way they could outrun them. He shouted to Rayor, who either did not hear him—the pounding of the Roanstors feet was deafening—or ignored him.

Rayor started pointing as he ran. There was a mound in the field with a slight hole in it.

Does he mean to hide in there? Surely, we both cannot fit in there … perhaps not even one. He's mad! Mad!

Rayor signaled for Sebastion to run in front.

Sebastion did so without coaxing and put everything he had left into the space between him and the hole. It felt as if the Roanstors were pounding their legs into the ground just behind his own feet.

Just a few more steps and I will dive! He flung himself into the hole.

Luck was with them because the interior was enormous. Sebastion rolled, bouncing off rocks and debris. It seemed to take forever for Rayor to dive into the hole with him.

Sebastion grabbed his hand and started to pull him further away from the entrance.

Rayor smiled a huge grin … and then it disappeared, and his hand was ripped out of Sebastion's as he was pulled from the hole.

Sebastion yelled and dived for Rayor's hands again, but he was gone.

He felt around the hole frantically and found the sword. Taking a deep breath and brushing the hair from his eyes, Sebastion stared at the exit a moment longer, and then he charged. He emerged, yelling and swinging his sword like a man possessed.

Rayor was suspended several feet from the ground by one leg by the Roanstors. Another was coming toward it, its front legs starting to instinctively slash in apparent anticipation of another meal.

Sebastion picked up a nearby rock and hurled it at the second beast.

The rock bounced off the Roanstor's shell with no apparent effect, but it did get the monster's attention. It turned its huge antlike head toward him and chirped angrily.

"COME ON, YOU UGLY BASTARD!" Sebastion yelled at it.

"What are you doing?" Rayor yelled from high in the air and upside down. "GET BACK IN THAT HOLE YOU IDIOT!"

Sebastion ignored him and threw another rock. This time it bounced off the shell and flew sideways, hitting the Roanstor in the eye.

Giving a high-pitched scream, it rushed toward Sebastion.

Its eye ... That rock hurt its eye.

Sebastion reached into his boot, pulled his knife, and let fly. The blade struck its mark, directly in the center of the same eye the rock had hit.

The giant insect screamed and reared up on its hind legs. It took several steps backward before it lost its balance and tumbled onto its side.

Sebastion looked up at Rayor, who had seen what had just happened and was pulling a knife from his sleeve as he dangled. The cloak hanging down over him made it difficult, but he managed to turn to face the Roanstor. As he met the giant's head, he saw two outer eyelids close over its eyes.

"Tricky," Rayor sighed.

Suddenly, he had an idea and pulled a package from another sleeve and frantically started to unroll it. He nearly dropped it as he pushed himself off the face of the Roanstor, which was trying to shove him into its salivating mandibles.

He finally opened it and blew the yellow powder into the monster's face.

At first, nothing happened. The two just froze, waiting to see what would happen.

Abruptly, blood shot from his captor's mouth, soaking Rayor. He was falling. He hit the ground with a thump, and then everything went dark.

Rayor woke to pounding and … something more. At first, he couldn't make it out. It sounded like singing—no not singing more like … *screaming!*

Rayor sat up, and for a moment, the world tilted. He put his hands to his head to settle it, and then the screaming started again. Shaking his head, he looked around.

The Roanstor he had blown the powder at was on the ground, twitching. It was not dead, but it was not doing well either.

Screaming again!

"What?" Rayor said, holding his head.

He looked over and saw Sebastion slashing the other Roanstor's leg and then moving quickly around it. The small blade still stuck out of one of its enormous eyes, the outer lid only half shut over it. It kept spinning, trying to catch Sebastion, but every time it did, he would move inside its blind spot. It would take a swipe but always missed. The monstrous creature was actually screaming in frustration. It was getting dizzy and looked close to toppling over. So did Sebastion, for that matter.

Rayor had no idea how long this had been going on. He could have been out for minutes or hours.

"Take off your blanket and attach it to the leg on its blindside … just enough so it gets a glimpse," Rayor instructed, holding his head and not getting up.

Sebastion immediately understood the plan. He took off the blanket that was rolled up on his back and threw it at one of the legs. It stuck to the spiny leg instantly. At the next spin, he ran off out of its vision and joined Rayor.

The Roanstor screamed again and kept chasing the blanket he took to be Sebastion.

"Are you all right?" Sebastion asked Rayor when he got to his side. "I thought you might be dead."

Rayor grunted. "Not that lucky, I guess."

Then they heard the pounding of those legs again.

"The third one…" Sebastion gasped breathlessly.

Sore head or not, Rayor was up, though stooped over, running nonetheless.

This time they made it back to the tree before the third Roanstor could see them. They had stayed low, but when they looked back, they saw that they were no longer in any danger. The third Roanstor had been stuffing itself with meat while the other two were squaring off with Rayor and Sebastion. It had only come toward them to retrieve more pieces of meat that had flown across the field.

"No reason to push our luck," Rayor whispered. "Let's get our things and get the puckering dark out of here."

Sebastion did not need to be convinced.

***

Many hours and miles away, Sebastion began the questions again. He was not sure Rayor would answer, but he needed to know.

"What were they?" he asked.

Rayor had poured some water over his head to wash away some of the blood. Most were from the Roanstor, but not all.

"Some say they were created by a wizard to act as sentries to his castle. The story goes that he couldn't control them, and they killed him and destroyed the castle."

Rayor rinsed his mouth out and spat. "Whatever they're made from or by whom, I think I'm going around them from now on."

"Me too!" Sebastion agreed.

Rayor gave him a funny look.

"A wizard, huh? I didn't think they really existed," Sebastion noted in a skeptical voice.

Rayor looked back with a raised brow.

"Did you think giant insects existed?"

Sebastion shook his head.

"Looks like you don't know everything," Rayor said in a matter of fact tone.

"Why were they doing that with the meat? You know… stuffing it into themselves."

"I believe that is where they store food. The Crango deer would have left the field long ago if the losses were too great. The Roanstors take only what they need."

Sebastion pondered this. "You mean the … uh, Crango deer knew about those things and still stayed?"

"Of course, no other predator would come close to that field."

"That big dog did," Sebastion countered.

"Look how that turned out for him. No, those nasty deer have two things to worry about in that field, Roanstors and old age."

They walked on like this until dusk when they found a dry spot, and without even bothering to start a fire, they absently ate dried meat and fell asleep, exhausted. No one sat watch that night. Instead, they slept as if dead to the world.

Both were sore and mentally drained from their encounter with the Roanstors.

Very little was said after that as they traveled, but Sebastion could tell there was more on Rayor's mind than the Roanstors. He still felt worn out and weary though, so he did not push the matter.

Two more days of uneventful walking later, they arrived at their destination.

Chapter 6 – The School

The school was big. Everything seemed to be made of mortar and stone. The walls that stood around it were tall and menacing. Sebastion could not help but wonder if the walls were meant to keep people out or to make sure they stayed in. The old man that had brought him there had been gracious enough to let him stand on the hill awhile and take in his new home, just a short distance away.

Their weeks of travel together had been the best times of Sebastion's life. His head would swim with Rayor's stories. It was like the traveling would disappear and he could see the things the man described. Like he was actually there. He did not want it to end.

Rayor put his hand on Sebastion's shoulder and gently urged him forward toward the school. A thick forest lay in front of them before they would arrive at the entrance of the school. The entire area was covered with trees and vines. The school itself was the only structure for as far as the eye could see.

Sebastion lifted his nose.

"Rayor, what is that smell in the air?"

The old man's face crinkled into a smile.

"What does it smell like?"

Sebastion bowed his head, closed his eyes, and concentrated.

"It smells like meat cooking and fresh bread … and at the same time, like sweat and something rotting."

Rayor chuckled and gave Sebastion a playful kick in the rump to keep walking.

"You'll see soon enough, boy."

As they approached the school, it seemed to disappear into the forest. The walls were so thick with ivy that you could walk right by it. Rayor walked as if he knew exactly where he was going, so Sebastion followed closely, not wanting to get lost among the trees.

Sebastion was getting an uneasy feeling that someone was watching them. He looked around cautiously, but saw nothing.

"Your instincts are correct, boy. We have been watched since we entered the Forest."

Sebastion was getting nervous.

"Don't get anxious. We belong here," Rayor said flatly.

Sebastion noticed Rayor had said this louder than was necessary.

Coming to a part of the wall that was slightly less covered with ivy, Rayor reached through the vegetation and moved his hand in a sequence of patterns.

The wall moved in with a soft, grating sound. He said something in another language into the waiting darkness, waited a moment, and then walked confidently into the empty space the wall had occupied just a moment ago.

Sebastion just stared at the place the old man had walked through. He didn't know if he should follow or not.

An arm shot out of the darkness and pulled him in. It was too quick for him to resist, but Rayor's voice spoke quietly into his ear.

"Walk slowly and make no sudden movement. There is something strange going on here."

With that, he grabbed Sebastion's wrist and moved cautiously forward.

They walked for some time before they came to a stairway. The only light was coming from the holes and cracks in the mortar of the stone wall. Only a few stairs were visible before they disappeared into the darkness.

Rayor pulled Sebastion along as if he had walked these corridors all his life.

Sebastion, sure he would fall, tried to keep up with the old man in the darkness. If he tried to slow down, Rayor just pulled him quickly along.

In the blackness, Rayor began to slow and finally stop.

Barely able to make out his companion's dark form, Sebastion watched as the old man put his head against a wall and listened for some time.

He reached forward, part of the wall opened, and once again he pulled Sebastion into a room and closed the secret door behind him.

There was slightly more light here, and Sebastion looked to where the door had been just a moment ago. He could find no sign of entry whatsoever.

The room they were in was small and smelled of flour. Crates and barrels were everywhere, filled with fruit and vegetables.

Sebastion's stomach began to growl.

Rayor gave him a nasty look and threw him an apple from a nearby barrel. "Hurry up and eat that, before your stomach gets us killed."

Sebastion wolfed down the apple as quickly as he could.

"Are you quite finished?" Rayor asked, tapping his foot impatiently.

"Yes ... sorry."

Rayor just frowned at him.

Sebastion could see the old man's forehead wrinkling in what he hoped was just impatience with him.

"Ok, this is what we're going to do. On my signal, we are going to leave this room, and you're going to follow right behind me. You are not going to stop and gawk or anything of the sort, no matter what you see. You are going to follow me and do exactly what you are told. Do you understand?"

"Yes, sir," Sebastion answered softly. "But where are we going?"

"We're going to see why nobody's around to greet you in your new home. Now, silence." Rayor opened the door, and they moved forward.

The light in the room beyond the door was bright, so they had to take a moment to let their eyes adjust. They found themselves in a large kitchen. A pot of water boiling over was causing the flames from the fire to hiss and crackle. The whole kitchen looked as if the people had left whatever they were doing in a hurry.

Rayor moved quickly to a corner that contained a small stairway that went both up and down.

"This is what the kitchen folk use to go about their business without disturbing the *important people*." His voice had a funny tone when he said, "important people."

Sebastion didn't understand, so he ignored it.

They went up the stairs, with Rayor leading and peering around every bend before going on. As they came around what seemed to Sebastion to be the hundredth bend, they began to hear voices off in the distance.

Rayor did not stop; he just kept moving more quickly towards the voices.

As they came to an open door, Sebastion could feel the fresh air rushing past him. The old man poked his head into the room and signaled for Sebastion to stay where he was. Returning moments later, however, he waved Sebastion into the room.

A large window that was wide open on the opposite wall from them illuminated the room, which was full of comfortable chairs and many vibrant, ornate tapestries.

Sebastion stared at one of the tapestries, lost in the depictions of knights and naked maidens. His jaw hung open, and he could not have turned away if his life had depended on it.

Rayor was at the window, intently watching something below. Without looking at him, Rayor motioned Sebastion to the window.

When Sebastion did not come, Rayor looked over and saw him looking close-up and intently at an image of a rather well-endowed woman depicted in a tapestry.

The old man rolled his eyes and made a hissing sound, trying to break Sebastion from his stupor. When that didn't work, he quickly walked up to Sebastion and slapped him hard on the back of his head.

"What is wrong with you?"

Sebastion could not think of anything to say.

"Come here and take a look out the window," Rayor commanded, annoyed.

Sebastion walked to the window, through which he heard voices. He poked his head out and nearly knocked Rayor over as he jumped back.

"Are you mad, boy?" Rayor caught his balance. "This stupid dark, blasted boy is going to kill me," he mumbled under his breath.

The old man grabbed Sebastion by the scruff of his neck and pulled him slowly to the window.

Sebastion's eyes were wide, and his hands shook, but he did not resist. They both peered into the street below.

There were many people gathered there, in fact, more people than Sebastion had ever seen in his life. So many faces and voices! He was overwhelmed by the sheer magnitude of it all. The entire population of the school was in the courtyard, and one man was standing on a barrel trying to quiet the crowd. The crowd was angry, and they were shouting and waving their fists at the man.

Sebastion looked across the courtyard and saw even more people staring out from large windows, like them. They seemed to be more his age. They seemed very serious and even a little angry with the people below. Sebastion moved to the corner of the window so as not to be seen.

Suddenly, the crowd began to part, and everyone fell silent. A man was walking in the middle, and the people were parting as if he was cutting right through them. He walked up to the man on the barrel and said something quietly.

The man hopped off and sprinted back into the building.

The people whispered again, but the man only had to turn around to have silence again. No one made a sound.

The man was short and very thin. The skin on his face was so tight you could see every angle of his bones. Thinning dark hair mixed with gray was tied tightly behind him. His eyes were set back and shaded by heavy eyebrows.

Sebastion could feel the power of that gaze even from up in the window.

The man wore all black, with a long black cape that flowed like the wings of a bat when he walked.

"What is the meaning of this distraction?" his deep voice boomed, low and commanding.

No one said a word. Everyone looked at one another, but nobody said anything.

"You have disrupted us with this display, and I will know why."

He stepped forward and fixed the entire crowd with his piercing gaze.

"WHO..." he roared. "Who leads this ... interruption of yours?"

Sebastion noticed that there was a younger man in the crowd that everyone kept looking toward. Finally, after several prods by the people surrounding him, the young man stepped forward.

He kept his eyes on the ground as he spoke.

"Sir, we have a grievance that we must make you aware of."

"Yes?" the man in black sneered, staring down at the young man like a bird of prey ready to strike down a pigeon.

Sebastion looked to his companion, the old man he shared the window with, and saw that he had drawn his hood over his face and was just shaking his head in disapproval.

"This is going to end badly," he heard Rayor mumble.

The young man who was the obvious, but reluctant, leader of this crowd was wringing his shaking hands together as he studied the ground at the feet of the man in black.

"What is this grievance I *must* know about?"

The awkward leader took an uncomfortable moment before answering. "Sir, for some time now we've asked that someone investigate the deaths that have been happening..." He swallowed so hard that they could hear him from their window on the other side of the courtyard. "Um ... consistently over a year now, sir."

Sebastion looked to the windows and saw the sullen-looking children talking to the man that had been standing on the barrel. He was handing things out. The children, after receiving what was being handed to them, quickly returned to the window, obviously hiding something from view.

The man in black crossed his arms and stared down at the leader of the crowd. "And what is it you want me to do about this?" he asked.

The leader took another uncomfortable moment.

"We want you to find the person responsible for these murders." The leader was getting more confident each time he spoke.

"We have decided that we will no longer perform our duties until this matter is resolved."

With that, the leader of the crowd looked back at his comrades and gave them an encouraging nod.

The man in black shot his hands out and began making movements in the air.

Immediately, five arrows flew through the air, landing neatly in almost the same spot in the chest of the leader of the crowd.

The surprised leader stood there with his eyes wide and staring at the arrows, shafts protruding from his chest.

The crowd was shocked into silence.

The man in black stepped forward and put his finger on one of the protruding arrows and gave a gentle push.

The young, reluctant leader fell onto his back—dead. His eyes were still open and staring upwards.

Sebastion felt like they were staring directly into his own.

"Listen to me, you impetuous insects!" The man in black seemed to be growing in size as he spoke.

"I have not brought you all here because of your housekeeping abilities."

His upper lip was lifting into a snarl.

"You all are here because no one else would have you. You are the undesirables, and I have agreed to take you in!" He stepped forward with his eyes ablaze.

The entire crowd took a step back.

"You are all murderers, thieves, rapists, and worse. Do not think you are ever in a position to make demands of ME!"

His hand shot into the air once more, and the children in the building stood, pointing their arrows in the direction of the crowd.

"Is there anything else I *must* know?"

The crowd did not move, and everyone was silent.

"If there is nothing else," the man in black said with contempt oozing from his lips, "I will have my lunch in the library." He smiled. "It seems we have guests." With that, he looked directly at Sebastion and Rayor in the window.

Sebastion gasped and stepped back.

The old man stepped forward and nodded slightly from beneath his hood.

As they stood silently together, waiting in the library, Sebastion noted it was cooler with the heavy curtains covering the windows. The many books that lined the walls fascinated him. And there were paintings everywhere. His head was buzzing from the events of the day. He was still trying to process the fact that he had watched a man die just moments ago. It seemed so unreal.

A rather timid servant entered the library, announced that the master of the house would be with them shortly, and asked them if they would like some wine.

The old man said yes and requested some fruit for his "boney companion."

The servant left, and the old man removed his hood, letting his sewn-in strands of white hair once again fall down his back.

Sebastion could not keep his knees from shaking, and his palms were cold and clammy.

Rayor pointed to a nearby chair, and Sebastion sat thankfully. He knew he did not want to meet this man from the courtyard. He wanted to go back to the safety of the forest.

Sebastion looked up and saw a sword hanging above the fireplace. It was so beautiful. It made Keeper's sword seem more of a stick or a knife for cutting bread.

The old man saw him studying it and waved him toward it.

"Just look. Don't touch."

Sebastion was across the room in seconds, studying the giant Claymore.

There was an audible "swish," and the man in black clothing was standing in the room.

Sebastion was taken by surprise, and his instincts took over. He moved like a cat to a pillar and stood there, still, trying to make himself disappear.

"And to what do I owe this pleasure?" the man in black with dark eyes asked Rayor in his deep voice.

"Serin, I am here because I have done what you have requested and brought the boy."

"And what of the troll we put in charge of him?" Serin asked.

Rayor paused.

"He has run off. I do not know where he has gone or why he has left."

Sebastion realized they were talking about Keeper.

Serin made a crooked smile.

"I would say he left because he didn't take to having knives plunged into his feet."

Rayor looked to the floor and took a deep breath.

"I found his company ... distasteful." he said.

Serin's half-smile disappeared.

"I do not care what you find distasteful. You were not given orders to harm any of my men. However, I do know the circumstances, and he had no right to attempt to destroy my property."

Sebastion surmised that the "property" meant him. He did not like this man dressed in black and did not want to stay here.

Slowly, he moved his head in the direction of the door. He calculated the best way he could leave this library and this "school" and never look back.

The servant came into the room with wine and fruit. He poured three glasses and offered the men theirs. He left the room as quietly as he had come.

"What is wrong with the boy? Why does he look so sick?" Serin asked.

"Your *troll* has been overdosing him with the poisons. I believe he was trying to cause an accidental death so that he would longer have to care for him."

The man in black scowled and walked to the window.

"He probably was not the best caretaker, but he made up for it in other ways. I see the boy already is far better at concealing himself than the others of his age."

He looked directly at Sebastion.

"Come, let's have a look at you."

Sebastion's breath caught in his throat. The realization that Serin, the man in black, knew he was there the whole time made the hairs on the back of his neck stand up. He began to move forward, slowly.

Serin stood like a cat ready to strike.

Sebastion's heart was beating so hard he thought it would pop right out of his chest.

"He looks more like an animal than a boy," Serin observed.

It was true. Sebastion had been traveling for weeks, and his hair was long and full of knots, not to mention pieces of leaves and sticks from sleeping on the ground.

His clothes were all too small and nothing more than rags. His boots were an old pair that Keeper had abandoned for new ones. He was covered in dust, and his gray eyes were barely visible from beneath his bangs.

"This is what all this trouble has been about?" Serin wondered aloud to no one in particular.

"The boy has already bested your man on the practice field," Rayor said, with just a hint of pride.

Serin just grunted and grabbed the boy's arm. He pinched the skin much like Rayor had when they had first met.

"I am surprised he has grown as tall as he has, considering the amount of poison he's consumed."

Serin looked him over like he was some beast to be purchased at a market.

"He is nearly as tall as I am already."

He frowned.

"This may prove to be a problem. You say he bested my man, did you?" Serin asked the old man.

"That's right. They were in a practice round, and I noticed that the boy was holding back. I suggested that he put more into the fight and so introduced a ... catalyst."

Serin's eyebrow lifted.

"What kind of catalyst?"

The old man cleared his throat nervously.

"Uhh ... a small dagger," he answered, with an insignificant nod.

"I see," Serin acknowledged. "And?"

While the old man continued his tale, Serin never showed any reaction but also never asked him to stop. When Rayor got to the part about hitting Keeper in the backside, Sebastion thought he saw Serin lift his brow in amusement. When the story was finished, however, there was no hint of humor on his face.

"We will be eating at sunset. You will both join us. The servants will show you where you will be staying and provide you with whatever you need to clean up."

With that, Serin left as quickly and quietly as he had come. The black cape he wore filled with air, and he looked more like a bat flying from the room than a schoolmaster.

The same servant who had brought them the wine and fruit earlier escorted them through the school to where they would be staying. Rayor and the servant had to pause many times as Sebastion would stop, gawking at a tapestry or a suit of armor. Soon they arrived at a dormitory-like room.

The servant, obviously annoyed from all the delays, unceremoniously bowed and left.

The room was small and the beds were plain and looked hard, but to Sebastion, everything was luxurious compared to what he had been used to.

Rayor looked Sebastion up and down and shook his head. "This will not do," he said. "We need to find a barber and some clothes before we go to eat with the others."

The old man dropped his bags on the floor and motioned for Sebastion to do the same, and they left the room.

People stopped and stared as they walked down the narrow halls. Sebastion and the old man were quite a sight.

Rayor was wearing his hood, and even his hands were concealed beneath his large sleeves.

Sebastion looked more like a wild animal than an adolescent boy. His strides were long, trying to keep up, and his head was darting everywhere to take in as much as he could.

Rayor stopped and turned to Sebastion.

"This is no good. We are disrupting everyone. These imbeciles are too interested in us. You'd think they've never seen an old man and a boy before," he thundered for them to hear.

A boy of around Sebastion's age walked up to the two of them.

"Are you two lost?" he asked, wrinkling his nose at them.

"Servants are not permitted in this part of the school. If the House Master finds you here, you will surely share the same fate as your companion in the courtyard." He spoke to them as if they were insulting him by just being there.

"We'll take that under advisement, *boy*," Rayor answered with disdain.

"BOY!" The boy's face turned bright red in anger. "Who do you think you are?"

The boy made a grab at Rayor's hood but, before he could touch it, Sebastion shot forward and struck the boy in the stomach.

Collapsing to the floor, the boy gasped for breath.

Rayor grabbed Sebastion's arm and pulled him away quickly.

"Why did you do that?" Rayor asked angrily.

Sebastion walked with his head down as they hurried away.

"I have met boys like this before and ... I thought they would kill you."

"Ridiculous!" the old man said, shaking his head.

The crowd of boys that had been watching the confrontation was now helping the boy up from the floor. They were talking angrily and looking in the direction of the old man and Sebastion as they made their quick retreat.

Returning to their room, they secured the door behind them. Rayor pointed to the bed, and Sebastion sat down. The old man anxiously paced the floor. "That is not a very good first impression for your peers to have of you."

Sebastion stared at the floor and tried to look chastised, but he was not sorry he had hit the boy. He remembered the boys in the forest and had no intention of letting them do their evil to Rayor or himself. Not ever again. That is why he had trained so hard with Keeper these past few years.

"Never again," he whispered to himself.

"What was that?" Rayor asked.

"Nothing," Sebastion replied gloomily.

"Fine, we will summon a servant, and we will have a barber come to us. We will instruct them to bring water to wash and some clean clothes ... that fit."

With that, Rayor grabbed a red rope and pulled hard.

Moments later, a servant was at the door. It was the same servant that had seemed annoyed at them earlier.

"What can I do for you?" he asked, rather rudely.

This was a wrong time to be giving Rayor attitude, and he reached through the doorway and pulled the servant into the room. Sticking his head out the door, he looked up and down the hallway. He then closed the door and walked quickly to the servant, who was now brushing off the place where Rayor had grabbed him. Grabbing him again in the same spot, the old man pushed the servant hard against the closed door.

The servant was lifted several inches into the air. His face nearly disappeared into the old man's hood as they whispered.

Sebastion could not hear what they were saying, but the servant's body seemed to go limp as he hung against the wall like a rag doll.

Rayor finally dropped the man to the ground, and he fell to his knees. He looked up at the man in the hood, stood up, and quickly left the room.

Very soon afterward, there was a light knock on the door, and Rayor cautiously opened it. Several more servants entered with everything Rayor had requested and more.

Sebastion noticed that the rude servant was nowhere to be found. The band of servants measured him all over. At one point, he pushed a servant's hand away and would have done more if Rayor hadn't slapped him on the head again.

"Let them do what they're here to do, boy."

Sebastion lifted his arms and let them do what they wanted.

There was another light knock on the door.

Rayor moved quickly to it and asked who it was.

"The barber, sir," answered a deep but feminine voice.

Rayor opened the door, and a middle-aged, very plump woman came in, causing Sebastion's jaw to drop. He could not take his eyes off her.

She was the most beautiful thing he had ever seen. She had a white bonnet on her head, and her dress was threatening to burst from her gigantic midsection. She bowed and smiled wide at the old man. She was missing nearly all her teeth.

Rayor just pointed to Sebastion, who was still standing with his arms out at his sides and his mouth hanging open.

She saw the wild wolfish look on his face as he stared, fascinated. She gasped and stepped back.

Rayor rolled his eyes and pushed her unceremoniously in Sebastion's direction. He had to put some effort into it and didn't know if it was because of her apprehension or her significant size.

As the woman barber worked on Sebastion, he could not help but stare unabashedly at her vast bosom. She had to continually push his head down when he tried to look up at her.

"If you keep this up, I will end up chopping off your ear," she said, embarrassed but gentle.

"I don't mind ... uh ... Ma'am."

She smiled her nearly toothless smile. "You'd think he'd never seen a woman before," she told Rayor.

"I don't believe he has," Rayor said in a matter of fact reply.

She stopped for a moment before she continued.

"What of his mother?"

"Stop asking questions and finish with your business," the old man said sharply.

The woman quickly turned back to her task.

Sebastion was smiling up at her, and she gently pushed his head back down again.

As Sebastion was being cleaned up, Serin was in his office sitting behind a large desk, his dark-booted feet up and his hands resting behind his head. He was staring up at the ceiling, deep in thought, smiling and quite satisfied with himself.

Someone quietly entered the room, and Serin, not even bothering to look up, told the intruder, "I told you I was not to be disturbed."

"I have no care of that, Serin," came a raspy reply.

Serin stood up quickly to confront the rude servant, only to find himself clasped by the throat and thrown back into his chair. "What is the meaning of this?" he yelled.

He tried to get up again, but before he could, the stranger in the long, deep-hooded, red robe stuck out a scaled, crooked finger at the man in black. Serin was frozen in his chair. As much as he tried, he could not move.

"What type of witchcraft is this?" he asked, struggling to make his body respond.

"The kind that will introduce you intimately to your entrails if you don't close your mouth."

The stranger's voice had an accent that Serin had never heard. He noticed the finger he held out was misshapen, with gray skin like a reptile, though he could not see any of the man beneath the robe.

"Listen to what I have to say, and you will be back to your puny life in a moment." The stranger's entire body shook as he talked. It was as if the speech was causing him excruciating pain.

"Who are you, and what business do you have with me?" Serin demanded.

"It does not matter who I am, but my business here is deathly important!"

"Okay. What business?" Serin asked, trying to sound more angry than scared.

"You have a boy here... "

"We have many boys here. Take your pick. What's your type fat, thin, blond? What's your pleasure?"

The stranger spoke some words that Serin had never heard before. He started to feel his head fill up with something. His nose started to run and he couldn't clear his throat fast enough.

"You will listen and only shake your head yes or no. Do you understand?"

Phlegm started running down his face, and he was coughing all over himself instead of speaking. However, he did find that he could move his head, so he shook it up and down in response to any questions the thing in front of him asked.

Back in his room, Sebastion was staring at himself in the mirror. He could not believe it was his own image staring back at him. He was wearing clothes that fit him, and his hair was cut short and combed into place.

Rayor came up behind him and also looked at Sebastion's image.

Sebastion could see Rayor's eyes in the reflection. They were wide and filling with tears.

The old man quickly turned away and walked to the other side of the room.

"Rayor, are you all right?" Sebastion asked, concerned.

Rayor stayed quiet for a while before answering.

"You remind me of someone I knew a very long time ago," he said, without turning around.

Clearing his throat, he walked back to the mirror and smacked Sebastion hard on the back of his head.

"OUCH! What was that for?" the boy yelped.

The old man was smiling now inside his hood. "That was for making me have to drag you all the way here to this forsaken school."

The wrinkled man brushed his hands across his cloak. Small bits of dirt and twigs fell to the floor.

"Prepare yourself, we'll be having dinner with these imbeciles."

***

A servant knocked on the door of Serin's office to remind him it was time for dinner. It was common for the master to lose track of time, and if they did not tell him of his appointments, they would be in a great deal of trouble. The servant knocked again, but there was no reply, so the old servant poked his head into the room.

"Master, are you here?"

He heard faint coughing and, concerned, he entered the room.

"Master?" the servant inquired again, respectfully.

Serin popped his head up from behind the desk. His face was covered in mucus, and whatever had once been in his stomach from lunch. He was still spitting on the floor behind the desk.

"Get out!" he gasped.

"Yes, of course," the servant said, his eyes focusing on the floor to avoid looking at his master. He bowed and quickly left.

Dinner was somewhat late that evening, and Serin did not ask Sebastion any further questions. Still, Sebastion was glad Rayor was there. He would have hated being alone with that man.

***

Two weeks passed and Sebastion was still searching for a way to get out of the big school. He disliked the other boys. He preferred being by himself to being in the company of his classmates.

He would occasionally sneak over to the other side of the school, where the girls were, to sit and watch them. He could watch them for hours.

Whenever he was missing for too long, Rayor would find him and tell him how stupid he was for running off.

Sebastion did not care, though. He could not stand the constant studying. He was learning which plants could be used for what, how much poison is enough to kill a man of a certain weight, what were the points on the body susceptible to a mortal wound... He found the studies dull and very boring.

The teachers insisted that he spend extra time catching up with reading and writing to be at the same level as the other boys in his class. His text was good because he had been reading Keeper's books, but he had never had to write anything in his life. Therefore, he would get frustrated and daydream about ways to escape the school.

He hated weapons training at first. He was in a class with boys of his own age, and they were clumsy and not up to his ability.

It was not long before the teachers decided to have him train with the men instead. This, he found to be much more rewarding. He was even able to practice with the sword, and he was rarely beaten.

Some of the men resented the fact that a boy in his mid-teens was besting them.

"This boy does not belong here with us!" they would complain.

But he was as tall as many of them and, soon enough, they forgot his age and came to accept him because of his skills.

Sebastion did not care one way or the other. He just wanted the practice time with the sword.

His most-hated class was dissecting the body of the man that had been killed in the courtyard. He had even pressed the teacher on why they would need to know what was inside a body.

The crippled old man had looked up from his sewing of the rib cage, obviously annoyed. "If you are going to be an expert at what you are to become, you need to know what exactly you are doing ... outside and in."

Since that exchange, the bent old man had Sebastion come in front of the class and work on the corpse regularly. The cruel old man would have him plunge a knife into the dead body's heart, liver, or other sensitive places. He would then have the boy explain to the class why that wound would be fatal.

Sebastion hated the feel of stabbing that body over and over again.

The only good part of his existence at the school was Rayor. He had stayed with Sebastion in the dorm room they shared and would tell stories at night about Knights and great battles of the past. He would describe strange creatures that lived in the forest far to the East, insisting that these things existed and that, one-day, Sebastion would see for himself.

Sebastion would dream of going off on adventures of his own. He hated the school and everything it was about, but Rayor's stories always made him feel better.

His dreams were of traveling and seeing these magnificent creatures and fighting in great battles. Still, his days always brought him back to the reality of the school.

As much as he loved the old man's stories, he decided that he would run away from this place as soon as he could. When an opportunity presented itself, he would be gone. This was the promise he made to himself.

Early one evening, Sebastion was sitting on the wall looking out over the forest. He would sometimes see a deer far below, walking and busying itself with feeding on the moist grass.

He wished he could be like that deer. He wanted to be free and be able to go and do whatever he wanted. He was sick of having people tell him what to do. He wanted to run far away and never see another person again. He liked being around Rayor, but the old man was always keeping track of him and making sure he went to his classes. He wanted to be on his own. He no longer wanted to be watched and evaluated. He wanted to be free, like the small brown deer below him.

The sun was going down, and he knew everyone would be going to dinner soon. He sighed and started back to his room, walking through the courtyard with his head down, deep in thought.

A boy stepped out of a dark corner of the yard.

Sebastion saw the boy but ignored him as he always had in the past. He wanted nothing to do with the people at this school.

"Hey!" the boy yelled.

Sebastion kept walking.

"What, you too good to speak to me?"

Sebastion just rolled his eyes and kept moving.

Three more boys stepped out of another corner in front of him, and he had no choice but to stop.

He suddenly started to have flashbacks to the time in the forest, but this time he was getting angry instead of scared.

They surrounded him, smiling but not making a sound.

Sebastion crossed his arms and stared directly at the boy that had spoken to him.

The cocky boy was smiling and looking very confident. "So, you decided to stop and speak to us lowly people, after all?"

Sebastion didn't say a word. He just stood there and returned the boy's stare.

"I know you know how to talk. We have all heard from you in class. Though you never even knew we were there. What makes you so special? You don't look so special to me."

The boy walked around Sebastion, looking him over.

"I see a skinny nobody that grew too tall."

Sebastion looked at the other boys as they laughed at him, the memories coming back stronger now.

"Are you finished?" he asked.

"Not quite, Bones. I think that's what we're going to call you because you're nothing but a bag of bones. What do you think of that, *Bones*?"

"I think it is time we went to dinner." Sebastion tried to step through the ring of boys, but every time he tried, one stepped in front of him, and he stepped back into the center of them.

It was becoming evident what they had in mind, and he was mentally preparing himself for what was almost certainly coming next.

Sebastion's attention, however, was momentarily caught by the sight of a man on a balcony above. As he turned his head back to the band of bullies, he was struck just above his ear. He fell to his knees, clutching his wounded head.

"You missed, you idiot!" one of the boys whispered harshly.

"It's not my fault, he turned his head at the last second!"

"Don't just stand there, hit him again until he's out cold! You know who is watching."

With that, the boy who hit Sebastion the first time kicked him in the side of the face.

Sebastion rolled on the ground, writhing in pain and put his hands out in front of him to ward off any other blows.

"He won't pass out!" one of them said excitedly.

The leader of the boys rolled his eyes and waved the rest of the boys into the center. They all started kicking and hitting Sebastion as he curled into a fetal position. This went on for some time before there was a loud clap from the balcony above. Serin made some moves with his hand, and the boys quickly left the courtyard.

Sebastion lay in the courtyard very nearly unconscious now. He was lying in the dirt, covered in his own blood and vomit. He could not catch his breath and thought he was going to choke and die. Still, he noticed it was starting to drizzle, and it felt cool against his cheeks. He could not see from one of his eyes and wondered if he ever would again.

Pulling himself to a sitting position, he spat blood onto the ground. He tried to clear his head. He saw from his one eye that there was a puddle of water forming not far from where he sat. He rolled onto his stomach and pulled himself to it. The cold water from the puddle was helping, and soon the feeling that he might be sick again started to go away. He didn't think his legs were severely injured, but a particularly cruel boy had continuously kicked him in the groin. He was not sure that even if he were able to stand, he would be able to walk. Nevertheless, he had to get out of there.

Serin watched from above as Sebastion slowly limped out of the courtyard. He had meant for his boys to only knock him unconscious. He wanted to see if there was anything on the skinny bag of bones from which he could discover the reason for the importance others placed on him.

He knew very well that if Sebastion were to die, it would go badly for him. He certainly did not look forward to another meeting with the creature that had visited him in his office; yet he had to know why this boy was important enough that the vile monster had come to him.

Curious as to why the boy had not cried out or even lain there until someone found him, Serin watched but with no intention of helping. A very strange boy, indeed, Serin thought as he stroked his long, pointed chin and watched the skinny boy limp away.

Rayor was sitting at a table alone. He usually ate there with Sebastion, but today the boy was nowhere to be found. He lifted his head slightly as a group of boys came in late for the meal. They seemed even fuller of themselves than usual.

This particular group was Serin's favorites, and they let everyone know it. They never had to go to the kitchen to fetch their meals. Instead, they would have the younger boys do their bidding. This group was the underlying ruling class here at the school. When Serin was not around, they were the ones that ran things, for better or worse.

The old man watched as they whispered and threw mock punches into the air. One of the boys curled up and whimpered, mockingly. This set all the others into a laughing fit. Rayor was starting to feel uneasy. None of the boys would even look in his direction. He decided it was time to see where Sebastion was.

Sebastion was getting sick on the side of a building when Rayor found him. He ran over and grabbed Sebastion's shoulders to steady him. Sebastion, startled, drew a small knife from his sleeve. Rayor just grabbed the knife out of his hand and put it in his pocket.

"I see you are getting acquainted with the locals," the old man said gently.

"My chest hurts," was all Sebastion could get out.

"Don't worry, Sebastion. It's going to be all right."

Rayor picked him up as if he weighed no more than a feather and walked briskly back to their room at the dorm.

Lying in his bed and staring up at the ceiling with his one open eye, Sebastion's entire body felt numb. His head felt light and surprisingly good. He was having a hard time even remembering what had happened. He could just lie there smiling, for reasons he did not know, with his split lips looking up at the ceiling.

He could see that Rayor was busying himself, stirring up yet another mixture of herbs and powder. Sebastion was hoping it was something like what he had already been given. Instead, Rayor put a paste-like substance on cuts and bruises on his face. He looked furious from what Sebastion could see of him beneath his hood. He couldn't remember Rayor ever wearing his hood inside their room before.

"Rayor, why-r are you sh- so angry?" Sebastion tried to not slur, but he couldn't help it.

Rayor scowled at him from beneath his hood and continued to apply the strange, foul-smelling paste.

"Are ye angry at me?" he asked.

"Don't be stupid, boy. You are just feeling the effects of the poppy milk I have given you."

"I like the poppy, uh ... milk," Sebastion said with a smile.

"I'll bet you do," the old man said with a half-smile of his own.

"Rayor... " Sebastion said.

"Yes?" The old man was absently concentrating on his task.

"Am I like other people?"

Rayor's hands stopped. "What do you mean?"

Sebastion shifted his weight on the bed to face him. "I don't wanna be like thosh others."

Rayor went back to what he was doing and said nothing.

"Rayor, I h- ate thosh boys," Sebastion said, sleepy now.

Rayor lifted Sebastion's shirt to view the damage. His face turned even redder under his hood. Sebastion could tell, even in his current state, that he was becoming dangerously angry.

"Don't be a- ngry," Sebastion said. "I don't mind."

He smiled with his teeth stained with blood, and his lips swollen and split.

Rayor leaned in close and looked him in the eyes.

"There will be a time very soon when you will."

Sebastion tried to shrug, but found he could no longer move his shoulders.

"A time very soon... " Rayor said, more to himself than to his patient.

***

It was days later that Sebastion was finally able to eat his meals with the other boys again—well, at least in the same room—but he always sat alone. He could not eat anything hard, as he still experienced shooting pain from his teeth every time he bit down.

The side of his face was swollen, and he had to walk bent with his arm covering his bruised ribs.

He was healing quickly, though. He no longer saw blood when he urinated. He still did not see well from his left eye, but Rayor said that too would be back to normal when the swelling subsided.

The boys that attacked him would always laugh and point at him as they ate. He would ignore them as best he could and concentrate on just chewing on the right side of his mouth.

He found that he was hungrier now than he had ever been. Even though Rayor would bring him even more food throughout the day, it seemed as though he was always eating but never getting enough.

At first, he was slow to get back to where he had been in his training, but with time he did finally get back to normal. Rayor had started his own regimen with Sebastion as well. At night, he would come to the room with a tray of food and put Sebastion through his drills. It started with his hand-to-hand fighting routines. The school had its own version, but Rayor's was more precise and refined.

Every night before bed, Rayor would watch as Sebastion did many exercises to build up his strength. The old man himself would even participate in some. Sebastion's body was healing and, in fact, he was feeling healthier than he had ever felt before.

Almost before Sebastion realized it, a year and most of another had gone by at the school. The boys had mostly ignored Sebastion as they attended classes. In weapons training, Sebastion was still training with the men and never had to deal with the cruel boys. The men had nicknamed him "The Wolf" because of his unique fighting skill.

Rayor was particularly impressed with the name. He thought it appropriately described Sebastion's way of barely moving in his defensive moves, but be a blur when on the offense.

"Much like how a wolf would fight," Rayor would tell him, smiling.

Sebastion thought it quite reasonable, as that was the way he had been taught in the beginning by his Keeper.

Rayor would get angry when he said that. "Your 'keeper' was an idiot and a lazy fighter." In fact, Rayor would get very red with anger whenever he spoke of Keeper.

"You have been taught a lazy man's style, but you have turned it into something different. Something … better. You should be proud and give no one else credit for your ability. There will be no more talk of that bent little troll."

Sebastion always swelled with pride when the old man would say something nice to him. He was not used to it and felt a little uncomfortable, but he liked it, nonetheless.

At mealtime one cold and damp day, all the boys were gathering to collect their plates of food. Sebastion always waited until the others had gotten their food before getting his. This was the best way to avoid the band of boys that were always first in line. Sebastion had begun calling them "the first boys," not only because they were always first in line, but because they were first in their own eyes and those of Headmaster Serin as well.

As Sebastion came to collect his dinner this day, one of the first boys was late in arriving. The boy tried to push Sebastion out of the way as he made his way to the food, but Sebastion did not budge. This boy was husky and short. His light-colored hair was cut short, and he always had a cruel, crooked smile on his face. He fixed his small eyes on Sebastion and looked him up and down.

"So '*Bones*', I see you have put some meat on ya."

Sebastion just ignored him and held out his plate as a timid-looking man placed a scoop of potatoes on it.

"You! Servant," the husky boy said to the timid man. "Don't think we haven't noticed you giving more food to 'Bones' here."

The man stepped back and stared at the ground. It was true; all the kitchen people were especially nice to Sebastion. They would always give him more food and prepare something for when Rayor would come in the evening.

The boy stepped toward the servant, who again retreated a step.

Sebastion saw the butcher in the back of the kitchen. He was not looking up, but Sebastion could see the man's neck was getting red from anger.

"If I ever find out that you are giving 'Bones' more than *we* think he needs, I will be sure to suggest that you be the next servant to disappear."

The timid man did not move, but the butcher's head shot up for just a moment. Sebastion saw he was squeezing his large butcher's knife so hard his knuckles were white.

The "first boy" turned to Sebastion.

"So, now that you've put on weight, you think you can stand up to me."

"I'm sorry, are you standing?" Sebastion said, without meeting the boy's eyes.

The butcher let out a snort despite himself.

The boy's face flushed in anger and embarrassment. He pointed to the butcher.

"You got something to say, *servant*?"

The boy said the word 'servant' as if it was the most disgusting thing in the world. With that, he walked up to the first timid man and slapped him hard in the face.

The poor man had been just standing there, trying not to be seen. Now he crumbled to the ground and started to sob.

Furious now, the butcher lifted his knife and stepped forward.

Before another step could be taken, Sebastion grabbed the boy and flipped him over his back with all his strength.

The other children in the school were going about their meals as usual. The popular boys were flipping their vegetables from their spoons at the younger boys. The younger ones knew they would just have to take the abuse. If they tried to stand up to the older boys, they would surely be beaten and, even worse, ostracized from everyone at the school. They knew already that boys that did not fit in here would eventually go missing or worse. They kept their heads down, just thankful that the cruel leader of the boys was not there today.

Then there was a hard slap that came from the kitchen, and all the boys looked in that direction. In the next instant, the cruel leader of the boys came sailing through the kitchen entry and landed hard on his back.

The dining hall went silent.

Rayor had been eating quietly by himself in a corner, waiting for Sebastion, as he always did. Beneath his deep-hooded cloak, he raised a single eyebrow in surprise as he, too, looked up from his not so exciting potato something he was eating.

Sebastion walked confidently out of the kitchen.

Rayor's face crinkled into a wide grin.

So, it's time to see if this wolf bites.

Sebastion was angry now ... more enraged in fact than he had ever remembered being. Very few people had ever shown him kindness, and the timid little man that had served the food was one of them who had.

The boy that Sebastion had thrown to the ground was recovering and beginning to catch his breath.

Sebastion stood over the "first boy" leader with his arms crossed, now no longer resembling the emaciated wild boy that had come to this school. The extra food and training Rayor had inflicted on him had done wonders for Sebastion.

He was taller now. Though still very thin, his body was becoming hard with lean muscle. His black hair had grown long again and was neatly brushed behind him. His face had become hard and emotionless, but his eyes glared like fireballs when he was angry. A year ago, the other boys would have fallen upon him in a second, but he was a different person now.

Serin had slipped silently into the large room, quickly taking note of what was going on.

The chubby boy on the ground got up slowly and moved to where the other boys were standing, watching him.

Sebastion faced his attackers from more than a year ago. They stared at each other, sizing each other up.

Serin shook his head in disgust.

Rayor smiled like a lion watching its cub make its first kill.

Serin cleared his throat, and everyone looked toward him. He moved his hand in the air, and this time Sebastion knew precisely what it meant. The silent language was a prerequisite at the school, and learning it was not a choice.

Rayor moved like a ghost to Serin's side.

"It's five against one, Serin. You can't be serious!"

Serin smiled his cruel grin. "I know ... and yes, I am."

The group circled Sebastion much as they had more than a year before. This time, however, they were no longer boys but on the verge of becoming young men and, therefore, much more competent fighters.

Sebastion stood in the center of them, very still, with his arms crossed, looking calm. If it were not for the rage in his eyes, one would think this was just another day in the big room for him.

The gang of boys exchanged smirks at Sebastion's confident demeanor.

Sebastion recognized the boy who had kicked him so many times in the groin. He clenched his jaw tightly, trying not to spring forward. He knew this would become a brawl and decided to use surprise, at just the right moment, to his advantage.

Finally, lunging forward using the balls of his feet like he was taught, Sebastion smashed his fist into the unfortunate boy that had inflicted so much pain on him.

The boy stiffened and fell backward like a fallen oak. It happened so quickly, the others didn't even have time to react. The fallen boy lay still on the ground after falling with a loud thud.

"Ok." Rayor looked at Serin. "Four on one is better."

Serin ignored him, frowning and crossing his arms, clearly annoyed.

The others exchanged surprised looks and then fell upon Sebastion. They came on him clumsily, throwing wild punches and kicks whenever they were close enough.

Sebastion used their clumsiness against them and, continuously moved, first behind one boy and then another.

The band of bullies became confused and then frustrated as each tried to be the one to knock Sebastion down in front of their schoolmaster.

Serin was angry now, shaking his head in disgust.

The group finally backed off to catch their collective breath.

Sebastion again crossed his arms and stared back at them. His chest was barely moving, and his demeanor was still totally relaxed.

A crowd had gathered in the room, making it difficult to keep the area where the boys were fighting open.

At the far wall, a group of men with whom Sebastion trained were jabbering and exchanging money. Serin was signaling to one of them.

Sebastion was unable to catch the meaning behind the subtle movements of Serin's hands. The man to whom Serin had signaled looked at Sebastion with a strange expression that might have been sympathy and then disappeared into the crowd.

Rayor was talking quietly but vehemently with Serin. He was pointing at Sebastion and pointing his other finger at Serin.

Serin raised his hand to stop him.

"I don't care about the consequences! This is my school, and I will not be made the fool by anyone!" he yelled.

At the same moment, the man he had signaled to came back with four swords. Keeping his head down, he handed each of the young men a sword, keeping one for the boy on the ground.

Sebastion looked toward Serin, who returned his gaze with a wink.

Sebastion could not understand why this man hated him so much. He was excelling in all his classes now, and he had never caused any trouble … until now, that is.

Rayor had both his hands in his sleeves and looked ready to kill everyone in the room. His face was pale inside his hood, and his light eyes seemed to glow in a ghostly way.

The group of four remaining boys confidently spun their swords in their hands.

Sebastion did not have a chance, unarmed now against four boys trained with swords, and now the previously unconscious boy was getting off the floor, shaking his head. He figured he could at least incapacitate one with the knife he had in his sleeve. He was sure this would be the end for him, and yet he was calm as if he accepted this.

He didn't want to die, but he did not mind it either. Except for his contempt for the people around him, he felt numb. It felt like what was about to happen was beyond his control, so he decided to just go with it and let what was meant to happen, just happen.

The four boys stepped forward, and Sebastion stepped back, reaching into his sleeve. There was a crashing sound behind him, and he turned slightly to see what it was.

He saw that a thick broom was sliding across the floor from the kitchen. It stopped right at his feet. He looked into the kitchen to see the butcher and the timid man, whom no one else could see from where he stood.

The butcher gave him a slight nod.

Sebastion returned his nod and quickly picked up the broom.

He twisted it sideways and broke off the broom piece with his foot. This left him now with a sturdy staff.

As he faced the four boys with the makeshift staff in his hands, the crowd of people cheered loudly. The older men he had been training with were chanting, "Wolf! Wolf! Wolf!" Soon the other people in the crowd were shouting as well.

Serin was glaring at the crowd, nearly mad with anger. He looked over at Rayor, who returned Serin's cold look.

Rayor's hands came out of his sleeves in a blur. It was not daggers that Rayor let fly, however, but a series of movements. His fingers danced their message before he slipped them back into his large sleeves.

Serin's eyes narrowed, and his thin lips pulled away from his teeth like a snarling dog. The message Rayor had sent was simple but directly to the point. He had simply signed "time to make them pay."

The small group of boys circled Sebastion from all corners. One lunged forward and went through a series of cuts and thrusts, each deflected easily by Sebastion's kitchen broom handle.

He remembered his fight with Keeper years ago and let each blow from the sword be redirected rather than allow the broomstick to take the entire force. This technique worked to throw the boys off balance.

The "first boys" were taking turns, obviously trying to tire him out and wait for him to make a mistake. However, the attackers were soon out of breath.

Sebastion, having increased stamina from his training sessions after a full day of school and using what he had been taught, was expending as little energy as possible. Now was the time for him to take the offensive.

One of the boys moved in and swung his sword at Sebastion's head. He deflected the blow to one side. When the boy stepped forward, off balance, Sebastion spun the broom handle and struck him on the head. The boy went down with a thump.

The crowd of onlookers went wild. There were more people exchanging money now. Many were looking none-too-happy as they handed over coins.

The three remaining boys looked as if they were not at all interested in continuing the fight. One was the short leader, and he was breathing hard from the exertion of trying to get behind Sebastion's defenses. He looked over at Serin and immediately wished he had not.

Serin looked ready to kill the nearest person available.

The three decided that it was better to take their chances with Sebastion than to face Serin's wrath.

They moved forward and flanked Sebastion. They started swinging their swords feverishly, looking for an opening to strike.

Sebastion was a blur as he went from one to another, blocking each blow of their swords. Pieces of wood from the broom were flying into the air.

The crowd was silent now as the boys fought at a fantastic speed.

Sebastion made a last-minute block, and the broom cracked down the middle. It bent inward and hit the side of his head when the boy's sword wedged itself into the broom. If it were free, Sebastion would have lost this fight and his life at that moment.

The boy, unable to free his sword to inflict the fatal blow, took advantage of Sebastion's predicament, spun, and kicked Sebastion in the ribs.

Sebastion went down, and the other boys moved forward quickly, raising their swords to finish the job.

Everyone in the crowd, including Rayor, sucked in a loud breath, anticipating the apparent inevitability.

Sebastion, on his back, pulled the broom apart, leaving two pieces, one of them a point. He thrust the pointed half into the leg of the closest "first boy."

The boy screamed, dropped his sword, and grabbed the protruding piece of wood.

Sebastion rolled, grabbed the boy's sword, and turned to face the remaining two bullies.

The "first boys" looked at the ground where a puddle of blood was growing, the one still recovering from the first blow of the broomstick exchanged glances with the leader.

The other one dropped his sword and ran with the others, not liking the odds now. That left only the leader, and he looked none too happy to be facing Sebastion alone. And even worse, to be facing Sebastion with a sword in his hand.

Sebastion reached up to where the broken broom handle had hit his head. He looked at his palm, and it had blood on it.

The leader was slowly moving backward, complained,"What would come from killing me?".

The chubby boy's voice cracked.

"I am not the one who ordered us to attack you ... either time!"

He was becoming frantic now.

Sebastion only looked at him.

"Not me. It was—"

Two knives flew through the air and landed deep in the boy's throat. He gurgled, looked at Serin, his eyes big with shock, and fell to the ground. It took several minutes of choking and gurgling before the boy finally died in front of the crowd.

All eyes turned to Serin.

Straightening himself, he walked to the center of the room with his head high. He swept his gaze across the crowd, letting his cape flutter out dramatically as he had in the courtyard.

"Fighting is absolutely prohibited on these grounds. You all know the rules." He swept an accusing finger across them. "The guilty parties will be punished as I see fit!"

His finger stopped at Sebastion.

"Seize this boy and bring him to my office NOW!"

Two guardsmen walked timidly to Sebastion.

Sebastion, having had enough of fighting, could not take his eyes from the dead boy at his feet. He dropped his sword, and they grabbed him and escorted him away.

Rayor's eyes were mere slits in his face as he watched Serin leave the room.

Chapter 7 – Friends in the Dark

In the cold, dark, damp dungeon, the only thing that kept Sebastion from sitting directly on the befouled stone floor left by the previous inhabitant was a small amount of straw. He sat in a corner with his head in his hands. He was contemplating his escape. Even if they did not let him out, he would find a way to escape this school that he hated so much. This was going to be the last thing he would endure here. Though he felt for the people that worked here, the people that ran it were terrible, and he wanted no part of it. He just wanted to return to the forest. He couldn't get the look in the dead boy's eyes out of his mind.

He wondered what Rayor was doing and if he was trying to find a way to get him out. He feared that Rayor would be very angry with him. Some of those boys he fought with could be dying or could have already died by his hand. He knew that a head strike could cause death much later. He had not actually killed the leader of the "first boys," but he was not sorry that he was dead, though the look in his eyes haunted him.

Serin had always been cruel to him, and he knew the schoolmaster had something to do with the boys attacking him. Perhaps before he escaped, he would pay Serin a visit. He could use some of the things he had learned at his school. Maybe he would pour poison in Serin's ear as he slept or plunge a needle into the base of his neck when he least expected it.

Sitting in the damp, dirty dungeon, Sebastion worked out all sorts of nasty things he could do to the schoolmaster. The training in this school allowed his mind to explore many different scenarios that would find the schoolmaster dead or … dying miserably. He just could not believe that, once again, he was in a bad situation being around people. He was absolutely done with being around people. He stayed because he was around Rayor, who he now considered a friend. But he could not endure anything else in this terrible place. No, he would not stay and die here. He would not give that dark blasted headmaster the satisfaction!

In his small cell, Sebastion started pacing. He had already pulled on every bar he could reach, to see if any were loose, with no luck. He had tried to push several small sticks into the lock, thinking he could pick it, but that too had not worked. Beginning to feel desperate, he stepped back to think. He cocked his head to one side, thinking he heard breathing from another cell not far from his.

"Hello?" he whispered.

No one answered.

"Is someone there?" he tried again.

Still, there was no answer.

He then heard the sound of a guard coming. No mistaking that. He retreated to the back of the cell and waited.

The hulking figure of a guard appeared in front of his cell.

"Ye're a pretty one ain't ya, boy," the guard said, wiping something from his chin with the back of his hand.

Sebastion did his best to ignore him and stared at the ground.

"Don't say much, do ye?" The guard looked him up and down.

"Leave him alone, Mishkif," called a voice from another cell.

"Shut up, ye old traitor!" the guard yelled. "Me and this here boy needs to get along, we do." The guard made some kissing noises and left.

Sebastion was starting to understand just how bad things were now. Sighing loudly, he put his head back into his hands. He needed to get out and away from this place.

***

Rayor was furious. He knew Serin was behind the beating Sebastion had received more than a year before, but he had hoped his suspicions were wrong. He knew Serin to be a cruel and self-absorbed sadist but not a fool. His whims could cost them everything.

Storming through the hallways, he made his way to Serin's office. Several times people got in his way, and he unceremoniously brushed them aside as if they were gnats.

As he approached Serin's office, two guards stepped in front of him. They puffed out their chests and crossed their spears in front of him.

The old man moved quickly, and the guards did not have a chance. Both fell to the ground, hardly even slowing his approach.

Drawing his knife in the same movement, Rayor flung open the door. Then he froze, not expecting the sight that was before him.

Serin was floating several feet above his desk. He was clasping at his throat, desperately struggling for breath.

A man completely covered in a long crimson cloak stood in front of him. Even his hands were hidden beneath the cloak's long sleeves. The man turned to Rayor, obviously surprised.

Serin fell heavily onto the desk with a thud.

The cloaked men faced each other. Neither could be seen from within the hoods that hid them. The only difference between the two was the color of their clothing and the long white hair that was sewn into Rayor's hood and ran long against his chest.

Rayor spoke first. "I have no quarrel with you. I am here to … speak with Serin about a private matter."

The mysterious man did not move or speak.

Serin was catching his breath again and slid off the desk, trying to get his feet beneath him. He pulled something from his desk drawer.

Rayor tried again, becoming impatient, "I am here to settle a matter with this fool," he explained.

The strange man lifted his head slightly.

Rayor could only see two red glowing orbs from within the hood. He stiffened but did not move.

Oh, *this just keeps getting better and better!*

He returned his knife to his sleeve.

"I see you have found me," Rayor said, letting out a deep sigh.

"It is not you I have searched for, Sir Killian," the stranger said in a rough rasping voice that sounded more like a hiss.

Serin could not believe what he was hearing. Could the old man who had been working with him for years really be the legendary Sir Killian? It could not be true; Killian would be nearly a hundred centuries old or more! This man was old, but surely not over a hundred centuries.

"The schoolmaster is mine to deal with," the stranger in the crimson cloak hissed.

Rayor stepped closer to the stranger.

"He has threatened to destroy everything we have worked for."

"He will be dealt with, Killian."

"I *will* ask you to stop calling me by that name," Rayor snarled.

Serin had been staying very still and quiet up to this point. He had now decided it was time to react. He stepped forward and hurled a dagger he had taken from his desk drawer. Let's see how this monster deals with steel, Serin thought, letting a hint of a smile touch his lips as the knife flew from his fingers.

The knife landed squarely in the back of the red-robed stranger's head. The man in the crimson cloak did not react; he remained facing Rayor as if nothing had happened.

"Where is the boy now?" the stranger asked.

"I believe this imbecile has placed him in the school dungeon," Rayor said, indicating Serin.

The stranger nodded.

"As good a place as any," his body trembled as he hissed out his words.

"You plan to keep the boy in the dungeon then?" the old man asked.

"He will be kept alive for as long as we will need him," the stranger replied, not even acknowledging the protruding dagger at the back of his head.

Serin was desperately looking around the room for a way out.

"As agreed, Killian, finish what you have been asked to do. Interfere and your fate will be much worse than you can imagine."

With that, the stranger turned slowly to face Serin.

Rayor sighed deeply, then turned and quickly exited the room. He could hear Serin's screams from the office all the way down the hall. Nevertheless, the old man felt no sympathy for the schoolmaster.

Deep inside his hood, Rayor scratched his chin nervously.

Fine mess we are in now, 'ole, boy. The boy is locked in a dungeon under the school, and now the idiot schoolmaster knows my real name, not to mention we have an under-wraith to contend with. Great ... that's just puckering great.

Rayor pulled his hood back from his head as he walked, rubbing his hands up and down his bald skinhead, trying to push away the pressure that was building there. He did not notice the people stopping to stare.

Few people ever saw Rayor's face. To them, he was a mysteriously cloaked man that could be seen walking around from time to time. To see him now with his hood down, completely bald, with his long white hair falling down his back and sewn into his hood was quite a sight.

Rayor did not care. He walked through the halls, utterly oblivious to everything around him. Stopping at one point, he leaned against the wall and put his head back. The stones that made up the wall there felt cool and soothing on his skin, and he closed his eyes and concentrated on clearing his mind.

A strange thought popped into his mind. Rayor lifted his head, surprised. It was a saying his brother had always used. A wave of dizziness nearly knocked his legs out from underneath him, and he was grateful for the wall behind him. He did not like memories, and immediately tried to shut the door that had somehow come ajar in his mind... But still, the saying kept coming back.

Sometimes you have to go backward to go forward.

"Stupid saying and a stupid memory!" he said out loud.

He pushed off the wall and continued walking, now even angrier than before.

***

By early the next day, no one had brought Sebastion food or water. He was using a corner of the cell to relieve himself. The man in the cell next to him could not be coaxed into speaking again. He was very hungry and, more than that, his mouth and lips were now dry from thirst. The blood from the wound on his head had become hard and dry. He knew it needed to be cleaned or he would run the risk of infection … especially considering where he was. He needed to get out of this cell.

He was again thinking of what he would do to Serin when the guard returned. He was holding a tray of water and a bowl of what looked to be food.

"You back there, sweetheart?" the guard asked.

Sebastion decided he was too hungry and thirsty to ignore him and risked stepping forward.

"AH! There ye' are, lad," the guard said, smiling. His teeth were rotten and discolored, and only a few were left.

"We gonna be friends, then?" The guard started making groping motions in the air in front of him.

Sebastion retreated slightly into the cell.

"No. Not friends? Then ye' won't be needing this here food, will ye'?" The guard put the tray down far enough from Sebastion that he could not reach it. "We'll see how long it takes before we become friends, my li'l princess." He laughed all the way down the hall.

Sebastion heard the big door closing behind the guard. He ran up to the bars and reached as far as he could. He was still a stride length away from the tray.

"You'll have to use your head and not your fingers, boy," said the man in the cell next to him.

Sebastion was startled, as he was not used to the man next to him speaking. "Wh- What do you mean?" he asked.

There was a long silence, and Sebastion wondered if he had heard a voice at all.

Then it came again. "What do you have with you in that cage?" the man asked.

Sebastion looked around. "I don't have anything but some straw and some loose rocks." He heard the man sigh at him.

"Are you wearing any clothes?" he asked.

Sebastion was getting suspicious. "Yes. I have clothes."

The man coughed. "Don't be worried. I do not have the same interests as that half-wit guard. Now, take off your pants…"

"WHAT!" Sebastion cried out.

"Listen to me!" the man raised his voice. "Take off your pants and tie your boot to the end of one of the legs."

Sebastion did as he was told.

"Now, throw your boot *carefully* beyond the tray."

Sebastion threw it and nearly tipped the water jug over.

"Carefully, I said!"

The jug righted itself without spilling much.

"Now, GENTLY pull your pants forward."

Sebastion followed the instructions and, to his surprise, the tray started moving forward. Soon it was within his reach. He grabbed the water and drank nearly the whole thing at once. What was left and half a bowl of some kind of gruel he pushed over to the cell.

"Why are you giving this to me?" said the man in a confused voice.

Sebastion seemed surprised by this. "You helped me get it, so you deserve your share."

"My share?" the man seemed even more confused.

"Yes," Sebastion said.

"I'm sorry; it's just that it's been so long since I've seen any sort of compassion," the man said quietly. He reached over and took what was left on the tray. "I don't mean to scare you, but ... you need to get out of here soon. Mishkif is ... a terrible person."

Sebastion did not know what to say.

"Are you a thief or a slave?" the man asked him.

Sebastion was taken aback.

"Neither!" he said.

"Oh, I see," said the man. "So, what brings a fine lad such as yourself to a place like this?"

Sebastion began telling his story. He told the man everything. It felt good talking to someone, and it passed the time. He even told him about the boys in the forest and about the animals he considered to be friends.

The man was very attentive and encouraged Sebastion to go on.

Day turned to night and then day again. Sebastion slept a little but then went on.

The guard had not come back, but the man in the cell next to him would hand him the jug of water from time to time, and surprisingly there was always more.

Sebastion did not question it and was very thankful to have it.

***

Rayor continued to pace his small room. He was deep in thought and half-crazed with indecision. While he walked, he would slash the air in front of him with a small dagger he had in his hand.

"My only concern is for myself!" he mumbled as he paced the room. "Why should I give a damn about this boy? No matter who he is!" This last bit always quickened his pace and made his face turn red.

Rayor had not slept and could not find the appetite to eat. Guilt was slowly sinking its ugly claws into him. Servants had come to his room and asked him to go to Serin's bed chambers, but Rayor had been turning them away. It was not long before one of the servants became irritable about Rayor's refusals and demanded to knowwhy.

Rayor stopped pacing for a second and knocked out two of the unfortunate servant's teeth. When the servant left the room, bleeding, Rayor laid the still bloody teeth in front of his door as a warning to the rest of them.

He knew why the servants kept coming, but he was in no mood to speak to Serin. Besides, Rayor thought, if he was still alive, he most likely would be with the under-wraith, and he certainly was in no hurry to see that thing again.

***

It began raining and water was slipping in through the cracks in the rocks of Sebastion's cell. He had to continually move to avoid sitting in a puddle, knowing sooner or later he would have no choice but to get wet. In fact, with the water bringing with it everything that was in the cell, soon he would be sitting in his own filth.

The massive dungeon door opened followed by the unmistakable sound of the guard lumbering in.

"Sebastion?" It was the man next to him.

"Yes?" he whispered.

"Do you still have that small knife in your boot?"

That surprised Sebastion. He couldn't remember telling him about that. In fact, he had forgotten it was there himself. Did he say his name? He figured he must have mentioned it at some point.

He reached in his left boot, and he did have it. "Yes, I have it but—"

"Quiet! We haven't much time. When that filthy guard comes for you, you must do whatever it takes with that knife. Do you understand me?" The man sounded desperate.

"Yes, I understand."

"Good. You do whatever it takes."

The guard was now at the bars of the cell, looking around for the tray.

"Did those bloody rats get ye' food, boy?"

The guard was swaying, obviously drunk. He looked into the other cell next to Sebastion's and scratched his head.

"Could ave' sworn there was another one of ye' in der."

The guard continued standing there, scratching his toussled hair and staring into the cell next to Sebastion's.

"Now dat I think on it there ain't been no one there for months. Hmm?"

The guard nearly fell as he turned his attention once more to Sebastion. He smiled his rotting grin once again.

"Today, sweetheart, we get to be *good* friends, we do."

***

Rayor was unable to take it any longer, He decided that if he was to be damned, then so be it. He could not let his only living relative, his brother's grandson, and his great-nephew rot in a dungeon to be used as a tool and then tossed aside.

Damn the consequences! he decided. I am going to free the boy and escape this godforsaken school. He would tell the boy of his true lineage. The old man knew the consequences would be horrendous, but he felt that he had no other choice.

Rayor, once known long ago as Sir Killian of the House Loyal, had decided to take a different course of action than the one that had been laid before him by the one he served. He would not put the boy in harm's way again. If they wanted to torture him, then so be it. The bastard Lord Bashor would have to catch him first. Besides … I already lived long enough, and death would be a welcome thing! Smiling from the thought, he left the room.

Walking confidently, Rayor headed down the halls towards the dungeons. For the first time in many years, he held his un-hooded head high as he walked with purpose.

The servants gasped as they looked upon him. It was not so much that he was now uncovered but the look of single-mindedness he now wore like armor. He was striding down the halls like a solider with a mission, feeling better now that his mind had been made up. One servant even bowed his head as he passed him.

He would finish off what was left by the under-wraith, killing Serin and get his nephew away from here.

The old knight turned away from the dungeon to take care of Serin first. There was no use having his nephew see what he was about to do.

***

In the dungeon, the huge, hulking guard had finally found the keyhole with his clumsy drunken fingers and opened the cell. He stepped in and closed the door behind him with a loud bang.

Sebastion stood as far back as he could, with his back against the damp wall.

Still smiling, the guard stopped to look at him.

"You're a tall one, ain't ye'?" He laughed as he strolled forward. He spread his arms wide, like a spider, and danced ahead, moving his face closer to Sebastion's. His breath was as rotten as his teeth.

Sebastion, overwhelmed by the stench of wine and what smelled like rotten meat, turned his head away.

The guard punched him hard in the face.

Sebastion went down on his knees.

The guard grabbed him by the hair and yanked.

"LET ME GO!" Sebastion yelled as loud as he could.

The guard laughed.

"Yer a feisty one. I like 'dat."

Sebastion pulled the knife from his boot and plunged it upward with all his strength. The little knife went deep into the fat guard's groin.

The guard screamed, let go of Sebastion's hair and stepped back. He reached between his legs and pulled the knife out. Blood dripped to the ground. He tossed the little knife aside and looked at Sebastion, his eyes wide and full of hate.

"You're gonna make it up to me for 'dat, princess."

Sebastion was still on the ground and the guard ran forward, kicking Sebastion in the ribs.

Sebastion felt himself being lifted into the air, and then he landed heavily back on the ground. All the wind had been knocked out of him. He lay on the ground, gasping and holding his chest. As he lay there, with his face on the wet rocky ground, he could see the knife just behind the guard. The guard attempted to kick him again, but this time Sebastion was too quick and deflected most of it using the things Rayor had taught him.

He slid between the guard's legs, the wet and slimy rocks helping him push far enough to reach the knife.

"Oh yer a sly one ain't ye'?" the guard sneered, turning.

Sebastion rapidly flicked the knife into the guard's face.

The colossal guard stiffened with a look of shock in his remaining good eye. He reached up and screamed as his fingers felt the hilt of the knife in his eye. Sebastion got off the ground and threw all his strength into the butt of his hand as he jammed the knife further into the man's head. The guard stood with his hands at his side for what seemed an eternity before falling onto his back, dead.

Sebastion looked at the dead guard for a few shocked seconds before searching him for the keys. He opened his cell and went over to his friend in the one next to him. He looked in, but there was no one there.

"Hello?" he called. "Are you there? It's me; we can escape!"

There was no answer, and Sebastion got an overwhelming urge to run. In fact, it felt as if someone was actually pushing him to go. He wanted to stay and search for the man that had been so kind to him, but instead, he ran.

As he reached the outer hall, he saw a small table with three empty skins of wine. There was a tiny fire and a cloak hanging beside it. He grabbed the cloak, put it on, and ran for the door.

The stairs leading up were narrow, dark, and quiet. He went up with his back pressed against the wall. The cloak, made for a fat man, was too large for him, and the hood kept falling forward, blocking his view.

Opening the door at the top of the stairs, Sebastion looked out. There was no one around. He started walking and remembered something Rayor had taught him. The old man's voice came to him in his head, "When you find yourself somewhere people don't think you should be, walk as if you've been there all your life. That is, don't go too fast or too slow. Don't walk as if you don't know where you're going. Even if you pass the same spot ten times, it's better to do that than to keep looking around like a lost puppy."

Widening his strides, Sebastion kept his hood on and walked with unfelt confidence. It was not unusual for a hooded man to walk these halls, so he stuck out his chest and crossed his arms. He was tall enough to be taken for an older man, even with the cloak being as big as it was. He could see only a few feet of the floor beneath him, so he followed the wall, hoping it would lead somewhere familiar.

At that very moment, Rayor was pressing his ear against the door of Serin's bed chambers. A skinny, bored guard had been standing in front of it a moment ago, but he now lay unconscious on the ground.

The old man pushed gently, and the door opened. Having let himself in, he stepped cautiously through. The only light was a small fire in one corner of the room.

He crept quietly to the bed.

Lying there was Serin, staring straight up at the ceiling and not blinking.

"You do tend to come at the most inopportune moments, Sir Killian."

Killian jumped, not expecting Serin to speak. He had thought for sure the headmaster was dead.

"Don't be startled, old knight. Your suspicions are correct. Serin, as you knew him, is quite dead." Serin was still staring straight up and not moving ... except for his lips—ever so slightly—as he spoke.

Rayor recovered his composure quickly. "If Serin is indeed dead, then to whom do I have the pleasure of speaking to?"

Serin's head moved ever so slightly toward Killian, but his eyes never changed.

"You do not remember me?" Serin said in a familiar, mocking tone. "Was it not I who brought you here? Was it not I who took you in when there was no other place to go?"

Rayor's eyes nearly popped out of his head. He fell to one knee and did not say a word.

"Do not think that I do not know what is in your heart, old friend," Serin said seriously. "You have the look of a traitor ... a look you have had before, as I remember."

Killian breathed out a heavy sigh as those words twisted inside him. The last thing he wanted to do was to confront his master, whom he had served for so many years. However, he was committed to what he had to do.

Without looking up, he said, "I must deny you. I thought I could do what you asked, but I cannot. The boy he looks so much..." The last he said as an afterthought. The old man brushed a hand across his eyes. "He is my brother's grandson."

"I KNOW WHO HE IS!" Serin yelled. "I am not concerned with who he is but with WHAT he is!" Spit was drooling from the corner of Serin's mouth, leaving a long path from his mouth to the bed and finally the floor. The eyes still stared upwards, but they were very wide now. The dark one speaking through him was outraged.

Rayor stood and looked into the eyes of Serin's possessed body.

"I am sorry to betray you ... but you cannot have him."

Serin's eyes opened, even more full than they had been.

"CANNOT!?" he yelled. "DO YOU FORGET WHO I AM?"

Rayor brushed his hands across his bald head and sighed softly again.

"I do. I know that this will end badly for me. I know that an eternity of pain is what I have to look forward to." Rayor looked down and studied his old, wrinkled hands. "You-" he took a deep breath. "you just cannot have him," the old knight whispered softly.

Rayor stood, crossed the room quickly and pulled a sword from the wall above the fireplace. He locked eyes onto Serin's.

"Yes, I do know you. I know you better than you think. I also know you have not quite taken over this body."

The thing that possessed Serin tried to move his arm, but it only twitched.

"STEP AWAY, KNIGHT!"

Rayor steadied himself and hoisted the sword over his head. It took two chops before Serin's head dropped to the floor from the bed and rolled a short distance, stopping face up.

"Do you think this will stop me? YOU FOOL!" The decapitated head said.

Rayor was surprised but not shocked. He picked it up by the long black hair and waited for the twirling head to rotate back and face him.

"I know I cannot stop you. But I sure as the dark can slow you down." Rayor said looking into the dead eyes.

With that, he flung the decapitated head into the fire and turned to leave the room. A calm and confidant voice came from the fire.

"I *will* find him." said the voice from the fire.

Not before I do, Rayor thought to himself as he left the room, lightly closing the door behind him to not attract anyone's attention.

In his own attempt to avoid arousing attention, Sebastion had made it to the corner of the large kitchen. He had come in quietly and unseen. Unfortunately, he found many people there, preparing for the evening meal.

Bruised and obviously having been beaten, the butcher stood in the corner of the kitchen.

Sebastion felt a wave of guilt wash across him. The man had most certainly saved his life by sliding that broom to him. He must have known he would be punished, but he had done it anyway.

The butcher must have sensed Sebastion staring, for he looked right at the young man.

Sebastion dipped his head, letting the hood fall all the way forward, covering his face, but it was too late; the butcher had seen his face beneath the hood and was coming over. Sebastion frantically looked for the nearest exit.

"That you, sir?" the butcher asked.

Sir? Maybe the butcher did not know it was he, after all. Sebastion cleared his throat and spoke in the deepest voice he could muster.

"What can I do for you?"

The butcher looked at the ground.

"We here just want to tell you that 'dat we appreciate what you did for ... for Tibin."

Sebastion was taken aback. Tibin must have been the timid man that the cruel leader of the boys had knocked down. He did not know what to say.

The butcher gingerly put his hand on Sebastion's shoulder.

"You have friends here," he said.

Sebastion looked up, letting the hood fall back slightly.

"But it is I who should be thanking you," Sebastion said.

The butcher looked at him, surprised.

"If you had not tossed out that broom, I surely would have been killed."

The large and muscular man's belly bounced as he chuckled.

"The way you fight? I somehow doubt that." He winked. "But, you're welcome, all the same."

Taking Sebastion's hand, the butcher shook it and saw blood on it. "Are you hurt?"

Sebastion ducked his head again, hiding inside the cloak.

"It isn't mine," he said in a low, quiet voice.

The man raised his eyebrows. "I see. It seems trouble is attracted to you. Will you be leaving us, then?"

Sebastion shook his head, yes.

"Then you'll be needing provisions."

The old butcher started yelling orders, and all the kitchen help went to work, putting together whatever they could find for the young man. Soon a backpack appeared from nowhere and was packed with provisions: everything from food to small pans to cook in. It was nearly overflowing with what the kind servants could find.

Sebastion shook hands with everyone in the kitchen, and they each had a warm smile for him. He was amazed by their kindness. He didn't know what he had done to deserve this, but he was happy to have it.

At the end of the line stood the large woman who had cut his hair almost two years before. Impossible as it seemed, she had become even fatter than before. Her cheeks were red, and she had a smile on her face, albeit her eyes were sad.

"So that's it then, huh? You'll be leavin' us to fend on our own?" She winked at him.

Sebastion just smiled, and before he could turn to leave, she wrapped her arms around him and squeezed. A lightning bolt of pain shot out from his ribs, but he enjoyed the embrace all the same.

The huge woman let go of him and gave him a big wet kiss on the cheek.

Smiling, the boy slung the backpack across his shoulder and headed for the storage room. He opened the door, stepped in, and closed the door gently behind him.

The kitchen servants exchanged confused glances as they waited for him to come back out. The big woman called to him through the door, but there was no answer. The butcher carefully opened the door and peered in but there was no sign of him.

On the far wall, there was an arrow marked in flour. On closer examination, the butcher saw a tiny latch hidden there. He smiled and chuckled to himself as he wiped the arrow away with his sleeve. He stepped back into the kitchen, his big belly bouncing as he laughed again.

The other servants were still exchanging confused looks and peering into the closet, more confused than before.

***

In another area of the school, Rayor was moving down the stairs to the dungeon like a possessed spirit. His gray cloak blended into the darkness. At the bottom of the stairs, he listened for the guard. There was no sound. A small fire had been built some time ago and was nearly out. Three wine skins lay on the table, empty, and the door leading to the cells was open. Rayor's heart skipped a beat, as he thought of a drunken guard and Sebastion alone.

He stood straight and pulled a dagger from each of his sleeves.

"Please do not let me be too late," he whispered to himself.

In the darkness, he could see a body lying on the floor of the cell.

"Oh, no!" he gasped out loud.

He ran to the body to find the guard lying on his back, dead. Killian noticed that blood was running across the rocky floor from between the guard's legs. A bad wound, but not mortal. When he got to the guard's face, he saw that a small knife was deeply imbedded into one of his eyes.

A small smile started to spread across the old knight's face.

Upon further inspection, he saw that it was indeed Sebastion's knife.

The old man started to laugh. He sat down on the cold, wet ground. Resting his back against the cell, he laughed until tears came to his eyes.

"RUN, BOY! RUN!" he yelled between fits of laughter. The sound of it echoed off the stone walls.

Two guards walked past the door at the top of the stairs. Hearing the laughter, they went to investigate.

Chapter 8 - Freedom

Sebastion thought he knew the way back to the place where he had grown up, but he had no desire to go back there. With no idea which approach would be best, he just picked a direction and headed that way. He was feeling freer than he ever had in his life. He figured he had learned enough between Keeper, Rayor, and the school to survive alone now.

However, survival was not enough. As the days passed, he realized that he was lonely. He missed the company of Rayor, but there was something more he wanted. He wanted someone he could share his thoughts with and other things as well. He felt, more than he knew, that there was more out there than what he'd seen already. He wanted to see the ocean he had learned about in school and ride in a boat instead of just a ferry. He wanted to have adventures like the characters in Keeper's old books and Rayor's stories when they travelled together.

One thing was quite sure: he would never go back to that school. He was determined to find his own way without being told what to do and when to do it. He did not like "the art" and would not become what they wanted of him. He would be free even if it meant he would die.

Nobody will ever tell me what to do and who I must be again. The thought played over and over in his mind, giving him confidence as he traveled into the unknown.

As weeks passed, Sebastion traveled by many small villages and towns. He had not wanted to enter any of them, but now his supplies were getting low. He could keep eating what he caught, but his stomach was craving cheese, bread, and milk. Thus, he sat on a hill overlooking a large town trying to build up his courage. He knew he had put off the inevitable for long enough.

Sebastion studied the town for every way in, out, and around, trying to push down his fear with concentration. He knew exactly where he wanted to enter, spotting what looked like a market, and where the closest exit was from where he would come. Hoisting his pack over one shoulder, he started down the hill. His feet carried him forward, but his heart urged him back to the safety of the forest. The weather was cool, yet sweat ran long lines down his back.

The town had a long wall surrounding it, but there was no guard at the entrance as Sebastion entered. He was immediately accosted by smells he had never experienced before … his head was swimming with them. There were horses and horse-drawn carts everywhere. Standing, gawking, just inside the wall, he was sure the town had not been this big when he had looked down from the hill.

A group of men walked by him.

"You lost, kid?" they laughed, without stopping.

He knew he was drawing too much attention just standing there staring, so he walked quickly to where he remembered the market to be. He couldn't help turning his head back and forth, trying to take in everything his senses could pick up. Rayor had said this is precisely what you should not do in a situation like this, but there was so much happening. He was mesmerized by all the activity. He couldn't believe how all these people lived together, all working together.

He saw a man who was sitting on the ground.

The man held a handout to him, causing Sebastion to step back, startled.

Looking into the palm of the man's hand, he saw nothing. He thought maybe the man was asking for help getting up, as Rayor had done many times, so he grabbed the man's hand and gave it a pull.

"WHAT?" the surprised man yelled. He was now standing before Sebastion, who had a very pleased look on his face. "What do you think you're doing?!"

Sebastion took a step back, surprised. Not understanding the man's angry tone.

The people on the street started laughing and pointing at the now-standing man. The man's pant legs hung low and unconnected. The beggar had been hiding his perfectly good legs behind him.

Sebastion looked at the man and realized what he had done. His face flushed almost as red as the apparently not-crippled man's. Turning, he hurried down the street as quickly as he could without drawing too much more attention to himself. He knew things were not going well so far.

The market area was full of people who were pushing and shoving. There were lines of carts selling everything from fruit and meat to live monkeys. Sebastion knew what he needed and found a shop that sold dairy products and flour. He entered the shop cautiously.

The store had many customers, and nobody had noticed him coming in. A pretty girl was wearing a stained white apron and standing behind what he surmised to be the owner. The man was giving her orders, and she would leave to grab things from the shelves for him. Neither of them noticed him as he slipped to the back of the store.

Never having been in a shop before, he had no idea what to do now. He watched the customers come and go. He studied what they said and how they received their items. When he felt confident enough, he got into line; however, he was getting more and more nervous as he got closer to the counter.

He held his hands tightly together to keep them from shaking. He wanted to run, but he knew he had to learn how to do this. Despite his nervousness, he was having trouble keeping his eyes off the girl behind the counter; he tried to keep his head down.

He concentrated on his muddy boots as he moved forward. Then he risked a look and saw that the girl was staring back at him. He could feel his face burn and knew he was turning red.

The customer in front of Sebastion said, "Thank you," turned and left, and suddenly it was his turn.

He had been practicing what he would say in his head the whole time he had waited. "I would like flour, cheese, potatoes, tobacco, flint—".

"Hold it! Hold it!" the shopkeeper said with a smile. The girl, too, was smiling up at him, which just made him feel even more nervous. "One at a time, sir. You said you wanted flour. How much would you like?"

Sebastion was stumped. "Uh. Enough for me?" he replied, like a question. He realized he sounded too unsure of himself and said, "I am traveling alone," and then immediately wanted to kick himself.

The shopkeeper sighed and put on a patient face. He wiped his face with his hand and smiled.

"How long will you be traveling, sir?"

Sebastion wished the girl would stop smiling and staring at him.

"I don't know," he said.

"How about five bags of flour, sir," the shopkeeper said, an edge coming to his voice.

"That will be fine, thank you," Sebastion answered, trying to deepen his voice.

"Would you like me to estimate the other materials as well, sir?" the shopkeeper seemed hopeful with that.

"Y- yes, please."

The shopkeeper, without turning, announced what he wanted the girl to get, but she could only stare at the tall young man in front of her.

"Did you get all that, Sara?"

She did not answer.

"GIRL! MOVE YOUR BUTT!"

The girl jumped with a squeal and went to collect the goods.

The shopkeeper looked Sebastion up and down and frowned.

"How will you be paying for this ... sir?" He hung heavy sarcasm on the word "sir."

The woman standing behind Sebastion grunted and rolled her eyes.

The servants at the school who had prepared his bag had stuck many colored rocks into it. They had said they were as good as money.

Sebastion grabbed one of them and showed the shopkeeper, hopeful.

A strange look came over the man's face.

"Is ... is that real?" he asked breathlessly.

Hearing the shopkeeper's reaction, the girl came over. Her jaw dropped open as she stared blankly at the stone in Sebastion's hand.

"Where did you get that, boy?" the shopkeeper asked, suspiciously.

Sebastion was getting very tired of being called a boy. Every time someone would call him a boy, they meant it as an insult. He moved closer to the shopkeeper.

"I think I preferred 'sir,'" Sebastion said, locking the shopkeeper's eyes in a stern gaze.

The shopkeeper took a step back.

"Is this rock enough to pay for what I want, or is it not?"

Blood was rushing into his face again, but this time it was not from being embarrassed.

The shopkeeper looked at the stone again and swallowed hard.

"Yes," was all he said.

The woman behind Sebastion made a throaty noise of disgust.

"Enough to buy this store and then some," she said under her breath.

The shopkeeper gave her a sharp look.

"I don't want the value of the stone, only what I need and..." Sebastion looked around, and the shopkeeper shot another nasty look at the woman.

She was smiling now, thoroughly enjoying herself.

After some time of pointing and collecting his goods, Sebastion left the small shop barely able to carry what he had ended up purchasing. He had also traded the jewel for all the money the shop had in its register. The stones brought more of a stir, and he did not want to draw more attention to himself. As he left, he could see the shopkeeper and the pretty redheaded girl through the window jumping up and down with joy.

The girl turned in his direction and caught his eye. She smiled and waved.

Sebastion flushed, gave a half-wave, and walked on, embarrassed. He was feeling good about himself, however. He had acquired what he needed and more from the small shop. He was pleased with himself, but he didn't want to push his luck. He knew he should count himself lucky to be on his way safely, but the appeal of the town was overwhelming. He wanted to go back to the market and perhaps buy something else.

There had been a man who was selling swords and knives. Perhaps he might check out those weapons. It seemed he had enough with the coin and the colored stones from the school.

Suddenly, turning back toward the market, Sebastion noticed a man following him. He took some other streets to see if it was just his imagination, but every turn he made, the man did so as well. The man was obvious and made a lot of noise, and Sebastion could tell he was not good at going unnoticed.

At one point, Sebastion found an alley and ducked into it. It was full of garbage and smelled of rotting food, but he waited for the man to take the corner. When he did, a surprise would be waiting for him.

The man was indeed startled to find Sebastion standing there and took a step back. He pulled a dagger from his belt.

"Hey, where'd you get all that stuff?"

The man was dressed in a uniform that made him look older than he really was. His voice, however, gave him away. He and Sebastion were about the same age.

"I bought these things," Sebastion said defensively, sticking his chin out and crossing his arms as well as he could with all the things on his back.

"How would I know that? Maybe you stole those things."

The man in the uniform put the knife away and placed his hands on his hips like he was scolding a child.

"I don't care what you know," Sebastion said, this time with anger in his voice.

Just then, the girl from the shop turned the corner. She had been running, and he noticed her full figure for the first time as her chest fought for breath.

"There you are," she said, running up to him and grabbing his hand.

Taken by surprise, Sebastion tried to pull his hand back, but the girl held on with an iron grip.

"Who is he, Sara?" the man in the uniform asked her.

"This is my cousin from Hampshire. He, uh, is from my mother's side of the family." She gave the young man in the uniform a big smile, and he smiled back.

"Okay, then." He turned to Sebastion, "Make sure you stay out of trouble. We don't like troublemakers in this town."

Jabbing a finger at Sebastion, he tried to look menacing but just made himself look even younger.

Sara rolled her eyes at him and pulled Sebastion toward the road. She had to let go of his hand so he could lift the other bags he had put down in the alley.

Being this close to her, he thought she smelled good and he could not stop thinking about how the skin on her hand that had held his had been so soft and warm. His hands were full of calluses and scars from his training. He hoisted the bags over his shoulder, and as he did so, she slipped her arm under his. This time he did not object. As a matter of fact, he felt lightheaded and woozy. When his head began to clear slightly, he noticed that she was leading him farther into the town.

"Hey, where are we going?" he asked, looking around.

"We're going to my house." She smiled up at him.

"What?" Sebastion pulled away from her. "I've got to get going! I can't stay here."

"What is your name?" she asked.

He stared at her and thought she could be the most beautiful thing he had ever seen.

She had long red hair the color of fire. Her eyes were the deepest green he had ever seen. She was small and thin but still had curves. She was wearing an old blue dress that she had obviously outgrown. Her bosom was threatening to rip the front of the simple dress. He wondered if she had been wearing this dress in the shop. He could not remember now.

Her face was turning as red as Sebastion's as he stared at her.

He knew it was rude of him, but he just couldn't help himself. There were a few girls at the school, but none were like her.

"Hello? You still with us?" She snapped her fingers in front of his face.

With considerable willpower, he returned his eyes to hers. Still, he couldn't keep from smiling.

"Yes ... uhh ... sorry."

She smiled and put her arm in his again.

He smiled dumbly down at her as they walked. "Aren't those bags heavy?" She asked.

He couldn't even feel them right now.

***

Sir Killian of House Loyal, known to Sebastion as Rayor, sat in a cell with his head in his hands. It had been raining for days, and he was sitting in a puddle that had formed there. The guards who had found him had not bothered to remove the body of the guard Sebastion had killed before locking the door, and it was starting to smell very bad. Killian hardly noticed, however, as he pondered what was going to happen to him now.

He had cut his ties with the only one who would have helped him. Having carried the weight of guilt for longer than a normal man's life span, death was just a dream he'd had for longer than he cared to remember. The shame he wore covered him more thoroughly than his long gray cloak, for he had long ago betrayed his only brother.

They had once been so close to one another; it had always been just them and their father. They had lived in the same home together for years. He had been there when his brother's wife gave birth to Sebastion's father. He had held him in his hands and watched as he took his first breaths of life. His brother's boy would have one day become a great man destined to do great things, but he too had been betrayed ... not by him but by the one he now served.

Killian had held on to this guilt for so long it was now part of him. His heart had twisted, as he became a servant who represented everything he had sworn to fight. He had always suspected Bashor had chosen him because of his lineage. Some perverse twist of fate to have the man who had betrayed the family continue now to betray the next of the lineage that was nearly gone.

Rubbing his old, wrinkled hands across his hairless head again, Killian thought he might as well stay in this cage, where he belonged. It would be a fitting end for a traitor like himself. I've now betrayed both sides, he thought, laughing miserably. It would be an excellent end of things to spend the rest of my life in a cold, wet cell.

"I know you," came a voice from the cell next to him.

Killian was startled and instinctively reached into his sleeve. He was sure all the cells were empty, but his.

"WHO'S THERE!" he yelled out, but there was no answer. Killian thought for sure he was losing his mind.

"I know who you are," the voice said again.

"I don't know who you are and you, for sure, have no idea who I am," the old knight grumbled.

"Oh, but I do," answered the voice.

This time Killian ignored him and went back to the dark place in his mind.

"Kil, you know what you must do."

The knight shot up like a cobra.

"What type of trick is this?! No one calls me that!" The knight was furious. "Who's there? Identify yourself now, or I'll come over there…"

He was so angry that his knuckles turned white as he gripped the bars of his cell.

One of the guards came to see what the commotion was about.

"Who is there in that cell?" Killian demanded of the guard.

"Where?" the guard asked, giving the knight a confused look.

"In the next cell, YOU MORON!"

The guard was getting angry and stepped forward.

"Listen, you crazy old man. If you don't watch your tongue, I'll cut it out."

The old knight reached through the bars and grabbed the guard by the shirt and pulled him towards the bars. There was a loud crack, and the guard fell to the ground. Killian searched the guard, but there was no key.

Sitting on the floor and putting one foot under the guard's body, the old man called out to the other guard.

"Hurry, this man is having some sort of fit."

He started lifting the guard on the floor up and down with his foot, faster and faster.

The man's body shook as if it was in some sort of seizure.

Killian righted the body's twisted head and lifted an eyelid as if he were checking for something.

The other guard ran in and saw his companion having convulsions on the ground. It looked as if the old man was trying to help him. He ran over to see what the matter was. When in range, Killian used the bars of his cage to render this guard unconscious as well.

He was still angry when he opened the cell that was next to his. He checked every corner but found no one. This was the cruelest of pranks. He thought it could be some sort of torture that Lord Bashor had thought up for him. However, they would not know that name. No man had ever called him that but one, and that man was dead—killed by the old knight himself. It had been a nickname only a very few used and almost all long ago gone. A shocked king had called him that as he looked down at a sword plunged into his chest.

"Kil, not you…" had been his last words. Hot tears made their tortuous way through the many wrinkles in Killian's face. He wiped them away quickly.

"Kil, you know what you must do," the voice had said.

It was evident to him now that it had come from within his own tortured mind.

I know what I must do, all right.

He would find the boy and keep him safe from his dark master, Bashor.

I was a knight to a king and a brother who was killed by my own hand. I know I am an abomination of what a knight should be ... but I'll be thrice damned if I'll let the boy be taken and used by that monster.

Killian did not even bother to disguise himself as he moved silently through the school. He collected his things and headed for the kitchen.

The kitchen was empty as he entered it and went into the closet. The closet, however, was not.

He was surprised to find two of the boys who had fought with Sebastion standing close to each other and looking very frightened. Even worse, the secret door that led to the outside was wide open. The two boys were staring into the darkness as if they expected a demon to walk out of it.

Hearing someone moving in the darkness there, Killian waited to see who would appear. He put his hands to the hilts of his knives.

What came out of the darkness, however, was not a demon, though from what Killian saw on the boys' faces, they would have preferred it. The butcher walked out of the darkness, a very hard look on his face.

"Sir, could you please help us?" one of the boys asked of Killian.

The butcher hadn't noticed Killian standing there and looked surprised.

"Now that Serin is ... no longer with us, have the caretakers turned on the children?" Killian asked him.

The butcher frowned and crossed his arms across his massive chest. "The caretakers, as you call us, have been disappearing for some time now." The butcher turned to give the boys a look that made them both look down.

"Seems they have been directing their training on the ones that work here."

Killian saw the guilt wash through the two boys' faces. There was no question that they were guilty.

"One of those who has disappeared," the butcher continued, "was my wife. And her silver bracelet now adorns that bastard's wrist."

Killian looked over, and the boy slowly let his long sleeve cover it.

"There are many here who have not yet gone as far as these here. Will you also reap your revenge on them?"

"We are not killers," the butcher said.

Both boys sighed visibly.

"Yet," he added for their benefit, "this place is not a school, but today there will be some hard lessons learned. Consequences will be the lesson today, I think."

Killian shook his head, understanding. He could tell that this man was a good man and that things could be much worse for the boys. Killian headed for the no-longer-secret door.

The butcher held out a hand, and Killian, instinctively, almost cut it with a knife.

"One thing ... eh ... Rayor, I think it is. The boy ... the boy you were with. He's special, isn't he?"

Killian turned to him, surprised. "What do you mean?"

The butcher visibly struggled to find the words. "You know ... he's ... different. We all felt it being around him. He's ... special somehow."

Killian thought on that before nodding.

"Yes, he is."

The butcher nodded, agreeing.

"It was he who showed us the door in the wall here. When I opened it, I knew immediately that it was here that these creatures ... " he jammed a thumb at the boys, "were doing their business. I needed to only wait and they showed up. They even tried their business on me."

Killian looked over and did see many red spots on the boys that would eventually be bruising.

"The boy ... I think without knowing it ... led us to them."

Killian nodded again and disappeared into the darkness beyond the door. As he traversed the darkness, he thought about what the butcher said. "He's special." Yes, there is something about him that makes things happen. It will be no easy task keeping him safe, I fear. This is going to be a long and dangerous journey. He sighed again as he felt for the walls beside him in the darkness.

***

At this point, Sebastion was barely able to remember his own name as Sara led him to a small red house in the middle of the city. All the houses on that block looked the same except for the color. Most were falling apart, and some had completely crumbled. Sebastion heard a splash and turned to see a woman pouring a bucket of filth out her window onto the street. He suddenly had a strong feeling in his gut that he should leave.

Sara had to physically pull Sebastion to the front door. He was feeling the weight of the bags now, and he was trying to get them into a more comfortable position.

"Why have you brought me here?" he asked testily. He did not mean to be abrupt, but his nerves were taking over. He was trying very hard not to look down at her body. One of the buttons to her dress popped while walking, and his eyes were drawn to it like a moth to a flame.

"My father and I just wanted to have you over for dinner. Your generosity at the store will help us get back on our feet," she said.

He looked down at her, confused. He tried to concentrate on her eyes.

"Why are you, uh ... not on your feet?"

She giggled, which made another button on her dress threaten to give way.

"Come, on," she said, looking up and batting her eyes at him. "Let's go in and see if father needs help with dinner."

He looked deep into her eyes and smiled, no longer resisting as she pulled him into the house.

The interior was neat and full of interesting things on the walls. Sebastion walked over to a painting and studied the blue water.

Sara walked over and took his hand.

"I painted that before my father and I moved here. That is the sea. Have you ever seen the sea?" she asked.

Sebastion just shook his head no, without taking his eyes away.

"Maybe one day we could go together, and I could show you my homeland."

She was smiling and holding Sebastion's hand with both of hers. She leaned on him as they studied the painting together.

He was a little uncomfortable with all the touching, but he also didn't want it to end.

The shopkeeper walked into the room, and Sara jumped away, but not before the shopkeeper saw them.

Sebastion thought he saw a flash of anger in the man's eyes before he smiled broadly and spread his arms wide to greet them.

"Ah, our young traveler has come to our house." He walked up to him and patted him on the back. He put his arm around Sebastion and led him to the kitchen.

"When was the last time you had a home-cooked meal, heh?" he asked Sebastion with a friendly grin.

Sebastion had to really think about that. He supposed it was not since Rayor and he had eaten with the ferry master. Every other meal since then had been prepared at the school.

A wave of guilt washed over him when he thought of Rayor. He missed the talks and stories, but he knew Rayor had his own reason for taking Sebastion to the school, and if he was to remain free, it would have to be on his own.

The three of them ate the most substantial meal Sebastion had ever seen. When he was sure he could not possibly eat another thing, the chubby shopkeeper kept piling it on.

Candles lit the room, and there was a pleasant smell of spices in the air.

The shopkeeper's daughter sat across from him, and he couldn't help staring at her as she sat there delicately putting food in her mouth. She was the most beautiful thing he had ever seen. His head would swim, and his heart flutter, just looking at her. She kept her eyes down and concentrated on her meal. The shopkeeper cleared his throat from time to time, and he snapped his head down and back to his plate.

"So, my boy. What fine name has been bestowed upon you by the Gods?" The shopkeeper asked.

"Huh ... Sebastion asked, stupidly.

"Your name," Sara whispered.

"Oh— My name is Sebastion," he said without thinking. He physically winced as he realized he had given his real name.

The shopkeeper did not miss the reaction.

Rayor would have slapped him painfully on the back of his head.

"Ahh, Sebastion, is it? A fine name if ever there was one." The shopkeeper pushed away from the table and rubbed his ample belly. "And what brings you here to this humble city?" he asked.

Sebastion did not know what to say. He surely could not tell the truth. What would he, or more importantly, Sara, think of him if he were to say he was running away from a school for assassins? He had to think quickly.

"I ... uh, am looking for ... adventure," Sebastion finally said lamely. He remembered Rayor's stories of young men venturing out, looking for adventure and fortune. He, too, was young, so this made sense to him.

Sara started to laugh softly. She lifted her head and smiled at him.

Sebastion flushed and looked down at his overflowing plate.

"Adventure ... I see," the shopkeeper said, leaning back and crossing his arms over his big stomach. "Where did you come by those precious stones you have?"

Sebastion decided the shopkeeper was asking too many questions, so he decided to change the subject. "How long have you and your daughter lived here?" he countered.

The shopkeeper looked surprised at that and gave Sara a look. She dipped her head down.

"We have been here in this town for almost a year now." He looked up at the ceiling as if he was deep in thought. "We had decided to have an adventure of our own, so we moved here."

Sebastion tried to listen to the shopkeeper as he went on about how beautiful it was where he came from and how they both missed it.

Sara kept her head down the whole time.

After some time, Sebastion politely thanked the two for dinner and got up from the table to leave. He was feeling tired and wanted to put some miles between himself and the town before sleeping.

As he stood up, father and daughter exchanged a look.

"Hold on there, my boy ... eh, Sebastion. We can't have you leaving now. Its dark out, and there is a curfew here. No one is allowed to walk the streets at night. There are some horrible people out at this time."

"Don't worry; no one will see me," Sebastion said after thinking for a moment.

Sara and her father exchanged another look at his confident reply. She walked up and took Sebastion's hand in her own soft and warm grip.

"Please, Sebastion. Could you just stay the night?" Her eyes were wide, and she gave him a soulful look.

"W- well ..." he stuttered. "I guess I'm really in no hurry."

Sara's eyes lit up, and she lightly bounced up and down on her toes. She still had the all-too-small blue dress on, the contents not lost on Sebastion. He looked over at the shopkeeper, who was smiling but seemed none-too-happy at Sara's reaction.

The girl helped Sebastion carry his bags to the spare room. He had to grab the big pack back from her, as she almost fell over from its weight.

The room she took him to was clean and had little furniture. Leaving for a moment, she returned with some warm water in a basin so he could clean up. She stood in the doorway as he took off his shirt.

Sebastion started to take off his pants when he noticed she was still there. He looked at her, and she smiled strangely and left the room.

The water was warm, and it felt good to get clean again. It had been many days since he had been able to scrub himself clean, and even longer since he'd had warm water.

What remained of the water, he poured over his head and washed his long, black hair. He toweled off and went to put on his old clothes, only to find new clothes neatly folded on the bed.

He flushed with embarrassment as he realized that Sara must have come in when he was naked, scrubbing his hair. It was not just the fact that she had seen him naked but that he had heard nothing of her coming. He was impressed with her stealth. He had not even heard the wood floors creak.

He quickly grabbed the clothes and put them on. The shirt fit well, but the pants were much too short. He looked ridiculous in them but had no choice, as Sara had taken his clothes.

He quietly poked his head out the door. He wanted to find Sara and get his clothes back or at least the pants.

Creeping into the hall, he tried not to step on any loose boards. He heard quiet voices coming from what must be the shopkeeper's bedroom. It sounded as if they were arguing. It seemed to him that the shopkeeper was struggling to keep his voice down. He heard what sounded like Sara sobbing quietly. Then he heard only the shopkeeper talking. He moved forward to see what was going on and put his eye to the keyhole.

The chubby shopkeeper was holding Sara in his arms and looking down at her. Sebastion had not a lot of knowledge about families but still, it did not seem the shopkeeper was holding Sara as a father should. She was pressed against him and staring up at him. The shopkeeper seemed to be very angry.

Sebastion suddenly felt guilty spying on them after they had been so nice to him. Leaving the keyhole, he returned to his room. He was rather excited about sleeping in a bed again. This was the most enormous, most comfortable-looking bed he had ever seen. The beds at the school had been nothing like this.

Curious about it, he got down on his knees to see what held the bed up.

Sara opened the door and looked into the room.

"Sebastion?" she called softly when she didn't see him.

He popped his head up, and she jumped, startled.

She laughed merrily at being scared, and he watched her smiling.

Standing up, he walked around the bed, and she started laughing even harder. Sebastion realized she was laughing at his far-too-small pants. He understood what he must look like and started laughing as well.

"I just wanted to say goodnight," Sara said, still trying to control her laughter.

"Good night," Sebastion smiled back at her.

Sara left and Sebastion crawled gingerly into the soft bed. When he finally laid into it, he thought it must be like sleeping on a cloud. No matter how long he lay there, however, he could not get comfortable.

The bed was too soft for him. For the last few weeks, he had been sleeping on the ground, and the bed was just too fluffy. Finally, he pulled the blankets off the bed and made himself a spot on the floor.

It was not long before he could hear the loud snoring of the shopkeeper. He couldn't help thinking how strange and wonderful it must be to be in your own house like this ... to be able to come home to your own place and be safe and enjoy all the comforts that came with it. He liked this little house, and he liked the shopkeeper and his daughter too.

They asked a lot of questions but they were very kind to him, and he had enjoyed laughing with Sara this evening. It had been a long time since he had laughed, and it felt good.

His mind went to Sara again. As much as he tried, his thoughts always went to the lovely daughter of his host—except when interrupted by his incessant snoring.

He had never heard anyone snore so loudly. Even if he had been able to sleep, it would have been impossible to remain asleep with all that noise.

Sebastion heard light footsteps coming from the hallway. He peered under the bed and across the floor, and he could see someone's feet on the other side of the door.

The doorknob turned quietly. Sara's delicate little bare feet carried her almost silently into the room, and she closed the door. She gasped as she saw that the bed was empty. Coming around, she found Sebastion on the floor looking up at her.

"Are you all right?" she asked him in a whisper.

"The bed is too soft," he said, just as quietly.

She smiled down at him, wearing a sheer nightgown and nothing else. There was a candle lit in the hallway, and the light under the door framed her body as she stood there.

His eyes drank in her silhouette in the darkness, as she stood there quietly letting him look her over. When he got to her eyes, she was staring just as intently back at him. He had an urge to stand, but he was not sure his knees would bend.

Sara moved her small delicate hand upward and traced a line up the center of her chest. When her hand slowly arrived at her throat, she unfastened the only button that was there and gently pulled the gown from her shoulders and let it fall to the ground. She did not move but stood there naked, allowing the young traveler to study her.

Sebastion's hands were shaking with anticipation. She slowly descended to her knees, and he thought his heart was going to jump out of his chest. He thought she smelled like flowers and spices. It made his head spin.

Reaching out to him, Sara took his hand and gently placed it on her firm breast.

Sebastion's head felt light and he couldn't think. Her skin was soft and warm.

She let out a soft sigh at his touch and licked her thick red lips.

Sebastion sat up and pressed his lips hard against hers.

She gently pushed him back down, lying down with him.

The shopkeeper snored even louder. The raspy gurgling noises he made sounded angry and almost inhuman.

Sebastion and Sara forgot about the noises and the shopkeeper altogether as they explored each other for hours.

The sun was peeking out of the sky when Sara, sweat glistening on her skin in the soft light, grabbed her nightgown and headed for the door. She stopped halfway and ran back to Sebastion to give him one more deep kiss.

Never dreaming he could feel this good, Sebastion lay back down on his blankets, his hands behind his head. A big smile spread across his face, and before he even realized it, he fell asleep on the floor, completely exhausted.

The shopkeeper woke him a few hours later by opening the door without knocking and poking his head in. He must have seen Sebastion's legs sticking out on the floor.

"Come on, Sebastion, my boy. We have a fine breakfast waiting for you."

In fact, Sebastion could smell many things cooking in the other room.

The shopkeeper was looking at him curiously as he noticed he had slept nude.

"I wanted to save the clothes you gave me for today," he said, smiling up from the floor and feeling the blood coming to his face as he lied.

The man shrugged and left Sebastion to get dressed.

Sebastion hurried to get his clothes on. He wondered if Sara was up already. He tied his hair neatly behind his head with a leather strand that had been left with the clothes. He very much wanted to see Sara again. She was all he had dreamed of as soon as sleep had taken him.

He walked out of his room and to the table, where she was already serving her father. Sebastion tried to catch her eye several times, but she busied herself with filling their plates. When the shopkeeper pushed himself away from the table, he once again crossed his arms over his large belly.

"Well, I have a favor to ask of you, Sebastion."

Sebastion looked up from his plate.

"I would like to ask that you help me with a side project I am working on."

The shopkeeper stood up and motioned for him to follow.

They both walked onto the front porch. The old boards creaked and cracked as they walked. On the road, people were walking, and some were on horseback; they were kicking up a lot of dust, all going about their business. The shopkeeper pointed to a boarded-up building across the dirt road.

"I purchased that building the same time I bought the store you have already seen," he said proudly. "Now that I have more money," he winked at Sebastion, "I would like to open this one as well."

He turned a pleading eye to Sebastion.

"Would you be so kind as to help me rip off the boards and remove some of the junk inside?"

Sebastion thought about this.

The man crossed his arms and studied the building across the street.

"Of course, you would stay with Sara and me until you're done," he said without turning.

Sebastion, without hesitation, agreed.

The shopkeeper gave him a happy look, though Sebastion could have sworn he also saw a flash of something else. He was not sure what it was, but he definitely saw something else come over the man. Then the chubby shopkeeper smiled and put his hand on the young man's shoulder.

"In that case, you may call me Khan," he said, squeezing Sebastion's shoulder and giving him a shake. "This means a lot to both of us. We should have that building clean and open in no time."

Khan saw a flash of disappointment come over Sebastion and added.

"Of course, there is setting up the store after that."

Sebastion smiled despite himself. He stared at the old run-down building, not seeing a bit of the shopkeeper's dream. His mind was back on the previous night and filled with anticipation of what this next one might bring ... and the future and the nights following.

Working on the building across the dusty roadside with Sebastion every day, Khan was always kind to him. Sebastion found it strange that Sara and her father never had to go back to the shop. He had it in his mind to say something. Still, he didn't want to appear nosey, and the subject never came up naturally in conversation. Instead, each day was the same, and each night was the best he'd ever had. In the evening, they would eat and make light conversation. After dinner, Khan and Sebastion would smoke their pipes on the porch while Sara brought them wine. In the night, he would experience great angst, wondering if Sara would come to visit him. He would listen for Khan's loud snoring, and usually, just a few moments later, he would hear Sara's light footsteps outside his door. Every night, Sara would come to him, and they would spend the dark hours together until the night changed to early light, near sunrise. As the sun barely beamed its first light, she would pick up her nightgown and run silently back down the hall.

Their secret encounter was already on the second week before Khan mentioned the tired looks and the yawning at the table.

"You two look very tired," he said, looking at them both suspiciously. "Perhaps we should slow the pace some." He was speaking to them both but looking fixedly at Sara, who looked up at Khan and then quickly back down.

Sara never even flirted with Sebastion when Khan was around. She would always serve her father first and be by his side when she was not serving him wine. Khan seemed to just take it that they were working too hard in the abandoned building.

When Sebastion looked up at Khan, the portly double-chinned man would smile, but underneath Sebastion was sure there was a touch of anger. He liked this man very much, and he felt guilty deceiving him, but he could no easier stay away from Sara than breathe and eat.

Feeling something on his leg, the young dreamer almost jumped out of his skin. Khan gave him a look, and Sebastion just smiled.

"Sorry, just thought of something."

He turned back to his plate as Khan went on, describing what he wanted to do with the building. Meanwhile, Sara's foot went up Sebastion's leg and further. He looked up at her, but she was intently cutting up a small piece of meat. Khan was talking about the positioning of the products in the new shop now.

Still, Sebastion was finding it very difficult to follow his conversation. He would put in an appropriate "Huh-huh" and "Yes, that sounds nice" to keep up. But his attention was really on the soft foot pressing on him beneath the table.

"Sebastion, are you quite all right? Your face looks flushed, and you just don't seem to be with it this evening."

Sebastion flushed a deeper red.

Sara was smiling wickedly into her food.

"I ... ah ... I am just a little tired this evening. I think," he stammered.

Sara would not let up, so Sebastion shifted his weight in the chair away from her.

Khan shook a sympathetic head at him.

"I think you should run off to bed straightaway, then. No use in getting sick, for we have a lot to do." After a pause, he continued.

"Off you go, then."

Sebastion knew he could not leave right at that moment. If he excused himself, Khan would know what they had been up to.

"Uh, first, can you tell me about the ocean a bit more? I have always wanted to go there."

Khan laughed and reached over to slap him on the back.

"Always thirsty for more, aren't you?"

Sebastion smiled and looked over at Sara, who looked up, mischievously, for a second. Khan went on about the boats and the strange people that would show up on them in the ports.

Feeling Sara's foot again, Sebastion pushed slightly away from the table.

Khan, lucky for Sebastion, was lost in his thoughts of his homeland as he rambled on.

Sebastion gave Sara a quick, exasperated look.

She just pouted her lips at him.

Khan continued to spin his tales, and they laughed together and made jokes, but Sebastion and Sara kept exchanging quick glances.

One evening, Sebastion was cleaning his room, and he noticed that one of the straps on his pack was unlatched. He pulled the bag all the way out from under the bed. The things inside were not in order, and it seemed as if someone had gone through the compartment containing his money.

There was a hidden flap that included the jewelry the servants had packed for him. When he looked inside, he found nothing missing, but it was obvious someone had been searching through the pack itself. He didn't want to even entertain the thought that his friends could have gone through his bags. Still, he couldn't ignore the possibilities.

He decided to conduct an experiment. Pulling a jeweled ring from the secret compartment, he placed it deep within the pack, on the bottom. He then washed up and waited for the inevitable evening visit with Sara.

She came into the room in her sheer nightgown without speaking a word. Now she was no longer taking her time to come to him. She would just let the gown drop to the floor and jump into the blankets with him, giggling quietly.

They came together that night as they had every night, and soon after they finished, Sebastion fell into a deep sleep, all thoughts of the pack and its contents forgotten. He dreamed of staying with Sara and Khan. He and Sara would run the shop with her father. He could use the other jewels he had in his pack to buy a house of their own. She was the most beautiful thing that ever happened to him, and he knew he wanted to be with her more than anything else.

Sebastion had learned a little about love through Keeper's books and through conversations with Rayor. He was sure that what he had with Sara must be that because, for the first time in his life, he was happy. He had never even known he could feel the way he felt now. He knew he had only been there a short time, and there was always a voice in the back of his mind, Rayor's, of course, that told him to be careful, but being here felt so good, and he wanted to give in to it.

His dreams spun images of life in the city with his new family. He enjoyed them almost as much as his activities just before.

The next evening, Sara was in an excellent mood and full of lustful energy. They rolled around together with great exuberance. She was insatiable. Finally pleading with her for a rest, Sebastion rolled onto his side, breathing hard, sweat drops running down his back and face. His eyes met Sara's, and he noticed they were the brightest he had ever seen them, and her moans had been so loud he thought Khan would wake for sure.

He lay there for some time, staring into her eyes, losing himself in them. He reached out to move a long lock of sweat-soaked auburn hair from her cheek and smiled at her.

Sara gave him a wicked wink before getting up and finding her gown.

Lying on his back on the floor with his hands behind his head, he watched her leave. He loved watching her move, and he took in the full view of her in the moonlight as she moved across the floor. He had to push over to his side to look around the bed when she got to the door.

When she had silently reached the door, Sara turned to look at him over her shoulder. She wiggled her rump once for him before disappearing into the soft light coming from the hall.

Sebastion breathed out a happy sigh. He was asleep almost as soon as the end of his sigh left his lips.

That morning, as he was dressing, he remembered the ring but immediately tried to put it out of his mind. However, Rayor's voice was there again, "what would it hurt to just look, boy?" The Rayor in his head was just as irritably insistent as the man himself. Finally, he decided if it would make silent that voice, he would just quickly peek in the pack.

Getting down on one knee, Sebastion looked under the bed. He found that the entire pack was missing. A cold wave of goosebumps ran up his back. He searched the room to see if they had moved it, but the bag was nowhere to be found.

When he had exhausted his search of the small room, he decided he would simply ask Sara and her father. They probably wanted to wash it or some such thing. He swore to himself for being so paranoid. He had finally found good people and he was letting his head get filled with negativity.

He finished dressing and went downstairs, but Sara and Khan were nowhere to be found. He searched the house, but they were gone. The now-familiar feeling once again crept up his spine.

He heard people's voices outside and went to the front porch. Sara and Khan were in the street, talking to men in uniform.

Sebastion knew something was wrong as soon as he saw them. He looked at Sara and could see her face was swollen and it looked like she had blood at the corner of her mouth. She was wearing a dress that was too small for her again, and it was ripped and dirty. She had to hold the front together to keep herself from being exposed.

The sight of her like that hit him like a fist to the stomach. Sebastion jumped off the porch, wanting to sweep Sara into his arms and be damned if her father didn't like it. The look on his face, witnessed by the growing crowd of people standing around, was grim and raging as he leapt over the railing.

Sara cried out and fainted into Khan's arms.

Khan went to one knee, holding her and rocking her back and forth. "THAT'S THE MAN!" he yelled out, pointing an accusing finger in Sebastion's direction as he hurried toward them.

Sebastion stopped and looked around, confused, and trying to see the person Khan was indicating.

"That's the man that raped my wife!" the shopkeeper yelled out again, pointing directly at Sebastion this time.

The uniformed men started forward, drawing their swords.

Sebastion stepped back. "Sara?" he asked, wonderingly, stepping slowly backward.

She opened her eyes and pointed, "That's him! That's the man that … that attacked me!" she yelled, recovering quickly from her faint.

That was all the men had to hear; a look of hatred washed over their faces.

Sara looked around the men rushing at Sebastion and lifted her hand to show off the ring he had put in the bottom of his pack. She winked, smiled in that wicked way Sebastion had loved, and gave Khan a hard kiss on the mouth from within his embrace.

Sebastion's head felt as if it were floating above his body. He and Sara were falling in love, just like the couples in Keeper's books, weren't they? The questions started coming fast to his head. Why did father and daughter sleep in the same room? Why did they bring him here in the first place? If that was not his daughter and she was his wife... Why would they do this?

Two of the uniformed men grabbed him by his arms. The questions in his head kept coming and he did not resist trying to understand it all.

This can't be right.

They pushed him down onto his knees.

This must be a mistake. How could she do this to me? I would have happily given the jewels to her if she had only asked for them.

By the dark, he would have even gone out and stolen more if that had made her happy.

What was it that Khan had said? Did he say, "my wife?" ... and the kiss...

I can't think.

A young man in uniform, the same one that had stopped him in the alley weeks earlier, stepped in front of him now. He looked Sebastion up and down with that same disgusted look on his face that he had had when they met.

"How could you defile such a pure and respectable woman?!" He backhanded Sebastion and then coughed hard and spat what came up into Sebastion's face.

The officer looked over his shoulder at Sara, who gave him a pitiful look before burying her face into Khan's shirt, whimpering.

Khan stroked her hair, whispering softly to her.

Sebastion felt the blood run down the corner of his mouth.

The officer found new rage as he watched the couple's sorrowful exchange.

"Bring the prisoner to the side of the house."

The two guards standing over Sebastion hauled him up, and the boy-officer smacked his prisoner on the head as they walked.

This time, Sara was watching intently, and the officer thought he saw a satisfied look in her eye. He took it to mean that she was getting some satisfaction from seeing her attacker punished. She was also losing the battle of keeping her dress covering herself, and that only fueled the officer more. The two strong men holding Sebastion pulled him to the side of the house and pushed him to his knees again.

Sebastion could only stare at the ground, trying to make sense of it all. He wanted to put it together, but his mind would not allow him. He refused to believe it. He wanted so much to have things the way they were that he would not let his mind accept it.

There must be some explanation... They would not do this to me.

"Tear open the back of his shirt," the young officer commanded.

The two uniformed men holding Sebastion exchanged confused looks.

"Sir, this man has not been seen by the council yet," one of the men said, so quietly that it was almost a whisper.

"SILENCE!" the young officer yelled in what he hoped would be a commanding voice. The effort was lost, however, since it came out like a whiny child. "Don't question my orders!"

The men holding the prisoner looked at each one before one shrugged and start tugging as Sebastion's shirt, "That's it, tear it open and give me your belt. NOW!"

Chapter 9 - Miska

The tent was warm, too warm. She could feel the sweat rolling down her midsection and disappearing off to the sides. It tickled, but she was in no mood to laugh. She had been traveling in this scorching heat for nearly a month, and she was sick to her stomach of it.

Miska was no stranger to traveling and frankly enjoyed seeing the country as any respectable young Demsy woman would. In fact, the entire troop had been moving from one place to another for longer than she could remember. It was just the damn insistent heat that was making everything she did so unbearable.

Usually, at this time of night, she would sit by the fire with the other Demsies, young and old, and tell stories. She loved the stories the older folk would tell about how things were when they were in their prime. She knew that the stories were mostly made up or vast exaggerations of the truth, but she loved them all the same.

A large fly landed on her hand, and she shook it furiously.

Her little dog, Dung (her father had always said, "The dog ain't worth a load of dung," so that had become his name), poked his head up and gave Miska a lazy look.

"Oh, don't you start with me, Dung!"

The little black-and-white dog put his head back down and went to sleep.

Miska, however, lay awake on her back with her arms and feet crossed, scowling up at the tent. She was wearing only a small white slip that was now drenched in sweat. Of course, like all Demsy girls, her neck, wrists, and ankles were adorned with an array of beaded jewelry. She loved these beads, but today they just felt as annoying as the thick heavy air.

Her hair used to be very long, black, and full of curls. It would flip all-around when she danced as if it had a life of its own. But on one of those days when the heat had been too unbearable, she had chopped off her hair in a desperate effort to cool off. The long hair had been like wearing a fur hat all the time. It seemed to her that she was always brushing and grooming it, so she didn't miss it after she cut it short with her sharp little knife.

Miska's father, however, had been furious with her. He knew her hair was a vital piece of the enticement that kept the village men coming to their shows. He had to grudgingly admit, though, that even without her lengthy hair, she was still stunning to look at. Sometimes her father would stare at her and cry and tell her how much she looked like her mother.

Miska hated when her father did that, as it always led to him spending days drinking and being impossible to deal with. The people at the towns would feel uncomfortable around him and be less apt to spend their money on the shows. It was, after all, bizarre to see a huge and overweight man sob and share stories of love and loss.

Miska had always enjoyed the life she led, apart from the episodes with her father's depression and drinking. As a girl, she would dance for the townspeople, and they would exclaim how cute she was and give her and her father money. She was a natural dancer and loved performing in front of people.

As she grew older, she found that the kind women who had once given them money and tweaked her cheeks now looked at her disapprovingly and sometimes were even hostile.

Still, as the women stopped coming to see her dance, the men came in their stead. It became something totally different, but she didn't mind because she still loved to dance, and her father was always there for her.

Most men liked the fantasy, and that was enough for them. There were rare times, however, when some overeager man "forgot" the rules. And they were dealt with by her father, who sometimes reminded her of a grizzly bear rather than the sweet and oft-weepy man she loved.

Just then something or someone hit the tent, fell with a grunt, and then went running off again.

Miska sat up straight, and Dung started to growl.

"Quiet, dog! I can't hear."

Another thud. She was sure now it was a person falling again and then getting back up.

She was listening so hard now that she could hear her own heart pumping in her chest. She recognized the sound of her father snoring in the tent next to hers. His snoring had been the reason she had her own tent, though it was only minimally helpful since her father still insisted that she put hers right next to his own.

"It's for your own protection," he would say, though she knew very well he could sleep through almost anything. The only thing that could wake him from the deepest sleep was the smell of food cooking on the fire.

Miska gingerly untied the straps to her tent door and opened it just enough to peek out with one eye.

Dung poked his nose out and sniffed the air. He growled and, with his tail between his legs, he crawled back into Miska's abandoned blanket.

"Coward!" she accused the small dog in a whisper.

Poking her head out, she was slammed by the scent of something very foul. She nearly retched and held her hand to her nose to keep her from smelling it again. She thought she could see, not far off, a lump of something that had not been there before. The moon was full, but there was still was not enough light to see what that lump on the ground could be.

Miska was not new to danger; as a Demsy, you learned to be cautious, and as a Demsy woman that dances for a living, you learn to master caution. She could hear some of the others whispering somewhere off in the night and, sure that if she cried out they would hear, she moved forward to investigate.

The smell became even stronger as she approached what looked like a man. His hair and body were covered with mud and what might be blood. She could not tell if the man was hurt from all the mess he was covered in. His hair was long, greasy, and had twigs and filth hanging from it.

She was about to touch him to see if he was alive when she noticed the telltale signs of a slave. The man's neck and wrists were covered with scars from wearing shackles.

Knowing that interfering with someone's slave was a severe crime, she began to back up.

The man gasped, took a deep breath, and tried to stand up. He didn't even notice her kneeling there beside him. He slowly turned his head in Miska's direction.

As his eyes met hers, Miska covered her mouth to keep from crying out. His face was bruised and cut in many places. His lips were split and looked to be rotting, and there were large bags under his eyes. But the thing that shocked her the most was that this man could be no older than she was. His body was a battered mess, but his eyes were those of a child.

He stared at her, and tears ran down his cheeks, clearing lines down his dirty face. "Am I dead?" he asked her in a hoarse, soft voice.

Miska couldn't speak.

"You are her," he said, not as a question but as if he was sure of it.

Tears started to run down her own cheeks now. The man that was really a boy of maybe fifteen turns reached into his rag of a shirt and pulled out a Talisman. It was a simple stone with the Lady of Light's profile etched into it.

"I have never forgotten," he said to Miska. "I have done terrible things to stay alive."

He began to sob heavily, his shoulders bouncing as he cried.

"I do not deserve to be here in your presence." He wiped his nose on his filthy, ragged sleeve. "Why did you leave me there and let them do those things to me?"

An arrow shot past Miska's head and pierced the boy's chest. The arrow went so deep that she couldn't even see it and would have thought it her imagination had a hole not appeared that was now beginning to leak blood.

The boy still stared at her as if nothing had happened.

"May I go home now and see my family? My mother... " He began to sob again.

Another arrow flew past Miska, nearly nicking her ear. This time she could see the shaft protruding from the boy's shoulder.

His gaze never faltered. He locked her eyes as if he was holding her head still to stare.

"Please... " he begged. Blood started to run onto his chin, and he coughed. "You may forsake my soul, Lady, but please ... please let me see my family one last time."

Heavy footsteps were coming from behind her.

The boy's eyes were becoming glazed and distant. He gurgled on the blood in his throat, trying to speak. He held his filthy battered hand out to her, and she took it.

For a brief second, she saw life return to the boy's eyes, and a smile flashed across his blood-soaked lips. A single breath escaped him as his hand slipped from hers, leaving her holding the talisman now.

The boy fell face first to the ground.

Miska jumped as a heavy hand grabbed her shoulder.

She was forcibly pulled up and turned around to face a large man in leather armor. He was wearing a metal helmet that covered most of his face. His eyes were hard as he looked her up and down.

Miska realized that she was still wearing just her sweat-soaked slip. Becoming very conscious of it, she quickly wrapped her arms around her chest.

"Maybe we should teach this girl not to meddle with other people's property, eh?" His smile was cruel as he looked down at her. He ran the back of his hand slowly down the side of her breast.

As Miska tried to position her arms better to cover herself, the man was lifted into the air and suddenly sailing twice a man's length across the clearing. Now, where the armor-clad man had once stood was Miska's bear of a father, looking very angry.

"What is the meaning of this?" he yelled, glaring at the man now lying on the ground. Like ghosts, more armored men silently appeared out of the darkness of the forest. They circled Miska and her father without saying a word.

Miska pressed against her father, and he put a protective arm around her. Looking up at him with big, brown frightened eyes, she looked for confidence but instead she saw the worried look on his face.

Miska's father bent down and whispered into her ear.

"If this goes badly, run as fast and far as you can."

She started to object, but her father gave her a look she had rarely seen but knew instantly. It left no room for argument. She nodded and stared at the ground.

For the first time in weeks, she no longer felt hot. A coldness was creeping overe her body as she stared blankly at the ground, trying not to make eye contact with any of the men that now surrounded them. She couldn't believe that just a moment ago she had been lying in her tent complaining to Dung about the heat.

The soldier her father had thrown had recovered and was walking up to them. He looked outraged and more than a little embarrassed.

"I will tell you the meaning of this old man." He got very close to her father's face, pushing up onto his toes to meet his eye. "This whore has disrupted our work."

Miska saw the back of her father's neck turn red when the soldier called her a whore.

"Your work, aye?" her father said, raising an eyebrow. "My pardons then."

He smiled without the anger leaving his eyes. Miska's big father was just tall enough to exaggerate the act of looking down at the man as if the man were a child.

"I jumped to conclusions and believed my daughter was being accosted by brigands."

He stepped back and gave a sweeping bow to the soldier, who looked around, at a loss for words.

"My humblest and deepest apologies."

He was careful enough to add the slightest bit of sincerity to confuse the soldier even further.

"You mock me, old man!" the soldier replied angrily. Turning to the others, he waved them forward. They broke their surrounding formation and came around to face the big man.

"Wait!" Miska's father urged, gently prodding his daughter behind him. "There is no need to blow this out of proportion... " His hand behind his back, he waved his daughter off, but when he did not hear her footsteps, he turned to her.

Miska was crying, shaking her head. "I can't," she mouthed to him.

"Run!" he said in an urgent whisper.

Miska's father turned to the armored men and walked forward to meet them. He was no match for five armed guardsmen; however, his intent was not to defeat them but to give Miska enough time to run away.

He charged, but very quickly they had him on the ground and were beating him with the flats of their swords.

Miska started to run but stopped. She had glanced over her shoulder and saw her father being beaten. Unable to leave him like that, she ran to him and tried to pull the guards off of him.

The lead guard caught the Demsy girl by the wrist and backhanded her hard in the face. The sound of the slap made them all stop and turn to see Miska rolling on the ground, holding her face in her hands. There was blood already seeping from between her fingers as she covered her face.

The guard with the cruel smile licked his lips and started walking toward her.

"HOLD!" a loud voice shouted from the forest.

The soldiers froze and turned toward the place in the forest where the voice had come from. A short, bald man with a thick black beard stepped out from the darkness. He wore dark sleeveless leather and had tattoos all over his arms and on a good portion of his head. His demeanor was relaxed but deadly, and his eyes were small and cruel. On his belt hung a short whip that looked worn from much use.

"Leave the girl. Where is the one you were hunting?" He commanded the men.

Four soldiers turned to look at the guard that had initially grabbed Miska away from the now-dead boy. He turned a shade pale and looked at the ground.

The little bald man searched the ground with his eyes. They finally came to rest on the pile of rags not too far off to his left.

"FOOLS!" He swore and spat vehemently on the ground.

Walking quickly up to the lead guard, the angry little man grabbed the collar of the guard's leather armor and yanked the man down to meet him face to face. "And how do you propose to repay me for the property you have destroyed?"

Through the small slits between her fingers, Miska watched. She thought it strange that this little man would treat a large and scary man like the guard in this way.

Perhaps this strange man will help me in some way.

The pain shooting through her gave her the idea to exaggerate her injury in hopes of getting some sympathy. She knew the likelihood of that happening was slim, but she was out of options.

While she was at it, she looked over to see if her father was all right. He was not moving, but his chest was visibly rising and falling as he lay still on his back. *He's alive!*

The little bald man with the whip at his hip ran his hand through his beard, thinking as he looked down, concentrating on the dead boy. Sighing deeply, he threw his arms down at his side and started back toward the forest.

The guards visibly started to relax as he made his way back the way he had come. He stopped suddenly, however, and everyone shot upright, including Miska, who was now in a sitting position but trying very hard to be invisible. She was startled less by the little man stopping short than by the reaction of the others.

The strange man turned and fixed his vicious, small-eyed gaze on Miska. She hadn't realized that she had removed her hands from her face at some point and quickly put them back up to hide from the man's intense stare.

The scary little man looked her over as she sat on the ground.

Her father groaned, and she could hear him swearing. He sat up and spat blood onto the ground.

"I am Ishma," the little man said, "and I believe we are going to become better acquainted."

Miska's father was struggling to stand now. "My daughter has nothing to do with this," he said. The words sputtered blood from his lips.

One of the guards stepped toward him, but Ishma waved him off.

"Sir, the girl was seen helping the boy," the lead guard said confidently.

Miska felt her face grow red as she realized the man was trying to set her up.

"THAT IS NOT TRUE!" she shouted.

Ishma looked at her again with his eyebrows raised in mock surprise.

"This one is full of fire."

The armored men laughed, looking down at her.

Her father tried to come to her, but two of the men grabbed his arms.

With authority, Ishma stepped into the center of the clearing to address the growing number of Demsies awakened by the noise.

"This girl has committed a terrible offense," he shouted, dramatically pointing an accusing finger at Miska.

The Demsies were exchanging worried glances.

"She has interfered with the capture of a runaway slave."

The guards shook their heads from side to side to emphasize the seriousness of the crime.

"You all know the penalty for aiding a runaway, don't you?" Ishma spoke louder now, trying to catch as many eyes in the crowd as he could.

The Demsies began to talk nervously among themselves. They were not many, and most were too old or young to do anything about the situation. Miska's father had always been their constant protector. Still, now with him outnumbered and being held by the armored men, they seemed unwilling to act.

Miska stared in disbelief as her people; her family of Demsies, agreed with the scary little man.

Ishma waved the two men off her father, who took their hands off of him with a dangerous look.

Lumbering slowly to his daughter's side, the big man knelt down and gently put her arm in his.

"They know they cannot do anything to us without risking the entire troop. They are not fighters, and there is no telling how many more guards there are in the forest," he said sadly. "It's not because they don't love you, Miska."

An elderly Demsy woman, whom Miska had come to know as a grandmother since the old woman had helped raise her, stepped forward.

"Please master, show these humble servants of light your mercy."

Ishma raised his eyes to the sky as if deeply pondering her words. He scratched his chin as though he wrestled with the old woman's plea.

"The law in these parts plainly states that those aiding a runaway slave will be immediately put to death." He spread his arms out wide. "What can I do?"

Miska breathed in sharply.

"They mean to kill me, Father? He can't be serious."

She looked up at her father.

Her father looked back down at her with sad eyes. There was still blood at the corners of his mouth, and bruises were already appearing on his cheeks.

Miska couldn't help but think her father looked very old at that moment. She had not noticed all the gray in his beard until now.

He smiled bravely down at her.

"I do not believe that they mean to kill you, my daughter," he said so miserably that Miska did not feel any better.

"What then ... " she already feared the answer.

Instead of answering, Miska's father took a deep breath and stood up straight, coming to his full height.

"You must be brave, little one." He winked down to her.

Ishma suddenly opened his eyes wide, as if startled by a revelation.

"Of course!" he said, snapping his fingers. "The girl could take the place of the one that was killed. That way, all is even, and she could live!"

Miska's father snorted like a defiant bull at this.

The strange little bald man fixed the much larger man with a menacing stare.

"Either that or we spoil that tender throat with a blade, big man."

Miska's father quickly dropped his gaze to the ground.

"The girl will leave with us, and this matter will be forgotten." All playfulness and mockery were gone from his voice now, and he turned to leave, snapping his fingers to the guards nearest Miska.

"One moment, sir?" her father asked in a loud voice.

Ishma turned with a raised eyebrow, surprised at the big man's interruption and tone.

"I would like to accompany my daughter ... um, into your service, that is."

A guard whispered something into Ishma's ear. It was the guard her father had flung across the clearing.

Another of the guards started laughing and shaking his head at Miska's father.

Ishma turned to the guard.

"Something funny?"

The guard stopped immediately.

Ishma walked up to the guard that had laughed and faced him.

"If you can throw this big fellow to the ground, he will say goodbye to his daughter tonight forever."

The guard smiled.

"But ... " Ishma continued, "you will only use what the gods have given you. No weapons."

The guard's smile faded slightly.

Miska's father smiled back at him, raising his eyebrows up and down on his massive brow.

Throwing down his weapons, the guard charged the large man in a rage.

Miska's father caught the guard by the throat, stopping him in his tracks. He lifted the guard several feet from the ground with one hand, while he raised his other massive fist high and struck the guard hard on the head, denting his helmet.

As he let go, the guard fell heavily onto the ground, unconscious.

Ishma, looking amused, waved the other guards to bring them both.

Miska turned instinctively toward her tent to gather her things, but the guards grabbed her and pushed her in the direction of the forest. She started to resist, but her father hissed between his teeth and shook his head at her. It was then that she really started to understand what was happening.

Suddenly there was barking, and Dung broke out from the crowd and ran forward.

A guard turned and, smiling, raised a crossbow in Dung's direction.

Miska gasped when she saw the guard taking aim.

Just as quickly, a young girl appeared seemingly out of nowhere and ran forward to scoop up the little dog. The girl was no older than six and was the most beautiful girl Miska had ever seen. She was sure she knew every child in the troop, but she had never seen this girl. She would have remembered a child like that for sure.

The guard also looked shocked and lowered his bow.

The beautiful little girl walked back into the crowd. When she was almost out of sight, she turned and gave Miska a small, sad smile that should have crushed her heart, but surprisingly she felt slightly better. Realizing that the wounds on her face no longer hurt as much, she touched her face and then looked back to the girl again, but she was gone.

The guard holding Miska's arm again pushed her towards the dark looming forest.

The guard with the crossbow was shaking his head as if waking from a trance.

***

The rocking motion of the cart that was fashioned as a cage in combination with its filthy inhabitants was making Miska very nauseous. She had to stick her face out as far as it would go through the bars to get to the fresh air. Her cheeks ached from being pressed so hard, but she didn't care. Anything was better than the smell in the cart. Her father sat beside her with his back against the rusty cold bars. He didn't even seem to mind the awful smell inside. He was actually snoring and looked quite content.

Yet she could feel the firm, warm grip her father had on her leg. She was trying to concentrate on being angry because anger was better than being scared. She would much rather yell in anger than whimper in fear.

When first they were put into the cart, the other men gave her wolfish grins. One man even tried to grab for her, but her father was too quick and knocked out a few more of the man's rotting teeth. With every turn of the cartwheel, Miska was more clearly understanding the desperateness of her situation. She wanted to cry, but she did not want the people in the cart to think she was weak. She squeezed her eyes shut and pressed her forehead hard against the bars. The pain helped keep her angry, and that held the tears away.

Ishma was riding ahead of the caravan of slave carts. He rode a large black stallion. He must have thought the big horse would make him look more imposing, but it only made him look like a child on his father's horse. The guards would joke about it, but only in dark corners and very far from him. As small as the slave trader was, the guards knew better then to provoke him. Even just looking at the cruel, tattooed, and evil appearance of the little man could freeze the biggest man in his tracks.

When the slave master disciplined the slaves, he would do it with such joy that it sent fear into not only the other slaves, but the guards as well. The older guards told stories of Ishma … things that would make the most seasoned guard cringe. It was said that Ishma had once been a slave himself but had killed his owner and everyone who knew who he was. Some said he was a slave on a ship far to the east and that the boat had sunk. They say he came to shore in the west in a raft made of the corpses of the dead. These people would tell the tale that Ishma had stayed alive by drinking the blood of the drowned inhabitants of the wreck. They were just stories told by bored men around a fire but, when looking into his eyes, it was hard not to believe the little man was capable of the things in the stories.

The guards always kept away from Ishma when they made camp, and that worked well enough for the little slaver. Some said they could hear him in his tent late at night, filing his teeth to points, but no one was curious enough to go see for sure.

The fact was that nobody knew the truth about Ishma, but every one of those guards was sure he was something none of them had ever seen before … or wanted to. The bald head and tattoos were not uncommon in these parts. Still, Ishma appeared to be nearly completely covered in tattoos, with designs twisting in sharp angles that could make one dizzy. His little hand was always checking the whip at his side as if getting some kind of sweet satisfaction in just knowing it was there.

He rarely spoke other than to give orders, and he showed neither pity for the slaves he sold nor remorse for his part in their situation. To some of the guards, he seemed to enjoy their suffering in some twisted way.

But regardless of the slaves' conditions, Ishma was very careful not to injure them in any way that would be physically apparent. He was an expert at this. Most of the blows he inflicted were in the hairline or in some other inconspicuous place on the body. He knew too well that these people were his currency; he did not want to "damage the merchandise," as he would sometimes say with his crooked, evil smile. The man took his job as a slaver very seriously and meant to get them all to the city and ready to be sold in one piece.

The guards called the small caravan to a halt, as they did from time to time. They pulled the slaves from the carts and let them stretch and relieve themselves along the side of the road. While the slaves were out of the wagons, the guards replenished the hay inside. The women and the men were separated as they were led to the brush next to the road. Miska's father looked especially worried at these times. He at first resisted, but soon found it was hopeless and not worth the fight, so he just watched very closely from his side of the road.

Miska was chained to two other women on either side. The guards connected them together each time they were brought out of the cart. The woman attached to her left ankle was middle-aged, and always gave her a sad, kind look. The other on her right ankle was a giant of a woman. Her arms were twice the size of the biggest section of Miska's thigh. The large dress the woman wore seemed ready to burst at the seams. Her hair was cut short, like Miska's, but instead of looking feminine, she looked more like a soldier. If it had not been for her enormous bosom, she could have easily been mistaken for one of the guards that were watching over them.

Together they squatted behind a large bush not far from the road. Miska looked longingly at the forest off to the side, but she was chained, a guard stood close by, and there was no way she would leave her father behind.

She was the first to finish and stood unthinking of the chains, and it jerked forward with her. The large woman threw up her arms and lost her balance. She had to shoot her hand backward to catch herself and doing so put her hand into her own stream of urine. Without moving it, she looked straight up at Miska with fire in her eyes. Miska tried to take a step back from that dark look, but her chains prevented it.

The mountain of a woman pushed off the ground and stood, holding her hand in front of her.

"What do 'ya think I'm going to do with this?" She asked, looking down.

Miska only stood there, looking up at the large woman's wet hand. The woman smiled menacingly down at her.

"Let's see if they cut out your tongue, shall we, because if they didn't…" She smiled wickedly.

"No!" Miska gasped.

"Ah, ha! I see you're intact after all." The woman smiled more widely now.

"No way, lady!" Miska said, shaking her head, now fully understanding what the woman meant.

"Lady!" the large woman barked, growing angrier. "Do I look like, or better still seem to be in a predicament that would warrant me to be, a *lady*?"

She grabbed Miska's shirt with her clean hand and pulled her close.

"I could easily break your pretty little back in under a second."

Miska believed her. Her knees were shaking as she was suspended in the air with the woman's one hand. She started to hear the little slip she was wearing rip and worried that she would have nothing left to cover herself if she was even going to survive the monster of a woman's wrath.

"HEY!" yelled a guard as he came over to Miska and the woman. He stepped in something and looked down and cursed vehemently. "Violet put that girl down, or you'll walk behind the cart the rest of the way, ya will, I swear it!"

Violet looked at the guard and then at Miska as if she was thinking it over.

"Violet…" the guard said in a warning tone.

Suddenly Violet pulled Miska close to her and gave her a big wet kiss on the mouth. She then dropped her to the ground, where she fell like a rag doll. The other woman immediately started to help her up again.

The guard came forward and started poking Violet in the chest and going on about how she was on thin ice and this was the last straw, she'd be answering to Ishma next.

Violet soothed the guard by rubbing and patting his back and talking gently. It was evident that the guard liked her, and soon he was calm and turned to lead them up the hill again. When the guard turned, Miska saw that his back was wet from where Violet had been cleaning her hand. Violet looked down at her and winked. Miska had to hold her slip closed now as Violet had stretched it out so much it was nearly wide open.

Chapter 10 – The Run

The thick leather belt bit into the skin of his back as he was held on the ground, Sebastion's arms twisted behind him, by two guardsmen. Each time the belt connected with his flesh; his head became clearer. The feelings of betrayal and then the stinging realization he'd been played the fool, finally being replaced by red-hot anger.

SLAP! Sebastion could hear Sara giggling as the young guard spoke to her over his shoulder. She did not even care that he was being tortured right in front of her.

SLAP! He barely felt that one.

Sebastion opened his eyes. Ahead of him, up on a hill, was the tangle of trees he had stood by wondering if he should risk coming into the city. It was off in the distance, but he recognized it.

He had thought he could belong here with Sara. He had thought he could fit in. He had thought he could be free and never be what Keeper and Rayor had tried to make of him. The school had wanted him to become a monster. It was beginning to look as though their goal was right, as though that's what everyone wanted … what everyone was!

If it is a monster they want … if it is what they all want…

The two guards holding his arms exchanged startled looks as he began to pull his arms forward and stand. The officer holding the belt tried to beat him back down by whipping him more violently, but every strike of that belt seemed to give Sebastion more strength.

He hated these men, and nearly every person he had ever met. He was done with trying to fit in.

It is time to show them what they have created!

He was nearly at a complete stand now. The guards were eyeing each other nervously as they tried everything to force him back to the ground. One of them was punching him repeatedly in the stomach, but that had no effect.

A crowd had been watching excitedly as Sebastion was beaten for a crime he did not commit. His back was toward them as they waited now in silence while he rose from the ground with the two guards desperately trying to push him back down.

The boyish officer with the belt stepped forward and punched Sebastion in the back with everything he had. His captive, however, only flinched for a moment from the blow and then seemed to gain strength from it.

Sebastion let out a roar of fury and pulled his arms free of the men's grip, his arms and legs becoming a flurry of movement. Each move was so ingrained in him that they came without thinking.

He moved as naturally as a breeze through the trees created for one purpose and one purpose only. Bones were crushed, blood was spilled, and two guardsmen fell within seconds to the ground, like dolls broken and discarded by a child.

Sebastion turned to face the crowd and the two who had betrayed him.

Several people stepped back from his stare, and many women sucked in their breath and covered their mouths.

His lips were pulled back in a snarl. His hair, now out of its binding, was wild and he clenched his fists so tightly that his nails bit into his flesh. But more than that, it was his pale gray eyes, wide and full of such fury that it seemed he had gone mad with it, that made the crowd freeze and watch. Even the young officer with the belt in his hand could not move.

Sebastion's eyes searched for Sara, the girl that he had thought he loved and had thought loved him in return. That very same girl that now watched as he was beaten, unjustly, in front of her eyes. He found her in the crowd and stepped forward.

Sara turned as white as the soft sheets on which they had made love, and her breath caught in her throat. A small puddle started to gather at her feet.

Khan backed away from her and looked ready to run.

Sebastion stopped in his tracks, starting to take in what had just happened. He straightened and ran his fingers through his hair, making it look even wilder than it had before. He looked back at the twisted, broken bodies of the guards.

"HE'S POSSESSED!" yelled out a woman. The crowd was also coming back to their senses.

"Call the Guard!" yelled someone with a high-pitched voice from behind him.

He turned to find the young officer standing there, looking terrified and ready to bolt. He was still holding the belt in his hand, and Sebastion looked at it, feeling the welts now stinging his back.

The officer saw him looking at it and dropped it quickly, spreading his hands.

"Don't hurt me ... p- please," he begged in his whiney voice.

Sebastion looked back at the crowd to find that Khan had run and left Sara still standing there staring at him, frozen with fear. The anger was fading and being replaced with such sadness that his knees felt weak. He stared into Sara's green eyes ... the same eyes he had thought he could spend a lifetime being lost in. His heart felt as if it was being squeezed so hard it would never work again.

"Go! You must go! NOW!" yelled the familiar voice in his head.

He looked around for a way to run.

"He's going to flee!" People in the crowd started to pick up rocks from the road. "Stop him!" A rock flew by his head.

He turned and ran toward the town's center; he was on the opposite side of the big gate.

Some of the crowd tried to follow him, but his long legs carried him quickly through the streets. Dogs picked up the excitement and were barking, and people were shouting as he flew past them. Houses and markets were a blur as he gave all he had to his legs. A well-dressed man came around a corner, and Sebastion sent him crashing into the filth of the street.

The large opening in the wall that surrounded the town was filled with carts and people coming in to sell their wares. A huge wooden cart almost filled the entire opening.

Sebastion didn't slow, however. He jumped onto the seat and ran down the back with his feet moving even before they hit the ground.

It was not long before he was passing farms, and soon after that, there was only forest all around him. Still, he ran.

When he thought it safe, he stopped to drink from a stream. He crashed his face into the water and sucked in as much as he could. Then, rolling onto his back, he breathed in deeply, finally getting enough air into his burning lungs. But that didn't last long. As soon as he could breathe more easily, he got up and ran again.

He was not even sure in what direction he was running. He fought to keep thoughts from overtaking him. He only concentrated on the next step.

Days went by. When he found water, he would drink, and when his legs gave out, he would give them a short rest before continuing. When he was hungry, he would eat whatever presented itself, which mostly consisted of roots and insects. There were rare times when he found a fish or berries, but not often, and he didn't bother to cook or clean what he ate. The fire would take too long to make, and he wanted to keep moving.

Days turned into weeks and weeks to months. Sebastion was becoming comfortable with living like an animal. He carried nothing with him and spent all his time hunting and looking for water. He would stay only a short time in any one spot. If there was any sign of civilization, he would avoid it.

Eventually, his appetite made him pursue larger game, and he was now eating small mammals and lizards. Each area presented itself with a different food source.

A beard had started to grow on his youthful face, and the clothes he had put on that last day in Sara and Khan's house were becoming ripped and filthy from sweat and mud.

He fashioned furs to take the place of his torn clothing, and that provided him with sufficient warmth and protection from the elements.

He was finding that nature provided everything he needed. The needle he used to sew the furs was one he made from the thigh of a rabbit and the thread was from the gut of a rat. Everything he could need, nature had provided. He always moved forward, away from where he had been but toward no destination.

At times, he would accidentally pass close to civilization. He would smell the cooking meats and sweet things in the air, but he would always avoid these places as though death itself lived there.

One particularly wet week, he stopped to make his bed under a large pine. It would provide some shelter if it rained again, and the needles on the ground would make a soft bed, drier than any other he'd find in all this dampness.

Near to the tree, strange mushrooms had grown. He had been taught a lot at the school about vegetation and the mysteries they held, but as he traveled, he saw things in the forest he had never seen before. Trees and plants changed as the days went by and moved on. Even the animals were different, though he thought they still tasted pretty much the same.

He had not had much success with food lately, so he decided to chance the mushrooms. He ate only one and waited to see if it stayed down. When nothing bad happened, he gobbled up the rest.

Having come to appreciate the value of taking a few things with him, he now pulled the furs he used to make his bed. He actually made a nest, more than a bed, and curled up close to the base of the tree.

Sebastion found what he recognized to be bear scat in the general area, and he placed the only weapon he carried nearby. It was a hardwood stick with a sharpened bone embedded and tied onto one end.

Then it began, as it always would. Images of Sara started coming to him. As much as he hated it, her face would always appear in front of him. He hated her and her father ... or whoever he was. Yet, he still missed her. When he had these thoughts, they always made him feel worse than before, and they drove him farther and farther away. He figured the farther he got from Sara, the less he would miss her.

So far, it was not working well.

He rolled over onto his back and tightly shut his eyes. He fought the hotness in his face, but in the end, the tears won the battle. He did not weep openly, but only let the traitorous tears run out of the sides of his eyes. And he did not wipe them away; he thought it was better not to acknowledge them at all.

Looking up into the branches of the tree, Sebastion decided that this tree was very odd … very odd indeed! If he moved his head from side to side, he could make the branches form faces.

He did this for some time before he started chuckling to himself. Though he kept telling himself to be quiet, he kept laughing. Soon he was having a rather heated discussion with himself about whether his left hand was larger than his right as he extended them above him.

Suddenly he jerked up straight.

"Oh, no!" he cried out to no one in particular.

He quickly crawled over to where the mushrooms were growing. He stared at the place where he had plucked them from the ground.

"Don't think I don't know what you are," he said to the ground, then pointing an accusing finger. "I've been taught about all sorts of things, you know." He leaned more comfortably against the tree.

"You fooled me with those little red dots, though. That was pretty tricky of you."

No sooner had the words left his mouth than his head suddenly felt like it was spinning, and he fell over sideways, passed out.

Sebastion felt himself flying above the trees. He didn't see the trees as much as feel them under him as he flew. He knew he must be dreaming, but the wind on his face felt very real.

Up ahead, he saw light, and he was flying right to it. The wind was loud in his ears, and the tree branches brushed against his belly as he flew.

As he got closer, he could see a clearing outlined by the light. It was covered with yellow grass, and in the middle of the clearing, there was a young girl. He could see her standing there looking up at him, expectantly. Her arms were crossed, and she waited there patiently.

She was the most beautiful child he had ever seen. She wore a loose white gown with puffy sleeves at her sides. Her long, dark hair hung down to the middle of her back. Her skin was pale, and her eyes were large and full of life.

Sebastion hung in the air in front of her. They stared into one another's' eyes without speaking. He was starting to feel awkward, floating there, unable to move.

"You're dreaming, Sebastion," the girl said in a confident woman's voice.

"I know," he replied.

She smiled up at him, and he felt suddenly warm and safe. There was something so familiar about this strange child. She stepped closer, lifting his head with a delicate small hand to stare intently into his eyes.

"There is so much of your father, and of course, your great grandfather," she said in that strangely mature voice.

Sebastion's eyes lit up. "You know my family?" he asked the little girl, excited.

"Oh, yes," she replied. "And not long from now you will be acquainted with them ... especially your uncle," she said, smiling sweetly up at him.

She cocked her head to the side as if trying to look deeper to see what he was thinking.

"I see you also have a role to play in something else." Her smiled faded. "So sad," she said, and her eyes began to fill with tears.

Seeing this, his heart hurt. Sebastion wanted to comfort the beautiful child, to take her in his arms and tell her everything would be all right.

She reached up and touched his cheek, and his suspended body tilted down to meet her touch. She took his face in both of her hands and gently kissed his forehead.

Sebastion felt as if a great weight had been lifted off of him.

"Come find me," she said, her nose nearly touching his now.

The beautiful young child suddenly jerked her head sideways to look past him.

"You must wake up now, Sebastion," she said in an urgent tone.

"What is it? Can't I just stay here with you? I don't want to go back there. I hate it there! The people are cruel and they... "

"Shhh," she interrupted. "You must wake up, child."

He thought it strange that she was calling him a child. He started to say something more, but she pulled her hands from his face, and instantly he was flying backward as fast as an arrow. He yelled and grabbed at the branches beneath him. The rush of air around him was so loud it hurt his ears. He tried to cover them, but the pressure of the wind kept his hands out before him.

And then it all stopped.

Sebastion opened his eyes. He was still lying under the big pine tree where he had passed out. He sat up with pine needles stuck to his head. He sensed movement through the branches from the corner of his eye. He grabbed his club.

Crawling forward on his hands and knees, he ducked his head carefully to look under the low-hanging branches that made up his shelter. Two large brown eyes met his. He froze, gripping the stick tightly.

"Why are they all just skin and bones?" A deep voice asked in his head.

Sebastion flung himself back and against the tree base, eyes bulging. He started shaking his head violently.

"Not to mention this one has obviously lost his senses," the voice said again.

"STOP!" Sebastion cried out, banging the palms of his hands against his ears.

The large brown bear stuck his head under the branch. He had a strange, surprised look on his huge face.

"GO AWAY, BEAR!" Sebastion yelled at him, shaking his head back and forth in an attempt to clear it.

The bear let out a massive sigh and pulled his head out from under the branch.

"I must be just as senseless, thinking a smelly and obviously mentally incapacitated human would hear my thoughts."

"Looks like we're both crazy then," Sebastion mumbled under his breath, still banging his ears with his hands.

The large bear head was back under the branch in an instant. This time his huge jaw hung open, and his brown eyes were as big as saucers.

Sebastion looked up and couldn't help but laugh. "Okay. Now I know I'm still dreaming," he chuckled, sure he was still in some kind of mushroom-induced dream.

"Can you hear me, human boy?" the bear asked.

"I am *sick* and *tired* of everyone calling me a boy! But, yes, uh, Bear, I can hear you just fine," Sebastion said confidently. "You see," he started to explain, "I ate some mushrooms earlier, and I have already floated over the forest and spoken to an Angel of some sort." He spread his arms out wide to articulate flying. "So, it's not so unusual to be speaking to a bear, you see?"

The bear lumbered around the tree to where the branches were higher and unceremoniously plopped down on its enormous rump. Sebastion could see him better now, as the bear turned to face Sebastion with its eyes still big as it stared.

They sat there for some time, looking at each other. The bear was the biggest Sebastion had ever seen or at least the fattest. His head alone was the size of a boulder. The bear's eyes were intelligent and seemed to be sizing Sebastion up as well.

"So," said the bear. "A human that hears me when I speak."

Sebastion thought about that for a moment. "If you know how to speak," Sebastion said to the bear, "why is it I only hear you in my head?"

The bear opened his large mouth, and his thick black lips rose above his gums, exposing some very long sharp-looking teeth. He started to bounce his head up and down, grunting.

Sebastion looked at the bear in shock as the realization came over him that the colossal beast was actually laughing.

"You humans are really too much," the bear said, regaining his bear-like composure now. "I know you *people* like to think that your chattering is speaking; however, I am here to tell you that just because you can, admittedly, do clever things with those fancy paws of yours, that in no way implies that you do anything other than squawk as a means of communication. Just because you can't hear something with those sorry excuses for ears does not mean what you don't *hear* does not exist. Such impudence!"

The bear put a superior look on its face, looking for a response.

"This is not happening," Sebastion said more to himself than the bear.

"That figures," the bear said back with a huff.

"What?" Sebastion asked defensively.

"I find a human that can speak, and it has some sort of head injury."

"I do NOT have a head injury!" Sebastion replied angrily. "I have eaten some mushrooms, and this is some type of poisonous effect or something. THAT'S ALL!"

"I see," said the bear. "What if I were to tear off one of your arms ... or a leg, perhaps." The bear lowered his head in a threatening manner. "Would that convince you I am really here?"

Sebastion thought about that. "Okay, umm, Bear. What if I asked you a question that I couldn't possibly know and only you could," Sebastion countered, scratching his dirt-covered chin while thinking it through. "Then I would have to accept the fact that you are a talking bear."

"Speaking bear," the bear corrected.

"Yes, eh ... speaking bear."

The bear shook his head from side to side. "How did your species ever evolve? If only I know the answer, how would what I tell you prove I'm a speaking bear?"

Sebastion had to admit that the bear had a point.

"Perhaps you should just tell me how a person such as yourself is here in the middle of the forest by himself?" The bear suggested.

It was not long before Sebastion found himself telling the bear what had happened at the town. The bear would stop him here and there to say, "You're kidding... " or "That's terrible... " or prompt him to "Please, go on," when he seemed hesitant to continue.

Realizing that this was similar to the conversation he had had with the man in the cell in the dungeon, Sebastion decided that since the bear was just a reaction to the mushrooms, his mind must be using his experience with the man in the cell to make the bear seem real in some way.

The big brown bear became annoyed as Sebastion paused to consider whether he should tell him what he did to the two uniformed men in the town. Finally, frustrated by the long pause, the bear spoke up.

"Do you truly believe you are sitting in front of a large bear having a rational conversation?"

Sebastion shook his head no.

"Then, since I am only a figment of your tiny, chemically polluted mind, what harm could come of it?"

Sebastion thought about this, studying the ground. When he looked up at the bear, he spread his enormous front paws wide, cocked his head to the side, and smiled. Sebastion started to laugh. He made a mental note to find more of those mushrooms to take with him.

He told the bear the rest of the story, leading up to this moment. The whole time, he spoke only to the ground, trying not to make any eye contact, even if it was a bear. When he finished, he looked up, expecting the bear to have vanished, but there he sat, looking rather sad.

"That explains it then," the bear said.

"Explains what?" Sebastion asked, looking back at the ground.

"Why those men have been following you."

Sebastion's head shot up.

"WHAT!?" He was worried but then calmly thought it through.

"Hold on one minute," Sebastion said, sighing in relief. "This whole thing is not real, so those men can't be real, right?" He addressed the big fat brown bear sitting across from him.

"Well, Sebastion, you sure have broken down the logic here, haven't you? Such a clever boy," the bear replied sarcastically.

"However, no matter how you want to look at it, there still are about three rather fixated men following you."

With that, the bear jerked his head to the side and started scratching his furry nether regions.

"No matter how often... " he looked sideways at the skinny boy in front of him, "I have fur there..." he continued scratching and grunted, "uh, it always itches!"

Sebastion didn't even hear him. He was scratching his chin, deep in thought. "I think I'm still under the influence of the drug in those mushrooms," he finally said.

"This again?" said the bear. "How about if I could convince you that not only are you not dreaming, but you are actually here talking with me ... eh, a bear, that is?"

"Speaking," Sebastion corrected him.

"What?" The bear stopped scratching and looked at him.

"You said you don't *talk* but rather *speak*, remember?"

The bear shook his head, acknowledging.

"Perhaps you are not as thick as I thought. Now back to my proposition. How about if I could convince you that not only are you not dreaming, but you are actually here *speaking* with a bear?"

"Well, bear," Sebastion began, sarcastically, "It would be quite a feat to be able to do that."

"Oh, indeed it would!" replied the bear, drawing up his lips in another silent fit of laughter. "Okay, Sebastion, now pay attention," the bear continued, wiggling his hindquarters as if preparing himself for something. "The thing is, I am more than just a bear, and I will be *speaking* to you from time to time." He lowered his head to make the point. "Do you understand what I am saying?"

Sebastion did not remember telling the bear his name. It's my dream, so why should it not know my name? He thought. However, Sebastion was taken aback by the sudden change in tone. Suddenly this huge, friendly, and likable bear was very serious as it looked at him for a reply.

"Yes, bear. I understand. You will be talking to me from time to time,"

"In fact, we have already spoken. Can you guess where?"

With that, Sebastion couldn't help but let out a short snort as he tried not to laugh.

The bear rolled his eyes at him. "Do you at least comprehend the words I have spoken to you?"

"Yes, yes, bear. You're more than a bear, and you will contact me from time to time. I get it. Oh, and we have already spoken, right?" He was giggling uncontrollably now.

"Okay. Now for the unpleasant part," the bear said, getting to his four huge feet. "Please remember that you are a good, kind young man, and no matter what things befall, you must remember to believe in yourself." The bear shook his huge body, sending fur flying everywhere.

"There are men following you, and if they catch you, they will most likely kill you. I imagine it has something to do with what went on in the city. By the obsessive way they pursue you, I can only assume that you have killed someone they cared about or even a family member. Pick up your belongings, Sebastion."

Sebastion picked up his pack made from sticks and fur and his wooden stick, as he was told to, eyeing the bear suspiciously.

"Now comes the convincing, yeah?"

The enormous brown bear charged forward, teeth bared and snarling. He let out such a roar that Sebastion's heart nearly leaped from his chest, his eyes went wide, and he pressed his back against the tree. The bear rose onto his hind legs, which brought it to a towering height.

Sebastion was so frightened he couldn't move.

Like the softest whisper, the voice was in his head again, and it said, "Run!"

The trees and pricker-bushes kept slowing him down as he ran. The sun was going down, making it difficult to see the roots and twigs sticking up from the ground. More than once, he had to pick himself up and rub a swollen knee.

It was not long before he began to hear dogs barking behind him. It seemed the harder he ran, the closer the dogs were getting. He tried eluding them by running up a stream, but the mossy rocks were slippery and slowed him down even more.

The dogs were getting closer, and Sebastion knew he had to think of something.

If the bear was right, these dogs belonged to the men that were following him, and they could only be from the city where he had killed the guards. He was getting scared, but he knew that if he could only shake the dogs from his scent, he could hide.

The dogs were very close now, and he decided that it was no use trying to get away from them. He took off his shirt and, with the help of some branches, stood it up to the height of a man.

By their sounds, about three or four hounds were chasing him. Their frantic barking got louder as they got closer.

Sebastion hid behind a boulder as the dogs turned the corner. He gripped the wooden stick with the sharp bone on end. The dogs were the biggest he had ever seen. Their long legs carried them over the ground like some kind of predatory ghosts. He had not expected them to be so large, but he knew what he had to do.

The dogs lunged and tore his shirt to pieces.

With sweaty, shaking hands but a determined disposition, Sebastion ran toward the dogs with his weapon raised high above his head. I'll have to be fast and accurate. I'll only have one chance at this.

Just as Sebastion came within arm's length of striking the first dog, the bear burst into the clearing. It rose up on two legs and bellowed a challenge to the dogs.

The big canines were only fazed for a moment and then, excited to meet the unexpected challenge, theycharged the bear from all directions. Sebastion couldn't be entirely sure, but the big bear seemed to wink at him as it turned and ran, with almost all the dogs chasing after him.

One dog, however, did not run after the bear.

The massive hound stood facing Sebastion, studying him with big, brown intelligent eyes. The dog was so large that dog and man nearly looked eye to eye.

The hound had nearly knocked Sebastion over when the bear had appeared and startled it. Still, Sebastion could see from looking into its eyes that it was not frightened.

It began to growl deeply and dropped its head carefully, watching him.

Sebastion tightened his grip on his stick but gripping it was getting more difficult because his hands were now soaked with sweat.

The dog made a half-hearted lunge, and Sebastion stepped quickly to the side.

It was apparent now to Sebastion that at this point he was dealing with an intelligent foe that was taking its time and sizing him up.

Sebastion was plotting his strategy to get within striking distance without getting mauled, when three men walked cautiously into the clearing. All three were smiling and, by the looks of it, had no intention of calling the dog off. Instead, they got into comfortable positions, leaning against trees, and prepared for the show.

The hound's eyes never left Sebastion's as it circled him, looking for an opportunity to strike.

Sebastion tried to concentrate on everything he had been taught. Never had he been trained to fight an animal. He knew the dog would be quicker than any man. He committed himself to the fight as he had been taught and looked for weaknesses. The hound was smart, but Sebastion could tell it was also overconfident, for it was letting Sebastion get closer than he should have. He faked a couple of slips, downplaying his abilities, and giving the dog more confidence while getting closer still.

Again, the dog lunged, and Sebastion slowed his reaction so that the dog nearly bit into his cheek as it flew by him. The large dog moved forward and jumped again, but this time Sebastion was ready.

He manipulated his stick with the sharpened bone and shifted his weight so that the dog would fly past him, but then he could use its own weight to tear a gash into its side with the sharp part of his weapon.

The hound yelped loudly and limped a distance away.

An arrow shot out and knocked Sebastion's stick from his hand.

Sebastion looked up from his aching hand to see all three men walking forward, looking very angry.

"I'm going 'ta enjoy ripping you apart, boy," the largest of the men said in the same accent Sebastion recognized from the town he was running from.

"Hold!" yelled one of the men in a commanding voice. "If we kill the boy, we don't get paid."

"Wrong," the large man said, pulling a curved skinning knife from his belt. "We will get paid slightly less if he is dead ... but we will get paid."

They started to argue, and all three came together to discuss whether Sebastion lived or died.

"If we let him live, how are we to transport him all the way back?" They thought about that.

The shorter one, who seemed to be the leader, scratched his dirty chin, thinking.

"It would be harder to transport him if he were dead. Especially since that damn bear ran our horses off five days ago." They all shook their heads, agreeing, and concentrated on the predicament at hand.

Sebastion was nudging closer to his weapon.

"I got it!" one of them said, smiling triumphantly.

Sebastion jumped and nearly bolted.

"We will kill the boy and then chop off his head." The leader smiled back at the other two men like he had solved some grand riddle.

"That way, we can prove that we caught the murderer, and we don't have to lug his body with us." He smiled.

The other two men looked back at him skeptically.

"Come on! It's perfect!"

The large one started shaking his head in agreement when the other shot up a finger and cursed.

"Do we still have the ax?" he asked in a tone that already answered the question.

"Nope. It was with the horses," the larger one replied gloomily.

The man who had the original idea was growing red in the face.

"We don't need any damn ax; we will use your sword." He shot his hand up to silence any more debate as one of them started to open his mouth. "And if your sword is not sharp enough, we will just have to work at it. We got nothing but time."

All three shook their heads in agreement and turned back to Sebastion ... who was no longer there.

Frantically, they started looking around. "There!" one yelled and pointed.

Sebastion was halfway up a hillside.

"After him! Go!" They took off in his direction, running hard, not noticing that the big dog had taken its last breath and died silently in the brush close by.

Sebastion was nearly at the crest of the steep hill when he saw tiny streams of liquid meandering down from the top. He thought it strange, but he had no time to ponder it.

He was pushing his legs as fast as they would go. He could hear the three men behind him yelling curses at him, and he hoped none was smart enough to remember they had a bow.

When Sebastion finally reached the top of the hill, his legs screaming from the steep climb, he slammed into a large woman squatting on the ground. She nearly fell backward into her own urine, but she saved herself by throwing her arm behind her to catch her balance. She had an odd look on her face when her hand sank deep into the urine-soaked mud. Standing up quickly, she looked outraged.

She was by far the largest woman Sebastion had ever seen. She had to be several inches taller than he and weighed at least twice as much, perhaps even three times. She kept glaring at her hand as if she couldn't believe what had just happened as if it had happened before.

The woman balled her wet hand into a fist and slammed it into Sebastion's face. He fell to his knees, covering his cheek.

His three pursuers came over the hill and were quickly on him. One grabbed his hair and pulled his head back, and another pulled an old sword from his belt and lifted it high.

Miska, who had been witnessing the whole thing from the ground, gasped and covered her mouth. She stood and tried to back away, but the chains prevented her from moving.

***

"Hold that sword!" a loud and harsh voice commanded.

The man held his arm up as he looked to see where the voice was coming from.

Ishma sat atop his large black stallion, angrily staring down at the three men. "How dare you put my property at risk!" he yelled down at them. His eyes blazing.

The three women slaves lowered their gaze and stepped slowly back in unison.

The man holding the sword lowered his arm, and the men began exchanging confused glances.

Sebastion still had his head pulled back, but the man holding him had slightly loosened his grip. He considered trying to get loose and was reasonably sure he could probably get free and even fend off the three men hand to hand. Shifting his gaze sideways to the strange-looking bald man on the big horse, he decided he should wait and see whether or not this man would help him before he risked it.

Ishma shifted his weight in his saddle, looking them over.

"Bring this young man to his feet," he commanded.

Cautiously, the three did as they were told.

Ishma looked Sebastion up and down, taking his time.

Sebastion was bare-chested and had never felt so aware of his body before. He self-consciously crossed his arms in front himself.

"How much?" Ishma finally asked the men holding the prisoner.

The three men exchanged more confused looks.

Growing visibly annoyed, he started tapping his fingers on the saddle, and the bald little man repeated himself, this time louder and slower, "HOW-MUCH!?"

"We can't—" one of the men started, but the shorter leader brushed him aside and stepped in front.

"How much do you offer, kind sir?"

Ishma, looking as if suddenly he was in deep thought, and said finally, "Ten silver."

Two of the men gasped, and their eyes lit up. The man in front shushed them, waving a hand.

"How about fifteen silver?" he asked, his voice cracking slightly.

Ishma paused again as if thinking it over once again. "Interesting offer, but how about ... I chop off your feet and watch as you eat them?" he countered, in the same bargaining tone.

The man in front took a step back as Ishma smiled down at him, baring his sharpened teeth.

"From the look of your boots, you've lost your horses, yes?" He looked the three over again. "And by the look of your sword, you've lost most, if not all, of your supplies." His smile faded from his face. "Your accent tells me you're from someplace far from here ... probably from a small town in the North, yes?" He leaned toward them in his saddle, "Tell me, do you have any family that would miss you?"

All three started sputtering out stories of large families and people that were waiting for their safe return.

Ishma half smiled and leaned down, extending his arm. He put ten silver pieces into the hands of the nearest man.

The man looked up to Ishma. "You need to know this boy is a killer," he said gravely.

"Really?" Ishma replied, raising an eyebrow.

"He killed three guards barehanded," the man explained, giving Sebastion an evil look.

Liars! It was only two! Sebastion was still on his knees and tried to look as innocent as he could.

Ishma looked him over again.

"Stand up straight, boy."

Sebastion did as he was told.

"You're tall, but you sure don't look like a man that could have killed three guards with his bare hands."

Ishma snorted a short laugh, dismissing the notion.

Turning his attention back to the three men, he simply and quietly commanded, "Leave now," and urged his horse forward.

The three looked at each other and then at Sebastion, who was standing there looking and feeling lost, not sure what to do next. The one that was standing in front shrugged and turned to leave. The others followed.

Sebastion watched them go but heard someone coming behind him. He turned to see two large guards walking toward him with chains in their hands. He weighed his options. Behind him were the three men that wanted to bring him back to that town, dead, and in front of him there were ominous chains. He chose the chains, figuring he would escape just as soon as the opportunity presented itself.

The guards searched him roughly, wrinkling their noses at him as they did it. His hair had grown long, and he had patches of hair on his face. He looked more like a wild animal than a young man and was sure he smelled as wild as he looked.

"Killed three guards with your bare hands did 'ye?" one guard scoffed, shoving him forward.

"This one needs to be cleaned up, and I haven't the patience or the stomach to do it," the other said, and the first guard grunted his agreement.

"I got an idea!" the second guard said, with a cruel look in his eye. "Violet has already taken a likin' to him; let's have her do the washing, then. It be woman's work anyway." With that, he spat on the ground near Sebastion's feet and laughed.

"Only problem there be Violet ain't your typical woman. She'd just as soon kill 'em as clean him," laughed the first guard.

Sebastion realized who they were talking about and looked in Violet's direction. She gave him a wink and a sinister smile. He wanted nothing to do with that giant woman and was now getting worried.

The second guard scratching his beard, thinking, and said, "Well, there are three of them chained together; maybe the other two will keep Violet from killing him."

They both nodded in agreement, chuckling, and put the shackles around his ankles. Neither wanted to touch the dirty boy with their hands so the two guards pushed him along by kicking him in the backside.

They laughed the whole way to the stream, where the three shackled women waited for them. None of the women were happy about this new duty, but the large woman that Sebastion had pushed into her own urine seemed even less pleased than the others.

As he arrived and stood in front of the women, Sebastion turned red as he began to understand what was going to happen to him. This caused the guards to chuckle and snicker even more.

Even the women were starting to look slightly amused at his obvious discomfort.

Sebastion's head was still swimming, and he wasn't sure if it was the mushrooms or the fact that in just a short time he had gone from possibly being killed to now being washed by three women ... not to mention that not long ago, he had been "speaking" to a giant bear. He snickered to himself at the strangeness of his situation.

"Something funny, dirtball?" one of the guards asked. He stepped close to the young man from behind and pulled his pants down to his knees.

Sebastion's eyes opened wide as he covered himself as best he could with his hands.

The two older women started laughing. Miska turned her head away, feeling bad for the boy. Her face was red, not because of the naked boy, but because of the way he was being treated. The guards could see that this young man was embarrassed, and they took pleasure from his awkwardness, and the women were no better than the men.

"Can we get started then?" the kind middle-aged woman inquired.

The guards paused a moment and then started laughing even more hysterically than before.

Sebastion stole a look from the ground to see the woman who had spoken. He noticed that the one in the middle was not laughing and was staring at the ground looking angry.

She seemed different than the others. Shorter and much younger, she wore a simple white dress of some sort, and her hair had been cut short.

There was blue and red beaded jewelry all over her body, and the ones on her ankles could not cover the fresh cuts from the chains. He thought the shackles must be very painful for her.

She looked up at him and, for an instant, they locked eyes. Sebastion almost immediately looked back to the ground.

Her eyes ... so Kind.

Stop, Sebastion! You're acting the fool again!

Miska couldn't look away, however. She thought the dirty boy with the wild hair was absolutely beautiful. His eyes were bright and smart but tainted with such pain. In that small space of time, she felt her heart do summersaults in her chest.

She couldn't help but think how much he reminded her of the boy that was killed in front of her just a few days earlier. This one was different, though. His eyes seemed to look right through her. She felt, in that short glance, that he saw her soul.

Miska noticed the laughter had stopped. She looked around to see that everyone was looking at her now. The women had disapproving looks on their faces, and the guards started pointing at her and elbowing each other.

"What's the matter, you never seen one of those before?" Violet asked, wrinkling her nose.

"Well, of course—" Miska started, but thought it better to stay silent.

"Into the water, rat!" yelled a guard, kicking Sebastion hard in the backside.

Sebastion tried to gain his balance by stepping forward, but the chains and the pants around his knees prevented him. He fell face forward into the shallow water, scraping his bare knees hard on the rocks and crying out before being submerged.

"Hey!" Miska yelled.

One of the guards looked in her direction, and all humor left his face. He looked her up and down, standing there at the water's edge.

Violet grabbed both women by their arms and walked them into the cold water.

"We have work to do here, ladies."

The guard's narrowed eyes followed Miska into the water before he turned to leave.

Violet leaned close to Miska's ear. "You're too skinny to be picking fights with them guards, pretty one." With that, Violet slapped Miska on the back of her head.

"OUCH!" Miska responded angrily.

Chapter 11 – The Old Knight

Killian's heart was beating fast in his chest, and he was wringing his wrinkled hands together as he stood in the middle of the dirt road. He knew this road well but had not seen it for many years. As boys, he and his brother would ride their horses along this very road and discuss the great adventures they would have when they were older. He couldn't help the great guilt that washed over him when he thought of his brother. It was like a huge ocean wave slamming him down and grinding him into the sharp stones beneath. All he could do was stand there and wait for the crippling feeling to recede.

He had been born two years before his brother, Talion. Still, he would be second to inherit the small kingdom, and great responsibility weighed heavily on his brother's shoulders.

While Killian had been able to spend long hours hunting or practicing the sword, Talion had been studying politics and the essential things a king should know. Though he also suspected it had something to do with his lineage, the fact that he was second, it was more than fine with him. The mother that had raised him for a few short years was not his birth mother. His mother had had difficulty carrying a child and he was the product of a bargain between a healthy woman, whom he never met, and his father's seed. Talion was a great surprise to their parents and to him. A wonderful surprise.

Killian was never much of a student, but he was an accomplished soldier. So it seemed to become apparent early to his father that running a kingdom in a political world was not for this son. Talion, on the other hand, was very astute in his studies, and the inner workings of the ruling came naturally to him.

Killian stared down that road, fighting for memories and, at the same time, trying to push them back. He remembered that the people had loved his family, and the king and he and his brother had loved them back. His head began to ache, trying to recall those old thoughts from so long ago after so long pushing them away.

The Great King bestowed a great honor upon his father for his courage and loyalty in the Eastern Wars. His father had been a great knight, never leaving the King's side, even when all others thought the king would die from a terrible wound earned fighting in a particularly bloody battle. At that time, the Great Kingdom of the West had been ready to forget their wounded king and anoint another king when, as the story was told so many times, Sir Bastion whirled into the meeting hall in full armor.

He had declared that the next one to dismiss the true king as dead before he had indeed passed would find his head on a pike outside the king's rooms. One outspoken advisor from a wealthy house had the misfortune of not taking Bastion seriously. He laughed at the threat and told Bastion he was wasting his loyalty on a king that was as good as dead. The story was that Killian's father had drawn his battle-weathered sword from his hip and taken the man's head off right there in the meeting hall. Some say there are still bloodstains on the great oak meeting table to this very day. It was then that Sir Bastion, Killian's father, had earned the name Sir Bastion The Loyal, and later he became King Bastion of the Eastern Barriers.

Killian had heard these stories hundreds of times, though lately, even these were hard to recall. Standing there, his eyes peering out from deep within the hood of his cloak, the long strands of white hair flapping wildly behind him, he felt as if his feet had been planted there in the road. They refused to move forward. Then he heard the sound of many horses galloping behind him.

As if waking from a dream, Killian slowly moved to the side of the road. Memories cropped up in bits and pieces, and he thought of the times he and his brother had wrestled and exchanged mock insults. Though older and stronger from all his time outdoors practicing the sword and spear, he would let Talion win at times. He was sure his brother knew, but he had never said a thing. They had loved each other, as brothers should.

They made plans for when Talion was to be king. Together they would venture deep into the wilds beyond the vast forest - like their father had. They would build a great host of soldiers and conquer lands where barbarians, elves, and beasts dwelled.

Their plan was always to do this together. Knowing they were two halves of the same coin, they would share their adventures and the spoils, and people would sing songs of the two sons of the Eastern Barriers.

Talion would never put himself above Killian in their stories. He would say 'we' and 'together.' That was the kind of brother he was. The sort of king he would be one day be. That is until the brother Talion loved and trusted more than anyone else would one day rob him of the life he was meant to have. A single tear ran down Killian's wrinkled face deep inside his hood there on the side of the dusty road.

I do not want these memories anymore! Go back to the place you were, and do not come back!

As much as he hated feeling the guilt, a part of him longed for those memories and the days he was with his family.

Five armed soldiers came riding by. They stopped suddenly when they saw an old man standing silently and still by the side of the road. One of the soldiers slowed and rode close to him.

"Ho, there ol' man. What business do you have here?"

Killian did not pay him any attention and, lost in thought, stared straight ahead to where his home had once been so many years ago.

"I said." The soldier tried again, clearing his throat. "What business do you have here?"

The soldier was growing impatient and desperately trying to get a handle on his horse that wanted to keep up with the others. When Killian did not answer again, he looked back to his companions, who were now stopping and throwing inpatient looks his way.

"OLD MAN! CAN-YOU-HEAR-ME!" He yelled out, thinking perhaps that the old man could be deaf.

Killian finally raised his head slowly and looked them over one by one. He noticed that they were wearing mismatched armor, and their cloaks were patched with animal hide in many places. He saw that some of them had swords at their sides that seemed to be rusted right into their scabbards. Looking into their faces, the men themselves were no better. The ones that seemed old enough to fight looked to have not seen battle for many years, if ever.

Some had stomachs so that large they hung over the front of their saddles, but there was no mistaking the insignia on their chests or on their torn flag. It was the black gauntleted fist crisscrossed by the Great King's swords that represented honor, strength, and loyalty. The gauntlet fists was the symbol that represented his father's kingdom. They were once the fists that protected the empire from whatever came out of the forests in the east. Though by the look of the soldiers, Killian suspected they couldn't defend themselves from anything.

"There be thieves and worse on these here roads. I suggest you go back where you came from or come with us," the soldier said loudly, thinking it was the yelling that got the man's attention.

"I can hear you just fine. There is no need to shout like a damn fool," Killian answered back. The other riders starting laughing, and even the soldier addressing Killian started chuckling at his retort.

"I see." The soldier said back in a more normal voice. "And where might you be headed, kind sir?" He asked sarcastically, crossing his hands on his saddle and smiling.

"Where I am headed is my business, and I think you and your *mighty* companions should get back to the barracks before it rains," Killian said. The riders looked at each other confused.

"Why should we get back before it rains?" One of them asked. Killian turned to face the man who spoke.

"Because from the look of your armor, you will finish rusting and be stuck here forever." This sent them all into laughter.

"Perhaps Baran could rust his member into an upright position and finally use it for something other than pissing." One of the soldiers offered, still laughing.

"I don't know what you mean there Feckles." The soldier that must be Baran spoke up, "It works just fine with your sister." There was a round of 'ooh's' and wincing at that.

"Baran?" Killian said, cocking his head, thinking.

"Yes," Baran answered suspiciously.

"I seem to recall a Sir Baran from the great house of the Bull." Killian went on trying to think hard, remembering. The small group exchanged surprised looks. The big knight in the mismatched armor leaned forward in his saddle and looked down at the old man.

"He happens to be my grandfather; The Lady rest his soul." The others nodded agreement at this.

"What of it, old man?" He asked in a dangerous tone. Killian scratched his chin, getting lost in his memories again.

"He was a good man. Very competent with the sword and loyal to my father." When he realized he had said this out loud, he cleared his throat and tried to compose himself. All of them were staring at him wide-eyed, Baran most of all.

"Are you saying you knew my grandfather?" he asked. Killian tucked his hands into his sleeves and bowed his head to hide in his hood again. He spoke up in a humble old man's voice now.

"I have decided that I would very much welcome your assistance in journeying to the Eastern Kingdom. Your lordship's willing, of course."

The closest guard 'hymphed' at him and waved a dismissing hand. Baran was still staring at him suspiciously.

"Come on now, Baran. The old pucker probably heard of your grandfather in a story or something." They all started moving up the road again with the old man following behind as best as he could. Or at least as best as he wanted them to believe he could.

The group of armed men decided it would be faster to share a horse with the old man than to continually slow down and wait for him. Killian thanked them graciously and made a great display of effort straddling the horse behind one of the men.

He was growing anxious, knowing that soon he would be back in the place from which he for so long was shunned. As they got closer, the more he questioned his plan. He was not a man that got nervous easily and was irritated with himself.

Stupid old man! You know you should be at your best, not having your heart race like a virgin maiden on her wedding day. Damn this place! He thought to himself, trying to find courage in his anger. The man on the horse in front shifted his weight in the saddle and looked back over his shoulder, surprised.

"Either you're very excited about being on a horse, or you're a well-armed old man."

Damn!

"As you mentioned earlier. There are many things on this road, and an old man like myself must be careful."

"Uh, huh." Was the soldiers' only skeptical reply. The group rode on in silence after that, and Killian was thankful for it. The men peered into the forest on the side of the road and studied the tracks in the dirt. They were obviously out here searching for something. When Killian's father was king, they were continuously scouting the forest for whatever might decide to come from the Eastern Forest that shouldn't be there.

The road to the front gate was up ahead now, and Killian was having trouble keeping his composure. The gate was overgrown with weeds and vines. The hinges looked so rusted that they would probably crumble to dust if anyone would dare to close it. Garbage littered both sides of the street, and the smell that came from it made him want to retch.

"May I walk the rest of the way, sirs?" He asked the men and hopped down from the horse before they could answer.

"Are you sure you can make it?" One of the men asked. The baggy armor made him seem older, but Killian noticed he looked to be no more than a boy of maybe sixteen cycles or so. His armor was so ancient that Killian couldn't even recognize it. He tried to speak in his best feeble voice.

"It's not far, and my old back is giving me trouble from the bouncing on this damn boney horse." He knew he had made a mistake as soon as his words left his mouth.

"Not far?" The man who had spoken to him first alongside the road asked. "Have you been here before?"

Killian swore silently to himself from under his hood.

"Oh no, sirs. I can smell the sweet smell of cooked meat from here. When you have lived alone for as long as I have, you can smell food from miles away."

He made an 'mmm' sound and rubbed his belly with a shaking arm. He could tell the party was not totally convinced, but they turned and headed towards the outer gates anyway. Baran moved slowly up to the front and leaned close to the man leading them.

"I think d's one should be brought directly to Lara. What you think?" He asked. The man in front glanced behind him.

"Yes, I think there's more to dis' old man than meets the eye," the leader replied. "Don't spook him. Let's get him within our walls before we question him." He looked back again to see if the old man was falling behind and noticed he was gone. The leader pulled the reigns in hard, and the horse reared. The rest of the party looked around to see what the matter was.

"Where'd he go?!" The leader called out, pointing to where the old man had just been. The rider who was riding in the rear seemed confused.

"He was just there!" He said. The leader's face turned red with anger. "Just find him. GO!" He yelled.

"He's just an old man." The young man with the old armor piped in. "He couldn't have gone too far."

"Not too OLD to slip away from you!" The leader yelled. "IDIOT!" The young man bowed his head shamefully and started searching for the old man, knowing that couldn't have gone very far.

Killian was very angry with himself. He had made so many stupid mistakes he felt like slapping something. He knew he had to be careful to not be seen. He was so angry that he had to kick the tree he was hiding behind. Pain shot up his leg, and this only made him more upset. He started quickly slipping from tree to tree and soon he was far off in a wooded area. He was sure the men took him as being too old or inexperienced to cover this much ground so quickly.

The trees that grew near the wall were dense and overgrown with thick weeds. The men would have to get off their horses and look for him on foot. He was betting they were so fat and poorly conditioned that they would give up halfway to where he was now.

Besides, he knew these walls surrounding the kingdom better than anyone. He was taken aback by his memory now of the wall. He hadn't realized that these memories were even still there. Even his dreams only showed his home as a blurred vision, at best.

It's like I've never left.

Sometimes he would stop and stare at one spot as a memory flashed into his head. Trees had fallen, and all kinds of vegetation had grown, but so much of it was still the same. He heard the voices of the men and pulled his thoughts back to what he was trying to do.

The truth be told, this *kingdom* was really a large fort surrounded by a large wall. Most of the people that lived here had some semblance of soldier training or was the family of a soldier. The Great King had called it a kingdom only to give Sir Bastion the Loyal the title of a King.

He was his most loyal knight at one time and deserved the title in his eyes, or so that's what everyone thought. King Bastion was really the commander of a large fort of soldiers that kept the Easternmost section of Torenium safe from attack … and, more importantly, to the king, Sir Bastion out of the great city.

The Eastern Wars had left a significant scar upon this land, and the nobles needed a competent, battle-hardened leader to watch to see if the Easterners were to rise again. Nobody wanted the job, and many knights refused the post.

The Great King at the time had no choice but to ask his most loyal knight, knowing he would not refuse. It was said that the Great King even entrusted Sir Bastion with his greatest treasure as a reward for his loyalty. It was The Crystal Eye of the Gods that some said could allow the one who owned it to communicate with the gods directly.

Killian had seen the amulet many times and even played with it when he and Talion were young. It was just a simple crystal hung on a chain. He had never seen anything special about it.

His father would always tell them how important it was and to respect The Eye, but he and his brother would just roll their eyes, laugh, and make jokes. Never had his father said they could not touch it or even play with it if they were careful. They just thought it another one of the Great King's gifts to make him not feel so guilty about sending his most trusted knight off to the edge of the world.

Another memory flashed before Killian's eyes. It was of him and Talion spending many days being punished for their horseplay and antics. Their mother had died giving birth to Talion. So, it was up to the castle caretakers to make sure their punishments were carried through. They always suggested quite passionately that the King should separate them when being punished, but the King would not hear of it.

He would say, "If those two were ever separated, they would become twice as bad as they already are," but Killian knew better. It was because they were growing up without the discipline that a mother would bring. Their father was there when he could be, but he was busy being the king and leader of the soldiers. The only one they could rely on was each other. Even when they were being punished as children, they watched out for each other.

There was a time when Talion had mistakenly tipped over a vase that was a present from a wealthy nobleman. The head servant was furious. He had heard the noise coming from the hall and ran to investigate.

What he found was Talion standing over the vase looking very sorrowful. But that did nothing to curb the little man's vicious temper.

There were already stories around the castle of him beating the maids and terrorizing the kitchen help. He was a short, skinny man that had a high receding hairline and a long pointy nose like a ferret. When he got angry, he would squint his eyes and point his ridiculously long nose at the one who was about to catch his wrath.

That day he was pointing that nose at Talion. His brother was trying to pick up the pieces of the vase, but the head servant ran over and hoisted him up by the collar. It was not unusual for the castle servants to do this as they were really the boys' surrogate parents. But in this instance, the man pulled him up like a man ready to beat another man.

The angry ferret man balled up his fist and pulled back to deliver a blow. But before he could, Killian was there with a corner of the broken vase pressed hard against the head servant's throat.

He didn't say a word, but the skinny man let go of Talion and spread his hands. Talion ran off, leaving only the two of them in the room facing each other. Killian, seeing his brother was safe, dropped the broken piece of the vase and met the little man's stare. Killian was no more than thirteen cycles at the time but was already taller than the man that stood in front of him.

"You are playing a grown-up game, boy," he remembered the man saying. Killian had said nothing but only returned the man's stare, ready for whatever came next. It was then that he realized not only how much his brother meant to him but also how far he would go to defend him.

He shook his head, trying to shake the old the memory out of him. He realized that the men could have snuck right up on him while he was daydreaming and put a sword through him.

What puckering dark is wrong with me?!

He concentrated and focused. He knew of a place where he and his brother would sneak in and out of the wall when they were young. He was not sure if the place still existed after so much time, but it was worth a try.

He needed to get into the castle, and with those sorry excuses of soldiers looking for him, he'd better be quick. His plan was simple. He would sneak into the castle, find the Eye of the Gods, wherever it was and then trade it for Sebastion's life. He knew Lord Bashor wanted it. He had no idea why or how bad, but he was running out of options, and for some reason, his gut was telling him that this just might work.

The problem was that he also knew Bashor wanted Sebastion, and he did not know which one he wanted more. What he did know was that he was prepping Sebastion for some task.

After that task had been performed, Killian had no idea what Bashor had planned for him… It could even be death. Killian had not spoken to Bashor directly about Sebastion. Still, from what he had heard and what he surmised; the puckering bastard had something evil planned for his ... whatever he was.

Nephew ... great nephew? GODS!

The boy was family, and that was all that mattered. He had to admit to himself that trading the Eye of the Gods was a long shot and would probably get him killed, but it was all he could come up with right now, and he had to do something. If he could only convince Lord Bashor that it was the Eye he wanted and not the boy.

Thinking back, he was not exactly sure why he would always tell Bashor that he could not locate the Eye when his master would ask him to retrieve it. Perhaps it was because he didn't ever want to come to this place again and relive the memories. His head was hurting with everything going on, and he was getting close to where he remembered the loose rocks to be. As he came to the spot, he saw the entire side of the wall had been covered over in fresh mortar.

Damn! Is anything going to work out today?

There was a sharp, crisp blast of a horn, then another. He recognized the meaning immediately. He had grown up knowing the meaning of those signals. It was the intruder alert.

Oh, that's just great. DAMN! DAMN! DAMN!

Chapter 12 – Chains

Sebastion had to admit that the cooling water felt good as he lay face down in it. He could see the round flat rocks on the bottom. He thought it would be nice to just let the water wash over him and never come up again. From his vantage point, he could see three sets of chained feet walking towards him. Each of their steps sent up puffs of dirt on the bottom of the small brook.

One set of feet was much bigger than the others. The small pair in the middle was adorned with blue beaded jewelry that wrapped around the ankles several times. When those feet would move, he could see the raw red skin underneath the shackles. That must really hurt, he thought to himself. Sebastion felt someone grab his hair on the back of his head. Then he was yanked up hard. He took a deep breath and coughed out some of the water.

"STAND UP, YOU STUPID BOY!" The large woman yelled at him. "The water is too shallow for you to drown. Get 'ye feet under you, and you can stop that thrashing about too."

Violet spat angrily, grabbing his shoulders and centering him. The hair pulling hurt so bad he saw stars. He wanted to hit the big woman in the face. He quickly got his feet under him and wound up, as best as the chains would allow, to take a swing and found himself face-to-face with the girl who had the pretty feet again. He knew this because she had the same blue beads around her neck and wrists.

He thought her face was thin and pretty, but it was her eyes that Sebastion could not look away from. They were big, brown, and beautiful. He shook his head to try to clear it and realized what he must look like standing in a stream being held up by his hair by a large woman with his arm locked back, ready to throw a punch. Worse yet, he was completely naked except for his pants around his ankles. He dropped his hands quickly to cover himself. He gave Miska a shy look before trying to reach down for his pants. She let a half-smile touch her full lips and shook her head at him.

He couldn't reach his pants because the large woman still had him by the hair. He turned slightly to look her straight in the eye. She was tall for a woman, but Sebastion was still half a head taller, and she was reaching up to hold onto his hair when he stood.

"Let go." He said in a severe tone. They stood there, staring at each other for some time before Violet finally let him go. She was smiling, but Miska thought it looked forced.

"I would hate to anger you, my prince, but those pants will have to go," Violet said.

"They won't come off past the chains," Sebastion grumbled back, giving Violet a dark look.

The three women surrounded him then and went to work scrubbing. He just stared straight ahead, going somewhere else in his head. He tried to think of anything else but what was happening to him right then.

Miska worked out the knots in his hair. "By the Lady, have you ever combed this out?" She asked him in a quiet and disgusted voice. He said nothing, staring straight ahead at the forest he wanted to be back in.

"Where did you get all these scars?" She tried again. Sebastion ignored her. Violet backed away and took on the role of ordering the other woman where to wash.

"He probably got them from getting caught stealing." She said in an all-knowing tone.

"I'm no thief, woman," Sebastion said under his breath.

"Just ignore her," Miska said, soothingly combing his long hair into a tail now and tying it back with a piece of leather she had pulled off her wrist.

"I'm no thief." He said again to Miska only. She stopped for a moment and looked at him and into his eyes. She saw his eyes were full of pain but there was also truth.

"We are all the same here." She said sadly back to him. He turned his head to look at her. He thought that she was beautiful and seemed kind, but he had been fooled before by a pretty face.

"We are not the same." He said, turning away again.

"Oh, I see." Miska took his remark to mean that she was beneath him because she was a Demsy. Throughout her life, people had always looked down on the Demsies because of their life without walled boundaries.

"I can see you're much better than I am. Maybe you're a prince or even a Great King? And I am just a lowly Demsy? Is that it?" She asked with anger rising in her voice. "Well, I got news for you 'Prince of Dirt'; we are both equals now. Here I am a slave, and so are you!"

She jerked her last knot into the strand of the leather binding. Sebastion flinched from the pain. Miska stood as best she could with the chains and put her hands on her hips.

"He is done. Can we go back now?" She asked Violet.

Violet smiled down at her.

"' Afraid it's not up to me, little one. Not even up to the Prince of Dirt here." She laughed. She whistled at the guards and pointed at Sebastion, who was in the middle of the pond with his pants around his ankles. The guards came to meet them.

Sebastion had no idea what the pretty girl was talking about, and he had no idea why he felt guilty about something he didn't even know he did. He did not mean to insult her.

All he meant was that he was not like other people. He shrugged and pulled up his pants. He had to admit it felt good to be clean again. He made his way out of the pond the best he could with the chains. The guards grabbed his arms and pulled him towards the wagons where Ishma was waiting.

Ishma was leaning against a covered wagon, smoking his long pipe, when they arrived. Sebastion was surprised that the man was even shorter than he had first thought. Though he did have to admit that Ishma was broad in the shoulder and looked fierce with his tattoos and shaved head.

"So, it seems there is something underneath the filth. What have you got to say for yourself, slave?" Ishma emphasized the *slave* to make the point that he was his now.

Sebastion just stared at the ground, not saying a word.

"The silent type, I see. The problem with that is I can't tell if you can speak at all. If you can't speak, then the price for selling you goes down." Ishma took a significant drag off his pipe.

"Can you speak, slave?" He waited patiently for Sebastion to answer.

"Yes, I can speak." Sebastion finally answered quietly.

"That's good, but we have another problem," Ishma said, looking Sebastion up and down again. "You obviously have not had a decent meal in a very long time. I can't get top money for a tall young twig, can I now?"

Sebastion did not say a word. Ishma turned to the guards.

"You will give him double rations, and he will pull the carts with the horses half the day, each day." He waved them all off then and continued smoking his pipe. They put Sebastion in the same cart as Miska and her father.

"No funny business," one of the guards said, smacking Sebastion on the back of his head and winking at Miska. When their meal came, he was surprised at how much they gave him. His bowl was full, and he was given a half loaf of bread. The other slaves eyed him jealously.

"It seems to be the Prince of Dirt comes with special privileges," Miska said to her father. Her father snickered, winked at her, and went back to his bowl.

Miska's father had already lost much of his weight and had dark circles under his eyes from not sleeping. At night he would stay awake as long as he could to watch the other slaves in the cart. He did not much like the way they looked at his daughter when they thought he was not watching.

Now he had another male in the cart with them. He feared that one day he would sleep too soundly, and the worst would happen. That was what always kept him awake. He knew he was a very sound sleeper, and it scared him to no end. He tried several times, giving this new boy his fiercest look, but the skinny boy never looked up from his food.

A guard yelled, and the carts started moving. Sebastion nearly fell over from where he was sitting. A good portion of his food ended up on the floor. One of the men in the back of the cart slowly moved forward in his direction.

"Hey, boy. How about you share some of that food, heh? Surely you can't eat all of that yourself." He said, smiling a crooked smile. Sebastion tried to ignore him, but the man was insistent and getting closer.

"Come on now, share some with me, and I'll be your friend. Everyone needs friends, don't they?" The man said, touching his leg.

"Leave h-" Miska started, but before she could finish, Sebastion struck the man hard in the face with his fist. Sebastion did not speak a word and continued eating as if nothing had ever happened. He did not hit the man hard enough to do any damage, just enough to let him know that he would be best to leave him alone. The man recovered quickly and moved to the back of the cart, grumbling and swearing under his breath.

Miska watched, surprised and a little frightened, but it was Miska's father that was the most disturbed. He had seen this boy bat away a grown man like he was a fly. What would happen if this boy decided one day that he wanted his daughter like he did that food he was gobbling down? He would need his strength, but to have it, he would need to sleep. But if he slept, what would stop anyone from taking whatever they wanted? He sighed and rested his head against the cart, the bags under his eyes tried to pull his eyes closed. How am I going to keep her safe? He thought miserably.

***

The next day, Sebastion was dragged out of the cart before they started moving. One of the four horses was unhitched from the team, and Sebastion was chained there taking its place. He was glad to be out of the cart. Being outside in the forest for so long had heightened his senses, especially his sense of smell, and being in the carriage was torture for him.

One of the guards had given him an old shirt, and he had tried to bury his nose into it all night, but the shirt had been only slightly better than the cart. There were times throughout the night when he thought he would be sick. And that was not even mentioning the threatening looks the big man with the girl kept staring into him all night. Now they expected him to pull the cart like one of the horses.

One of the guards chained him into place and leaned in close.

"If Ishma finds that you ain't pulling your share of this wagon, he'll put you over there in the covered wagon with the Beast." The guard jabbed a thumb in the direction of another cart, laughing, and gave him a shove.

Sebastion looked over at the covered wagon, wondering what he meant about a beast. His curiosity was soon forgotten when the whip cracked, and the horses started moving.

He was behind one of the two horses upfront. He tried to push, but it was hard keeping up with the pace. He had to jog and push at the same time. They had taken off the chains on his ankles, but it was still awkward having his wrists chained. He hated being locked up in that filthy smelly cart and so decided he would do his best here with the horses with the hope that if they saw he was trying, they would be more apt to keep him outside.

It was the middle of the day when the guards pulled the carts over for a break. The slaves were filing out to relieve themselves on the side of the road. Sebastion was on his knees, resting his head against his arms. His whole body was numb, and his heart was still racing. One of the guards came over and started unchaining him. Sebastion looked up and thought he saw a hint of respect in his eyes.

"Didn't think you had in 'ya, lad." He said. "I think Ishma wanted you to give up so he could teach you a lesson. I believe you have ruined his day." He gave him a half-smile.

He helped Sebastion up and brought him over to where they were handing out water. The three chained women were in line as well, and Miska caught Sebastion's eye. At first, she looked sympathetic but then rolled her eyes at him, looking away. He drank the water the guards gave him and sat on the grass as the other slaves took turns getting their water. He hoped they hadn't planned on hooking him up again. He didn't think he could go more than a short while before passing out and being dragged.

"Oye, You slave!" Ishma yelled from atop his horse. "Your duties are not over. Get back to those horses." He said, pointing with his whip. Sebastion started to get up, and a guard came over to his side.

"Sir, if he does too much and gets wounded, his value *will* go down."

Ishma's face turned red. "Do not lecture me on how to care for MY slaves!" He yelled, considering what the guard had said. "Put *it* back with the rest of them." He said, finally yanking his horse's head away from them.

"Looks like it's your lucky day, boy." The guard said with a smile. "Not many get to anger him and get their way." He winked. He started pulling Sebastion towards the carts when Ishma yelled back to them.

"Hold!" He rode back. "I have something else for this slave to do." He said, smiling. "He will clean and feed the beast. This will be your duty every day after you have done your time with the horses." Ishma beamed as he rode off again.

Sebastion turned to the guard, confused. The guard just shook his head sorrowfully and brought him towards the covered wagon.

The wagon was the same size as the others, but it was covered with a large tarp. The guard instructed Sebastion that he must uncover the cart only on the side, facing away from the slaves.

"If they saw what was in there, they would all get spooked, and we would never get them calm again," he explained.

The guards around the cart all kept a reasonable distance away from it. When they were told that Sebastion was the one to care for the beast, as they called it, they all looked physically relieved and started laughing and patting him on the back. One of them handed Sebastion a bucket full of dead rats with a relieved expression on his face and pushed him towards the cart. Two guards lifted the tarp on one side with long sticks.

"This is how it's done. Don't expect us to do it again." One of them said, averting his eyes to not look inside. "An evil thing." He muttered and spat on the ground.

The tarp still covered half the cart, so it was dark, but he did see something sitting in the back. The smell of feces and rotting flesh smacked him in the face like a fist. The scent in the slave's cart was pleasant compared to this. The guard gave him another shove, and he moved forward with his bucket of dead rats. He moved in close then and peered inside.

"I wouldn't get that close," the guard warned.

The creature inside lifted his head and looked back at him. Its eyes glowed green, reflecting the light. Its ears were long and pointed on top of its head, and from what he could see, a light fur covered most of its body.

It was built mostly like a man only slightly shorter and very thin. It sat there with its legs crossed underneath it much like he sat in the slave cart, Sebastion thought. All he could do was stare at it in awe.

He had never seen anything like this creature in the forests and was fascinated by it. The beast returned his stare, its eyes never leaving his. Finally, it blinked, and Sebastion took a step back startled. The animal's lips curled up slightly, revealing long sharp white teeth much like a man's but much longer and pointed.

Did it just laugh at me? Sebastion thought, unsure.

"Okay, boy ... enough gawking and get to working." The guard said, already moving away. He quickly explained to Sebastion what he must do as he walked away hurriedly.

All he was to do really was clean out the cage and throw in some fresh rats, though the rats he was holding in the bucket were far from newly killed. He looked at them and was glad he didn't have to eat them. The guards left him long sticks to rake the cage and told him to toss the rats in when he was done.

Sebastion took the sticks and started raking out the filth. It was grossly obvious that it hadn't been done in some time. The beast just sat there, watching him curiously. Once when the stick with a rake on the end came close to the creature, it absently batted it away. Sebastion nearly jumped out of his skin when the creature's claw-like hand hit the stick. The beast rolled its lip up again, seeing this.

"Yes, very funny," Sebastion said out loud to himself. The beast's ears perked up, and he gave Sebastion a confused look.

A guard came cautiously up behind him. "Here," he said, pushing a tray at him. "Finish up and eat your meal. Apparently, you're to be getting more than the rest of us, so don't be wasting it. Ye' hear?" The guard lifted his hand to give Sebastion a smack on the head but looked over at what was in the cage and thought it better to move away. He left, muttering under his breath.

Sebastion carefully threw the rats into the cage and sat to eat his own meal. The beast got up and walked on two legs to the front of the cage and put its claw-like hands slowly around the bars.

Sebastion stopped mid-bite and watched. He was shocked by how much it moved like a man. He bit down on the broth-soaked bread, and it watched him. It would, at times, look at his bowl. It's no wonder it is looking at my food with the rotten rats that they were feeding it. Sebastion ate what was in his bowl but saved most of his bread and hid it in his shirt.

He got up to put away the long sticks, and when he was close enough to the cart, and sure no one was looking, he slowly reached into his shirt and tossed the bread to the beast that was now watching him very closely. It caught it right out of the air and hid it behind him.

"What are you?" Sebastion asked, too low for anyone to hear him. The beast's ears twitched, and the lip curled up again for an instant. It then slowly got up and walked back to its spot in the back of the cage. Sebastion covered the wagon, and the guards escorted him back to the other slaves. He was so tired from running with the horses that he fell asleep the instant he was in the cart, bad smells and all.

There was a point when the cartwheel ran over a large rock, making it jump so that he opened his eyes slightly. Across from him was the pretty girl that hated him. She was leaning against the wall with her legs crossed in front of her. She had acquired a shirt somewhere, and it was tucked into her stained white skirt. It was hot, and she had many buttons undone.

He could see that the sweat was running down her neck and disappearing between her breasts. He saw that around her neck hung a talisman of some kind. It seemed to be a flat stone with the profile of a woman. It did not seem to go with the rest of her beaded jewelry. When his eyes moved up to her face, he found she was looking right back at him. She raised her eyebrows as if to say, 'what are you looking at?' But it was her father who leaned into his line of vision and gave him a menacing look. Sebastion let his eyes close again, and he drifted quickly off to sleep again.

He dreamt of Rayor and their adventures together before the school. He put his mind there often when he wanted to forget. Those times were the best in his life. Rayor was more like a father to him than anyone had ever been. He considered him family and felt guilty when he thought about how he had left him there at the school.

But he also felt anger. Rayor had been the one to bring him to the school in the first place. He hated it there and Rayor knew he did, but still, they had stayed. Even after he was nearly beaten to death by the other boys there. There were times when he would think of the leader of the boys, the knife sticking out of him. That would always lead him down the path of the men he had killed, and before he knew it, he would see their faces, and he would wake up breathing heavy and sweating.

This night he did not dream of them, however. Tonight, he dreamt of Rayor and the Roanstors. Only this time, the Roanstors had the face of Ishma, and instead of stuffing meat under their shells, they were stuffing the bodies of the slaves into it. He saw the pretty girl with the beaded jewelry down a hill, and she was calling to him, but he could not move. He looked down to find that Serin was there on the ground, holding his ankles. The Ishma Roanstors were getting closer to the girl, but as hard as he struggled to get to her, Serin held him tight. He looked over, and Rayor sat with Keeper laughing and watching as the Ishma Roanstors were nearly on top of the girl now.

Then there were two glowing green eyes in front of him. It was the beast, and he was stretching his clawed hand towards him. Before he could think, he took its hand, and he was pulled out of Serin's grip. He woke instantly, finding his hand was outstretched towards the roof of the cart. But no green eyes were looking back at him.

***

Killian knew of another spot where he could get into the castle, but he wanted to avoid it if he could. He leaned against a tree, trying to think of any other way in. The more he thought, the more he got frustrated. He could hear the men not far off now. It would not be long before they would find him if he lingered much longer. He cursed his luck and the mortar around the loose rocks. He and his brother used this spot to get through the wall often, but now it seemed this was not going to work.

Killian took a deep breath and silently moved through the trees. *This is going to be much more difficult than I had anticipated.*

He was feeling the ache in his head getting stronger. He knew exactly where he needed to go, but he would have instead gone back to Bashor's castle then the place he knew he must go now.

I don't know why I thought this was going to be easy. What did you think this was going to be, a fun little family visit? You are a puckering, stupid old man! I'd be better off crossing swords with a dozen of The Great King's Western Guardsmen than this. DAMN THOSE ROCKS!

The small cave he knew of was not far off, and he did not have any problem getting around the men who were looking for him. It seemed the Eastern Guard no longer used the dogs in their searching, or they thought one old man was not important enough to rouse them.

By the looks of the men, Killian suspected that they might have eaten them, along with the decent horses, long ago. It had been a long time since he was a soldier, but he would not tolerate those swollen bellies, from old or young! He would have those running drills all day and eating grass before that ever happened. It was a dark damned disgrace to his family's name.

The small cave was right in front of him now. He looked at it for a moment to gather his strength. He looked side to side for anything that would keep his attention there instead of going in. When he found none, he closed his eyes and listened, still nothing. He pulled the sword from under his cloak and quietly made his way to the small entrance.

The cave was small; they had found it long ago when they were little and exploring their home, and he suspected it was more used as a roadway for the rodents that lived within the walls. He went to his knees and slipped into the small hole that was the entrance. He held his sword in front of him and hoped that nothing meaner than he had taken residence inside. He thought it ironic that he should be entering his old home in the same way and place that he had left it so many years ago. He crawled and slithered like a snake through the cave. There was no light and Killian had only his memory and the feel of the rocks to guide him.

The rain had found its way into the crevasses, and Killian was getting soaked to the bone. He thought to take off his cloak, but it was the only protection against the sharp rocks that lined the top. There was a time or two that Killian thought he would get stuck, but he twisted and turned like a worm to get through.

***

Baran was riding slowly on his horse through the brush. The others were on foot, but he preferred the ability to look over the vegetation in case the old man tried to make a run for it. He was studying the ground, perplexed, but it had nothing to do with the lack of prints below.

The old man spoke as if he knew his grandfather. That would be impossible as that would make this old man a one-time Eastern Guard, and there are no Loyal Guards unaccounted for. All Guardsmen names are carved into the castle wall, and as they pass on, the carvings are filled with silver ... at least they were. Now it was silver-like paint as silver was far too expensive. Even the Guardsmen whose bodies had been gone missing in battle would be far too old to be this man. I don't like mysteries, Baran thought, scowling down at the ground, looking for tracks.

"How can a puckering frail old man disappear without a trace, like d's?!" He said out loud at no one in particular.

The men with him only shook their heads, just as frustrated, and continued searching. What was it the old man had said precisely, Baran scratched his thick beard? He said, my Grandfather was competent with the sword and loyal- why would the old man say my Grandfather was loyal? Of course, he was loyal ... no, there was more. Baran sat up in his saddle and looked up at the sky.

He was rubbing his thumb up and down the hilt of his sword. He played it over again in his mind, trying to figure out what he was missing. He was not that fond of remembering and struggled with it in his head. The old man had said, 'Sir Baran was competent with the sword, and loyal ... loyal to ... what was it ... loyal to ... my ... father. That was what he said! Sir Baran was competent with the sword and loyal to my father. Baran proudly looked at his companions, very satisfied with himself for remembering the whole thing.

"Did you find anything?" One of them asked.

"No, no, I just remembered da't all."

"Did you remember that you are very fat and ugly, also?" Feckles said, strolling by him. Baran gave him a sour look and went on with his thoughts. It didn't matter what his friend Feckles said. He had remembered what the old man had said, and that was what mattered. It was a strange thing to say, though. His Grandfather, Sir Baran, was loyal to only one man. He was sworn to the Eastern Guardsmen and to King Bastion. Why would the old man say such a thing? 'Loyal to my father'. If that were to be true that would make him the once good King Talion and if not him then... Baran's eyes opened wide, and he sat up straight in his saddle. But that would be impossible. No one lives that long. But what if...

Without saying a word, he turned his horse quickly and galloped back to the Castle. The rest of the men watched, confused, as he left.

"That man gets stranger by the day," Feckles said, shaking his head. "Everyone, keep searching!" He yelled to the other men. "He probably forgot his third lunch." He mumbled to himself.

***

Killian had been crawling for some time now. His knees were raw and bleeding, and his hands were cut in many places by the sharp rocks littering the ground, but he crawled on. He could feel the cooler air and knew he was getting close. Soon a soft light was filling the small cave. He slowed and listened but heard nothing but the dripping of water somewhere off. He rounded a corner and saw the opening. He lay on his stomach and moved very slowly to the edge like a stalking cat after a mouse.

Soon he was extending his neck and peering over the ledge. He was halfway up a high wall. So, he was at a vantage to see the large room lit by two windows on either side.

The small windows were barred but let in enough light so he could see. The opening he was peering through was so small it looked almost impossible for a man to fit through. Still, Killian had gone this way before and twisted his head sideways and started wiggling his body to get through the hole. It was going be a long drop down, but if he hung from the ledge, it shouldn't be too bad.

He twisted and turned to position himself right, and all the time made every effort not to look at what was lying in the middle of the room. He concentrated only on getting through the hole and grabbing the ledge. Because of his positioning, he would have to get his head and most of his body out first. He wiggled and twisted until half of his body was through the hole. Using his arms to leverage himself, he peered around the room, still not letting his gaze go to what was there.

When he was satisfied, he let his legs slowly drop down the wall. He rested his chest against the cool damp rocks and his head on his stretched-out arms, not yet wanting to commit to the drop. Of all the places to be in this castle, this is the one he would have least chosen. He sighed and wondered how long he could actually hang there before his arms gave out. He was quite strong, even compared to a young man, and tried to convince himself it might be an interesting experiment to see how long he could hang on.

***

Baran nearly jumped off the horse before it stopped. He handed the reins to a surprised boy and slammed his shoulder to the door. Inside, some of the Guardsmen were eating and leaning against the wall, quietly.

They became very alert when Baran crashed into the room. He looked them all over, one at a time, looking for someone in particular. The man he was looking for was sitting at a large table, frozen in the process of taking a bite of bread.

"Where is Lara?" Baran commanded.

The man at the table gave him a doubtful look. "Why is it any matter of yours?" He asked back. "And furthermore, Lara is busy working on a proposal to the Great King and not to be bothered." The man said this dismissively sticking his nose up in the air and returning to his meal. The man was small and wearing bright colors, obviously having a high opinion of himself.

Baran took off one of his mismatched gauntlets and marched forward to face the sarcastic little man. The man shifted in his seat but held his ground. Baran grabbed the man by the front of his tunic and lifted him above the table. There was a reason he was called Baran the Bull. The little man looked down at his dangling feet.

"I will not be provoked by an ill-smelling brute." He said, putting his pointy nose up in the air again.

Baran snorted and dropped the man bodily onto the table with a crash. He put his gauntlets back on and faced the crowd that was watching them with amusement.

"Does anyone know where I can find Lara? It's important!" He added the last as a plea, but the crowd exchanged confused glances. Baran shook his head, exasperated, and headed for the stairs. The little man rushed after him and pulled at his cloak in a meager attempt to stop him. Baran lowered his head and sighed miserably.

"Yes?" He asked.

The man put his hand on his hips like an angry mother would.

"You may *not* disturb Lady Lara." He growled up at him. Baran turned around and gave the man a look that made him take two steps back.

Whispering very low, Baran said, "Touch me again, and I'll hand you your entrails on a puckering plate." Baran smiled wide at him. The little man gasped and retreated hastily to his table.

The big knight ran up the stairs, opening each room without luck. On the highest floor, in the darkest corner, he tried to swing open the door, but this one was locked, and he took his frustration out on it by kicking it. The door swung open, and Baran saw Lara run across the floor nude. Her feet flip-flopped on the wood floor as she ran. Baran thought he saw a bookshelf sliding against the wall.

A hidden door.

Baran knew he should be looking away but could not help but watch Lara's frantic search for something to cover herself. She was a tall woman, sinewy, and very muscular for a woman, he thought to himself. She had scars on her body that looked like she had been in battles her whole life.

In Lara's desperation, she grabbed a curtain and ripped it from the window. The pieces that held the curtain to the window crashed to the floor at Baran's feet. She whirled at him, the curtain spinning around her like a bullfighter from the Great City, which Baran the Bull did not miss the significance of.

"Yes, Baran?" She said between clenched teeth.

"I uhh-uhh," He started.

"Baran, I am rather … indisposed at the moment." She said, smiling, but her dark eyes were filled with rage.

"Yes, My Lady. It's just that…" Suddenly Baran felt very foolish with what he was about to report.

"Please, Baran, do continue. If I stand here much longer like this, I'll catch a chill, and you will find yourself doing two double shifts walking the Castle Path."

Baran grunted, as he knew very well about walking the Castle Path. It meant he would be on foot walking around the outskirts of the wall from sundown to sunup. *Blast! Why do I not think before I react? Big dumb bull!*

"My Lady, Ww believe there is an intruder at the wall." Baran finally spat out. Lara's dark eyebrows came together in a frown.

"Who?" She demanded.

Baran tried to think before answering, but Lara cleared her throat and extended her hand, making small circles as a sign for him to hurry up.

"It is an old man we found on the road." He said. He could see her face flushing for the first time, but this was not from embarrassment.

"You have kicked in my door to inform me that an old man is loose *behind* our walls?" She said this almost in a whisper.

Baran was desperate now.

"My Lady, he said that he knew Sir Baran the Bull." He blurted out. Lara started to say something but stopped and thought before continuing.

"What did this man look like?" Baran started tapping his head with his fist, trying to remember. Lara tapped her bare foot on the cold wood floor, waiting for him. The curtain was scratching her skin, and the door remained open, so anyone passing by would see them. Worse, they would think she was here naked on purpose with this half-wit.

I should have married and never accepted this responsibility. Foolish woman!

Lara sighed deeply and leaned against the wall, waiting patiently for Baran's reply.

***

Killian had dropped from the wall and was now sitting in the dark, damp room, staring at his hands. He tried to keep the memories at bay. He concentrated on his hands, thinking he had lived longer than most men and fought more battles than one man should have to.

He reached into one of the many hidden pockets of his cloak and pulled out a talisman. It was a simple flat stone with the silhouette of a woman. He sighed and ran his fingers across the lines on the rock.

"If he knew I still owned this, he would have me 'reconditioned' all over again. Only this time more severely ... if that is possible." He whispered to himself. The clouds must have moved away from the sun because suddenly the room was brighter. A small window on top of the wall was letting in a bright beam of light. It shone down onto the wall across from it. A cloud moved across the sky, and the sunlight moved to rest on the sarcophagus in the center. "May the Lady help me and keep me strong." He prayed for the first time since being in the service of Lord Bashor.

"Hello, my son," came a deep, familiar voice from across the room.

Killian reacted quickly, drawing his sword and holding it before him. "Who's there?" He demanded.

"Always the soldier, Kil," came the voice again.

'Kil,' n*obody has called me that for a long time.*

"It would go far better for you to show yourself now than to make me find you," Killian said harshly.

"I am here, son." The deep voice said again. But this time, it came from behind the caskets. Killian squinted, peering through the beam of light, and indeed a tall man was standing there by the wall. Killian quietly made his way along the wall to have a better look. He pressed his back against it and held his sword out, ready for anything. Killian froze as the man came into view and stared in disbelief.

"It cannot be." He whispered.

"Your eyes do not deceive you." His father replied.

"This is a trick!" Killian said, searching the room with his eyes.

"This is no trick, my son." King Bastion said.

"Stop calling me that!" Killian snarled. "I am not your son. If you were truly the ghost of my fa- of Bastion, then you would know that I no longer have a father."

King Bastion's eyes flared and stepped closer to Killian, who pressed his back to the wall and raised his sword threateningly. "Do not come another step."

"I AM YOUR FATHER!" Bastion yelled with a gauntleted finger in Killian's face. His voice was so loud that it boomed off the walls. "Alive or dead, or anything that has or will happen, I will *always* be your father. I do not know what powers were put into action for me to stand here before you. *But* know this.

If you denounce me again, I will take you across my knee. Right puckering here!" Killian suddenly felt as if he was ten years old again and had made some mischief with his brother. All doubt drained out of him like a water-skin turned upside down. "

"I am sorry ... father," Killian said, lowering his sword. "I did not think it was possible to ever see you again ... or if you ever wanted to." Killian pulled the hood over his head and lowered his gaze. He heard Bastion sigh.

"Kil, we need to talk. I do not know how much time I have, and there are things you must know."

Killian shook his head from beneath his hood, not thinking he could bear what his father would say.

"Father, do you not remember what I have done ... what I am now ... and who I serve?"

"I know who you are." Another voice said from within the room. Not as deep as his father's, but all too familiar. Killian dared not look up. A coldness ran through him, and his knees began to shake.

"Please, this is too much." He pleaded. "Not you. I cannot face you." Killian put his hands to his face and began to weep as his sword clanked onto the floor, forgotten, at his feet.

Talion of House Loyal and brother to Killian stood beside his father, watching Killian's reaction.

"Father, perhaps this is just too much for him. Maybe we should leave and give him more time to process this."

King Bastion shook his head. "I do not know how much time we have, son. The truth must be told, and I think it must come from you." Bastion's youngest son nodded his head in agreement, staring at the ground, not wanting to continue. "This will be hard for him to hear. So much time has gone by for him."

Bastion sighed his acknowledgment. "He may have a part to play in all this. Though, I fear, it may be too late. He may be our last hope."

Bastion frowned and touched the crown on his head as if, even in death, its weight was heavy to bear.

"Tal, tell your brother now everything … everything. Do not spare my feelings nor my loyalty. It was my loyalty to the Great King that nearly destroyed everything, and it was that that shattered the one thing I should have protected the most … my family."

Bastions' shoulders drooped. "Tell my oldest son why I choose you to be King in the East, Tal. Tell him I have always been proud of him and that … that I am truly sorry."

Killian felt more than saw the King disappear from the room.

"Father?" He said, raising his head from his hands. Only Talion stood there now, looking very sad.

"Brother," Talion looked down with sad eyes, "You can't know the pain that lingers with him still, even in death."

Killian lowered his head, sliding against the wall and sitting on the ground with his knees against his chest.

"Tal, no words can I say-" Killian began sobbing again. "I am a traitor and a murderer of a brother I loved!" Killian heaved with every sob that seemed to come from his soul. Talion moved closer, sighing at his older brother.

"Oh, Kil. That's just it." He knelt down close to his weeping brother. "It wasn't you."

"What do you mean? It was!" Killian wept, looking up from his hands.

"There is much to tell you, brother," Talion said with a pained look on his face.

Talion, once the King of the Eastern Guard, took a seat on the ground next to his brother. A brother who had for so long been accused of murdering him.

"How is it that you are here … brother?" Killian asked between his fingers.

Talion smiled. "How is it that you are still alive after all these years, Kil?" Killian thought a moment and stared again at his wrinkled hands. "I am alive because I am cursed by Bashor." He answered.

"Wrong," Talion said flatly. "You are still alive because somebody, or I should say something, more powerful than Bashor wants it that way."

Killian cocked his head confused. "Who?" He asked.

Talion shrugged his shoulders, "All I know is our family; namely you, have a part to play in the future."

Killian was getting more confused. "Tal, what did you mean when you said it was not me who killed you?" Killian, for the first time, met his brother's eye. He thought he looked exactly as he did before he died. Perhaps a little younger and definitely more rested. His brother was tirelessly working as a king. "I remember the night we fought, and I remember ... what happened. It is *always* with me."

Talion shook his head. "What do you remember, Kil?"

"I remember everything. I play it out over and over every day."

Tears were coming to his eyes again. "I have betrayed not only you and father but myself. You were not only my brother, but you were my best friend and ... my King."

Talion made a derogatory noise in the back of his throat.

"Not much of a king. I do not believe our family was ever meant to be Kings. We are better suited to a knight's life, not one governing and posturing. Oh, how I envied you when you became a knight. Imagine that, a king envying a knight?"

Talion smiled, shaking his head, remembering.

"Alright brother, what do you remember of that night? What color were the clothes I was wearing? When you see me do I have the scar on my lip that you gave me when we were boys? Think of everything."

Killian started to think. He never tried to remember the details of that night. Instead, he was always trying to block them out. The memories were still there, but he never wholly entertained them long enough to search out the details. He had spent all his energy trying to bury them. He had no desire to bring them back. He did not want to be tortured by them here in his family's catacombs, surrounded by rock walls and speaking to his dead brother.

This was madness!

But something inside him was telling him that he needed to do this. He could not imagine how or why he was being allowed to see his dead father and brother, but he knew that he must do as he was told, and he must do it quickly. He closed his eyes and began to bring back the dreaded memories. He remembered his brother was wearing a red shirt with the insignia of the Eastern Guard, and he had on a flowing blue cape with fur sewn into the collar. He told Talion what he remembered, and his brother started shaking his head as he always had when he knew something and Killian did not.

"What?" Killian asked.

"Come on, Kil," Talion said, smiling. "When have I ever worn anything so ... Kingly?"

Killian lowered his eyes, thinking to himself.

"Do you remember the day before you supposedly killed me?" Talion asked.

Killian looked up at his brother.

I am having a conversation with my dead brother. I am genuinely crazed now.

"Yes, I remember the day before. We were receiving a royal messenger from the Great King."

Talion started nodding his head up and down. "Yes. What was I wearing when receiving this Grand Messenger of the Great King?" Talion asked in a sarcastic tone.

Killian started chuckling despite himself.

By the Lady, I miss you, brother.

"We told him the castle was infested with lice, so he would have to sleep outside beyond the wall." They both started chuckling now. "He was so angry he called us barbarians and said the Great King would take away your crown," Killian said.

"Yes- Yes Kil, what was I wearing, though?" Killian wiped his nose with the back of his hand, absently. "What you always wear. Father would say 'That boy would wear his riding clothes on his wedding d-'
The realization began to come to him, and Talion smiled.

"Why would I dress so 'Kingly' on just a regular day when I would wear riding clothes on my wedding day, as our father was so fond of saying?" Talion said this imitating his father's voice.

"What are you saying, Tal?" Killian asked. His brother put that ever-knowing look on his face that used to drive him crazy.

"I'm saying it was not you. Lord Bashor, or whatever he was calling himself at the time, tricked you into thinking you, um ... you know, killed me."

"If it was not me. Are you saying that, Bashor..."

Talion closed his eyes a moment before answering. "It was late, and I was preparing for bed. That meant going over papers and putting seals to letters. There was a knock at the door. I thought nothing of it and answered before asking who it was. As I opened the door, you were there- or I thought it was you. You asked to come in. I thought it very peculiar that you would be so serious. You came in and walked to the window as if waiting for something. I heard shouting and running on the stairs outside my door."

"This is not how I remember it," Killian said.

"I know, brother. Bear with me for a few moments more." Talion closed his eyes and went on. "The door burst open, and the next thing I know, a knife is plunged into in my chest. I see the guards' eyes go wide, not believing what they are seeing. I look up to your face, but it is not you. The skin became scaly, and the eyes glowed red like fire. I looked down at the knife in my chest, and it was your knife; only the hand clutching it is not yours anymore. I fall to my knees, and I hear the guards cry out, 'Killian, why!?' I try to tell them it was not you, but my life was nearly gone, and I was too weak. I did try to tell them, Kil. It was some vile creature I've never seen before. I am sorry, brother."

"…an Under-Wraith," Killian whispered, more to himself.

"Yes, Kil."

"But, my memories are so real," Killian said, holding his head.

Talion shrugged, "Is it so strange?" He asked. "Have you not seen stranger things than false memories?"

Killian nodded his head in agreement.

"But why?" He asked.

Talion wrung his hands together and looked up at the sky.

"Okay. This is a little more complicated. Do you remember how father got the title Sir Bastion The Loyal?" Talion asked.

"Yes, Tal. I am old, but I am not quite senile … at least I don't think I am." He gave his brother a look.

Talion knew that his brother was thinking that this could be less than what it was. "It's a gift that I am here."

"A gift from who?" Killian asked suspiciously. "When was the last time you prayed to The Lady?" Talion said seriously.

"Today was the first time since … since I can remember."

Talion smiled.

"No. Do you mean to tell me that the Lady-"

"You draw your own conclusions, Kil."

Killian just shook his head in amazement.

Talion looked up suddenly.

"Brother, I do not have much time left."

Killian nodded for him to go on, and Talion continued. Killian knew most of the story of how their father received the title of King but some things he had not heard before.

"As you know, the Great King was injured in battle so many years ago." Talion went on. "What you must know is his body was taken over by the Dark Mage. At one point, the Great King had asked father to give him a merciful death."

Killian was shocked to hear this now after so many years.

"Why have I never been told about this?" He asked, unable to keep the anger from his voice.

"Killian, you must know father wanted to protect you. He always was going to tell you everything. But … well, you know what happened. Please, I must finish within the time I have been granted."

"Sorry … sure, Tal. Go ahead." Killian's head was spinning with it all.

"Everyone believed the king had been healed. But father was suspicious. The other knights thought it a miracle of The Lady. It is said the knights wept and re-pledged their allegiance to the King, but father did not believe it. Soon he had convinced others at the Palace that something was wrong. The King had no choice but to prove that father was wrong in his suspicions and was truly the same king. The King had him sit with him to greet a possible suitor to be queen from a rich family far from the southern border."

"Yes, I know this part, Tal. Father met our mother then, right? They fell in love and moved to the Eastern Border, right?"

"Yes, brother. But there is more to it than that. The Great King didn't just decide that it was alright for them to get married when she was promised to him to be Queen of the Torenium Empire. He used it as an excuse to banish him to the Eastern Barrier. He used their love for each other as an excuse to send him away."

Killian started shaking his head. "That is not how it was. Always father told us … BOTH of us, that they married with the blessing of the Great King."

"*Only* after they agreed to come to the East and never come back to the castle again. Father now had something to lose, and he and the King knew it. He had no choice but to agree to leave. He had to leave the King in the hands of the dark mage. He had no choice but to swear to himself that he would one day return and kill the mage that now controlled his friend, the Great King."

"Are you kidding me with all this?" Killian asked, spreading his hands. "What does any of this have to do with me right now?"

"Father swore that if he didn't avenge his friend, the Great King, his firstborn would."

"So that is why his second born was to be king and not his first," Killian said, finishing for him.

"Yes, Kil. He always hoped you would be the one to finish the job he never could." Talion looked at his brother, sadly. "He still does."

"And what of the Eye?" Killian asked.

"Father heard that it could be used to draw out evil entities. It's supposed to have so many different powers that no one really knows what it can do."

"If there are any at all," Killian added.

"That's true."

Killian shook his head, feeling it ache from it all. "So now I'm supposed to either go suck out the evil with the Crystal Eye of the Gods or kill the Great King of the entire empire because it's not really him and because father swore it? Is that it, Tal?"

Talion nodded his head, acknowledging.

"This is a lot to take in," Killian said.

"I know, my brother, but time has limited our means in telling you this," Talion said sadly. Killian scratched his head, thinking.

"I can see how my memories could be false now, but I need to know how and why?"

Talion shook his head in agreement. "When you slept, the Under-Wreath put you under a spell. Those memories are what he wanted you to see. When you woke, it seemed so real that you had the urge to flee even before the guards chased you through the castle."

Killian nodded, taking it all in.

"That bastard Bashor needed you to get the Eye. As long as we had it, he knew that there was a chance we could save the Great King. He meant to use you to bring The Eye to him."

Killian rubbed his ancient hands across his bald head.

"I meant to trade The Eye for the boy's life." He said quietly.

"The boy?" Talion asked, confused.

"Yes, Sebastion. Lord Bashor has some interest in your grandson." Killian explained.

"WHAT! My what?" Talion stood up straight, his eyes big. "What are you telling me, Kil?"

Killian looked around, confused, and stood. "What do you mean?" He asked.

"Are you telling me?" Talion swallowed and composed himself. "Are you telling me that my son's child still lives?"

"Yes, I thought you would have known that," Killian said, apologetically.

Talion just stared at his brother, eyes wide.

"Tal, are you alright?"

Talion took the crown from his head and brushed his hand through his long hair.

"I thought the child was killed by the Great King when he was born?" Talion said.

Killian shook his head. "The Great King promised to keep the child alive if his great-granddaughter promised to tell where she was to meet Ryder. Your son was ambushed there and killed. I am sorry, Tal."

Talion frowned down at his brother. "I knew how my son was killed. I just had no idea his son still lived."

"There is more," Killian said quietly.

Talion looked at his brother, curiously. "The Great King went back on his word and killed the child."

"You just said he was alive. Which is it! Is he alive or dead?"

"Both, I'm afraid."

Talion shook his head from side to side, confused. Killian couldn't look him in the eye.

"There were two, brother. Sebastion had a twin. One was killed so one could live. Bashor erased the memory of Sebastion from his mother, at her request. We promised to keep him safe, and she agreed to forget him. We took him and have had him ever since."

Talion thought for some time, rubbing his bearded chin before turning back to Killian. "This changes everything." He said in a whisper. "To the seven hells with all these plans of saving the world. Our family has been used as pawns long enough." Talion suddenly started to shake.

"Tal, what's wrong!" Killian reached for his arm "Listen to me, Kil ... brother. You watch over your great-nephew." Talion now went down on one knee, obviously struggling against something that couldn't be seen. "You are his only hope. You are his only family. Bring him his grandfather's sword and do not let him be used as we were." Talion was now on both knees. "Kil, we will once again ride free together through the forest as brothers. No more of our family should have to suffer as we did ... as my son did." A tear ran down Talion's face, and he started to become translucent.

"TAL!" Killian cried out and tried to grab his shoulder, but his hand passed right through him. "NO!" He yelled. Killian could only watch as his brother began to disappear.

"Tal ... he looks just like father. He even fights like him. You'd be so proud." Talion smiled wide before disappearing, "Thank you. Keep him safe, brother..." Were his last words.

Killian suddenly found himself alone in the large cold room. He felt so emotionally drained and physically exhausted that he could sleep for a month.

So much...

He was tricked into thinking he had killed his own brother with false memories. Why, after all these years, did he not face those memories and see the truth. He was so angry with himself.

Too scared to see the damn puckering truth. Coward!

And now, the Great King is a puppet of Bashor? Somehow, he had taken over his body after a wound in battle long ago? Actually, the Great King should be long dead by then, so ... maybe that made sense too.

Damn it!

His father swore that he would either save his friend from the evil inside him with the Crystal Eye of the Gods or ... set his soul free by killing him. Was he supposed to kill the Great King?

Killian rubbed his head and slid to the ground again, thinking. No, this is all just madness. He was going to keep Sebastion safe, he decided. His brother was right; it had to be family first. Damn the empire to darkness! He was going to find Sebastion and go to some corner of nowhere where they could live out the rest of their lives. He was going to watch Sebastion and his young family grow, and he will be happy bouncing his nephew's babies on his knee. Puckering hell with this! He was decided.

* * *

Sebastion's body no longer ached like it did pulling the slave cart with the horses. It had been many weeks now, and he could feel himself getting stronger. The double rations and sleep helped as well. He was finding that being a slave was not that different from being at the school or even with Keeper. In fact, it was better. He was fed regularly and had a place to sleep. He found that the pretty girl with the big eyes would keep looking at him when she thought no one was watching. He mostly ignored her and her oversized father. It was strange that the more he left her alone, the more she seemed to get angry.

Sebastion couldn't understand why he let it bother him ... but it did. He thought he would try to talk to her, but the opportunities never came. Whenever he would get close to her, images of Sara would pop into his mind. Part of him missed Sara, and the other hated her so much he wanted to strike anything close by. He was determined to never let himself be in that position again.

Never again!

It was getting dark, and it was time for him to feed The Beast. He was finding this time to be his favorite part of his day. For some reason, when he was with it, he felt comfortable. The guards still treated the cage as if it was diseased. They would leave him alone when it was feeding time. Sebastion would always give the strange animal some of his bread and more that he saved from his dinner. He stopped using the long polls and reached right into the cage directly. Each day, he would hand the food off to the creature like it was a person.

He was fascinated by how many of its mannerisms were man-like. When he was alone with the strange thing, which was most the time, he just talked about this and that as if it could understand. He didn't like talking to the other people in the slave caravan.

Still, strangely, he very much enjoyed talking to the animal in the cart. At times, the beast would even look up with some emotion as if he understood him. Sebastion knew this was his imagination, but he did enjoy pretending at times that he was being understood.

Even though he was feeding it bread from his meals, he still placed the dead rats into the cage. He would put them off to a far corner, knowing he would only be cleaning them up later in the day.

After a particularly grueling day of pulling the cart up what seemed to be a never-ending series of hills, he was released and allowed to go about his nightly duties. The sun was going down earlier, and it was getting cooler. Sebastion could see his breath. He pulled the tarp from the cage that held the Beast. It was back in the corner as it always was.

"Hello, my friend," Sebastion said, hoisting up the tarp. "How are you doing today?" He asked.

"I wish I could convince Ishma to let you out for a while each day. I think he's afraid that we would get spooked or something or that you would run away. I know I would if I were you."

He looked around for guards, and when he saw none, he reached into his shirt and handed over the bread and some meat. The Beast regarded him with his big green eyes before moving quickly and gently to take the food and retreat to the darkness at the back of the cart again. Sebastion stared at it, wondering how something could look so human and yet like an animal at the same time. He sighed and started cleaning the cage. He saw the creature move his hand strangely, from the corner of his eye, and looked up. It was looking right back at him in a curious way. When it did nothing, he shrugged and started to turn away, but again the Beast moved its hands in a series of movements.

Sebastion, seeing the sequence of movements, froze in shock.
It can't be.

He started to regain his composure and laughed at himself for being an idiot. He just saw what he wanted to see. Still, it did it again, this time watching Sebastion very closely with those big intelligent eyes. It was signing the language of the hand that Sebastion had learned at the school. Those movements only meant one thing. It was signing the word *'Why?'*

Sebastion looked around to see if anyone was watching. The guards were far off eating their dinner and paying them no attention.

"Can you understand me?" Sebastion asked. The beast stared at him for a moment and, finally, after deciding something, moved its clawed hands. *'Why do you bring me food?'* It asked.

Sebastion smiled, letting out a short laugh. He looked around again and moved his own hands.

'I do it because you do not like rats.' He answered. The Beast took a bite of his bread before he started moving its hands again. *'My name is-'* and it spelled out the word M-O-R-A-K-Y-E. Sebastion couldn't stop shaking his head in disbelief. *'My name is...'* He started, but he wasn't sure he wanted to use his real name but this ... thing ... trusted him. *'My name is Sebastion'*

'Greetings, Sebastion. Thank you for your kindness. I did not believe humans had it in them.' Morakye signed. He even smiled that snarl of a grin at him. Sebastion thought about that for a moment before replying. *'I'm not sure they do. I do not consider myself one of them.'* Sebastion said, with the smile fading from his face.

Morakye nodded his head slowly as if he understood. *'From what you have told me, you have not been treated fairly by anyone thus far.'* Sebastion jaw dropped again.

'How do you know how-' Sebastion turned red as he realized how Morakye must have understood him all this time. *'Did you understand all the things I was saying?'* He asked, more than a little embarrassed. Morakye looked up from his bread and saw the expression on Sebastion's face and was taken aback.

'I meant not to be rude. If the other humans found that I could understand them, there is no telling what they would do.' Morakye spread his arms slightly and made a short quick bow that could only be an apology. Sebastion just watched, shaking his head from side to side again. *'Please, do not tell the others of our conversation.'* Morakye asked.

Sebastion snorted.

'They wouldn't believe me if I did.' Morakye still watched Sebastion for his answer. Sebastion realized what he was waiting for. *'Of course, I promise I will not tell.'* Sebastion said with his hands. Morakye physically relaxed.

"Hey, boy!" One of the guards yelled, "Are you sleeping, or are you cleaning."

Sebastion started cleaning out the cage as Morakye ate the rest of the meal Sebastion had brought for him.

The next day, Ishma kept all the slaves inside the wagons. They were passing some small villages, and he did not want to let them know what he was carrying. The guards had put large tarps over the carts to hide them. They were only allowed out when they were far between the villages. This meant that Sebastion had spent the entire day inside with the other slaves. He was nervous about having to deal with Miska's angry stares for that long.

It was the middle of the afternoon, and the hot sun was beating down on the tarps. Even in the coolor temperatures, it was making it very hot in the carts. Sebastion was doing his best to pretend to be asleep. Miska's father was fighting the urge to pass out. His shirt was soaked through, and his hair was plastered against his head.

"Father, we should be getting water soon," Miska said unconvincingly, in a sad voice. Her father just shook his head and tried to breathe. The man with the bad teeth at the back of the cart was observing them. Sebastion had noticed that he had not taken his eyes off Miska from the first day he was put into the wagons.

The man reminded him of a vulture circling a sick animal. Only this vulture wasn't after the dead. Sebastion thought of what it must be like to be a father and daughter here as slaves.

Miska sat close to her father, holding his hand and resting her head on his shoulder. He couldn't but notice the frightened looks she was making at the back of the cart.

Despite the temperature, she had covered herself the best she could. Her shirt was buttoned to the top, and her knees were tucked under her skirt. Only the tips of her bare feet could be seen. She even had her short hair brushed forward to hide as much of her face as she could. Sebastion, for the first time, saw that it was more than just the man in the back that was watching the two of them.

The women in the cart gave her cold stares, and the other men all watched her like hungry wolves. He was surprised that he had never noticed this before. Maybe it was because he was so wrapped up with his own problems and trying to avoid her angry looks that he just never saw the rest of the people in the cart with them. He couldn't understand why everyone seemed so upset. They were all in the same predicament. If anything, they should want to help each other. This only helped him be convinced he was somehow different from them. Then a thought struck him that made his stomach hurt. By not doing anything, wasn't he just like the others? Maybe he was becoming one of them. He did not want to be like all the cruel people he had encountered. What was happening to him? Was he becoming one of them?

He sat up and stretched as if he was waking up from a long nap. He made a point to flex his now expanding muscles. He looked over at Miska, and her father sucked in a breath. He tried to sit up to face him, but Miska held him back with one delicate hand.

"My name is … Sebastion. I come from a village far to the North." He said, trying to smile disarmingly. Miska and her father exchanged confused looks at Sebastion's sudden show of comradery. Miska gave him an unsure half-smile and nodded.

"I have read about Demsies but have never actually met one." Sebastion tried again in a soothing tone. This time both Miska's and her father's jaws dropped open as they stared back at him.

Uh, Oh. What did I say?

"You can read?" Miska asked, shocked.

"Yes." He answered, confused.

She smiled wide in a mocking way. "You mean the Prince of Dirt is an educated nobleman, then?" She said this with anger coming back into her eyes.

"Well, I guess I am," Sebastion said, smiling back at her with the same amount of sarcasm.

"Tell me, Prince." She went on, crossing her arms in front of her. "Why is it you seem to think you are above us?" She asked.

Sebastion thought he understood what she was trying to do. She was trying to use him to find common ground with the other slaves. If they all hated him, they would have something in common.

Fine by me. If they want to hate me, why should I care?

"Why?" he asked crossing his own arms now in front of him.

"Yeah, why?" She asked.

"Because I am not like you all here." He said, trying to sound superior. The other people in the cart started whispering and cursing at him. One old man even threw some hay that had littered the ground at him. "Furthermore." He went on, smiling even more sarcastically. "I find that the smell you all give off is offensive and not at all to my liking." He put his nose in the air like he had seen the teachers do when addressing the other students. The cart full of people were silenced. Miska's father started coughing, which sounded suspiciously like laughter. The old man who had thrown the hay started smiling and then started laughing, holding his stomach. Soon the rest joined in. Even Miska was covering her mouth, trying not to catch his eye.

"I find the odor offensive as well!" Said the old man holding up one finger as best as his chains would let him and pretending to be someone important. This was not what Sebastion had in mind, but it seemed just as effective. The slaves were patting each other on the back and making jokes of their own. Smiling, Sebastion looked over at Miska. She darted a look at the man at the end of the cart, her smile faded, and she again took her father's hand. Sebastion looked over at the man and he was not laughing with the rest of the slaves. He continued to stare, unabated, at Miska. His eyes were mere slants in his face, and they were consistently moving up and down her. He is going to be a problem, Sebastion was sure of it.

Chapter 13 – Dark Rock Castle

The room was warm and well lit, with many candles. Scrolls littered the many desks that lined the room. The walls were gray granite, but most of them were covered in slimy mold from the moisture that dripped everywhere. Off in one corner was a large tub that bubbled and steamed with blood. There was a light timid knock on the great wooden door. When no one answered, it creaked open slightly, and a small man with a grotesquely burned face peered inside.

"Master?" He asked softly, with a slur. The man no longer had much of his lips and saliva ran down what was left of his chin.

He tried one more time, but there was still no reply, so the burned man moved silently into the room. He was wearing a red robe that was filthy and rotting. Food and grease spots were so thick on his cloak that if it were not for the red color that adorned it as it hung loosely around his slumping shoulders, it would have been thought black. Flies buzzed around him and took as much from his flesh as they did the rotting food on his robe. He no longer had feeling in what was left of his face and so did not seem to mind the company of the insects.

He rubbed his burned hands together, nervously surveying the room. He turned his head from side to side, looking around, inadvertently opening the burn blisters on his neck. Puss ran into the neckline of his robe.

"Master?" He said a little louder.

The bubbles in the tub became more violent, and an emaciated hand that looked almost like a claw emerged. The hand gestured the burned man closer to the tub. The man took small unsure steps towards the bubbling blood. He was rubbing his hands together faster, and small pieces of skin fell off, leaving a trail on the ground below as he came closer to the tub.

"Ma- Master?" He asked quietly.

The clawed hand slowly submerged back into the tub.

"Why do you disturb me?" It was a whisper that filled the room. The burned man's head snapped up to a severed Boar's Head hanging on the wall above them. Did the whisper come from the Boar, he wondered?

"Master." The burned man said again, turning from the tub and the Boar's Head repeatedly. "One of your servants is ... eh, missing."

The mounted Boar's Head high on the wall moved slightly from side to side. Its eyes, now glowing red, focused on the little man. The burned man walked up to it, respectfully.

"Master, we have not heard from-"

"I know of what you speak." The Boar's Head whispered down at him irritably. "He thinks he is acting with free will, but his actions will only speed my plans."

The burned man nodded and smiled a lipless grin.

"Find the boy!" The Boar's Head whispered harshly. The red light in its eyes flared up and then went black. The burned man shook his head nervously and turned to leave.

"And bring me more blood." This time an Elk Head whispered the command in the direction where the burned man was now leaving.

"Y- Yes, Master." The man said, bowing to no one and closing the door behind him.

***

Melodia had made a small fire in the forest surrounding the dark castle. She sat there, warming her hands and watching intently. The walls were of dark stone and looked as if they had been pulled from the ground in which now stood a hulking structure of black rock. Behind it was a mountain composed of the same black material. The whole area looked as if a great fire had at one time burned the life from it. Even the forest she was now sitting in seemed to have been sucked of life. The trees were long dead, and there was not a single bird anywhere in sight. The only thing alive was the slick green and brown mold that was growing everywhere. She had a hard time locating dried wood that didn't have any of the slimy stuff covering it.

As much as she wanted to leave the place, she knew it was precisely the place that she was looking for. Her search was easy, and she wanted to believe it was The Lady that drew her to it, but she knew otherwise. Each step she took closer to this castle, the more she felt distant to her deity. She made an unconscious reach for the talisman that hung around her neck but stopped before her hand touched it. She would not try to take comfort in it as she knew this mission was not on her behalf, and *she* would most certainly not approve.

Melodia was here to free a murderer from the service of evil. She had no idea how she was going to do it or what she needed to do, but she knew what her heart was telling her. She was meant to be with Killian, and she would not let him down again. If she had to walk to that castle and take the life of the man inside, she would do it.

In fact, that was precisely what she planned to do. She had no stomach for skulking around and always found that she did better when meeting obstacles head-on.

She also had no desire to spend the night in the dark, dead forest. The sooner she did what she came to do, the sooner she could once again be with the only man she had ever loved. She let her head fill with memories of Killian when they had first met and tried to gather strength from them. She closed her eyes and let the memories wash over her, but as soon as they came, so did the memory of the look he had on his face that day when he had left her ... the look of such deep hurt that it would change him forever, or so she believed. He had trusted her with his secret, and she was unable to accept him because of it. She lived her life, helping others, and serving a gracious God that was known for love and empathy. But she couldn't help the one she loved... She had failed him. She was here now to fix that.

It is time to meet this dark master of yours, my love.

She kicked dirt into her little fire and prepared herself for the confrontation she was about to have. She flung her pack across her shoulder and started for the road that led to the castle. She hadn't taken two steps when she heard the sound of hoof-steps coming from not far off. She ducked behind a substantial rotting oak and waited to see who it was that would be coming to visit a place like this.

The forest was silent and her hearing good, so it took some time before the knight finally rode by. The knight was wearing his helmet and had his facemask down. His cloak that must have carried his insignia was folded and secured neatly behind him. There was nothing that gave away where this knight was from.

To a normal eye, it would have been nearly impossible to tell where this man originated, but Melodia was not normal. She was a priestess of the Lady of Light, and she made it her business to know things. The armor was vibrant, and even with the muck the knight had obviously tried to hide it with, there was no way tot stop the sheen on the metal underneath. There was not a spec of rust, and the man in the saddle rode high as if he was used to commanding. This was a knight of the Great City, and she was sure of it. There was no doubt. What was a knight of the Great City doing here in the middle of nowhere and visiting the home of Bashor? She was suddenly very intrigued by what was going on here.

She watched as the knight rode to the castle and stood outside the front doors without dismounting. He just waited there.

Finally, the big doors creaked open, and a small man in a dark red cloak ... or perhaps black, came into the entryway as she watched. They exchanged words, but even with her keen hearing, Melodia could not make out what was being said.

She thought about getting closer, but the trees were so sparse and dead that she was afraid she would have been seen. Instead, she strained her ears but could only make out their voices.

There was the deep tenure of the knight and the strange way the man in the cloak spoke. That one's voice seemed to be pained and unnatural.

She was getting frustrated and thought she might stick to her original plan and just walk right up. It was then that she saw the small man walk back to the door and reach in. He came back out with large saddlebags that seemed to be very heavy. The little man struggled to hand them up to the knight. The knight grabbed it from his hands, greedily. He then guiltily looked around the area. That's when he spotted her pack sticking out from behind the tree. She hadn't realized it was sticking out as far as it was.

She tucked behind the tree and squeezed her eyes shut.

Stupid girl!

She heard heavy hoofs heading out on the road again and at first believed it was the knight coming to see who she was, but as she listened, she found that the sound was moving further away. She peeked around the tree again and, sure enough, the knight was riding hard in the opposite direction. However, the little man was still there standing by the door, staring directly at her. The sun was going down, and she could only make out his silhouette now.

Well, I might as well get this over with.

She took a deep breath and stepped around the tree and headed straight for him. As soon as her boots hit the road, she started getting her confidence back. With each step she made in the direction of the castle; the more anger ran through her. Whatever waited for her in that forsaken castle- she was ready. She had not traveled all this way to be intimidated by a craggy rock or by a cowardly knight of the Great City. She was here on a single-minded purpose to free Killian from whatever bargain he had made with the man in the dark castle. She could see, as she got closer to the man, that there was something definitely wrong with him. He put his hood down, and the fading light reflected off his skin in an odd way.

Melodia faced the man, now a short distance away. They stood there looking at each other and waiting for the other to say something. To him, she was the most beautiful woman he had ever seen. She stood there in her green cloak, looking down at him like a conquering general.

Her arms were folded across her chest, and she had a very confident look on her face that he thought she must have worn a lot. She was like the image of some deity in a painting. He could not find a single word to utter. He could only stare at her through his nearly nonexistent burned eyelids.

He wanted to reach out to her and see if she was real. He even started to but saw a sudden change in her eyes that made him recoil. He couldn't help thinking that his master would be very pleased with him if he were to bring her to him.

If he still had all his flesh, he would have even kept her for himself. She must not have liked that look in his eye either as her right hand moved ever so slightly to her belt where a long knife was tucked.

Melodia fought another wave of nausea, looking at the man. He was the most disgusting thing she had ever seen. Every exposed part of him was burned beyond recognition and oozing puss from blisters that completely covered him. At one point, he even tried to reach out to her, and she thought she was going to be sick.

The flies buzzed around his head in a swarm, and she thought she even saw maggots crawling in the crevice that must have been at one time an ear.

She wanted to speak, but she was just too afraid of what would come up from her stomach. So, she waited there for him to say something. That was when she was able to recognize a look on the grotesque thing's eyes that couldn't be hidden even by one as badly misshapen and burned as he. The anger came back like a thunderbolt in the night.

"Are you Bashor?" She asked, sternly looking down at the burned little man.

He snorted a laugh that sprayed fresh snot onto his face from the hole that was at one time a nose. He didn't bother to wipe it off but instead took the opportunity to extend his hand again in an introduction.

"I am Grothar." He said, smiling up at her. She felt another wave of nausea but pushed it away with pure will.

"I am not in the least interested in you then. Take me to your master or whatever he is to you. I am here to see Bashor." Without thinking, she took a step back away from his extended hand. He looked disappointed and unconsciously reached up to his neck and scratched open a blister. She watched as red and yellow puss ran into the cloak.

"You don't like my looks, then?" He asked, smiling. She instantly wished he hadn't. "Maybe you find my master better company then, huh?" He started laughing and waved her inside the door. She could feel his sickening yellow, blue eyes on her as she slipped into the door past him.

"I's think you will be most welcome." He said. She stopped and waved him ahead of her to lead the way. He did as requested but gave her another disappointed look before leading her down the hall.

The castle inside was nothing like the outside. There were bright tapestries and rugs all over the floors and walls. There was also beautiful furniture for as far as her eyes could see. The foyer was bright and open. There was a window high up on a tower that let in light.

It was nearly dark, and yet there was light enough to light most of the rooms. Grothar led her through a large hallway to a staircase that was the biggest she had ever seen. It led up and then twisted. She couldn't tell where it went from there. Curious, she stopped to look up. The little burned man patiently waited for her to finish.

"This place is amazing." She said more to herself, than Grothar.

"The master likes nice things." He said, winking. She couldn't tell if the wink was meant for her or to chase away a fly. Further down the hall, they came to another staircase that was smaller than the first but not by much.

"Go to the top and push open the doors there. Master Bashor will join you shortly." He bowed slightly, grinning a sickly smile. She was glad to see him go and felt like she needed a bath.

At the top of the stairs, there were two large doors and she gently pushed one open. It led to a library the likes of which she had never seen before. The room was fully lined with books. There was a second floor that held even more. There were many soft chairs about the place where one could choose a book and sit for a long read. Melodia loved to read, and this was the best library she could have ever dreamt of. She supposed she could spend months here just going over the titles of the books.

There was a large table in the center of the room with wine and cheese. She approached the table and looked at what was there. The cheese looked fresh, and the wine warmed. She poured a glass and tasted it tentatively. Sure enough, it was spiced, and she could feel her whole body begin to warm. She took a piece of cheese and walked to the nearest bookshelf. She absently nibbled the cheese as she searched the titles of the books on the shelf. The section she was in now seemed to focus on philosophy, and she pulled one out that seemed to be of interest. Holding the large piece of cheese with her teeth, she opened the book and started skimming a page.

"Do you find my collection satisfactory?"

Melodia looked up from her book and almost replied but remembered the cheese in her teeth. She pulled the cheese out and smiled.

"Quite satisfactory."

Just then, the fireplace sparked to life. The man standing in front of it was quite tall. He was gaunt to the point that he looked almost sick. He had his black and gray hair cut very short, and his cheekbones were very pronounced as if he had been without food for a long time. His clothing was black and carefully tailored to his body, which made him look even more thin and frail.

"To what do I owe the pleasure, eh..." He gestured to her for a name.

"My name is Melodia, and I'm afraid I am not here for pleasure."

"Pity." The man said, smiling thinly.

Do all men always start and end with the thing between their legs? She believed she knew the answer.

"My name is Lord Bashor, and I am the master of this place." He spread his hands wide, indicating the walls around him. "If it is not pleasure you are here for, then what is it? What brings a Priestess of The Lady here to my humble home?" Melodia did not like the fact that he knew what she was but was also not surprised. Very few women presented themselves as peers to men, and Priestesses were among them. "You guess correctly on what I am, but it is not in *her* service that I am here."

"I see," Bashor said in mock curiosity. "Do tell?"

She put the book away and stuffed the rest of the cheese into her mouth. She took her time chewing and then swallowed.

"I am here in regard to Killian of House Loyal. Do you know him?" This time there was no mockery in the curiosity in the tall man's gaunt face.

"Indeed, I do." He said cautiously. She came to the table again and leaned on it.

"I very much would like you to free him from your service."

Bashor said nothing but stared at her oddly. A strange feeling ran through her.

"I see." He said finally. "I have to admit I didn't see this coming. A Priestess in love with a murderer ... who also happens to serve the Dark Lord, in his own way. My, My, what a predicament, my dear." Melodia suddenly felt violated, and cold anger ran into her veins. "I do not know how you came by this information of my feelings, but know this. They are my own and not your matter."

Bashor shook his head at that. "But you are wrong, Priestess. You are asking me to release a servant of mine. Does that not make it my matter, as well?" Melodia knew he was right, but that only made her angrier. "Please, there is no need to get angry. It is late, and I am still without my supper. Would you be so kind as to join me?" He saw the answer before the response came from her lips. "We could talk further on the matter you have proposed."

He knew he had her then. She agreed, and Grothar led her from the room without another word. He had his hood up now and wore gloves to cover his hands. Still, the insects flew around him and disappeared in and out of his hood.

She was led to a bedroom not far from the library. The room was huge, and a very soft-looking bed sat in the center of the room. Red drapes hung around it on all sides. There were no windows in the room, but there was a fire burning brightly off in the corner.

The burned man had said he would return for her in one hour to take her to dinner. She put her pack on the bed and sat down. The cushions on the bed were so soft, and she sank deep into it. Moments later, there was a soft knock on the door.

"Yes?" she called, but there was no answer. She went to the door and opened it cautiously. Outside on the floor was a washing jug and basin. She looked up and down the hall, but no one was there. She took them both inside and placed them on a bureau. She looked around and found towels folded neatly near the fire.

"Thinks of everything," she said out loud, retrieving the towels and putting them on the bed. She did not want to undress in this big room, no telling who was watching, but she had been traveling for some time, and washing would feel very good. She took off her clothes and scrubbed herself. She could feel eyes on her, but it was worth the warm water and smell of the perfumed soap. The towels that were near the fire were hot and felt good against her skin. She shook out her clothes and put them back on. She had to admit she felt better already. She picked up the knife from the bed where she had laid it and tucked it back into her belt.

Let's get this going. She opened the door and went out to investigate.

Chapter 14 – Shama

He was enjoying taking the shape of the fox. He was able to zip into and out of just about anywhere without being seen. His legs were strong if he needed to jump, and he could endure long travels without getting tired. Yes, he could just give himself more energy, but what fun would that be? The whole point of these changes was to feel closer to the natural order of things on the surface.

Well … that wasn't the whole point, truth be told. The reality was that the boy fascinated him. Ever since he had seen him being carried away in the arms of the horsemen, there seemed to be a connection. It was like he was drawn to the human child. At first, Shama was completely skeptical about the whole thing. Just a figment of his aging imagination. But it was when he was in his dragon form that he felt it strongest. It was like they were connected, and he decided to ignore any warnings by the blasted twins and see things for himself.

And luckily, he did! Between being nearly accosted by guardsmen in the dungeon to eating poisonous mushrooms … well, it was good that he was around. His corpse would have been rotting in the forest had he not put an antidote in the air around the idiot child!

Spotted mushrooms to snack on, indeed. Shama stopped and shook his little canine head a moment before trotting on down the dirt road. He looked up to see thick dark clouds overhead. Maybe he would sleep tonight as a duck? Ducks are very waterproof and keep amazingly warm with their feathers! Though he didn't want to get eaten again. He pushed the thought of his most regrettable time as a squirrel out of his head.

One of the not-so-great things about being a fox was their keen sense of smell. Not that there was anything wrong with a fox's sense of smell. Quite the contrary. In fact, this form was giving him many benefits along with having a powerful nose. Not even close to that of a bear but enough to be useful. The negative, however, was when he got too close to the carts holding the most, unfortunately, smelly humans. It was truly unbelievable to Shama that even in the Empire today slavery still existed.

Shama sneezed, and he stopped and wiped his nose with his paw.

Too close!

He let the carts move forward a bit before he continued on. He could not for the life of him understand how the boy could be finding enjoyment in being in chains?

He was at a school of his peers, surrounded by people and knowledge… Although the school was surrounded by rather unscrupulous teachings, it had to be for sure better than being in chains locked in a cart with other unwashed mortals.

He thought of Sara, and the Shama just shook his fox head. It was a good lesson, but a hard way to learn it. The smell of rot came to him, but before he could sneeze, he smelled what was in the last cage. His eyes perked up, and he started to trot again. One thing that he did understand was the connection between the boy and the Fangor. Shama had known many Fangors and, he must admit, he liked them all. Such an interesting species. They were not known to be particularly magical. Still, they had a very uncanny way of being around those that were. It was like they were somehow attracted to it.

There undoubtedly something happening here, and he wanted to watch to see what unfolded. Shama did not give much credit to prophecies or myths, but he did have to admit something was happening. It was almost like a buzz in the air. He was too old and had seen too much to miss it. Every few cycles, there was something that happens that changes the course of things. He felt it now. The question was, would it be for good … or something evil. It was there, but he had no idea which way that wind would blow. What he did know is that he wanted to see it up close. Life could get a bit boring, waiting around for things to happen in this world. He had to admit, it was a lot better than dealing with the twins. Though … he did have to also admit he liked looking at The Lady. He let the thought of her drift into his mind as he trotted behind the carts, trying to ignore the smells that kept making him sneeze.

The End

Torenium Chronicles

The Torenium Empire is void of magic as it is in the hands of the twins that balance light and darkness. The entire Empire is facing destruction by an outside human flesh-eating invading army. Will the prophecy be true and will Torenium be saved from total destruction?

Blood Demon: Book 2

Sebastion finds himself on his own as betrayal and violence follow him. Though he does find kindred spirits in the most unlikely of places. Killian has been mysteriously transformed back to his younger self and is now determined to save Sebastion from what's coming, even if it means killing the dark sorcerer he served for so many years.

Meanwhile, the Twin Gods plot against each other as they try to find the meaning of the prophecy and Shama, the Dragon, searches to learn what could be interesting about a boy aimlessly wandering the empire.

Death comes from the Eastern Barrier as Barbarian hordes feeding on human flesh wash over the land. The Torenium Empire is facing destruction, and nothing seems to stand in the man-eater's way as the cities burn and fall.

"Watch for the loyal, as he will come."

– Prophecy, source unknown.

Coming Soon!

www.ingramcontent.com/pod-product-compliance
Lightning Source LLC
Chambersburg PA
CBHW031724170626
46808CB00005B/1873